The Librarians of Alexandria

The Librarians of Alexandria

A TALE OF TWO SISTERS

Alessandra Lavagnino

TRANSLATED BY TERESA LUST

STEERFORTH ITALIA

AN IMPRINT OF STEERFORTH PRESS • HANOVER, NEW HAMPSHIRE

To a grand and glorious organism
on the way to extinction:
Alphabetical Order.

First published in Italian as *Le bibliotecarie di Alessandria*
by Sellerio editore, Palermo, 2002

The Librarians of Alexandria is winner of the Zerilli-Marimò Prize for Italian Fiction, sponsored by New York University and the Fondazione Maria and Goffredo Bellonci. Funding is made possible by Baroness Zerilli-Marimò, as well as through contributions from Casa della Letterature in Italy. The publishers would like to thank Baroness Zerilli-Marimò for her support of this publication.

The English language publication of *The Librarians of Alexandria* has also been supported by a translation grant from the Italian Ministry of Foreign Affairs.

Library of Congress Cataloging-in-Publication Data
Lavagnino, Alessandra.
[Bibliotecarie di Alessandria. English]
The librarians of Alexandria : a tale of two sisters / Alessandra Lavagnino ;
translated by Teresa Lust — 1st ed.
p. cm.
ISBN-13: 978-1-58642-099-4 (alk. paper)
ISBN-10: 1-58642-099-2 (alk. paper)
I. Title.

PQ4872.A83B5313 2006
853'.914—dc22

2005029901

FIRST EDITION

CONTENTS

PREFACE

I HAVE RETURNED to Alexandria in Egypt. I call it a return, even though it is my first time here, for I have memories of Alexandria. I have images, and the lingering scents evoked by the stories told to me by my mother, by my grandmother, and by my aunt.

By my grandfather, no, as he was not a storyteller. He read. He studied, and at the end he knew fifty-six languages. He used to say: *You have to work to learn the first ten; after that, they come by themselves*. He was always seated at a desk cluttered with books, with piles of books from floor to ceiling behind him. On his desktop lay his cat Sinesio, stretched out like the Sphinx.

I visited the site of the new library. The Public Library of Alexandria! Sponsored by UNESCO, designed by Norwegian architects. It will contain, the guidebook says, all of the five hundred thousand volumes that had been housed in the original ancient library. I asked myself how it would be done, but I could find no one to whom I could pose my questions. Would there be books or microfiche or tapes or CDs? And in which languages? Would there be texts in the ancient languages? And how would that be possible? Who would read Aramaic or ancient Greek, or the classical languages of Persia and Latin? Today in the city of the great

Macedonian the writing is all in Arabic, except for in the oldest quarters, where a few of the old street names remain. Hence, the Rue des Soeurs where several convents and children's schools had once been located; whoever passed through those streets a century ago would have been greeted by choirs of angelic voices through the *meshrebeeyeh*.

Hardly anyone speaks English anymore, even fewer speak French or Italian; as for Greeks, either from the mainland or from the islands in the Aegean, if they are there, they certainly don't make themselves known. Alexandria is not a city for tourists, and the vestiges of its days of glory have all but disappeared. But the Greco-Roman museum, which opened at the beginning of the twentieth century, is still visited by schoolchildren; the girls wear skirts or blue jeans, but also wear scarves to cover their heads.

In the days when my grandparents were living in Alexandria, there were two hundred thousand inhabitants. Today there are perhaps eight million. They live in apartment buildings of fifteen, maybe twenty stories, packed tightly into forty kilometers of coastline. But along the tranquil and endless stretch of beach a fisherman can still cast his net as in times past, standing in water up to his waist. And he can still catch fish, a couple of kilos with each toss of his net. The sea of Alexandria is still full of fish.

My name is Adriana. My aunt, Zia Margherita, is over ninety, and has outlived her memories. She passes them on to me as gifts, in bits and pieces. Her friend and neighbor in those days was Stelianì, a Greek Cypriot. My grandmother, Nonna Antonia, used to sing:

Stelianì once had a cat
And her name was Flora . . .

INTRODUCTION

"I WISH I COULD HAVE been called Margherita. Mamma wanted it that way, but Papa was against it: it was not a family name, he said."

"All right then, when we tell your story, we will call you Margherita, but no one will be able to recognize you."

"No one will recognize me?" she repeats. "Yes, I would like that very much," she says, breaking into an enormous, toothless smile. "But I don't have a story. My life has been pointless. Nothing but pointless." She begins to laugh. "And it is precisely because of its pointlessness that it will never end."

It must be her beta-blockers, I think. Ever since she has been living with the nuns, she has been feeling much better. Under their care, she receives her medications at regular intervals. Indeed, she is much better than when she was living in her own house, alone. If only she hadn't had her accident — it was never fully clear what happened — but I had to go to the Ospedale di Santo Spirito to claim her. It's much better this way. Here she can outlive her memories, and some of them maybe she'll even be able to forget. It certainly won't be me who brings them back up.

"I was the house fool," she says. "And sometimes, down deep, I actually enjoyed it. They used to tell me, 'It's too soon for these things,' and I believed them. Such a fool. The fact is that Mamma was never very fond of me, or my brother, either. She said, 'It would have been better if you had become a nun.' But Papa always said to your mother, 'You will be a great woman someday,' and she believed him!" Then she says, "But Alexandria was so beautiful! What a shame."

"Why didn't you ever go back?"

"Nooo," she dismisses the idea as crazy, unseemly. "How could I? They told me at the time that we would return, but it was a lie. And then it became impossible."

She herself does not know why. She is seated in her overstuffed chair, looking out the window. She hasn't used her hands since the stroke disabled her right side. They are getting better, though, her beautiful hands, still soft and white, but they don't do anything. The nuns have been taking good care of her. And so Margherita is outliving her own life, a life without a story, she claims. A life without children: this is true. A life that no man remembers, although perhaps an Arab somewhere has memories of her, but he would have to be more than a hundred years old by now.

She is telling me the story of her silly life, but I actually think there are many things that she has forgotten. She never asks me about my life, about what I did after moving away from her: my "real" life. I will never speak of it. Thus, every day that I spend with her I am forced, though I enjoy it, into a false reality that focuses only on her life or on my present life. Or else we enter into the dream world of my childhood, which was practically ours alone.

I was with her constantly, and we were always happy. Only one time, years ago, she said to me, "I always took you by the hand, so everyone thought you were my daughter, and nobody noticed me. Nobody." Then she pauses, perhaps so as not to offend the woman — no matter that this woman was no longer of this earth — who was noticed. And how they stared, for she was so beautiful! Her sister: my mother. She still thinks husbands can be found strolling down the road. She remembers, and her mind wanders through all the streets of Rome. And those of Alexandria.

❖

". . . and I would pass in front of the main gate of Villa Torlonia, on my way to my music lesson with my violin tucked under my arm, and if at that hour — and it happened frequently — Mussolini was leaving, inside his enormous black, shiny limousine, he would greet me with a wave of his hand. Because he himself was a violinist. And if I didn't have my violin with me, he wouldn't bother to wave. Maybe he didn't recognize me. Of course, he would have had more important things to think about!"

Or else she says, "There, our house had a balcony just like that one, but not so high above the street. When the camels went by, they would look inside the window. I was so afraid of those enormous eyes, so serious, and I closed the shutters. They had enormous teeth, those camels, they could really frighten you. And they bit, oh, how they would bite! They were always passing by, because at the end of our street there was a man who rented out camels —" And she started to laugh. "He gave them hardly anything to eat, poor beasts, they really did suffer."

"And what was it called, this street of yours?"

"That I don't know. I know where it is, I could get there, but the name . . . Maybe it didn't have a name, or at least I don't remember it. What would have been the use of a name, anyway? Papa had to go to the station to receive our mail from Italy. Cairo station, which was just nearby, underground. You could watch the trains passing from above. We lived under Moharam Bay, and our house was in a row with many others on the Mahmudiyah Canal. But not in the elegant part, farther up the canal, near the Antoniadis Gardens . . ."

Margherita knows the characters of the Cyrillic alphabet and, given an occasion to speak or read it, she would still remember a bit of Russian. And Bulgarian. She tells me, "My teacher, at the institute on Via Lucrezio Caro, was a beautiful woman, but she never adapted to the Italian way of life. She had two pupils: me and a colonel. He was a magnificent man, that colonel, but they stole him from me, too. When we were taking the exams for our diploma the teacher separated us so that we couldn't copy each other. She always wore a ribbon in her hair, a brightly colored bow, which wasn't the fashion then. How she turned heads in the street . . ."

Margherita spoke Arabic very well, and Greek; those were the languages of her childhood. In addition, of course, to the Italian she spoke at home, and the French spoken with the Franciscan monks from the church of Saint Catherine. Her confessor was named Père Quilici — pronounced *key-LEE-see* — and she made her confession to him every Saturday, the sins of a little girl.

"Then, when I was fifteen years old, we returned to Italy. The war was over, and my brother had come back. With half his skull rebuilt, but alive. And your mother had to go to the university. It was 1920. We went right away to see the relatives in Alatri and Fumone. You remember Fumone, don't you?"

Part One

ITALIAN CONCERTO

1. THE CANTERNOS

Ciociaria, Italy, 1870

PERCHED ON TOP of a mountain, Fumone was, and still is, the smallest village in Ciociaria. Among the houses nestled closely together, bunched as tightly as a cluster of autumn grapes, the roads climb the rock like a staircase. Inaccessible above stands the fortress where the imprisoned Pietro da Morone died with only two books in his possession; he who had been the angelic Pope Celestine V. Six hundred years later, who bothered to think of that anymore?

The medieval gate in the wall surrounding Fumone is so narrow that a donkey bearing a man and a bundle of kindling can barely pass through it; one of those beautiful chestnut-brown donkeys with their white muzzles and stomachs, their enormous ears and ample hips.

On the back of just such an animal the midwife had arrived from Alatri, guided through the labyrinth of the village by the cries of the laboring woman. Upon reaching the house, she set directly to work, and only a few minutes later, after the woman's loudest and most prolonged wail, she pronounced matter-of-factly, "It's a boy!" The father, Giacomo Canterno, and the grandmother, Nonna Erminia, raised their eyes and hands to heaven in thanks (though Nonna Erminia did so for only an instant) and in that moment they could think of nothing else. The midwife finished her chore and washed her hands.

Half an hour later the young Erminia, her black eyes hidden behind red ringlets, observed with grave concern that she had acquired a little brother. She burst into tears and ran away. There was a patter of bare feet across a tile floor that had just been washed but was already beginning to dry; it was ten o'clock in the morning and quite warm, especially for the twentieth of September. In those same moments the walls were being breached in the city of the pope.*

Upon seeing the child run off like that her grandmother said, "What's wrong with that one?" But she immediately put the question out of her mind, for at the time no one gave a second thought to the tears of a little girl.

The Piedmontese soldiers were entering Rome while in Fumone, Nonna Erminia had poured water and oil into a bowl and was whisking it with a fork, making an emulsion to administer to the newborn child in order to rid him, she said, of "all that black stuff" he had inside. The mother, meanwhile, had fallen asleep, the puerperal fever rising.

The infant was baptized Tommaso after his departed grandfather, and he soon grew strong, even without his mother. He followed his sister in her games, but he didn't have her red curls. She would say, "Come on, forget about them. Come with me." And Tommaso forgot about them, his father and Nonna Erminia, when they pressed him to be obedient, to tend the vineyard and the animals' fodder, to obtain a good price for their wine, and to select new land to buy: because there was plenty of money, and it was his duty, ever since Michele, the only male cousin, decided to become a priest. But at thirteen Tommaso, too, was in Alatri, with the priests, always reading his books and studying. So it went until eighteen, but not in order to become a lawyer, as his father wished. Or to become a priest,

* Victor Emmanuel seized Rome, and the city became part of the kingdom of Italy. —*Trans.*

which would have made his grandmother very proud. Merely because he enjoyed studying. Their hopes for him made feel ashamed, and he became increasingly withdrawn and silent.

The sister became more and more beautiful. And there came a day one spring, it would have been 1888, that a string of six mules descended the road from Fumone toward Alatri, the chests of her trousseau strapped across their backs. Behind them, with great dignity on her white donkey, followed Erminia, the lovely betrothed of a wealthy landowner.

The following year Tommaso fell in love, but with a married woman, and he wanted to kill himself. Ineptly, he managed only to wound himself, and he ultimately recovered, though not in the head, his family said. When he was finally back on his feet, he went before his father, his grandmother, and his sister, and he embarked on a lengthy but incomprehensible discourse from which emerged only one clear but absurd idea: he desired to be dispossessed of all his holdings, his lands, his flocks, and his vineyards. "I don't want anything," he said in conclusion. "Just leave me in peace. All that I am due to inherit, I want to give to Erminia and Giovanni. They can do with it whatever they wish. All I need are the things that will be useful in my studies." Giovanni was his brother-in-law. Tommaso would have just turned twenty-one. He loaded up an old cart with a few of his belongings, and with a handful of coins in his pocket he made his way down the mountain to Rome. He had known only Fumone with its clusters of houses cloaked in fog, and Alatri standing so proudly inside the wall that had surrounded it for twenty-five centuries. Rome seemed immense, dusty, desolate, and mind boggling to him. But only one thought occupied his thoughts: as soon as he found it, he would enroll in the University of Rome, which was then called La Sapienza.

In Rome, Tommaso Canterno found lodging with a family in the neighborhood known as Pantani ai Campitelli, where his monthly rent included his room, meals, and laundry. From the window each morning he watched the women passing by in the street, a basket covered by a blue handkerchief balanced on each head. They had turned-up chins and a vacant expression, they were old or almost old, and he knew some of them. He could smell, or he imagined he could, the cheese in their baskets. On their feet the women wore sandals called *cioce* after their region of Ciociaria, or else they wore nothing at all. He himself, after turning at the large factory beneath the Campidoglio, would walk to La Sapienza, just as he had always done between Fumone and Alatri, with a spring in his step. He was not yet accustomed to his shoes, and he wore them big, with thick socks and paper stuffed inside.

He walked all over Rome this way. Through the sinuous, dark, ancient streets, where the scents and sounds of animals and human beings were even more pronounced than in the villages of the countryside. He looked at palaces of unknown princes, but he knew about Boniface VIII and the Caetanis, the Della Roveres and other popes. He breathed the verdant air of the grandiose villas, he entered churches that were warm in winter but cool in summer, and only in these places did he love the city. He was blinded by the sun as he came upon the work sites of a gutted Rome that seemed stunned at being rebuilt into something so indecent and silly.

But on Wednesday, every Wednesday, as he returned from La Sapienza, he walked to that piazza that is neither too wide nor too narrow, neither too long nor too short, that piazza filled with every color and aroma: Campo de' Fiori. There he stopped at the bookstalls and bought books in all languages; he took them home, still on foot, a bundle in each arm held by clasped fingertips. When he received his doctorate in ancient languages he rented a cart and returned with it to his native village. He and his books, and never had so many books come to Fumone.

As a professor at the Ginnasio-Liceo Conti-Gentili in Alatri the following year, Tommaso Canterno boarded with his sister, Erminia. That year, 1895, a recent law of the new kingdom of Italy allowed *ginnasio* classes to be attended by male and female students. So in addition to the twelve boys taught by Professor

Canterno in the first level, there were three girls, who after great consideration were assigned to the first row, with a row of empty seats behind them. Outside, on the wall of the Ginnasio-Liceo Conti-Gentili, the solar clock showing real and mean time silently marked the passing of the days and seasons.

Antonia, who was sixteen, had gone to school in the fall and continued in the winter. To her delight she could finally understand the words — perhaps not all of them — of the Latin prayers that she knew by heart; but she did not tell her family that Adele and Maria, her classmates, had left school after less than a month. Nobody had asked her about it. At home, down at the Plaje, Antonia lived with her mother and younger brother. But not with her elder brother, who was about to become a priest. As for her father, Antonia did not remember him. He had gone to America many years before hoping to become rich, and only at that point had her uncles, who were canons of a collegiate church, forgiven their sister, Antonia's mother, for marrying a mason; a "lowly" alliance. The canons now took care of their nephews and niece; the eldest was already in the seminary, and Antonia would become a nun, which was why she was studying Latin. Her walk to school was a long journey through town, because the Plaje is a neighborhood of very poor houses, as dark as caves, spilling out of a large breach in the eastern side of the Cyclopean Wall. Antonia, all alone, walked all the way across Alatri, going first uphill then down. But she was not really alone, because she had her guardian angel with her. Perhaps everybody has one, but Antonia always felt hers close by, and talked to him. He was tall, blond, and smiling. She spoke to him with words; the angel answered with his silence, and she understood him.

One day when her husband was away, red-haired Erminia said to her boarder brother after the midday meal, "Look, this cannot go on."

"What?"

"People are talking."

"They are? And what about?"

"That girl you keep in your class . . ."

"That girl. What about her?"

"You are so smart and yet you don't understand anything. You are alone in class. Those others don't count."

Tommaso drank the last of his wine, stood up, and started pacing back and forth, back and forth — just as he did in class — with his hands behind his back. Once in a while he stroked his beard. Erminia gazed at those hands: white, too white. The problem was that her brother had wanted to study; that's what it was. And while she looked at her brother's hands, the minutes passed.

"So, people are talking. You were right to tell me." His voice surprised her. "It means that she won't come to school any longer as a pupil, but as a wife. Because that girl, I am going to marry her."

"What are you talking about? Marry her? That girl is from a poor family, she has nothing."

Erminia had made another mistake: a girl who has nothing and studies! Professor Tommaso was already running down the stairs. His sister called after him in vain. It was barely three in the afternoon and the winter sun was already gone from the Plaje. Antonia, her braid down her back, was rubbing with a bit of sand a clay cooking pot still redolent of celery and onion. She heard those long steps coming down the steep, stony path, and she stood with the pot in her hand, without moving, while her mother came to the door.

In Alatri, asking for a girl in marriage is done as it always was. The talk between the canons' sister, wife of the mason who had gone to America, and the young Canterno, born in Fumone and professor of ancient languages, followed the old conventions. Antonia remained hidden to listen; it was her great luck that her angel was nearby to give her courage while her mother, defying all conventions, objected. "But no! There are so many girls in Alatri!" Which was true. Antonia appeared from around the corner of the wall just as her professor said in a strange, unforgettable voice, "Yes, there are many. But I want this one and this one only." And with two fingers he took the girl's small hand, still red and wet, and she stepped forward, almost reluctantly. It was the first time — needless to say — that he had touched her. The angel remained behind the wall.

Then the mother's voice rose again. "But Antonia wanted to be a nun . . . her father is in America, we are poor people . . . her hope chest . . ."

"There is no need of a hope chest. I'll take care of that. All I need is time to write her father and receive his reply."

The wedding took place in June, with the blessings of her uncles and of her American father, by letter. Antonia stopped going to school; she herself could not have said why.

Erminia's house was large. "Where else would you want to go? I'll give you a room," she said. But Antonia's angel was ill at ease in that house; he came and went. Still, when Giacomo was born Antonia knew that she was happy.

She went to visit her mother with her baby in her arms, but her mother did not come to see her in Erminia's house. Antonia, who once obeyed her mother, now obeyed her sister-in-law and took care of her children, too. Only once did she say to Tommaso, "You do have a house in Fumone. Let's go there, at least when you are not teaching." He shook his head and that was it. He did not explain that he didn't want to return to Fumone because his cousin the priest had fathered a son within the confines of the village walls and had been forced to leave. Tommaso and Antonia remained in Alatri, in Erminia's house.

In the winter of 1898 a girl was born with the red curls of her aunt Erminia, who was her godmother, and they called her Maria.

Three months later a letter arrived from the Ministry of Foreign Affairs in Rome. It informed Professor Canterno of his selection for the position to which he had applied, and of the results in the exam he had taken without telling his wife. Tommaso had been awarded the chair of Italian and Latin at Alexandria's state *ginnasio-liceo* for Italians, in Egypt. He could leave immediately.

Antonia's milk stopped flowing and for two days and two nights Maria cried in hunger. To leave! And to go so far! Antonia had been to Frosinone once, to Fumone three times, and many times to Trivigliano, where an aunt of hers lived. She wished only to go to Rome one day to see the pope, but not right away. She had no desire to see anything else because, to be truthful, it was as if the rest of the world did not exist for her. And now, Alexandria! In Egypt, no less. All that sea to cross! For her the sea was only a vague strip far away in the distance that was visible from above Civita, like a meadow of light under the sky. She looked in horror at the map. Tommaso treated her gently, perhaps wanting to hide his own anxiety. He said, "Think how many people go to America to become rich; even your father . . . and America is so much farther away. Egypt faces our own sea. It's close, we will come back soon." He, who had once been rich, did not tell her, who did not understand money, that he had participated in the competition not to get rich, but out of a desire to meet people who spoke different languages: those languages he studied all alone in the evening, bending over the books he bought in Campo de' Fiori. Alexandria, a port city, was ideal for that — so he thought.

With her eyes wide open and her lips pursed, Antonia prayed, while the little one nuzzled her frantically for milk. She talked with the angel, but at first he did not answer and then he seemed to be on her husband's side, not on hers. So Antonia disguised her dismay as well as she could, and when her daughter was at last able to nurse, and she felt her breasts fill up again, she thanked God. Then she began to prepare silently for departure. But when she looked up from her daily tasks and rested her eyes on the mountains she had always known, and on the uncertain horizon where she knew the sea to lie, both mountains and horizon felt like enemies. So much so that she felt a new, resentful desire to change not just her home, but her very horizon. After a while she truly wished to leave, and then to land again, anywhere. She felt remorseful about that, too, and asked her mother for comfort and support. But her mother, who had taught her only obedience and sacrifice, told her, "You will do God's will," and Antonia, in this new detachment from her mother, began to mature anew. And when she sat on the cart that carried her toward the sea, her daughter held tight in her arms and her son by her side, she was quick to turn her eyes drowned in tears toward that emptiness. She did not turn back again to look at those who waved to her, or at the roofs, and the great walls of Alatri, dark and proud on top of its mountain.

The sea that Antonia saw was the one at Gaeta: glimmering and clear, it seemed benevolent to her. We don't know if some relative accompanied them to Naples; perhaps one of the uncles, or her brother Luigi who was a priest, too, by then. Antonia was not crying anymore, but her trip was an unbearable distancing marked by the water left behind by the ship: a laceration without respite from one strange port to another.

On a September morning the Canternos reached Alexandria without incident. A small, agile boat led the steamer through the narrow breakwaters into the great harbor, where ships of all sizes stood anchored in the dockyard; entering the Maritime Station of the Port of the Occident was never easy, and it became perilous if the sea was stormy. That morning the sea was calm.

Antonia knew that the following day she would give her husband, her son, and herself — but not the baby — the castor oil she had not forgotten to add to the already abundant luggage; any *ciociaro* knows that it must be done when changing air. She left the steamship feeling happy because the monstrous distance had finally stopped increasing, but in leaving that final vestige of her country she felt a further wrench. Once on land, with her daughter held tight and covered up against the sun and the little boy held by the hand, she saw only low, yellow houses far away. Tommaso said, "Wait for me," and walked with long strides along the quay to meet a man with a cart and a small, white donkey. He brought the man back to his family, and they were already on their way to the city when a voice called, "Mister, monsieur, signor . . . Signor Professore." It was the driver of a carriage, a real carriage, black and shiny, such as Tommaso had seen in Rome. The carriage came from the Italian consulate, and had been dispatched to meet the new professor of Italian and Latin for the royal state *liceo* for Italians. The man with the cart was allowed to follow with the luggage.

Alexandria, Egypt, 1899

Alexandria was a city, and Antonia had never known one. She did not see it. She smelled the air but did not see the houses of the Turkish quarter that they crossed, nor the graceful palaces made glorious by the sun all along the avenue of the Eastern Port. She did not see the azure sea where triangular white sails raced, etched sharply against the porcelain sky. She did not see the great Qaitbay Citadel, built on the promontory of Pharos, where the great lighthouse, one of the Seven Wonders of the World, had reached high into the sky. She did not see the white palaces with elaborately embroidered grillwork at their gates, nor the gardens filled with palm trees swaying in the wind. She hugged her daughter and looked at Giacomo, seated tranquilly in his father's lap, letting himself be taken to new places as he watched the horse, the driver, and the city. She had known that everything in that new land would seem foreign to her, except her children. Everything was beyond justification other than her duty of obedience to her husband, and in those moments he, too, seemed foreign to her. But *you will do God's will,* her mother had said. And this was it.

Far from the Western Port where they had disembarked, far from the Eastern Port and its avenue called the Corniche, but close to the center of the city stood their house, and it was beautiful. Too beautiful. The consulate had made all the arrangements for it. A tall, wrought-iron gate with a grate like lace opened onto a pure white staircase that led to the first floor through a garden filled with fragrant jasmine. The Canternos had one side of the villa; there were Italians living on the other side also.

That is how Antonia and Tommaso learned that there were many Italians in Alexandria, but none was like them, as if their distant homeland had come here to manifest its eccentricities.

Was it because their luggage was made up of bundles in addition to the chest, or because Antonia was timid and poorly dressed? Professor Canterno detected contempt in the ready kindness of his compatriots and colleagues, and in the courtesy the ladies showed Antonia. Alexandria, with its palaces, charming villas, and pinnacled theaters, was no doubt disappointed with that professor, so unassuming as to look like an immigrant, a penniless immigrant with no ambition. His young wife, with a daughter at her breast and a little boy hanging on her skirts, looked exactly like the peasant she was. They soon stopped going to the frequent parties offered by the consulate. With whom could they leave the children, anyhow? True, the signor had girls of various ages as servants, but Antonia did not know how to be "served." As for the other Italians, the workers and technicians at the port and docks, Tommaso soon learned he could not have them as friends because, as he said, they were anarchists, all of them, and half of them were illegal immigrants.

In their handsome home Antonia felt shame for months as she hung to dry the items her mother had woven with her own hands, but she did it. She wrote letters to her mother, knowing someone would have to read them to her, and she sent her skeins of the cotton she bought while taking long afternoon walks with Maria in one arm and Giacomo holding her by the hand. She would walk past Fort Napoleon, along a street lined with beautiful cottages on one side, its other side bordering a neighborhood where Greek and European workers lived, including Italians. Eventually she would reach the Nile, where black water buffalo rested peacefully and chewed their cud on the riverbanks, the same buffalo cows that gave her children their fragrant milk.

In truth, the river was not the great Nile, which does not touch Alexandria, but the Mahmudiyah Canal, dug a century earlier to provide water to the city. Beyond it, pastures and cotton fields extended to the large salt lagoon, Lake Mareotis, its banks covered with cane and papyrus. It was not the great Nile, that canal, even though it was also a child of the immense Delta, but it did look like a river, especially to Antonia, who had never seen the Tiber.

So during those walks completed before the fleeting descent of the sun, as she talked to Giacomo and the baby, as she sang or remained silent, Antonia told herself that she had not known the river of her homeland, but she knew the Nile. Antonia sang church songs and even opera arias, because that was the golden age of Italian opera.

She did not sing at home, though, for fear the neighbors would hear. They were a childless couple, and the wife had a sister who made people address her as "the marchesa." They had servants — two young girls — and after sleeping half the day, the couple spent their evenings and nights with company, playing cards and smoking, sending laughter and little clouds of smoke into the sky, which was azure, or yellow when the wind blew in from the desert.

One evening Antonia realized that even though she repeated her prayers mechanically, she had forgotten the angel. Not God, immense and overarching, but the angel, that almost constant presence by her side. Had he remained in Alatri? Or had forgetting about him sufficed to make him disappear? Only with time and great effort was she able to bring back their four angels, for they had become quiet and almost indifferent there, in "Alesandria" (that's how she always pronounced the name); indeed, the angels did not help her anymore.

Tommaso said proudly, "Giacomo and Maria will speak perfect, pure Italian. They are hearing it only from us; we have no excuse." As for him, he was learning other languages, developing with his natural talent and his mind a method of his own, which one day — in a sad time that was still far away — would be set down in writing for his son. After buying Andersen's tales in Portuguese, he taught himself Danish from a stack of dictionaries on his desk. And the house was filling up with books. During his daily walk to the market street called El Attarìn, which was the antiquarians' row, Tommaso bought new and used ones from the booksellers, all of whom he soon knew. But on holidays Professor Canterno escorted his wife and children to church — the great church of the Franciscan friars, Saint Catherine of Alexandria —

and then went alone, partly by streetcar and partly on foot, to the Western Port. Once there, he did not chat with the Italian and French dockworkers, with whom he did not want to socialize, but with the sailors, particularly those who came from the East. His was a strange, familiar presence that even twenty years later would have elicited curiosity: a tall man dressed as a professor but reserved by nature, coming forward on the quays of the large port to talk with men who wore diverse clothes and miens; many of them — smugglers or ex-convicts, since Alexandria was a city open and welcoming to all — had secrets to hide and could not imagine what in the world he wanted. He did not want anything, except to talk. He did not seem to understand that even talking was too much for them, even though he himself was a quiet man. But do we know the deep reason behind the human desire to understand other languages? It is perhaps the most powerful of all reasons.

And yet, the people closest to him loved him more than he imagined. The third year, when Antonia was pregnant again, there were knocks on the windows and doors throughout the part of the city where they lived. There was a tumult caused by a fight in the market square over a watermelon that was not sufficiently red. It was a small rebellion against the Italians and it had spread into their quarter. People ran screaming through the streets, banging on windows and doors. Excited Arabs reached their gate and climbed over. They came even to their door and someone said, "Him, not her." But Tommaso was saved by a neighbor, a shopkeeper who was an Arab like them. He knocked on the kitchen door, asked to be let in, and said quickly, "This way, this way. Leave your wife, don't be afraid, she will not be hurt because she is expecting . . ." He hid Tommaso in his own house.

The following morning Tommaso returned from his shelter. He was pale and said to Antonia, who was still awake, with Maria in her arms and Giacomo asleep beside her, "Let's leave this place. We'll go and live among them; that way we will be left in peace."

That same day Tommaso Canterno went on foot, alone, to the Arabic quarter, which lay beyond the Cairo railway near

Moharam Bay, along the Mahmudiyah Canal toward Bab el Gedid, the "new gate." He found a house there on a dusty yellow and gray dirt road shaded by large sycamore and mulberry trees. An immense sky in every tone of blue and yellow was turning red at sunset over Lake Mareotis. In that house, two months after perhaps saving her mother's life, Marta Canterno was born with the help of Arabic and Greek hands. She would become my mother.

The house on the banks of the Nile was spacious, and a balcony ran all around it. Half of the floor was inhabited by a Greek Cypriot named Stelianì and her family. The Canternos lived in the other half. The two balconies almost touched.

Stelianì once had a cat
And her name was Flora . . .

Stelianì's husband left early in the morning with a basket full of ring-shaped pastries on his back. Stelianì had made them in the evening with flour, water, anise, and a bit of sugar, then she had fried them at dawn. They were called *kollooras*, and the family supported themselves on *kollooras* and Stelianì's bobbin-lace. Stelianì also baked other pastries, such as *glookistàs*, which Antonia soon learned to prepare. Stelianì, too, learned things from Antonia, like how to wash and disinfect a wound, and how to stop dysentery. Antonia, Giacomo, and Maria learned to speak Greek from Stelianì and from her four children, Elèny, Antonio, Nicola, and Kliò. The house itself belonged to the husband of Settemunìra, a quick and energetic woman who had six children. The man also had another wife, called Bambi, who lived in the countryside; she was fat and infertile. The man used to spend two weeks in the city — they had a store on the ground floor — and two weeks in the country, where he owned a small piece of land. The fat wife and Settemunìra thought highly of each other and visited often; usually it was the country wife who came to see the city wife and her many children.

On the wall of the second-floor landing there was a picture of Saint Joseph with a lamp that was always lit. "Saint Joseph is a great saint, and we Muslims revere him," Settemunìra's husband explained to Tommaso Canterno. "Besides, you never know . . . ," he would add, raising his hands with a shrewd look.

At thirty-five, Tommaso Canterno knew about thirty languages. He always went to his school, and everywhere else, on foot. Ever since their move to the Arabic quarter the school was a long distance away; the tall, curved silhouette of the Italian professor Canterno, with a book in his hand and another in the pocket of his bulky jacket, with his swaying steps like those of a camel, soon became a familiar and even beloved sight along his route.

After Marta's birth, Antonia quickly became comfortable and happy in the new house, much more so than she had been in the rich quarter. She spoke Greek with Stelianì and Arabic with the neighbors, who held her in high esteem. Since she was generous with these families, sharing poultices, medicines, and customs from Ciociaria that were always efficacious on the young and infirm, she was believed to be a thaumaturge. When called, she came right away, full of compassion and ready for any horror. For instance, she was once summoned by the screams of a little girl. The child had just turned seven, and she had had something cut away that would never grow back, an operation to protect her virtue as an adult. Antonia would come running, but only if called, with lemon and water in a seeping unglazed earthenware carafe. She kept that cold water precisely for health emergencies, certainly not to drink, because Tommaso had ideas of his own, first among them the need to be immunized. Like everyone else, the Canternos drank water straight from the canal, unfiltered and at room temperature. When Giacomo was six years old and sick with cholera, Antonia cured him with a lot of lemon water.

They slept on beds made of boards with mattresses filled with cotton. Every morning Antonia spread the mattresses out on the balcony to air them out and keep the bedbugs from nesting in them. She propped the slick bed boards between the iron bedstead and the yellow brick floor, and Marta would slide down them, imitating her sister, Maria. Their mother stood watching them and thanked God.

The summer Marta, whom they called Martina, turned five, they all returned to Alatri to take Giacomo to the *ginnasio*, the same Conti-Gentili where his father had taught Latin to his mother. Tommaso was reunited with his father and sister, and Antonia with her mother, sister, and brothers.

Summer passed, and just before their departure for Alexandria, Antonia was sure that she was again expecting, for the fourth time. On learning this, Erminia said, "Leave Maria with me for a while. We'd be happy to have her, and besides, Giacomo will feel less lonesome with her around." They let themselves be convinced — why, oh, why? Because five weeks after they returned to Alexandria, right after receiving their first little letter from Maria, word came from Antonia's uncles, the canons: Maria had come down with meningitis and her soul had flown to heaven.

Martina did not know what happened, but she heard her mother's mournful cries and her father's screams, his head held high, like that of an animal howling to the sky. Her mother cried and ate next to nothing for months. But her belly kept growing like a separate object, a package set there. When her husband was not home she walked around the house doing nothing, disheveled and lamenting, then she took her belly with her two hands as if it were a ball, and cursed under her breath, "This one, what is this one for? You should have left me my daughter, that one . . . I don't want this one! What will I do with him? Take him back, why don't you take him back?" Then she would fall on her bed in tears, screaming "Forgive me, forgive me!" into the pillow, so that Marta was filled with terror. Then, finally, one evening Marta was happy to be sent to sleep with Kliò, Steliani's youngest, and during the night she heard screams — but it wasn't her mother, it couldn't be her — and in the morning they told her, "You know what? A new little brother has arrived at home . . ."

It was a girl. She would be baptized as soon as they returned to their homeland, and the godmother would be her aunt Erminia, who, back in Italy, should not feel that her brother and his wife held it against her for insisting that Maria be left in Alatri that fateful winter.

I wish I could have been called Margherita. Mamma would have liked that, perhaps out of devotion to the queen . . .

She was born in the summer, weak and weighing very little. The father would sit and contemplate for hours that latest creature of his, and he would murmur, "My little one, my little girl . . . ," as if he wanted to convince himself that he could love this other daughter, after Maria and Marta. Antonia looked at her husband, looked at her newborn, and cried. She thought of those little red braids buried so far away, in the cemetery in Alatri. She did not have much milk, but she was late in realizing it. The baby cried and hardly grew until Stelianì said, "Give her some other milk," and Margherita was fed with buffalo milk thinned with boiled water; perhaps too much water.

It was at that time that Halley's Comet remained fixed — and silent! — in the sky above our street for many nights. Bab el Gedid — which means " new gate" — looked like a giant nativity scene. But I don't remember all that. My sister told me about it, your mother.

Now that there were only Marta and the baby at home, Antonia found she had little to keep her busy, for in Alexandria's climate a newborn is not that much work. Slowly, in that calm atmosphere where the silence of despair and resentment had at last become resignation, in that silence inhabited by murmured prayers — while Marta played in the street with Kliò and her little Arab friends — the guardian angels came back to keep Antonia company. Margherita's angel was little, a cherub, who stayed close to Marta's angel. All her life Antonia saw angels and dreamed of people who had passed on. But she did not talk about it; not then. Those who see and know such things most often keep silent. And yet, years later, Nonna Antonia told me: "Listen, last night I dreamed of my sister Elisabetta; you did not know her. She died when she was thirty, while we were in Egypt, so I was not able to see her again. I dreamed that she was surrounded by light and she flew, flew up high. Then she said, 'Antonia, good-bye; I finished my Purgatory!' Then she disappeared. Now I don't have to pray for her anymore. She is praying for me now. Or rather, for all of us . . ." My grandmother corrected herself, a bit ashamed. I was fifteen then; there was the war, we lived in Rome, in the house at Prati, and she helped me translate Caesar and Livius. She certainly remembered the Latin taught to her by her professor in Alatri, and she had continued reading it. Really; she liked it.

Since God's name must not be pronounced in vain, Antonia mentioned it only to instruct her children. She sang:

Tutte le feste al Tempio
Mentre pregava anch'i – io

She attended mass, the sacraments, novenas, and Lent sermons with her children at the church of Saint Catherine of Alexandria. Her daughters took part in the processions inside the church and out in the semicircular courtyard, and the cries of the evening swallows blended with their singing. But God is One, and in addition to not calling Him directly by name, Antonia developed the habit, and even a penchant, for uttering the Arabic exclamation *Elhandulillàh!* which means, "Thanks be to Allah!"

Tommaso, now in full bloom in both mind and body, wore a beard and had light wrinkles in the suntanned skin around his eyes; by nature his complexion was fair and delicate. He had a very tender smile, full of goodness. His mouth was small, as it often is among the *ciociari*, and if it tightened in anger, Martina trembled. When she and her father went out together, her little sister stayed with their mother.

❖

My sister was intelligent and Papa expected much of her. Too much. That wasn't fair. I was the family idiot . . . and they let me be.

"Martina is going out with me," said her father; but after urging her, "Go on ahead!" he remained silent, and during those walks Marta felt alone and under observation. But as soon as they were out of the city he would say, "Here, I'll give you a present." The present would be a stone, and he would explain how old it was, and why it was all striped, and how it had gotten there from the river, and how that river was very, very long, much longer than it seemed. Or else a flower, and he would point out an insect that visited flowers like that one. In town he would take her along to buy books, and only then, among the crowds along El Attarìn, with its booksellers and musical instrument vendors, would he hold her by the hand.

He held her hand when it rained, too. Rain was a gift almost too precious to hope for, arriving suddenly to refresh and cleanse, to turn the cracked, dried-up street into yellow mud. And immediately the road would insatiably drink up the eddies of water that appeared here and there and then disappeared who knows where underground. Almost certainly they ran into the canal nearby, which was already swollen, cloudy, and steamy. And from the downpour the street emerged completely changed.

Later, during the long summer, Tommaso used to take his elder daughter to the pure white beach of Anfushi Bay, the promontory that jutted out into the open sea between the Eastern and Western Ports. Anfushi was far away, beyond the walkway known as the Corniche, and they had to take the streetcar on the Ramleh line — *ramleh* means "sands" — then walk through the ruins of the former Turkish quarters, where the second floors of the houses hung over the street from balconies supported by inclined beams, like a makeshift camp. Blue curtains hid the interiors from view, and heady odors emanated from within, mingling with the strong smell of the fish market.

Then, before reaching the dunes and the beach, there was a great field of lilies, dense, perfect, and intensely aromatic. They were taller than Marta; her father would pick her up and carry her on his shoulders. With a swift rustling he traversed that army of long, blossoming stems without speaking — their perfume was suffocating; it was as if he didn't want to spoil them, and at the same time, as if he wanted to ask their forgiveness with his silence. They reached the white sand beach and a group of large, smooth boulders that encircled a shallows to create a pool. Tommaso, who did not know how to swim, waded in cautiously, holding his daughter in his arms. When the water reached his waist — a frightening moment for her — he would dunk her in all at once. He was convinced it was unhealthy to enter the water a bit at a time. Then he let his daughter free and he played with her.

But one morning as they were entering the water and Marta was looking up from below at her father's tense face against the immense blinding sky, a net — large, black, and heavy — suddenly fell on top of them. Tommaso held his daughter tightly to him as he tried to free himself with the other hand, but he knew they were doomed. He shouted, a shout of terror without words, which he repeated until the oblivious fisherman appeared from behind the rocks and came to their rescue. It was the only time that Marta heard her father curse: ". . . you and your Prophet."

They were saved, but Tommaso's face remained pale for a long time. On their way back he said to her, "Don't tell your mother," and Marta felt guilty for that silence. Days later she was still looking at her father, thinking about that secret of theirs. It did not dawn on her that perhaps he himself had recounted the event to his wife.

While Stelianì's house glistened like a mirror, Antonia's was invaded by books. Strewn around at first, then piled in stacks, they spread out on the floors like weeds and climbed the walls like vines. Those that were buried and became irretrievable were forgotten, or perhaps were sorely needed and got bought again, because Tommaso never moved his books, or so it seemed. Antonia, who did not feel the need to put things away, lived surrounded by books in the big, sunny house on the Nile, making paths through them as if through an overgrown garden. There were books on top of the few pieces of furniture and on the trunks; there were books under the windows, some of which could only be opened partway.

Alone in the middle of the bedrooms, mosquito netting hung like ghosts; in the morning the nets were wound around the bedposts for a few hours while Antonia worked, singing nursery rhymes and arias to Margherita.

Martina slid on the inclined boards, which were becoming too short for her as she grew.

Stelianì's older children worked: Elèny at the cotton mill and Antonio as a shoemaker. The two little ones went to school. They could read and write Greek. Martina would sit on the house steps with Kliò and write on a small chalkboard, learning the symbols of that language she already spoke. But if her father saw her he would say, "You shouldn't tire yourself. Go and play!" and he did not move until she obeyed. So while Margherita was learning to walk on her weak little legs, the father's concern for Marta became possessive and jealous. Perhaps it was because Maria had died in Italy and Giacomo wrote letters that were too brief, or perhaps it was something else, but Tommaso suddenly poured all his love and affection onto Marta, thus taking it away, in one manner or another, from the others.

"It's time for Marta to go to school," Antonia would say.

"It's too soon. School is bad for little girls," her father would answer; and then he said to Marta, "I'll teach you whatever you want to learn." But Antonia bought a little chalkboard and some notebooks and gave them to Marta so that her daughter would not use up Kliò's things, not even the chalkboard. She gave her a pencil and told her, "This one is yours." As for the chalk, she found it in her husband the professor's pockets. He had Marta read and write occasionally, but he did not realize that Marta was learning far more than he taught her because Antonia, on the sly, was adding her own lessons to his.

❖

She was growing fast, Marta; when she was seven she looked nine or ten. She was eight when her father gave her a copy of Aesop's fables as a present. The stories were in Greek and she could read it. As he handed her the book, which was old and falling apart, he said, "It's yours, but you can't have it until tomorrow; I must sew it back together first."

"*I* will sew it," Marta exclaimed, and in a rush she pulled the book out of her father's hands, tearing it. He changed color and took the little girl by the arm, then placed her on his knees and spanked her on her naked bottom, as he had never done before. Then he left the house. Marta did not stay inside to cry; she couldn't. After regaining her composure, she, too, went out, and saw her father flee with those long strides of his. She followed him in tears, calling him, because she *had* to be forgiven. But he could not hear her — it's impossible that he could be so cruel as to not stop if he had heard her — and he moved rapidly away. Then a cart passed by, further dividing them and adding to the distance between them.

Just as the Canterno girls drank the Nile's water without even filtering it or keeping it cool in terra-cotta carafes, so did they find it was not a great sacrifice to be thirsty when they were perspiring. Nor did they need to find a cool breeze or stretch their legs under cool sheets if they were feverish. So Marta lay still in her bed, and everything was different, more special, when seen from under the mosquito net that also prevented the flies from landing during the day. One no doubt got well after an illness, and one emerged from it better than before, all the more so in proportion to the price of the suffering. When the fever disappeared, it was important to fast and wait to be hungry, "with genuine hunger," her mother said. But then, only then, her father, whether out of compassion or nutritional conviction, would do something forbidden: he would secretly bring Marta a big loaf of bread, fresh from the oven, hot and dark-crusted. It was not *el reghiff*, the round, flat bread that the Arabs bake, nor was it the "French" bread, white and smooth, that he bought downtown every day as he returned from school. Instead it was a real Italian loaf, baked dark and crusty to his specifications by Signora Ungaretti, from Lucca, the baker on Moharam Bay.* Tommaso would put that loaf under his favorite daughter's sheets, then look her in the eye and say, "Keep quiet, eh!" The loaf was wrapped in cloth to keep its black crumbs from scattering throughout the bed. Then Marta, guilty and innocent at the same time, would break the loaf with her hands — which was difficult, the crust so hard it hurt her fingers — and she would slowly eat it, savoring each aromatic, flavorful mouthful. Innocent but guilty, that is how she felt. Because when the two authorities looming over her seemed to be in conflict, as in times like this, the love she felt for her father, stronger than her love for her mother, even though it was mixed with terror, was tempered by pain and resentment. It seemed that her mother did not sufficiently respect her husband, like when she said, "He knows too many languages to be able to speak." She and her daughters spoke Arabic better than he, in addition to Stelianì's Greek. Arabic words necessarily indicated the food that was bought or prepared at home; Arabic and Greek were the expressions of everyday life, "my only life," Antonia would say. Her homeland, even though returning there remained her constant dream, was becoming ever more misty and remote.

Mina Mina Mìn!
Anà Sultàn!

Thus went the nonsense rhyme.

On the mulberry trees along the canal lived the silk butterflies. Marta and Margherita would collect half-grown worms and take them home. They kept them in a cardboard box with a few fresh leaves. The insects would eat, turning their tiny heads "always in one direction, always," and they quickly grew. They ate night and day, then they made cocoons on the sides of the box. In time the

* Signora Ungaretti was mother of the Nobel Prize–winning poet Giuseppe Ungaretti. —*Trans.*

sisters watched the clumsy butterflies emerge, unable to fly, and Marta would take them back to the trees along the canal.

I was rather delicate — says Margherita — and when I did not feel well and Mamma had to go out, Settemunìra would keep me company and tell me little Arabic tales . . . I knew a lot of little songs, too, all of them songs for dead children. Because when a child died, we children of the neighborhood went to sing in the house, in front of the dead child who was placed up high, surrounded by flowers like a nativity scene. Then we were given candy.

The time came when Martina stopped participating in the processions with her white veil and sweet-smelling pomelia flowers in her hair. Father Quilici's sermons, in the big Franciscan church of Saint Catherine, were in French. Marta stopped partaking in the little girls' processions because although she was still a little girl, she was becoming too big; she was growing both in height and in breast size. Her mother said only, "You are too old," and sewed soft and shapeless dresses for her, feeling embarrassed by that uncontrollable natural phenomenon. It was a change that certainly was noticed at home, no doubt with their homeland in mind, as Ciociaria had long been known for its wet nurses. In fact, Marta and Margherita would come to call the female bosom the *ciociaría*.

Marta was afraid of horses. One afternoon she stumbled and fell in the street just as a carriage was passing by, and a wheel crushed one of her legs. She managed to get home — it was only a few yards away — and she did not faint only because she did not know how. She was very pale, she bit her lip so hard it hurt, but she did not let anyone hear her because her father was home and certain things, she had been told, were not meant for him to know. Antonia, with a face as pale as hers, had her lie down in bed. The wound was ugly, and serious. So Antonia went to retrieve the Devil's Stone from her medicine box (a box with a smoking train painted on the cover; how could anyone forget it?). The Devil's

Stone was a white stick that made the flesh turn black by burning it. Even so, Marta knew not to make a sound until after her father left the house. When she was able to think again, she told herself, *If I could hide this, I can hide anything, anything at all!*

The Savory Note, Alexandria, 1911

When Marta was ten and Margherita five, Giacomo returned. Having finished *ginnasio* in Alatri, he would attend *liceo* in Alexandria; so his father had decided. Giacomo was sixteen, he was a man. He brought joy, music, and a new unimagined air of idealism to the house. He alone could build kites that remained high above Alexandria until the red sunset and beyond, held by an entire ball of cotton string. The bow of Giacomo's violin screeched sometimes, but almost always drew melodious sounds and long, harmonious arpeggios. With her plump, rosy face resting on her hands, Martina listened to him ecstatically. "You look like one of Raphael's cherubs," Giacomo would tell her, and she felt happy even though she did not understand, or precisely because she did not. She adored her brother and would have followed him anywhere he would let her go.

Giacomo took her to the opera, to see *Aida*, "Aida, in the right place," he said, and she didn't understand, knowing nothing about opera; but she said it was the most beautiful show she had seen in her life. Giacomo played Bach and Beethoven and would tell her, "Listen, listen to these Prophets. These are the Prophets, much greater than those of the Bible."

When Giacomo handed her a sheet of music Marta sang the melody, following those black signs with tails and recognizing in them a sequence that he was picking out on the strings. "You see? You can read music, see?" And pushing his soft curls away from his eyes, Giacomo spoke to their father about Marta, who was ten and looked thirteen. "Why don't you send her to school?" he asked. "Why do you let her grow up like a little beast? It's not right, it's not fair to her."

❖

The phrase *like a little beast* was an expression used by priests, Italian priests, but it was efficacious and appropriate. The father said nothing and went out, alone. When he returned home he told his wife without preamble, "Tomorrow Marta is going to school."

"*Elhandulillàh!*" Antonia exclaimed, and she ironed Marta's new blouse.

It was a wonderful feeling. She was in school, with female classmates and one — just one — male classmate, with professors and an immense blackboard, and she could learn, at last! She was taller than the other young girls and from then on she felt that she was Marta, not Martina. She had never set foot in a classroom so she was placed in the first grade, even though she could read and write Greek and Italian.

The following day her father called her and handed her a big book. It was the Georges, that grand dictionary of classical Latin. He said, "This is the most precious and sacred book of all. It's yours. Take good care of it. I will teach you how to use it, but after that, remember, do not ask me anything, because everything is in it."

Marta was happy. She was in school! She regretted only that those were hours she could not spend in Giacomo's company. She learned to be competitive with her female classmates, whereas the only boy (whose name was Leon, no less!) was truly pathetic. She had new girlfriends, whose homes and parents were in other parts of the city, on streets she did not know. She thought her classmates lived a life different from hers, a life different from that of the daughters of Stelianì and Settemunìra as well. And she was right.

Marta was good in school, although not right away. This was not because her father favored her in class or helped her at home; "Look in the dictionary" was his answer to all her questions. Nor was studying at home any less forbidden, or done less furtively, than before. "Don't get tired. Go and play," her father would say. But in the evening Marta now saw her father with a different eye as he did his schoolwork and prepared his lessons. He wrote out the assignments for the following day on separate sheets of paper, one for each student in his five classes; if he made an error with that minute handwriting of his, Professor Canterno would crumple up the sheet of paper without hesitation and throw it away. It was the only time his daughters ever saw him waste paper.

He was forty; his appearance, and his long, bouncing stride, with his hands behind his back holding a book, had become more majestic. Now that father and daughter were walking to school together, a new, but not easier, rapport developed between them during their long walks. She would have liked to tell him, *Go ahead and read, if you feel like it*, but she did not dare. And those silences brought back to mind the terrifying scoldings she used to receive as they walked through the streets. Though calmly delivered and rare, they were almost always unexpected, often incomprehensible, and at times undeserved. Her father's most explosive outbursts were saved for the home, frequently unleashed at night in the conjugal room. These were terrible fits that would keep Antonia awake all night crying and leave her downcast and silent the following day. But another day would pass — her daughters noticed — and serenity would be restored, sometimes even better than before.

It was during one of those walks that Tommaso Canterno saw inscribed in big letters on the wall of Fort Napoleon: MARTINA WANTS A PIANO. He saw it and did not slow his pace, but said only, "Where did you get the chalk? You didn't steal it from school, did you?" Not another word. In fact, Marta had always had chalk at home because her father stole it for her, albeit without realizing it, so at first she said no, then yes. She wanted only to have the scolding over and done with, but this time it did not come. It had been several months since she wrote those words on the wall, and her anxiety over his reaction had eased with time.

Two entire months went by before her father again said, "Get ready, we are going out." They went together, without talking, through Suk El Attarìn market until they reached the music store, where Marta watched her father buy a book, a large book with a pale green cover; it was the Peter's edition of Beethoven's *Sonaten für Pianoforte Solo*, all of them. The book was new, a rare purchase for him. Marta turned bright red and did not speak. On their way back home her father said, "Just like the man who bought the crop before the horse. The piano will come later." At that, Marta threw her arms around his neck and placed a kiss between his tender, smiling eyes.

That same year, her first in school, Marta read *Les Misérables*. For the first few pages, she looked up every word in the dictionary and transcribed it on paper along with its meaning, for although she spoke French she had never seen it written. Thus she learned French, which she would perfect with Monsieur Bocara, a Parisian. The class composed a poem for him:

> *Who doesn't know Professor Bocara?*
> *From one pole to the other his praise is sung.*
> *His vast knowledge and great virtue*
> *Make him beloved by* tout le monde.

For they were a most kind and gracious class.

Marta's friends at school were Editta Tagliacozzo, Luisa Fera, and Ida Latis. The Tagliacozzo girl was the youngest of four daughters of a widower, a rabbi, while Luisa's father, Professor Fera, taught mathematics and was the colleague whom Tommaso Canterno esteemed above all.

Our father was suspicious of all, absolutely all, the Italians he associated with. He used to say, "They are sectarian . . . anarchists . . . they are all sectarian . . ." He never explained more than that, and we would not have understood . . .

In fact, many of the Italians in Alexandria at that time were anarchists: the poet Giuseppe Ungaretti, for instance, who was the son of the baker in Moharam Bay, and Enrico Pea, his friend, who was a mechanic in the shipyards of Ras el Tin. But a sense that he was being persecuted took hold of Tommaso Canterno during those golden years in Alexandria, and once it insinuated itself, it permeated his soul, and it would be inherited by the gentlest of his daughters, Margherita.

Marta would see Editta Tagliacozzo again, more than half a century later, in the United States, where two of the four sisters, daughters of a rabbi, would find refuge after fleeing Rome.

Marta listened to her brother play, and one day she said, "Do you hear that? That is the savory note." She pointed to the note "sol" on his sheet music, but Giacomo did not understand. The following day he called Marta. "Listen now, and tell me which one is your 'savory note.' Isn't it present in all music?" She listened and then pointed to a "re." They tried again with a different melody. "All right," her brother said. "And here?" Another piece of music, and another savory note. Giacomo went to see his father. "Do you know what Martina is saying? That the third of the major scale, or the fifth of the minor, is the savory note. Marta understands music. You must let her study it."

On the other hand — says Margherita — I was growing up like a little beast, in part because I was frail and I went to school late, at the kindergarten run by the French nuns — the Sisters of Charity, the ones with the big white hats. That was when I learned all my French. From the nuns, and also from the friars, because Mamma took me to Saint Catherine's for catechism and to march in the processions dressed as an angel.

My best friend in those days was Fatma, a little Arab girl who lived below us. She was plain — she looked like her father — but she had a younger sister who was really beautiful. Her name was Nabaneja, and she was really a beauty. My brother, who was European and a bit harsh, did not want me to play in the street. But where else could I play? All of us, even Kliò, played in the street. And so when he went out and Fatma saw him disappear down the street, she would call me, crying out, "Tahàli tàchte!" which means, "Come down . . ." I can hear her now. But then Fatma and Nabaneja's mother died. She died of typhus. And Fatma, who was seven, was the one who had to announce her mother's death, shouting along the neighborhood streets, because that's the way it's done there; it's always the woman who announces a death, right after it happens, even at night, and Fatma was the only woman in the house after her mother died. Then her mother's relatives came — her family was from the interior, from Upper Egypt — and they took the two girls away. I did not see Fatma ever again, and I never heard anything more about her. Who knows why I think so much about her now? I think of her every day. Who knows, perhaps she is dead and comes to visit me . . . "Tahàli tàchte," she used to shout . . .

Margherita played all day with Fatma. She knew, however, when her father would be returning home, and she always went to wait for him on the balcony. She spoke Italian only in the evening, at home; she who knew all the little Arabic and Greek nursery songs. Short and dark-haired, with very delicate and refined features, she had large eyes like velvet, eyes that seemed to have come not from her parents but from Egypt itself. But while Marta at fourteen looked eighteen, Margherita looked like a seven-year-old when she was nine.

Now I will tell you a story from when I was really small. One day I was sitting in Papa's room playing with my dolls, which Mamma made of cloth, and Papa had a visitor, a friend and colleague. And while they talked among themselves and I played quietly, Marta came in. And Papa said, "This is my elder daughter. With God's help, I have given her beauty, intelligence, and culture in a much larger measure than my younger received . . ." I heard and understood, but I felt fine all the same . . . Or at least that's what I thought then . . .

At last Marta's father said, "Get ready, we are going out." And then, "We're going to an auction. That way, you can see what it is." They went up to El Attarìn, and in the grand, illuminated hall Tommaso Canterno bought a piano; a secondhand one, but a real Bechstein. "It's yours," he told his daughter. Marta was so happy she couldn't sleep all night and kept getting up to see if the piano was still there.

She took lessons from Maestro Papasiàn, a Greek from Greece, who had never had a student as talented as she was. He let her play whatever she wanted, guided by the remarkable ease with which she read music, a talent given to her by Allah. Since Marta owned Beethoven, she played Beethoven, and left exercises and scales aside. Her memory, too, was a miracle, and Marta went to her lessons without her books, playing from memory the musical piece she had learned at home. Her teacher listened to her with his eyes closed. "Brava," he would say. Six months later his pupil made her debut in the annual concert, and on the twenty-fourth of May, 1914, on the stage of the Great Alhambra Theater of Alexandria, Marta Canterno played the Sonata number 2, opus 49. Present in the audience were her father and mother; her brother, Giacomo, who ran to kiss her proudly; and her little sister, whose copper-blond hair was tied for the occasion with an enormous sky-blue silk bow.

Papa was moved and he went on stage to say a few words. He thanked Maestro Papasiàn, sang his praises, and mentioned that he had a large family — says Margherita.

Upon returning home her father called Marta, who was still inebriated by her success, by the lights and all the people, and he said, "You will be a great woman! You will do important things and you will not disappoint me!" Then he handed her a small knife. "Always keep this with you, right with you. If it happens that a man comes too close, if he wants to touch you, don't hesitate to use it. You are beautiful. Remember, you will have to be on your guard, you will always have to defend yourself."

Perhaps he told her other things we don't know, things she never told anyone; or perhaps not. But from that day on Marta always carried that knife, an object toward which she felt neither horror nor attraction, because it was small, and because it was her own. She even carried it when she was with her father. If only she had had it that time the fishing net almost killed the two of them in the warm waters of Anfushi! That time when Tommaso Canterno, an Italian, had dared curse Muhammad!

The house had two stories and, like all the others on that street, it had a little attic off the balcony, at the top of the last flight of stairs. The air in the attic was dry and hot, with a heavy, sweet odor, like honey. In addition there was the stench of chickens, because the attic also served as a chicken coop. One of Antonia's chickens had the vice of eating its own eggs right after it laid them. One afternoon Antonia told Marta, "I am going out. The red hen is going to lay an egg; keep an eye on her and take it right away." Marta forgot her orders, and when she went to the attic, too late, she found the empty shell and a bit of egg white in the nest. Furious with the chicken and with herself, she picked up the broom and beat the bird until it lay down, as if dead. When Antonia returned, she found her daughter next to the chicken, which was lying on its side with its legs outstretched and its eyes closed. She knew at once what had happened and said, "What have you done? You must confess."

For days Marta nursed the chicken, hand-feeding it, petting it, talking to it. Father Quilici in Saint Catherine received daily reports of the hen's recovery. When it was fully recuperated, it started laying eggs again but no longer ate them. Perhaps this was because it had been fed a different and more nutritious diet, but Marta had no doubts: the chicken had understood and learned a lesson. She had taught it. Years later, when the annulment of Marta's marriage was requested, her husband recounted the episode to the Ecclesiastical Tribunal of the Sacra Rota, saying, ". . . she is convinced that she taught a chicken, when she was a young girl . . ." "You must mean *trained*!" "No, Monsignor, really *taught*. And she wanted to do the same thing with me . . ."

But it's too soon for that.

The attic was also "the little birds' room." After tying a cord to the door that led to the balcony, Marta would lure the sparrows inside with bread crumbs, and from her hiding place she would watch them eat and hop about. Then she pulled the cord, locking them inside, and overcome with emotion she entered the room among those wings flapping in frightened confusion. She caught as many sparrows as she could, petting them and then letting them go. Ah, to hold those soft beings, fluttery and defenseless, but able to fly! It seemed to Antonia's daughter as though she held creatures of paradise in her hands. It was bliss. One sparrow that she had taken from its nest lived with her for years. For fun, it liked to slide down the inside of a watermelon rind; it would open its little wings a bit, raise its tail, and down it went along the cool and wet slide. She was enraptured by the bird's delight, and she let it climb again and again onto her finger, then placed it at the top of the watermelon slice to continue its game.

Ramadan lasted a whole month. The Arabs fasted all day half asleep, but at night they ate: small cooked fava beans, *falafèl*, *kollooras*, and big soup bowls of *moluhyia*, making a lot of noise in the streets. The Canternos, for whom those were not vacation days but school days, were kept awake, and they would fight. They quarreled over the eternal topic of their relatives, the priests in Ciociaria: the pride and avarice of Antonia's canon uncle; the excessive drinking of Don Luigi, her brother . . . "Well," Antonia would respond, "your cousin is even worse; it was because of troubles with the ladies that he had to go to America . . ."

That same summer of 1914 they took Giacomo to Italy. Having finished *liceo* in Alexandria, it was time for the beloved brother to attend the University of Rome and become a professor like his father. His mother and sisters accompanied him, and Margherita had to learn to wear shoes all day. Marta was silent the entire time she was in Alatri; in part out of timidity and weariness, for she was accustomed to her bed of soft African cotton wool and could not sleep on Alatri's noisy corn husks. She also kept quiet because she could not understand the jokes and allusions, the hidden, already suggestive, meanings in the games of her female cousins. There were so many cousins in Alatri, all of them beautiful. She was the most beautiful, but she was not aware of it. But Marta's presence caused quite a stir, and her silences were interpreted as a sign of pride. It was a sad stay for Antonia, who was able to cry for the first time over the small tomb of her daughter Maria, dead in her homeland, because they had not brought her back home to Egypt that dreadful winter. And it was a tiring stay, because of the enormous dinners the visiting emigrants could not escape. Margherita was taken by her uncle Don Luigi to a wedding, and people asked, "Whose daughter is she, this little one?" "She belongs to my sister Antonia, who lives in Egypt."

And throughout that interminable dinner, Margherita drank wine without knowing it. She had never tasted wine before, and they kept filling her glass until she had to be carried home. She almost died from it. From that point on, Margherita never touched wine again.

And Zia Erminia, who was so good, said to me, "Stay with me. You can see your mamma doesn't love you." Yes, I loved her, Zia Erminia, but how could I . . . and how could she — it didn't occur to me then — how could she make an offer like that, after Maria? How could I tell Mamma I wanted to stay? Besides, I didn't want to . . . Yes, I loved her, Zia Erminia; I felt sorry for her because so many of her children had died. Only my cousin Elisabetta was left, and the boy, who was little then. They died of dysentery, or measles. In those days measles was a fatal illness. Still, Mamma never really was fond of me. Or my brother, when you come right down to it. She used to say, "Why have you turned out like this, you?"

They returned to Egypt that year, but the return trip was not happy like the first sea crossing with Giacomo. Antonia did not sing.

After Giacomo's departure for Italy, life in Alexandria was not the same anymore. Two events took place: a world war and the death of Stelianì's eldest daughter, Elèny, who died of tuberculosis at eighteen. Stelianì's husband had died the previous year and the *kollooras* business had ended with him; the family did not survive Elèny's death. There was Kliò, who was learning to make hats, and there were the two boys, but of these only Antonio, the shoemaker, brought any money home. As a consequence of those painful losses, and for reasons of nostalgia, need, fatigue, or perhaps new illusions, Stelianì decided to return to Cyprus with her son the shoemaker and Kliò. Cyprus, which she had left as a new bride twenty-two years earlier — many or few as those years now seemed to her; at times they seemed both. Yes, in those years she had seen steamers large and small, and many white lateen sailboats coming and going to Cyprus, their large, triangular sails piercing the sky, but apparently only now did she realize Cyprus was not unreachable.

During one of those afternoons when she and Antonia were working side by side on their adjacent balconies, Stelianì said, "We are going back to Cyprus. My brother is there, and my elderly mother. Antonio and Kliò will go with me, but Nicola wants to stay to finish his studies; perhaps he's right, because he doesn't know Cyprus, it's not a homeland for him, for him it is nothing. But I do not leave with an easy mind; Nicola is sixteen, he doesn't know how to do anything, and the house is large . . ."

Antonia said, "I'll talk to Tommaso tonight." And the following day while they were sitting, as they had for fifteen years, in the chairs on their balconies, overlooking the heads, veils, and turbans of the passersby, she said, "My husband would not want to bother you while you have so many worries, but he says this: if you think you won't need the entire house, and if you don't have other plans . . . if you are taking your furniture to Cyprus . . . whenever it's convenient, you could perhaps lend him a few rooms . . . for his books. As you know, he never has enough space." Stelianì set her hands down on the pillow, and the shiny bobbins dangled below. Then she raised her eyes over the rim of her glasses and waited for the rest.

The rest came. "As for Nicola, we'll take care of him, if you want. He'll stay in his house, your house, to sleep and study, but the laundry is no problem for me; it would be as if I had Giacomo here. He will eat with us. If that makes you feel more at ease . . ."

Steliani just nodded; she was so moved, she could not work her lips to speak.

Ghosts

Once Steliani went home to Cyprus and Nicola joined the household, Professor Tommaso could no longer sleep. He kept seeing ghosts in the night. He had agreed to the arrangement out of a desire to have more space for his books, but as the night song of the frogs rose, a fear took shape within him, a fear of that boy, that man, alone in the apartment next door, and his daughter Marta still at home. By dawn, in the brief moment of quiet after the frogs went to sleep and before the gulls woke lamenting, a complicated structure of fantasies had risen in his head: that Nicola himself had convinced his mother, brother, and sister to go back to Cyprus, and Marta had conspired with him. When the sun came up, Tommaso Canterno went to look at his daughter — the traitor — who slept serenely. At fourteen she was a woman and she was beautiful. She had the gift of music, she knew Latin and mathematics, English and French. And he, with his own hands, had allowed that filthy male into his house, that low-down Greek! Worst of all, she had schemed with that goal in mind! She, his daughter, had betrayed him, he who loved her above all creatures!

Thus Steliani's departure precipitated a period of spying, persecution, suspicion, and tears. Marta was accused of flaunting herself and flirting, even though she did not know the meaning of the word when it was shouted in her face. Nicola was unaware, and the family wanted him to remain that way. To Marta's discomfort, he joined them at every meal and was the object of their kindness, for "a guest is sacred." She did not dare speak Greek anymore, with anyone. And she began to judge her father, always badly this time, as she learned of an evil she didn't fully understand. For Marta the word *virgin* was an attribute of the Madonna, and it had no other significance whatsoever.

That there was a war on, that his son, a university student, had written from Italy to say he was enlisting, along with everything else, seemed to mean little or nothing to Tommaso Canterno. He would say to Marta, "Why did you walk home that way? Why are you wearing your hair like that? Yesterday it was tied tighter. The door to your room is not closed. Where were you today? What route do you take to go to school? Who was it that greeted you on the street? And why did you answer?"

"He is my classmate; you've met him . . ."

"No, I haven't met anyone, and you mustn't meet anybody, either."

As for the war, he said, "It's just the newspapers' propaganda. They write those things to frighten people; they have their own interests, their hidden agendas. Don't listen to them; they are all sectarian. Don't buy them anymore, those newspapers; they serve only to destroy peace in the family." So the war in Europe served only to increase the silence among them, and at the same time his jealousy for his daughter rendered him merely annoyed by the concerns of others. Antonia prayed and, when alone, she cried. Her visits to Saint Catherine's became brief, and done in secret.

Margherita says, Father was in denial about the war, he did not want to believe that it was possible, that it was real . . .

Feeling persecuted at home, Marta went to study with the rabbi's daughters, the Tagliacozzos, until she finished at the *liceo*. Meanwhile, Margherita started at the elementary school. She liked school, but if she was afraid of being called on, or if she was anxious about her assignments, she would leave the house with her books under her arm and go to Saint Catherine's instead of to school. She sat there and said four hours' worth of rosaries while she watched the friars and counted the candles, betting on which of the wicks would die down first. All alone, she made up stories with marvelous plots, full of men and young women and evocative houses. Those were the golden days of cinema, and perhaps the most enjoyable time of her life.

They went to the cinema every Thursday, Antonia and her two daughters, escorted by Tommaso, who paid for their tickets and then returned home. They saw Charlie Chaplin, Harold Lloyd, Larry Semon, and Buster Keaton. There was Francesca Bertini, clinging to the drapes in love's despair. And when Margherita imitated Chaplin or Larry Semon, or pattered about, casting her eyes about like the chicken in *The Gold Rush*, she would make her father laugh. Nicola laughed, and her mother and sister laughed, for Margherita was still a little girl and anything was allowed. In some obscure way, it seemed to her father, to all of them, that she would never grow up; as if that was her duty, and their right. *This daughter of mine is for paradise*, Antonia thought.

When she was at the Tagliacozzos', Marta would put on her head one of those large hats that all the ladies wore back then, even her mother; the kind that Kliò made. With a tragic expression she would lean on the doorjamb and let an imaginary glass fall from her hand. Her friends composed a poem for her:

Martina Canterno is a schoolgirl
With sweet manners and a singsong voice.
She doesn't study Latin yet she learns it
And she drinks poison like Francesca . . .

Within two years Stelianì's apartment, whose floors were once immaculate, was invaded by books. Stelianì and Kliò came back to Alexandria a few times — to see Nicola, to get their things, and to cry on the tombs of Elèny and her father in the Greek Orthodox field, down on the Road of the Western Cemeteries; it was a large, long avenue shaded by mulberry trees near the mouth of the canal.

Marta was happy with these return visits from Kliò, her oldest, dearest, and most intimate friend. Stelianì and Kliò would arrive in the afternoon, and in the evening after Marta had already gone to bed — she always needed a lot of sleep — Antonia would stay up late talking with Stelianì, telling her the news of the last few months. Kliò stayed and listened. The following day the girls would spend all the time they could together, and Kliò would tell Marta, "I dreamed . . . you know what I dreamed? Guess! That you played in a concert at the Alhambra and everybody came to listen to you, and you played . . . Do you know what you played? The one that goes . . . Wait, I'll remember, yes, here it is, listen . . ." and Kliò would hum a perfect rendition of the first movement of Bach's Italian Concerto.

"Noooo! How is it possible. Really? You dreamed it?"

"Yes, yes, really. I am telling you!" Kliò would say, her dark eyes shining with mischief. Marta believed her because she took anything Kliò said for gospel truth. And she was pleased their friendship had remained so close, even after spanning the sea.

Perhaps it was his daily solitary walks through the city and along the canal or past the esplanade of Moharam Bay to the shore of Lake Mareotis, his hands and book behind his back and his eyes to the ground; or perhaps it was all the terms he read and contemplated in their various alphabets (for he had heard or spoken few of those languages); but Professor Canterno's mind seemed to be deviating increasingly from the real course of events. When Antonia said, "Giacomo hasn't written in such a long time . . . ," Tommaso would answer, "He will write. He must be busy." "What do you mean busy? Giacomo is in the war . . ." "Don't you believe it. The newspapers just say that to frighten us. Who knows what the governments want. It's all propaganda."

Didn't Tommaso see the warships in the port, or did he not know what they were? He would tell his wife, "I told you not to buy the newspapers anymore. Stop giving them your money." At first Antonia thought he said those things out of concern, to keep her calm. But several months later a letter from Giacomo arrived from a hospital. It said: "I am alive and well, but my head is not like it was before." And after her tears dried up, she noticed her husband's vacant look. Professor Tommaso was not even fifty years old; his wife said, "He has too many words in his brain to be able to think."

The day came when Marta completed her *liceo*; that remote and unacknowledged war had ended by then. The Tagliacozzo girls were returning to Italy and Marta said, "I am going with them. I want to study at the University of Rome and at Santa Cecilia Conservatory. Giacomo is waiting for me." She said those words after nights and days filled with fear. But her father looked at her and started pacing back and forth, as he did so often. His silence was leaden, and so was the sky. Then he said, "You're right. You know how to study and you must study. The best university for you is ours, the one in Rome. But I will not let you go alone. I'll ask to be recalled. We will all leave."

But the following day he said, "I talked to the school authorities and they cannot let me go now. First they must find a substitute. I cannot go back, not right away. But Marta must; I have made a promise to her and to myself."

"I will go by myself, with my friends. Giacomo is there waiting for me . . ."

"No," said her father. "Your mother and sister will go with you. You will leave and I will follow you as soon as possible."

Antonia blanched. Something must have happened for him to wish to get rid of all three of them. She was the one who wept, not Marta, who was happy her mother and sister would be accompanying her. And Margherita? Perhaps, but she never said a word, and to whom anyhow? Tommaso remained silent for days, then he said, "I will take care of the trip, of everything. I will write to Italy and say they must recall me because my family is leaving me."

And Antonia said, "That isn't true, I'm not leaving you. We are staying. I am not going to leave you . . ."

"You must. Don't you understand? That way I will fool them; I will be the one to outwit them . . ."

They could not help him. Silence spread through them like a disease during that trying summer, one of those summers that stifled all thought; Antonia almost forgot she would soon be leaving. And when Tommaso came home one day saying, "I bought your tickets. You are leaving in twenty-five days," Antonia wept, but not in his presence. She cried as if it were a natural thing, as if those tears were a seasonal rain. It had been a long time since they had spoken to each other at night, a long time since they had been close — ever since the date of Steliani's departure, or even earlier perhaps, from the day of Elèny's death. Because he had not sought her out, Antonia felt rejected. She accepted this in the same way the young girl from Alatri had accepted Egypt. Fortunately Stelianì had been there in those days. Poor Stelianì, *unhappier than me* thought Antonia, who had by then been able to transform Maria's death into an angel's return to heaven. She prayed. Then, red with shame for having to accept that new duty in obedience to her husband, a duty against nature and religion, she asked Settemunìra to look after the man she was about to leave. And Settemunìra, as jovial and calm as always, said, "Don't worry. My daughter Amina likes to iron, and she will do it for him. I will send her to your house to clean when your husband is in school." So Antonia nodded several times and swallowed her tears. In the entire world, not even in the faraway home country where she was returning against her will, there was not a greater friend than Settemunìra; she was sure of that.

Ibrahim

Amid the contention and incredulity surrounding preparations by the three Canternos for the journey, precisely on one of those afternoons full of astonishment and confusion, Tommaso received an unexpected visit. The caller was a very wealthy Arab who owned one of the finest homes overlooking the banks of the Mahmudiyah, up the hill from their quarter of the city. He was the head gardener of the Antoniadis Gardens, the most beautiful in Alexandria. He also owned stock in the Cairo–Alexandria Railway Company, or so he said, and the professor had no reason not to believe him. He said he had two sons and three daughters, two of whom were already married; the third was betrothed. He had come to ask . . . for Professor Canterno's permission. "After much hesitation, I have accepted a request from my second boy, Ibrahim, because I know that you are Christians and my son, naturally, is a follower of the Prophet. He asks me to ask you for permission to meet, on occasion, in the presence of her mother and according to all the proprieties of tradition, your younger daughter. He has had the opportunity to see her a few times with her revered parents while she strolled in our gardens. He has never talked to her, but he is burning with love. The boy is very serious; he is studying to become an engineer after he receives his diploma in Cairo and completes his training in Europe . . . The times are changing rapidly, your daughter is a flower, and certain barriers can be overcome . . . Our city is home to people of great culture, although diverse . . . There have already been marriages between Christians and Muslims. Naturally my wife and I would like for your daughter, who is so virtuous and beautiful, to consider the idea — who knows, perhaps someday — a possible conversion . . . Perhaps that would be in keeping with the long acquaintance your esteemed family has had with the people of this part of town, where you are so highly appreciated and loved. The girl . . . she has so many Arabic girlfriends, she knows our customs so well . . ."

Tommaso Canterno turned red to the root of his hair, then he grew pale. He stood up, and with great effort and a voice that sounded vexed in spite of himself he said he could not satisfy that truly honorable request. At least not right away; his elder daughter and his wife were preparing to depart for Italy for a time. "As for the little one, she is still so young," he said. "I hope that we can perhaps talk again about this in a year, at least a year . . ."

"Is the little one also leaving, then?" asked the man, and Tommaso chose to think the question contained the Arab's hope for release from his obligation to his son, an agreement he had made to be in step with the times, albeit with great reluctance.

"She is the one who wishes to accompany her sister and mother," he answered.

The other man bowed and quickly took his leave, and Tommaso decided he looked much relieved.

After the head gardener left, Tommaso started his customary pacing around the house. Antonia and Margherita, returning home, found him still mumbling to himself, "He is mad. People are mad! She is a little girl, a little girl! What in the world . . ."

"What happened?" asked Antonia.

"Margherita, go outside," said Tommaso. He said to his wife,

"None other than the head gardener of the Antoniadis came with a marriage proposal . . . or for a betrothal, let's say. For his son, the second one. He says that he is studying to be an engineer. He would like to be engaged to Margherita, can you imagine? And don't you go and tell her. I don't want entanglements and I don't even want her to meet him . . ."

"But his family . . . they lived near us . . . don't you remember? Of course they've met; they have known each other since they were little . . ."

"Keep quiet, you! That's all we need! I told him that you are about to leave. He was plenty relieved that I said no. You know one thing? They would have liked the girl to become a Muslim."

"But it's not right not to tell her," murmured Antonia.

Yet she did not tell her. There were only two more weeks until their departure. Did Antonia notice, or even Tommaso himself, that at dusk a lithe shadow stepped out of a boat as it slipped through the canal, and small stones hit the glass of a window in the house? It was not the first time that Margherita leaned over the balcony and secret words and gestures flew between her and the young Arab. Such things have happened for centuries; passionate, tender, and sorrowful feelings have been wasted in the perfumed nights, and destinies have been thwarted.

If I had married Ibrahim . . . sure, I was too young then, but what does that mean? Everybody is young at first, and then not young any longer. If I had married him my life would have certainly been different. And not so pointless.

The day of their departure arrived. *I will see Giacomo again*, thought Antonia, and she tried to add that joy to the confused feelings she had inside. Tommaso said again, "I will join you. I will follow you soon," but he seemed not to believe it himself. He repeated it on the dock. But from on board the ship they saw him become smaller against the yellow houses of the Mex and the white-and-green strip of the splendid Anfushi. The stretch of water that looked like burning oil in the sunset widened between them, and when they saw him again, waving the straw hat they knew so well, which now looked like a butterfly, each asked in her heart, *When?* As his wife, Antonia had already experienced every possible emotion for that man, but now she felt only remorse. And in those moments, so long and yet so brief, her heart answered that question: *Never.*

They were returning to their homeland, which for the girls was not their own; their destinies would intertwine with those of other Italians, who were different by birth and culture, by tradition and custom.

Rome, 1920

Giacomo was waiting for them. They didn't recognize him, and they couldn't have been expected to: a tuft of heavy, dark hair covered half his forehead. But his eyes, full of fire and life, were still the same; his smile was intact, and even more luminous. He adored his mother and his elder sister, his favorite. As for Margherita, "My little sister, I love you so much!" he said, hugging her and picking her up. He swung her through the air and gave her a moment of fright. "I love you all so much!" said that stranger. He had a husky, deep voice they did not remember. "And when is Papa arriving? When will I see him, my old *pater*?" He kept speaking volubly, this new Giacomo. Then a long, uneasy silence fell. Was it because of that tuft of hair? Or because they did not know whether to tell him everything, or nothing at all?

"But you, how have you been?" his mother was at last able to ask, almost disbelieving her heart's joy; there was her son, alive!

"Me? I'm fine, really fine, and not even as ugly as all that; someone likes me! My curly hair, see? It's not there anymore. They had to stitch my head up a bit because a Hungarian grenade burned it. So this hair — well, see it, Mamma? It's not the beautiful hair you gave me, but it covers the half forehead they sewed up. What does it matter? The brain is still there, and everything else, too. I feel like a lion, in many ways, you'll see . . . we'll do great things, great things! That's right; I'll tell you later. Papa, when he comes, will find a surprise, and you, too . . . Is this all the luggage you have? In a month I'll start in my new teaching post; I am a professor; like Papa, but in Rome, and do you know who helped me when I got back, and who wants me to be with him? A friend from Alatri, yes sir, an illustrious friend, Don Luigi Pietrobono, yes, the very same, do you remember him, Mamma? I haven't written Papa about it yet. And there is another thing I haven't written him about yet; so for the time being the surprise is all for you. What are you going to wear next Wednesday? Because it's going to be a great day, we are going to a wedding. That's right; your son and brother is going to get married, yes sir, we waited for you, we wanted you to be with us. What? You are not happy, Mamma? A holy matrimony, a new family . . . No, Don Luigi has nothing to do with this; the parish priest, or rather, the archpriest, of Alatri will marry us. Of course my wife is from Alatri, where else? The nicest and most beautiful girl in Alatri, you'll see. Her name is Caterina but we call her Cate . . ."

He pretended not to notice that Antonia had closed up in a gloomy silence. Giacomo had never in his life talked so much. Marta did not say a word, and there was no sound from Margherita. They looked speechless at their beloved brother. He was not himself.

Marta looked at him again, in the narrow courtyard, on the stairs damp from the humidity, and in the three small, dark rooms, all in a row, that were their new home at the Arco de' Ginnasi. Was this Rome? Tears of bitter disappointment, a sense of loss and nostalgia welled up within her. She remained silent. Then she stood as straight and tall as she could and steeled her heart; she could not weep or lament. It was because of her, because she wanted to study, that her mother and sister had torn themselves away from home, their beautiful home with the sky overhead, with the chorus of frogs, the lamenting gulls, and the perfume of the mulberry bushes on the banks of the great river. Marta pushed back her tears; she had to resist and win over this unknown homeland that seemed so hostile. She had to. It was up to her to save her sister and mother by becoming a great woman. *You will be a great woman*; the words of her father echoed in her heart.

Such a hasty, anguished return to Alatri was not easy for Antonia — before that Wednesday it would have been unthinkable. She felt an immense, indelible stain upon her, the stain of that forced wedding. At the ceremony, Cate's imposing father was present, the "insufficiently feared father-in-law," as he called himself, and Antonia marveled that such a man had let his daughter slip away. Her certainties were shaken. She was even more troubled when she went, furtively and alone, to weep over Maria's tomb, the daughter she had once left in Alatri out of duty. Was this her duty now, to return here? No, it could not be, because she had left her husband to return here; she had left him on the other side of all that water, alone.

Margherita fell prey to an endless slumber; she slept everywhere. In Alatri she did not know where to hide to avoid being seen, but who paid any attention to her anyhow? Who understood that she found everything fatiguing? In Alatri, where once she had almost died from her uncle's wine, the youngest Canterno lost her last bit of appetite, her desire to move, and her joyfulness.

On the way back to Rome she fell asleep on the tram, then while walking in the street she felt ill and her head spun. Once home, she discovered blood running down her legs, and if she did not scream it was because she lacked the strength. She washed, tidied herself as well as she could, and for two days she tried to hide; she was sure she had consumption; she knew that consumptives lost blood. That is what had happened to Elèny. It was hot in their small, dark apartment, and she slept wherever she could. When Antonia found out what had happened to her daughter, she said, "You, too? So soon? Why didn't you tell me?" but she didn't explain anything more; perhaps she did not even guess that Margherita was completely ignorant, or perhaps she was unhappy that her younger daughter had become a woman.

The four Cacciamonti sisters seemed to be one and the same. Three were named after the Madonna: Maria, the eldest; then

Annunziata and then Assunta. Finally, there was Caterina. They were, as the saying goes, each more beautiful than the other. They had handsome noses, which seemed to be the mark of their absolute self-assurance. Since they always stood and moved together, it was difficult to decide which was the most beautiful. They played on that, and not unconsciously.

The four motherless sisters, raised with anxious care by their father and many aunts, embodied the timeless blackmail *virginity for marriage*, with the added inducements of healthy teeth, shapely arms, wild underarm scent, and black hair twisted in heavy but soft chignons that promised long flowing masses for the bridal bed.

The Canterno girls were ignorant of such things; they looked on with trepidation and could not resist the four sisters who had suddenly and forcibly come into their lives and taken charge. Theirs was a different style, a word the Canternos had never heard before, but the Cacciamontis had, and they used it. They spoke of style, of fashion, and "common folk." They knew all the popular songs and sang them, from beginning to end and in unison, sitting on Marta and Margherita's bed. They actually had but one bed, and at night they slept one at each end. Before coming up to pay a visit the Cacciamonti sisters had bought a copy of *Canzoniere*, a popular journal with the latest hits; it had pale blue pages, with the strophes printed, who knows why, right in middle of each page, or else in two columns. The sisters wore high-heeled shoes, but they removed them immediately, throwing themselves on the bed and taking them off with a practiced kick of the heel; they would then lie dangling their feet, which were bare in summer and covered by stockings in winter. The elastic bands showed above their firm thighs (after all, they said, we're among women), and on the chair or the bed lay their handbags, full of what Antonia would have called — were she to mention them — their beauty powders. And playing cards. Each sister owned a pack, and they played solitaire on the Canternos' bed.

The need to play a hand came upon them with sudden urgency, and if one of the sisters could not find her pack of cards, she circled the minuscule apartment asking, "Who took my *carts*?" mispronouncing the word's ending for who knows what reason.

The four sisters — and one of them was the sister-in-law — were eagerly attentive in their care for Marta and Margherita. In their view, the two of them needed to be brought out of their shells, like beans in a pod. "You've got to come out of your shell, honey, or else . . . ," and the "or else" sounded like a threat. *Or else there won't be any husband* was what they meant, a quip so obvious it went without saying.

Certainly Cate had found a husband, but even Assunta and Maria each had a fiancé. In the House of Canterno that word had never been uttered; and even to say, or think of, a "House of Canterno" was a novelty, introduced by the Cacciamontis.

When Marta went to Santa Cecilia to enroll in the piano school, the classes were already full. She stood, unable to think or ask for anything else, red-faced and filled with a sense of guilt. "Signorina, what are we going to do?" asked the elderly secretary. Then he suggested, "Do you know where there might be an opening? In Professor Forino's cello class, but in the second level." Back home, with her cheeks still flushed, Marta murmured, "I need a cello!" surprising even herself. The thought had not occurred to her before, nor did she know that her father had already shipped her piano and it was traveling across the sea at that very moment.

Giacomo procured a cello for her, and so she found herself owning two instruments. They made room for the piano because Cate liked it, but the cello seemed even bigger. The Cacciamontis banged on the piano and Marta did not have the courage to lock it up, hoping they would tire of it. As for the cello, she hid it as best she could. In order to have enough light, she practiced while seated by the window overlooking the courtyard. There was a *liceo* class across the way, and during recess the boys looked up and watched Marta play, then clapped their hands. That was the price she had to pay for admittance to Santa Cecilia. And the cello, how much had it cost? She did not bother to wonder, because she was not accustomed to thinking about money.

❖

Marta truly was a hopeless cause, as Cate and her three sisters said. She left the narrow courtyard on Arco de' Ginnasi, crossed in front of the Chiesa del Gesù, walked along the Palazzo Altieri, and continued on, following ancient streets until she reached La Sapienza. She preferred those shaded streets to the new Corso Vittorio Emanuele, with its recently created open spaces. She followed two fixed itineraries: one on the left past the Minerva, and the other to Santa Cecilia by way of Sant'Ignazio, Montecitorio, and Campo Marzio. During two entire years Marta saw almost nothing else of Rome. She did not notice the obelisks in so many of the piazzas, and perhaps she did not even see the small one she passed every day, the one supported by a patient little elephant by Bernini, for when she walked she looked down at the ground. In fact she did not even know what an obelisk was, she who had been born in Alexandria, for at home and at school her father had taught her other things. Marta had not seen the Campidoglio or the Colosseum, which was still hidden by buildings. Nor had she seen the Tiber. Until, after months spent in Rome, Antonia acted on a lifelong desire and said to Giacomo, "I have never seen Saint Peter's, would you take me there?"

"What do you mean, Mamma? You should be ashamed!"

So, at last, Giacomo took his mother and sisters down Corso Vittorio Emanuele to see Saint Peter's. They crossed the bridge and when Marta saw the river below Castel Sant'Angelo she just said, "So that's it? This is the Tiber?" Her mother was silent and Giacomo almost felt ashamed of Rome's river, imprisoned between massive walls. When they finally emerged from the narrow streets of the Borghi and reached the colonnade encircling Saint Peter's Square, Antonia stopped a moment and murmured, "*Elhandulillàh!*" Immediately after, she said, "It's too big." They crossed that sun-drenched space and entered the basilica and Antonia again thought, *It doesn't look like a church, there is too much space, too much air . . .* During the days that followed, pleased that she had at last paid her ancient obligation, she said to Marta, "Go back, return to Saint Peter's, otherwise what will *Pardi* say?" *Pardi* being the old Ciociaria way of saying "your father."

Marta truly could not orient herself among the gloomy old houses and the severe ancient buildings. And the new ones seemed enormous and heavy, with armies of brown shutters clear up to the sky. The sky? There had been so much of it in Alexandria! This was not sky. Caught between awe and repulsion in the misty air of wintry mornings or in the violent summers, Marta did not raise her eyes toward that sun, which was capable only of peeking from behind corners or burning without respite from above the rooftops. She never looked up; the sky, and heaven, had betrayed her.

She suffered even more from the lack of space inside the house. After being forbidden — for two years — from moving about the rooms where she might encounter Nicola, Stelianì's meek son, she had hoped for some privacy, but she never managed to be alone. Cate, her sisters, and their relatives were everywhere. By now even her mother and her brother were "Cate's relatives." Marta saw only her mother's back. Perpetually busy with cooking, Antonia did not sing anymore, and Giacomo did not play his violin. Yes, Caterina was everywhere, either draped across a bed or running around disheveled. Or she would dress up, wearing too much perfume and too many accessories, and then go out on her errands, as she said. She would return laden with *mascarallìcchie*, which is what Antonia called small, useless items. Indeed, the tiny house seemed to be bursting with Cate's *mascarallìcchie*.

But in the evening, as Antonia washed the dishes from the dinner she had prepared, just as she had always done, Giacomo's wife seemed to bloom like a large nocturnal flower. Cate read out loud! Most often she read the D'Annunzio given to her by her husband. They formed a circle around her: Margherita on the same chair where she had been embroidering for hours; Marta on her bed, but sitting up straight for fear she would fall asleep if she lay down. Giacomo also sat on a chair, but astride it and facing the chair's back, his long, delicate hands cradling his face, that face that had fought a war, thin and mysterious under the long flowing hair that was not his own.

Caterina read, and because she was pregnant, she would occasionally spit into a chamber pot kept on a chair beside her. She read marvelously, with ample or soft or commanding gestures from her large white hands, and with expansive expressions on a face now breathtakingly beautiful. An hour, two hours: Cate did not tire, and neither did her two sisters-in-law, enraptured by that uncommon charm; for that woman, who was as young as they were, subjugated them with a spiritual power, after subjugating them in a quite different manner throughout the day. They loved her, now. Cate did not tire because she loved reading more than anything else in the world. But when she was done, she would sigh her last utterance of the evening, "Giaaa-co-mo!" and her husband would immediately shake back his hair, push his chair forward, and run the few steps to take her in his arms and carry her to bed. The group would part, perhaps without even saying good night. In the silence that followed, while the two girls readied themselved for bed, the pot with Cate's saliva had to be rinsed, and Antonia did it, thanking God for that new life.

When Giacomo's son was born, Marta was spending her days studying for her second-year cello exam, having skipped the first year. At night the baby cried and no one could sleep. Antonia explained, "He was born at night and so he needs time to adjust to our schedule; he's like a little night bird. We must be patient and thank God."

Margherita slept during the day, in a chair. Although her mother still bought quantities of fabric and thread for her (and oh, how Margherita embroidered!), she did not splurge, not on her, or on any of them. Money arrived regularly from Alexandria, but Tommaso's letters were litanies of questions and never mentioned how he was doing. How was he getting by? The preceding year Tommaso had said he would wait "until the rains came" and Antonia remembered the intense odor that awakened the senses after their deep sleep through the dry season, an odor containing essences of mud and distant sky. And she heard the sound of running water — water that had overflowed its banks, flooding the fields and roads while Stelianì's songs and the squabbling of the hens on the balconies filled the air. Tommaso had stayed behind to wait for his replacement, but also to organize his books. Now, in the darkness of the narrow apartment on Arco de' Ginnasi, Antonia could see with her own eyes the impossibility of the task: by then, Tommaso had tens of thousands of volumes that no one would ever read again, and Stelianì's house was filled with them, too. They were damaged by sun and humidity, by worms and mice. Tommaso was spending his days fighting the mice, building barriers of pepper, boric acid, and salt, but was he perhaps ashamed to write her about it? Or was he letting the mice build their nests in the house? She remembered when the cat had kittens in their bed and he had said, "Let her be!" No telling what messes Tommaso was creating! Antonia could feel her legs moving, wanting to run home, to Alexandria, to return everything to its proper place and then rest under the mosquito netting. Or perhaps Tommaso was not sleeping at night, and instead he walked along the banks until he grew tired, although he never tired. He walked with long strides until he reached Lake Mareotis, where he got lost among the tangled reeds and papyrus. He called for help, he called, but no one heard him. The seaweed in the brackish water was dark, dark were the banks . . . And what was there to eat at home? But perhaps Tommaso has his dinner at Stelianì's . . . no, Stelianì isn't there, she has gone back to Cyprus, Stelianì. There is only Nicola, but Tommaso doesn't like Nicola . . .

Antonia could not forgive herself for having left Tommaso alone, having abandoned the husband God had entrusted to her. Antonia had fevers but did not mention them; but if Cate's baby cried, she quickly dispatched the angel to Alexandria and ordered him, "Go see!" For no matter how crowded the house at Arco de' Ginnasi, Antonia's angel again had his place. Antonia had entered menopause and she was sure that every hot flash brought another gray hair. Soon she would be white all over, and not just sporting the gray streak above her forehead that had appeared after that day so long ago, when she was in Egypt and Maria had died in Alatri. But once the fever had passed, she knew she would not be able to — no, she simply could not — return to Egypt. She had to take care of Giacomo and Cate's baby. She also had to visit her mother, at first once a month, and then less often, up at the Plaje. She brought her a chicken she had bought in Alatri — where else? — because a bit of broth was good for the little old woman. And her husband? He knew what needed to be done. He had always known, for that is the duty of husbands. Antonia never thought that Tommaso might have another woman in Alexandria; she was never jealous of the man who, by divine will, was her master on earth.

The days following the birth of Cate's second child were filled with confusion. It was a girl.

"What are you doing with that *tarboosh* on your head?" Antonia would ask Giacomo as he came and went dressed entirely in black. Marta studied at all hours. The newborn girl was a little night bird, too. "We are building a new Italy; I have no time to spend with all of you," Giacomo would say as he headed down the stairs. And with that *tarboosh* on his head Giacomo had marched on Rome; although at home no one had understood what that meant.

Professor Canterno wrote from Egypt, "The three girls must study acting. The enclosed sterling pound will serve to pay for their enrollment at the academy. Let Marta take care of it." "What we really needed . . . ," said Antonia, but since she did not dare keep the news from them or disobey one of his orders, she handed the letter and the money to Marta. Cate exclaimed happily, "I like *Pardi*, I really do like him," and she took care of the enrollments herself. "Let the three girls go," he had written, and Caterina went. She spoke and read. She read, declaimed, and acted. Not so Marta, who said she did not like to speak other people's words. And Margherita? Margherita would perhaps have liked to act, since just two years earlier — and yet it seemed so long ago — she had been such a natural at playing Chaplin's hen and Larry Semon. But she lacked the self-possession to face strangers and she did not have the time. She had things to do at home. At home, of course. Even though her home had been in Alexandria. Alexandria, with its yellow walls and yellow floors, with the warm dust in the streets, and the rains, warm or cool, depending on the season. Sweet were the chats on the stoop with her little Greek and Arabic friends, those secret conversations, light and never-ending, which had left no trace except the memory that they had been the salt of life.

No, Margherita had no time to attend the academy. There was the shopping to do, the children to watch, and her trousseau to embroider. While she embroidered and hemmed, she thought of Elèny, the cotton-mill worker, and she pretended she was still living in Stelianì's house. For Margherita, the years following Elèny's death had perhaps never happened; nor had Elèny's death. Margherita embroidered, because one day she would get married, she knew it. In the meantime she dreamed of him, her husband. She felt him next to her, kind and affectionate, and she spoke to him. Perhaps that imagined ghost of her dreams resembled the angel who had once been such a companion to the young Antonia. Ibrahim had stayed in Egypt . . .

Cate, on the contrary, did go to the academy, every day. In the evening, if her husband could not accompany her, she went with her three beautiful sisters and their fiancés, or with colleagues and friends. Slim and beautiful, Cate knew how to dress, how to behave around people. She studied. Her voice, endowed with great tenderness and resonance, was cultivated and trained by her teachers and her own intuition, and she was led along the most promising paths of the acting profession and art. Caterina made sacrifices for her talent and ambition, as was inevitable — something her mother-in-law could not undertand — but on the eighteenth of October, 1924, she performed at the Teatro Argentina. Cate was an actress!

As she walked down the avenue with her sisters-in-law she pointed to a poster on the wall: "Look! See? There I am!" "Where?"

"What do you mean, where? There!" The name was not her own but a stage name. Her sisters-in-law did not like it, or perhaps they did. Her mother-in-law scowled when she learned of it and said, "But *Cate* seemed like such a nice name to me!" "What does it matter to you, I am still the same person, am I not?" Actually, soon after she asked to be called Marika at home. It was the beginning of the career of an actress who would become famous. In the evening she no longer read to them aloud.

Three years passed, then four, and the letters arriving from Egypt were long, but written in an ever-smaller hand. Antonia did not read them in their entirety anymore because she would have had to buy glasses, and those were expensive. When she saw that those letters were becoming more and more strange and distant, Antonia just rocked her little granddaughter all the faster, even though the chair was on the verge of breaking and the baby was more than two years old. She rocked the little girl and sang:

> *Mina Mina Mìn*
> *Anà Sultàn!*

Caterina wasn't there. In all her loveliness and with her handbag full of beauty powders, she was acting on the stage, she was having dinner with her colleagues, she was visiting with people who counted. Giacomo was happy and proud, or at least he seemed to be. Giacomo, who since October had been walking around dressed in black, wearing that *tarboosh* on his head and taking everything too seriously. Yet Antonia, who was never without a pot or pan in hand, would sing as she always had:

> *Tutte le feste al Te – empio*
> *Mentre pregava anch'i – io . . .*

during the quiet moments of days that were almost all serene. Margherita sought refuge in church when she could, just as she had in Alexandria when she hid at Saint Catherine's on the mornings she skipped school.

The Chiesa del Gesù was nearby and always open. Margherita liked to push open the heavy main door made of leather; once inside, she loved standing in the high-ceilinged nave permeated by silence, by holy singing and rustling. Of all the things in Rome, Margherita liked the churches the best, which had also been true of her father many years earlier. Churches where one could hide, especially at sunset, so as not to see that interminable hour, that last breath of the day, which in Alexandria had been brief and irretrievable. As the light and sounds were changing in the early moments of nightfall, she would return home, a disheveled and lively child, to find the windows recently closed and the great protective ghosts embracing the four-poster beds. Here in Rome, the tolling of bells on both sides of the river caused her profound anguish. The voices and the noises of the day had ceased — the machinery and calls of the workmen putting up buildings — and softer sounds, of distant cowbells, of mooing and bleating, were borne on gusts of wind. Perhaps that was the cause of her anxiety — hearing animal voices in that uncertain hour, but never seeing them. Was that it?

Margherita saw animals only when she went to Alatri. The massive oxen with long horns and placid eyes did not look like the "true" gray-black buffalo of her own countryside, with their horns covering their heads like a bonnet, but who wanted to hear about that? The milk was brought in by a peasant woman, who would say, "I'm just come from Campo Vaccino." But this milk from the cattle market had a different flavor, in fact it had no flavor at all, and a different flavor could be tasted when Antonia made *glookistàs* with Stelianì's old recipe.

And the river! Narrow, walled in, she had seen it only once, running swiftly near the church of San Bartolomeo on the Isola Tiberina, and once again her professor brother had to tell her the story of the Roman hero Horatius Cocles, for he always thought of her as an uneducated little donkey. Why was he the one, her beloved brother, who did not want her to study, whereas he had insisted that Marta have the opportunity?

Margherita was free to go out; no one ever said anything more than a generic "Be careful" to her. No one had ever told her,

Carry your little knife. They were not worried about her; hers was a comfortable destiny. Comfortable for them. And she didn't give a thought to any dangers, either, since she knew nothing of the outside world, she who already had so many fears inside.

There were no mosquitoes in the house in Rome, so one could sleep at night. But not Marta; she couldn't sleep because of her many obligations at school. As soon as she was in bed she fell into a profound sleep, but she woke after three or four hours, perhaps because of the cold, which never happened to her in Egypt, and she had to get up. She hated that. She dreaded it upon lying down at night, and she thought about it with horror during the day, because during those night hours the kitchen walls, which she had to walk by to reach the tiny room they called the bath, were covered with hundreds of cockroaches.

They stood immobile, the ugly beasts, and they moved their long, curious, sensitive antennae in unison. Those few that had been taken by surprise on the floor ran in silly confusion as the girl went by with her candle in hand. Marta crossed the kitchen with a hand over her eyes, but that was not enough to avoid the horror. Those silent sentries of the night, there were so many of them! What did they live on, and how? They certainly couldn't find nourishment on those walls. Intrigued rather than frightened by her moving light, they did not flee. Did they stay there by the thousands just for her, so that upon seeing them she would not forget them? It had not been like that when she was a little girl in Alexandria, where the large red cockroaches that occasionally flew in through the windows had seemed to her almost like cheerful little birds. Upon returning to bed, she managed to fall back to sleep, but it was an agitated sleep, filled with dreams. Only in the afternoon, when she could, did she manage to rest, to sleep for half an hour. Then she became a new person, her mind alert, stirring with plans.

They simultaneously wished for and feared their father's return. "When *Pardi* comes . . . ," Marta, Margherita, Cate, and even

Antonia would say, " . . . when *Pardi* is here . . ." And as the months and years went by, that eventual return had become more and more surreal and frightening. The more improbable it was — if the past was proof — the more mysterious and formidable it became. At first, waiting for their father had meant maintaining hope for the return of their lost well-being, and for a house — because it was impossible to fit him into the one they had. But as time went by, their selective memory of him focused on his most capricious and mad traits. So "When *Pardi* returns . . ." became the threat of new difficulties rather than the promise of better days.

He wrote, that is true, and his small handwriting had become even more minuscule on the paper, but he never talked about his work. Had the long-awaited substitute ever arrived in Alexandria? Even for Antonia, the idea of her husband's return was mixed with a sense of dismay. And she did not realize that Tommaso and his son had struck up a correspondence. Giacomo had not said anything, and she and her daughters did not know what was happening in the Roman ministries, where the new political climate had brought, among other things, an early fruit: the nation did not like to be represented abroad by professors of unproven Fascist faith. On learning this, Giacomo felt he had to defend his father as well as he could, while trying at the same time to convince him to resign and return to Italy where he could certainly obtain a position at the Nazareno. Tommaso remained oblivious and wrote: "The dean has made it clear — not very diplomatically — that I could return to Italy and change position . . . But the Ministry of Education cannot recall me because I am attached to the Foreign Affairs Ministry . . ." In another letter he wrote, "The ministry can send me and my family out into the street. I have neither the power nor the strength to react to that . . ." And later: "You know that I am a tenured professor of Classics, Latin, and Greek . . . It's true that I have been very interested in other languages and philologies, but I haven't published on them, and it is impossible for me to demonstrate it . . . I regret that you have spoken about my competence in other languages. It's important only that I be known as a professor of Greek and Latin, otherwise, based on simple affirmations without any proof, no one will trust you, and people might say that I am a charlatan . . . Dear Giacomo, I fear that all this is to my disadvantage . . ."

At the end of October, Antonia received a letter: ". . . I write this deeply dejected and filled with embarrassment because I am not sending, as promised, any money. It's Sunday, September 30, and I have not yet received my September salary. I was asked to sign the receipts for the usual sums, but yesterday I learned that there is a deduction of I don't know how much and the salary has not been paid; they tell me that they are waiting for a telegram. According to an earlier telegram from the ministry, which I did not want to tell you about, I am 'waiting for further decisions' . . ."

In a letter written the following day he said, "We could not have been more unlucky than this. I am told that I am 'released from teaching.' I am left without a salary. I won't come back to Italy. And I won't sell anything, not even my books. Without them, I could not teach anymore. Only by owning my books will I be able to live and send you some money from time to time. All of you have fulfilled, particularly Giacomo, all the duties of filial compassion. If we want to rise again — because if it's true that I have been relieved of my teaching we will indeed be out on the streets — you must pretend that I am dead. In other words, you must take care of yourselves. Marta must immediately look for work — giving lessons, a post in some school . . . You must not make even one lament about your fate. However, you must not ask for or accept subsidies, free lodging, or anything similar, because that would be the final ruin of all of us. As for protecting our daughters' honor, reread what I wrote on that subject when you first went to Italy . . . Make sure Margherita understands about the world's dangers.

"Be temperate in your speech. You must not say or write, or even think, an offensive word against anyone. Read the Gospels often. Take care that the little ones do not go out and face the many dangers of the streets . . ."

The little girl got a case of diarrhea that would not stop. It was summer, and they took her to Alatri — her mother and

Margherita. "This way you'll find a husband," said Cate. "I'll make the introduction; just don't act silly." Flocks of cousins, sisters, and future sisters-in-law went strolling arm in arm in the evening in the shade of the horse chestnut trees below the black Cyclopean Wall. They chatted about everything, vying with one another, "I . . . and she . . . and you," and they would tell Margherita, "These things don't interest you, do they? Shoes, dresses, fiancés . . . you want to become a saint, right? . . . And you'll leave us here to suffer . . ."

Margherita did not answer, at first because she did not understand. What was there to answer? She had never been good at understanding jokes and innuendo, except in the playful exchanges she used to enjoy with her little friends. But those games were light and of a different nature; their memory was sweet and blurred by the distance and dissimilar atmosphere. From within the walls of Alatri, how could one *really* remember the house on the banks of the Nile? "The salt of wisdom" she had heard the priest say at the baptism of Cate's children. *Salt that she had never been given,* she thought. Margherita's large, beautiful eyes were always looking down. Neither her mother nor her brother knew how to make her understand those dangers of the world; they did not even try.

After that terrible letter of the previous fall, Tommaso seldom wrote. From time to time he sent money. He lived on private lessons and translations. He did not need much to live. And without his teaching he had so much time on his hands!

By the fall of 1923 Marta had already passed her fifth-year cello exam. The only shame was that studying that instrument had diminished her remarkable ability to read the two staves for the piano. She passed her exams in Latin and Roman history at La Sapienza and made a beautiful showing on her Greek exam, where she read "in the modern style" as if she were talking with Kliò. The professor did not realize that his student was not actually familiar with Homer, because ancient Greek had not been taught at the *liceo* in Alexandria.

Marta wore clothing that was too lightweight for the Roman seasons; she could not adjust to European modes of dress, and she was always cold. But when she walked through the city, tall and beautiful, in the company of her cello, she was noticed and admired. She became a member of the Women's String Quartet at the Royal Grand Hotel where the patrons danced, smoked, and talked, and doubtless some of them even looked at the players. Marta did not see anyone; her uncomfortable, unfathomable "present" was nothing more than a bridge leading to an immense, marvelous future that was equally undefined, even in her dreams.

One spring evening she heard, "Look! There's Francesca Bertini!" and Marta Canterno missed a half beat. Suddenly she was plucked from that scarcely believable present back to the past, to those Alexandria afternoons. And she missed a beat again as she remembered:

Martina Canterno is a schoolgirl
With sweet manners and a singsong voice.
She doesn't study Latin yet she learns it
And she drinks poison like Francesca . . .

Now that her beloved yet feared father was far away no one called her Martina anymore. Francesca Bertini was right here in the flesh, under an enormous hat. She was even more surreal now than she had been on the screen, in that cinema on the corner of the yellow road in Alexandria.

For two years Marta performed in the new cinemas, under the stages of old, refurbished theaters: the Palazzo Altieri, the Salone Margherita, the Orpheus. She played the piano, not the cello, accompanying the comedies of Larry Semon and the dramas of the great Valentino. And with her eye she followed the action on the screen, the tears on heavily painted eyes, the galloping of horses; those films she had once watched as a spectator seemed so different and strange to her now! She also played the cello in the orchestra of Podrecca's marionette troupe, Il Teatro dei Piccoli, and she led the puppets at the piano in Aubert's *Puss 'n Boots* and Rossini's *Cinderella*. Marta, however, did not talk about her work at home because she was too tired when she returned. She handed her mother the money she had earned and Antonia would blush and whisper, "Later, when *Pardi* comes back . . ."

But one evening Antonia said, "Your sister-in-law has decided." Caterina alias Marika (Maria Katerina? They never dared to ask her) had come to the conclusion that it was "high time" to move. "Two connecting apartments that share a landing, I don't want the children to be taken away from their grandmother," she said. Marika needed a house where she could receive her colleagues, her friends, her "people who counted." "Too bad for those who don't know enough to move on, who stay fixed in one spot. No question about it, here there's not enough space!" Then the idea of the common landing disappeared and it was again one apartment, but spacious and new. "Good! Big families are my passion!" said Marika-Cate, now speaking like a Roman instead of in the dialect of Alatri.

They were on the fourth floor of a new apartment building, in the Nomentano district. It was higher than the trees at Villa Torlonia, higher than those at Villa Massimo, and in view of those at Villa Savoia. Yes, it was better than being in the country; this was the Rome of princes and centuries-old trees. The house was full of sun and the singing of a thousand birds. The streets all around, which were new or recently broadened, were still quiet, sunfilled, and contented.

So they seemed to Margherita, in the morning when she went out with the children to buy groceries, and in the afternoon when the air was scented with bay laurel as she went to Via Alesàndria to buy milk from the dairy maid and biscotti — nice and warm, fresh from the oven — from the renowned Fabbrica Gentilini, just a few steps away. From then on, and for her entire life, Margherita would serve the square petits beurres and the round Marias to her guests. The name was written on each biscuit in the singular, but it always made her think of the Cacciamonti sisters. In truth, Margherita loved "the three Marias," who came and sat their fannies down on her bed, as Antonia would say. After kicking their shoes from their feet, just as they had done in the other apartment, they would sing the songs of the *Canzoniere*. She loved the Marias, but she would not have said so to her mother and sister. And they loved her, "their little turtledove," and it seemed as though they took an almost sinful pleasure in training her.

"All right, we are going, and we're taking Margherita with us!" they conceded, or threatened, whenever they decided — for it was they who decided, and no one else — to go to the cinema. At first Antonia had objected, "Margherita must . . . ," but then she gave in. For Marika might have been offended if Antonia did not trust her sisters and their smiling fiancés with their softly pronounced *z*'s.

They no longer believed in *Pardi*'s return, even though they did not say it. But then Giacomo, who was not only an award-winning Poet of the Regime but also still a professor at the Collegio Nazareno, spoke to *Pardi*'s old friend, the rector, Don Luigi Pietrobono. He told him about the "family problem": the father who refused to return, with his books as the excuse.

"Certainly, indeed!" said the rector. Receiving Professor Canterno's vast library would be an honor and an endowment for the Nazareno. The books would be a gift, but the institute would take care of the shipping expenses. Once they were in Rome, the collection would be unconditionally available for consultation by all the descendants of the professor to the seventh generation.

"*Elhandulillàh!*" Antonia exclaimed under her breath. There were thirty-seven large cases, and on top of one of them — or at least that is how his daughters imagined him — was Professor Tommaso Canterno, called *Pardi*. He, too, was returning from Egypt after a quarter of a century, in the month of November 1925.

And now, before the Canternos make their acquaintance, it is time to see what brought a few other Italians to Rome, the capital, in the last decades of the nineteenth century.

2. THE MUCCIARELLIS

Ascoli Piceno, 1870

"WHEN PEPPINA TURNS fifteen I'll give a debutante ball," Nonna Caterina would say, and her promise sounded like a threat. The Marchesa Mucciarelli, born a Malaspina, paced back and forth in the deep green salon of her residence in Ascoli Piceno. At every turn her ample taffeta skirt rustled twice, first from the imperious stroke of her bejeweled left hand, and then as it swept against the high, stiff armchairs. In her right hand Nonna Caterina held a Tuscan cigar. "It helps me to digest and think," she would say, "and between digesting and thinking there is not such a great difference."

The Marchesa Malaspina pronounced her sententious phrases every day, undisturbed by the fact that she was repeating herself, whether she had an audience or not. She walked in her salon every afternoon, but on pleasant spring and summer days she walked in the large loggia running the entire length of the Palazzo Malaspina, which three centuries earlier had been a fort inside the city. Bloody and hostile was the era of its construction, and bloody and hostile was the Malaspina family. The architect, Cola dell'Amatrice, to whom credit is owed for the major buildings of sixteenth-century Ascoli, gave that palace an inhospitable air — or so it must have appeared to its enemies. But for those who would inhabit it he had wanted a high, open space that afforded a wide-ranging view over Ascoli, the City of a Hundred Towers, and its countryside. A place that provided almost a forest overhead, and archway pillars shaped like tree trunks with branches. In summer the servants hung curtains from those pillars for protection against the sun, and the long terrace became another salon with adjustable shade and a garden of flowering plants.

"Then, when I am old, you can put me in an armchair," said the eighty-year-old Marchesa Caterina. But in her palace the last of the Malaspinas did not have even one armchair, a comfortable armchair, where she could be placed one day, in a future that was certainly remote.

In its interior the palace had a gentle air, with its garden shaded by a beautiful sycamore, and the small loggias made cheerful by blooming climbers, by the games of the little girls and the dogs running about. The life of the two motherless girls was not sad. Peppina and Matilde played tag and hide-and-seek with the dogs. Nonna Caterina had four dogs, and they ate with her in the dining room, each with its own mat and small dish. "Better dogs than children," the marchesa used to say. "At least the dogs wag their tails for me."

Those were the years when Peppina, who was born in the Marches — which were still part of the Vatican state — was a thin adolescent and Matildina still a child. They did not understand or even try to grasp the meaning of the words of the great lady who was their grandmother. As for her sons, one was their father, the Marchese Alessandro, and the other one was an uncle named Gustavo, whom they had never met. He lived in Paris, and that name was just a word spoken disparagingly, as if their grandmother the marchesa were saying, *He lives in mud*. "That's because the pope has gone!" was her explanation for everything that went wrong, be it the actions of her sons, the death of a horse, a brick that came off the pavement, or a frost that destroyed the harvest. "The pope has gone . . . ," she explained, as if he had once been always by her side and at her disposal. Perhaps Nonna Caterina had never known serenity because it was not in her temperament. She had certainly not been serene since 1849, when an interloper named Garibaldi had come, "to stir up," he said, "the empty heads of my compatriots." And this, after two hundred years and more of comfortable and peaceful papal government and prosperity for the Malaspinas. The fact that this prosperity followed the pardon, granted by the pope, of her ancestors for transgressions that were none too small was something the marchesa failed to remember.

The Marchese Alessandro was seldom in Ascoli with his daughters; he spent most of his time "taking care of Ferrara," by which he meant the house and other matters after the death of his wife. Because the Marchesa Eleonora, rest her soul, had gone to heaven when she was barely thirty. Peppina had been eight, Matilde five, and Carlo just three. "Ahhh, your poor papa!" sighed their grandmother the marchesa when she happened to think of her son's widowerhood, or of other things, perhaps. And then, "We'll see with Carlo," she would add, placing her hopes in the last little marchese, who was being raised in Ferrara with his mild and already white-haired maternal grandmother, Nonna Emilia, the Contessa Agnelli. Carlo was still running around the vast floors of the Palazzo Agnelli in a long baby dress. "Carlino is fine with Emilia. Emilia is good," explained Nonna Caterina, unable either to forgo judgment or to remain silent. Since she liked to recount "the business of her family" the two girls listened to the elderly marchesa tell stories of the first Malaspinas, the ones from Tuscany. Two branches of the family — called Spino Secco and Spino Fiorito, from a distinctive detail in their family crests — had owned land and horses for centuries, "but if you scratched under the surface, at bottom they were all robbers."

As for the late Nonno Mucciarelli, her spouse, Nonna Caterina never mentioned him; either she had forgotten him or she had loved him too much. Nor did she speak to Peppina and Matilde about their mother. The little girls had a portrait of her, which they kissed every evening after saying their prayers. From the walls of the entrance hall, the Malaspinas of Ascoli looked down or smiled at faraway azure landscapes. At the center of the wall, above the fireplace, hung the portrait of seventeenth-century Monaldo Maria de' Marchese Mucciarelli, who wore a handsome red velvet suit and held the oval portrait of a cardinal in his bejeweled right hand. Next to him was a very delicate damsel with a plumed hat and a rose in her hand; who could she have been? But Matilde and Peppina never learned what feats Monaldo had performed, what joys or sorrows had crossed his long-gone life, because Nonna Caterina talked only about her own ancestors, the Malaspinas. So they knew only that the three thin, pale girls in three portraits on the wall were called "the Canary sisters" because they always wore yellow; but they never learned their fates, though given their paleness and very narrow waists they were probably tubercular. The three Canaries had magnificent heads of upswept hair above their unbelievably slender waists. When Matilde looked at them she held her breath and sucked herself in, but it was impossible to attain that shape. That the three Canaries also had faces seemed irrelevant.

In the dining room the table was always set, for dinner and supper. At dusk the stately grandfather clock struck the hour, for itself and the immense sideboards filled with sterling silver, which made clinking sounds from time to time. The marchesa was served breakfast in bed, while the two girls were allowed to take their meal in the kitchen with the servants. The cook, Emidio, prepared hot chocolate at eight o'clock sharp. The drink was so rich that if a drop of it fell on the white marble floor he would say, "Look at that, it's going to harden and turn into a chocolate kiss." But when the girls asked, "Emidio, what are we having for dinner?" he would answer, "Medicine, for your eyes." There was always a hint of playfulness in his voice, yet he remained obedient to his mistress, who believed that little girls need not be told everything.

The gardens extended beyond the sycamore almost to the banks of the Tronto, including a vegetable garden and a rhubarb patch for the marchesa and the girls, "because it's good for your insides, rhubarb is!" At the other end, against the south-facing wall, was a long espalier of mulberry trees, which thrived in the warmth and light of the sun. On one side were the servants' quarters and those of the gardener, to which a room had been added for raising silkworms.

"Saturno, this year I want you to raise four ounces," the marchesa would say, and Saturno promised, "I'll do my best, Signora Marchesa."

"Four ounces and I won't hire a worm man. I had a room built expressly for you; all that's needed is a little bit of attention and loving care. With one hundred grams of seed you should get three hundred and fifty kilos of cocoons, and not one kilo less. Anything above and beyond that is yours." Thus spoke the marchesa. And the girls said, "Saturno, will you call us?"

"I'll call you, signorine, I will. When the time comes, when the little worms are born, you can come to see them with the signora marchesa." It was a celebration Matilde looked forward to every spring, whereas Peppina did not like the silkworm room because of the intense odor, pungent yet sweet, given off by the silkworms.

From the end of April and on into May, the marchesa and Matildina walked down the sun-drenched pathway lined with rosemary bushes in full bloom. Hemp curtains screened excess light from the interior of the silkworm room, where shelves lined with wicker mats extended to the ceiling. There were two rows of shelving, surrounded by a corridor and with another corridor running between them. "Listen, listen to this silence!" Nonna Caterina would say to the girl, holding her thin little arm to keep her still. And in that warm, malodorous silkroom, with the pale light diffused by the curtains, Matilde listened to the soft breathing as it increased in volume every day, becoming a buzzing, a rustling, almost a song as the tiny beasts gnawed without respite.

The mulberry leaves were shredded for the youngest larvae, but were left whole on the branch as the silkworms grew. On top of the wicker mats life stirred and crackled; little yellow and black heads, silly and persistent, gnawed the leaves with an identical, repeated motion, the same motion from thousands of voracious jaws. Matilde stood right by the mats and drew her eyes close to the silkworms so that they appeared enormous, and in her fantasies they became frightful dragons. Then, while Nonna Caterina talked with Saturno, she moved away from the shelves and the silkworms became small once again.

"But Nonna Caterina loved us," Matilde would say years later. That *but* was meant to point out that the marchesa's feelings had been so well disguised as to require unearthing and interpreting. The marchesa, however, had displayed a more open affection to Matilde because the little girl was so small and delicate. So on snowy mornings, which made Ascoli silent and charming, Matilda was sent to school at the Dame Celesti in a sedan chair. The fabric lining the interior of that undulating little chamber had a pattern of flowers, red and faded; Matildina didn't know that such fabric was called damask, just as she did not know that it had been years since anyone — even in Ascoli — used a sedan chair. The marchesa seldom went out — only for certain secret charitable works — and she strolled in the gardens alone. But she wanted the girl to go to school until she was twelve years old. After that Matilde would study at home, just as she had decided for Peppina, because "education makes one a lady," and the daughters of her son Alessandro were destined to become true ladies. As for the young Marchese Carlo, when he visited Ascoli with his father, Nonna Caterina would look at him while turning him around in front of her, murmuring dubiously, "Provided he doesn't become a priest . . . or a physician who goes off to the Orient to heal the Chinese . . . ," and who knows where she got that idea.

Then came the day she decided it was time for Matilde to learn to mend, because a girl must be able to do everything. Nonna Caterina took an embroidered linen handkerchief in perfect condition, made a hole in the shape of a cross in the middle of it with her silver scissors, and then tore the hole open. Perhaps in the Palazzo Malaspina in Ascoli there was neither dress nor tablecloth that needed mending; or maybe the Marchesa Caterina would never have touched worn fabric with her own fingers, nor placed it in her granddaughters' hands; or else she wanted the girls never to forget that handkerchief of immaculate linen, which is in fact what happened.

Thus the two sisters grew virtuous and somewhat lonely, especially Peppina because at least Matilde went to school; their father was far away, their brother, too, and the servants kept at a distance. Friends? Who knows if the marchesa had any? There were, it is true, the cousins from Ferrara, but Chiarina and Norina, blond, plump, and identical even though they were not twins, did not play with them when they came to Ascoli. Rather, they remained timidly attached to the ample skirts of the grandmother that all four shared, "that saintly woman, Emilia."

Your grandmother Matilde told me these things; she called me Margheritina. And margheritina was also the name she gave the glass beads, the tiny ones, that she worked so well into handbags and embroideries. She even decorated whole cushions with them. She loved me because I was a little girl then, and looked even younger than my age. And how she liked to tell stories! She loved me, she did . . . Then . . . well . . . it was a shame!

In September 1861 when the Piedmontese troops entered Ascoli, and just over a month later when the Marches went from the Vatican state to the as-yet hypothetical kingdom of Italy, Nonna Caterina cried. But ten years later, when she learned that the Italians had entered Rome, the old lady only shrugged disdainfully. She must have thought everything would end right there, and after all, the pope had deserved it. However, she grieved when her son Alessandro said, "I am going to Rome to see what's happening," and did not return the day he had promised.

Two weeks went by and Nonna Caterina became more irritable and touchy. She repeated the old refrain, "Then, when I am old, you will put me in an easy chair," and she smoked cigars while pacing up and down the dark green salon and repeating, "Better dogs than children." One of her sons was always "in Paris doing stupid things." The other one, her favorite, had now "gone down to Rome to be taken for a fool." Nonna Caterina spent a lot of time behind closed doors in her salon, with two severe-looking gentlemen who were dressed in black and had arrived in a coach carrying large parcels of papers. The girls were not allowed inside and neither were the dogs. From behind that closed door, the irritated voice of the marchesa could be heard in waves, because of course she talked while walking back and forth, back and forth.

Then one morning she did not drink the chocolate that Emidio had prepared, and the doctor was called. Nonna Caterina's illness was brief: scarcely three days in bed, and there was no need for an easy chair. She died in silence at dawn on a snowy day after the archpriest had granted her the privilege of muffling the clappers of San Francesco's bells with rags. But who knows if she heard that silence? Who knows if in that head invaded by an unstoppable hemorrhage she did not hear instead enormous thunder crashes and wild tolling? Two hours later the Marchese Alessandro arrived, and then unknown relatives, while Peppina and Matilde stayed by each other's side more than ever. Emidio, the cook, kissed Peppina and Matilde's hands — the marchesine — surprising them with mute emotion. From that day on, there was no "medicine for the eyes" at dinner, and only the chambermaid remained at Palazzo Malaspina, but even she was preparing to return to her people. Scarcely a month later the father and the two daughters also left by coach, and three days later they arrived in Rome.

Small, cold, and dim, an apartment was waiting for them in Via delle Carrozze. Here the widower marchese and his two orphaned daughters felt their loneliness as never before. He explained that he had been lucky to find that small apartment almost overlooking the Spanish Steps. And he wanted to explain more, but the small, tired, and disappointed faces of his daughters made his words die on his lips. Every morning a woman named Cosimata arrived from the nearby neighborhood of Porto di Ripetta to do the housework. Then the marchese returned to Ascoli for a few days and asked the two girls not to go out; as a matter of fact, it was a command, even though that mild man could not give orders.

Cosimata would take care of all that was necessary. The girls did not ask the reason for that superfluous prohibition, and perhaps they did not even ask themselves why. When their father returned, the portraits from Ascoli came to stay with them: the pale Canary sisters, the other unknown and sad-looking ancestors, and the large, smiling Monaldo Maria de' Marchese Mucciarelli. There was also, even larger than Monaldo Maria, a beautiful Marchesa Caterina. On that street, in spring, Peppina turned fifteen without a debutante ball to celebrate.

In those days Rome was still the city of princes and their immense villas surrounded by majestic trees. The majority of modest dwellings, apartments, and domes were squeezed within the curve of the Tiber near the Vatican, in Trastevere, site of the ancient Ospedale di Santo Spirito. Only fifteen days before the *bersaglieri* entered Rome, on September 10, 1870, His Holiness Pius IX had gone to inaugurate the Fountain of the Acqua Marcia at Termini, the final official and ceremonial outing of the pope in the territories of his state. By that time the Rome–Frascati railway that began at Porta Maggiore, and the Rome–Ceprano railway that had its station at Termini, already existed, having been built by the Vatican state. Development of the city, with large tracts of buildings between the Quirinal and Termini, had also been initiated by the minister of arms of the Vatican state, Monsignor De Merode. The street that would become Via Nazionale was called Merode Street in his honor, but the large, incongruous buildings rising at the edge of the malaria-infested Campagna would become a hallmark of the Rome that would be referred to as Piedmontese, and later as Umbertine. There were some who wanted the new capital to continue spreading east, as De Merode had envisioned; others preferred growth to the west and north, along the right bank of the river, under the Vatican walls and Castel Sant'Angelo, where there were meadows and vineyards. The dispute would not be short or propitious.

In addition to the portraits of his ancestors, the marchese had brought from Ascoli the fruit of the sales that had probably shortened Nonna Caterina's life, and also the profits from the sale of Palazzo Malaspina: thirty thousand for his part of the land and forty-five for the residence. Of those seventy thousand lire the Marchese Alessandro gave fifty thousand to the most illustrious Signor Morpurgo, on December 22, 1870. With that sum Mucciarelli became the owner of 7,523 square meters of land on the right bank of the Tiber, under Castel Sant'Angelo. Of this, 2,143 were grazing land — valued at three lire per square meter — the remainder, cultivated as orchard, was valued at four lire twenty per square meter. The purchase of that land — the most illustrious Signor Morpurgo was absolutely certain, and Mucciarelli did not doubt it, either — was an excellent bargain: on that land where sheep still grazed and artichokes grew, buildings would rise for those who would be streaming in from the entire peninsula to create the framework of the white-collar class, the new bourgeoisie. Landowners in that area would soon become rich, as soon as the city planning projects for the capital were approved. The very same Signor Morpurgo, and now Mucciarelli also, were shareholders in La Società Immobiliare. Construction plans for the new quarter, which was already called Prati di Castello, were signed by the same architects who had designed the area around Piazza Vittorio, which had already been completed, fully developed and inhabited by that time. It connected the district of the railway station and that of the first ministries, which were also under construction, one on the Viminal, and two, extremely large, at the top and on the slopes of the Quirinal, on the road that ran from the most famous palaces of that hill to the ancient Porta Pia.

It was one of those rare Roman mornings when snowfall during the night rendered Rome's natives and old cats unhappy and skittish, but imbued the Romans newly arrived from the north with a childish sense of adventure and nostalgia. The Marchese Alessandro, who was one of the latter, said cheerfully to his daughters, "Children, today I will take you around by carriage, because Rome is more beautiful under the snow."

The city was silent, and the wheels of the carriage were the first to break the white layer over the cobblestones of the astonished Via del Babuino. "Look," said their father. "Look up, girls; look at the highest floors of people's houses, at the windows that let in the most light, if you want to know and understand who inhabits them. Today, under the eaves trimmed with snow, you'll see that they tell you even more." Did the girls listen? Perhaps so. They certainly kept their eyes well open to drink in the new Rome that looked almost — but only almost — like the severe but gentle city of Nonna Caterina. Because of the snow, Rome seemed more open and clear, while they remembered the other city as being small and dark. The girls shared these same thoughts without telling each other, as they sat straight and lovely near their father, who was dressed in black but more vivacious than on any other day. "Wait till you see this!" he said as they came upon the piazza with its obelisk at the center and four lionesses serving as fountains; and he turned to the driver, Tarquinio, who had become his devoted friend, "Take us around the fountain and then along the Corso, Tarquinio. Take us to Ripetta, then I'll tell you where to go next."

He did not tell his daughters where he intended to go. They looked at the simple houses on the Corso, at the small windows near the roofs, where a few windowsills were covered in white below shutters that were still closed. Who lived in those houses? Old owners and new renters, each with some discomfort. As the carriage took him and his daughters along the bright Corso, the Marchese Alessandro felt perhaps for the first time free from all guilt, and pleased with his decision to move his life and possessions to Rome.

Shortly before reaching the church of San Carlo al Corso they turned right, and soon they were in view of the Port of Ripetta. The water spouting from the fountain in the middle of the pretty rotunda ran slowly down icicles that were already melting. The river was green, the most colorful thing in sight. The opposite bank was nearby, beyond a few bare-branched trees, stretching out white and flat to the walled citadel of the Vatican. The glass panes of the Palazzo Belvedere reflected the sunlight, and above everything rose the Cupola: the city of the pope. Farther to the right, Monte Mario crowned by pines was also white. "Look," said their father, "look at that land dressed like a bride . . . ," and then, "Let's go, Tarquinio, take us to the bridge."

They passed the Palazzo Borghese then headed along Via della Scrofa and Tor di Nona, streets where the ancient odors had been quelled that morning by the snow, and they reached Ponte Sant'Angelo, which in those days was the only bridge in sight. It was the first time the two girls had ever crossed the Tiber. The red Castel Sant'Angelo seemed even larger as they drew close, and the pellitory-of-the-wall sprouting from between the old bricks and the white stone trim was deep green. Pointing to the dome on the left above the massed rooftops, the marchese provided explanations and mentioned names while his daughters paid only partial attention.

"At Easter we will go to Saint Peter's," he said, "but now look over there. Let's go, Tarquinio, go as far as you can." The driver guided the horse along walled-in paths between vineyards and vegetable gardens. From across the snow a mooing could be heard, answered by the distant sound of cowbells. "Let's go farther . . ." Slowly, they proceeded, almost to the riverbanks, again facing Ripetta. On the other side of the river, to the north and east beyond the domes and houses, rose the grand black trees of the Pincio and the villas of the Medici and Ludovisi families. Far away, behind the buildings and the trees of the Quirinal, rose the sharply pointed bell tower of Santa Maria Maggiore.

"Yes, that is Rome over there, but Rome will be here, too, you will see, on this piece of plain, and Nonna Caterina would approve," the marchese said softly. Then he paused for a long time, so long his daughters did not know what significance to attribute to it, though perhaps it indicated perplexity, for when one talks in the snow where snow seldom falls, everything sounds surreal. And he murmured, "There has to be a plan, and the one made by the architects is not the only one. Rome is not a vain dream. You see, daughters, this land . . . this land dressed in white today . . . part of it is mine . . . ours. There will be great buildings, and we, too, will have a house here, beautiful and large, although different from our ancient one in Ascoli. It will be for you, now that you are growing into women. In short, your future is here, yours and Carlo's." Thus spoke the Marchese Alessandro Mucciarelli to Peppina and Matilde. Then the carriage circled to take them back to the bridge in front of Castel Sant'Angelo and then home. Michelangelo's Dome shone freely in the sun. The snow on the roofs and streets on that Roman Sunday was already melting, and as the girls passed by, tears dripped down the vestments of the stone angels.

The neighborhood where they were living, under the open sky of Trinità dei Monti and the pines and orchards of the Medici villa, and near the soft and almost silent drip of the Barcaccia fountain, was called the English quarter. It was also the artists' quarter. So it had not been easy to find lodging there in Via delle Carrozze, for there were many Italians who wanted to become Romans in those days.

The cramped dwelling of the Marchese Alessandro had buckling floors, and in early summer there were fleas. Peppina remembered that kerosene would take care of these pests, so she used it. Nonna Caterina looked down from the longest wall in the small parlor, smiling perplexedly. In the portrait the Marchesa Caterina was no longer young. She wore a black dress with ample sleeves, a white lace collar, and cuffs — Peppina certainly could have made lace like that! — and she rested her hand on a windowsill (the one in the inside loggia that overlooked the garden with the sycamore). The signora's hand was almost entirely covered by folds of lace, and her hair, parted in the middle, was lightly covered by a veil made of black lace. Behind her generous shoulders hung a curtain of red velvet (which, Peppina and Matilde knew, was in the salon), and in the background beyond the window there was a landscape painting, of Grottammare. Yes, Nonna Caterina was there, and facing her were the old smiling Monaldo Maria and the lady with a plumed hat and a rose in her hand, and also the other ancestors, placed closely together and thus keeping one another better company than they had in Ascoli; as for light, even there, they had never had much of it. But the three Canary sisters — we can't separate them, poor things — were in the girls' room, and they at least enjoyed a bit of sun in the morning.

In the house overstuffed with furniture on Via delle Carrozze, Peppina and Matilde embroidered, sewed, and mended. Because now there really was mending to be done at home. They were not in dire straits, rather the opposite, but why not repair their clothes with the same hands that had made them? Their father's clothing was gray and black, but at home he wore a reddish robe. He cut his beard *alla Verdi*; his eyes were melancholic and often lost in space, even tending to cross at times. *When he is like that he is thinking of Mamma* was the daughters' secret belief, but they did not mention it even to each other. Peppina, who was sixteen, loved to read and had beautiful handwriting, which was sufficient, because "no one marries a bluestocking."

Peppina stayed home or went with Cosimata to buy the groceries. But Matilde was still in school and her father accompanied her every morning, by carriage in winter, and on foot when the weather was fine, down Via della Trinità, as Via Condotti was called then. Then they walked along the Corso, and Matildina always looked up at the balcony of a house inhabited by some of her father's friends. From that balcony, they had watched the horse races during their early days in Rome, and they had felt an excitement mixed with fear. That race of wild and terrified horses was no longer held because that section of the Corso, near Palazzo Chigi, was being enlarged. "Let's not go down there, Tarquinio, because it's too dusty for the little girl," said the marchese. And the carriage turned at San Lorenzo in Lucina and traveled along the peaceful Campo di Marte. "I don't want you to see the houses coming down," he told Matilde, "but later I'll take you to see the new ones rising"; for it was he who decided what she could and could not see. He had chosen the Palombella school for her, directed by Erminia Fuà Fusinato (in her old age Matilde often repeated that name with pleasure), and the school was located on Via della Rotonda. The windows overlooked the ancient, curving brick walls, and one of Bernini's little bell towers still rang the hour. There were about twenty young pupils, all from good families. So on foot or in the carriage, Matilde went to school every day, just as she had in Ascoli. But she never told her father about the times Nonna Caterina had sent her to school in a sedan chair, because without realizing it, she was a little ashamed.

During the summer of 1872 the architectural plans of the Most Illustrious Architect Antonio Cipolla were presented to the Most Illustrious Members of the City Council by the landowners in Prati di Castello, but the project had been postponed. "This time the Jesuits have won, with their expansion to the east, and the developments in the Esquiline and the Hills of Celio. But we will insist. It's now a matter of inserting the Prati project in the next city plan . . . ," said T., who was a friend of the Marchese Alessandro and also a good friend of Morpurgo's.

The following year, in July 1873, he said, "The plans of the engineer Viviani, director of the City Art Office, are excellent. You should have heard what the new mayor, engineer Pianciani, said about it . . . you remember him; he's a patriot, a follower of Mazzini . . . he knows what has just happened in Paris . . . He said that a city plan is necessary, and it must serve the public, but individual citizens should not and must not be prevented from profiting from it, too. That's what they did in Paris . . . and Paris must mean something, even though he, the mayor, did not mention Paris by name. As a matter of fact, he said he did not want to name the city he was alluding to, but you will understand . . . a follower of Mazzini, one of Garibaldi's men, and before that, you know, he fought in the war of 1848, he was at Custoza . . ."

Of the ninety thousand lire the Ascoli palace had brought in, the marchese's brother had taken precisely half to Paris. Now, two years later, the Marchese Alessandro's joy in the advantageous placement of his own share was sometimes clouded by doubts in his mind. But his friend T. would say "Foolishness," or "Wonderful!

So much the better!" And when the second project by Viviani was approved and even praised for its form, he said, "Good for us! There is only a small modification in the wording that pertains to Prati, but it is to our advantage. In fact the parliament has decreed that it must remain open to private initiative. We can build when we want, even right now! Tomorrow, today! The real estate company, La Società Immobiliare, will soon be starting up from what I've heard. And that company is us! We must toast to that!" They had a toast at the Caffè Greco. The Barcaccia gurgled clear, soft, discreet . . .

Three peaceful years went by and the marchese even grew a bit fatter, for his daughters and Cosimata were good cooks.

In Rome at that time there lived an old friend of remote Ascoli origin, Giulio Cantalamessa, a painter. Alessandro Mucciarelli was pleased to spend the mild summer evenings with him in what was then Rome's parlor, Piazza Colonna. Matilde, short and small-framed, did not look her fifteen years in 1876 when she began taking drawing and painting lessons from Maestro Cantalamessa; he was involved in the restoration of paintings belonging to the Borghese family. The maestro drove down in a carriage from the villa of the Borghese princes, or else he walked, his coat flying in the wind, through woods and lush green meadows until he emerged near the Fountain of Aesculapius where the ancient Muro Torto makes a tight turn. From there he would say, it was "just another little stroll," and by way of the Porta, Piazza del Popolo, and Via del Babuino, the painter arrived in Via delle Carrozze and rang the bell at the door of his young student. Since Signorina Mucciarelli took her lessons at home, she repeatedly drew the bell tower of the church of the Trinità dei Monti, which she could see from her window; one bell tower only, and by portraying a particular and rather strange image of the famous church she made it look like the bell tower of some obscure country church.

Matilde painted flowers and fruit, and more flowers, with honest nineteenth-century technique. She found the process pleasing, and with pencil and brush she tried to render the people closest to her on canvas. She painted without ambition or motive, almost without wanting the maestro to know, for he had not taught her portraiture. But when Cantalamessa saw how his student had portrayed her sister and father he said "Brava!" and was generous with his advice.

Traditionally, models would gather on the Spanish Steps nearby, waiting to be hired by painters and ready to go to their studios. But a girl from a good family certainly did not rely on such sources; and if Matilde was a good portraitist, it showed in the paintings she had done of her sister and father. Her father was delighted with his daughter's talent, for although he knew that a conceited girl would scare the men away and nobody would marry her, he agreed that "a girl must be able to do a bit of everything."

"Sit up, sit up, Papa," Matilde would urge her model when he let his head droop during the long sittings. She portrayed him several times with his melancholy, slightly crossed eyes and his short, double-pointed beard. But when Matilde sang, her father, yes, he who knew all the operas and could whistle them from beginning to end, would cry softly, "Quiet, you hurt my ears! Stop, you are out of tune!"

One evening in April 1876, the father said, "I have made a decision. I sold part of my holdings in the company, only a part. As for the proceeds, I will use them — not all by myself for sure — for an important work: something essential for the construction of the new development, and therefore our house; a project that will accelerate the plans and facilitate the construction work itself, reducing our expenses. Yes, we will build a bridge. A bridge that will go from Porto di Ripetta to Prati. It will be an important, historic initiative. Just think, girls: it will be the new Roman Bridge, after the last one built by Sixtus the Fourth, and it will be the first one of the new Rome. It will be an iron bridge, solid and quickly built, primarily for the transport of materials. The construction will begin within days." The father and his two daughters drank a glass of *rosolio* liqueur under the perplexed smile of Nonna Caterina — but for some time now they had not even noticed her.

❖

So every morning for two years Alessandro Mucciarelli went to help build his bridge. He would tell his daughters, "When it's ready I'll show it to you. Right now it's a construction site, which is not a place for young girls." But as time passed he seemed to grow tired of the bridge. He would say "We're almost there" as he left the house, but he no longer set out so early. Then at last he told his daughters, "It's finished," and he took them to see it. The old Port of Ripetta — with its grand staircase and charming rotunda with the lovely fountain — was unrecognizable, although it was still there. Where the fountain had once stood, a bridge with wood flooring was now departing from the rotunda, and there were no longer any trees on the other side — those trees they had encountered, black against the snow, on that Sunday long ago. Instead there was yellow, upturned soil, and empty space extending all the way to Castel Sant'Angelo and the Borghi, and to the pope's walls and palaces. They did not cross the bridge. They didn't even say *Shall we cross?* Instead they returned home.

From that day on, the Marchese Alessandro no longer seemed to have anything to do. He had built a bridge that for the time being, and as far as he was concerned, went nowhere. La Società Immobiliare had indeed begun construction, but not yet on his land, which had become smaller in size. In fact, most of the money brought from Ascoli had served precisely to build the bridge at Ripetta. And they needed that money to live on, too.

January 9, 1878, was a beautiful sunny morning. Alessandro Mucciarelli dressed in mourning and went to the king's funeral. The street he had taken every morning for years when accompanying Matilde to school was filled by a silent crowd traveling on foot to salute its first sovereign for the last time. TO VICTOR EMMANUEL II, FATHER OF THE NATION was written in large letters on the church's tympanum, and black and gold velvet panels darkened the spaces between the columns of the Temple of Agrippa, now called the Pantheon. Above the figuration in bas-relief, a large eagle with outstretched wings looked down fiercely. At the corners two angels with trumpets stood guard, and from the two Bernini bell towers mournful tolling pierced the crystalline air. Now that it was evident how meager were the proceeds from the sale of Palazzo Malaspina in Ascoli, Mucciarelli was filled with disappointment upon the death of the king who had bombed Porta Pia and destroyed the temporal power of the pope. That grande dame his daughters called Nonna Caterina — the woman he had been unable to call by name for so long now, perhaps out of remorse — could she have been right?

The carriage drawn by black horses passed through the silent crowd by way of the Piazza della Minerva, a beautiful sight under the bright winter sky, and even the Marchese Alessandro wept.

The cousins from Ferrara, Norina and Chiarina, ever more plump, pink, placid, and identical, sometimes came to visit and stayed for long periods of time. Carlo, on the other hand, was studying in Ferrara, and if he came to Rome it was only for a few days. Consequently their brother was the least familiar of their relatives, even though they loved him ardently. They were also jealous of him, for he met privately with their father in the parlor, locked behind doors that were otherwise always left open. Carlo lived in Ferrara and studied medicine, until — just as Nonna Caterina had prophesied — he left for faraway lands. But it wasn't China, it was Africa.

With their father's increasing silence the girls drew even closer together, strengthened by their companionship, and free to go about and think as one. "Is Papa dressed to go out?" they would ask, and the entire house breathed freely — yes, just as if the windows had been opened — as soon as the Marchese Alessandro went outside. Where their melancholy father went once his bridge at Ripetta was completed, the sisters didn't even ask. He would return at dinnertime with a newspaper for himself, and on the first of each month he brought the girls' magazine, *Giornale delle Fanciulle*, for them.

In the new capital the aristocrats had retreated into their ancient network of associates, which had become even more exclusive. True, the shopkeepers were courteous, but they were still "common folk," as Nonna Caterina would have said. Families who had come from other regions gathered only with acquaintances from their place of origin, as did they; but other than their friend Cantalamessa, it seemed only the Mucciarellis had come to Rome from Ascoli. The girls had their friends Adele, Enrichetta, and Margherita, so they did not complain. As for a husband, one was bound to come down from heaven sooner or later for each of them.

Instead it was the Marchese Alessandro, in April 1883, who played a mean joke on them by falling in love. "She was English and a good lady, actually," Matilde would say much later, "but we could not stomach her, and we felt that marriage was done out of spite for us. And we refused to admit that the poor woman really was a help to us. She had a little money and only later did we understand that it was she who helped our father, and not vice versa . . ."

No one ever called the new Signora Mucciarelli *Marchesa*.

3. THE FIESCHIS

From Genoa to Rome

THE LENGTHY GENEALOGY of the noble family descended from Fiesco, Conte Lavagna, has documented origins in the 900s. Fiesco's son was Rubaldo, whose son, Tedisio, was lord of various villages in Piedmont, which had been taken away from him by the Emperor Ottone by the year 999. Tedisio begat Oberto, who begat Pagano. Two sons were born to Pagano, Oberto and Rubaldo, who gave rise to two branches of the family in the first century of the past millennium.

This was the time following the First Crusade, when naval captains of the great seafaring republics acquired glory and riches by subduing infidels and pirates in faraway lands and nearby seas. Riches and glory were often accompanied by church offices. In 1243 the branch descended from Rubaldo produced, in the powerful person of Sinibaldo son of Ugo, the great Pope Innocent IV, formidable rival of Frederick II, the Swabian. Twenty years later his nephew Ottobono briefly reigned as Pope Adrian V; Dante placed him in Purgatory among the Avaricious.

Through the centuries we count seventy-two Fieschi bishops. The genealogy in our possession does not mention the women; however, we do know that in 1447 Caterina Fieschi was born. After marrying an Adorno, she left this life in 1510 and is now honored as

Saint Catherine of Genoa. But neither the documents at our disposal nor our memory would be sufficient to retell the political, financial, private, and warlike events that had the great families of Genoa, Liguria, and Piedmont as protagonists in the fourteenth and fifteenth centuries, and that is not the aim of this story. We will mention in passing the famous conspiracy of Gianluigi Fiesco against Giannettino Doria, the favorite grandson of the great Andrea, who held Genoa under his dominion. It was a conspiracy prepared with meticulous care and cunning by a jealous husband, with the support of Pope Paul III, but it ended very badly for both sides.

Alas, on New Year's Day 1547, when the signal was given for the planned revolt, Giannettino Doria descended to the port and was killed by a harquebus shot. A short time later that winter night, the head of the conspiracy, the young Fiesco, barely twenty-seven years old, was crossing the gangplank from the dock to the ship, his ship, when he slipped and fell in the dark waters. The water was not deep, but it proved fatal. Gianluigi was wearing a suit of armor, and no one was able to come to his aid; perhaps no one even knew that he had fallen. With Giannettino killed and Fiesco miserably drowned in his own sea, Genoa was once again squelched by the wrathful dominion of Andrea Doria, and that branch of the Fieschi family came to quick extinction, producing only two more generations and one last, belated cardinal.

As for the other branch, the one descending from Rubaldo's brother, Oberto, after dwindling for centuries — perhaps from generating too many baby girls — it seemed poised not only to preserve but indeed to pursue titles, nobility, and the family name. At the end of the eighteenth century we have a Lorenzo who had three sons, only one of whom entered the priesthood, and we see it expand anew.

The youngest of the three, Francesco Zaverio, born in 1783, begat Giovanni Battista in 1810. Having married twice, this Giovanni went overboard: he had three sons and many daughters, nineteen children in all. Whether or not those offspring would inherit the title — and they would not, since the head of the family remained the firstborn son — did not weigh unduly on the heart and fate of the eighteenth child, whom we shall call Giacinto. Giacinto was not curious.

We know little about the childhood of Giacinto, or of his two brothers and sixteen sisters, except that they ate standing up, because "there were so many of them, and the servants were too few, or too rebellious, to set a table for all of them at every meal." So they served themselves from large pots kept warm on a table placed against the wall, then they took their own plates to the kitchen and returned them to the sink.

Their father, Giobatta, was one of those men who do not turn white-haired. His hair, still black when he was fifty, framed a stern, somewhat melancholy face; that is how Matilde Mucciarelli would paint him one day, using an earlier portrait as a guide.

One morning in September, Giobatta, elderly but not white-haired, took the twelve-year-old Giacinto by carriage to the great convent of the Jesuits. He certainly subscribed to the notion that a father should hand over one of his children to the church, which would reward that child many times over in spiritual treasures and allow the patrimony to be given in its entirety to the firstborn, rather than to be dispersed in rivulets. The boy did not know the riches and influence of the Fieschis had been much diminished since earlier times, and perhaps the father did not want to think about it; no one had ever told the boy the ancient tales of his family.

Giacinto's possessions were contained in a small wooden chest. The air surrounding the hilltop cloister — and many were the cloisters in the hills — was cool, still, and sonorous. Thoughts seemed to bounce between the walls of the portico, to whirl beneath the arches, to run, tumble, and roll away. At times they became lost in that square opening to the sky. For two weeks Giacinto wandered in the cloister with other young boys dressed in gray like him; the gray of slate shingles, which were part of his family wealth, and which were covering the roof of the portico, just as they covered all the roofs in Genoa and the roof of his family castle, far from the city.

For two weeks Giacinto slept badly, waking early but still tired in the dormitory made stifling by thirty sleeping adolescents. When it was his turn to have his initial introduction to the Reverend Father Rector, and he was asked the ritual question, "My son, what intention prompted you to come to live with us, in this place devoted to prayer and study?" Giacinto responded, "Every intention, except to become a priest." The saintly Father Rector, who was an old man, smiled. He placed his plump, white hand on Fieschi's curly head and said, "That's not the answer, my son, not at all! You must answer 'to do God's will.' Repeat it with me . . . ," and the boy repeated it, finding the venerable old man's words correct and fitting. In truth, he gave God enough credit to believe that his own will was guided by His. So, convinced God was on his side, he behaved well in the seminary, calmly waiting for His divine will to become manifest.

One afternoon during the boys' daily walk in the city the chaperoning priest became distracted and Giacinto slipped out of the line. He hid for a while in a doorway, then went in the opposite direction from his companions. He walked down the steps of narrow streets where overclad women and men with faces smoothed by the sea winds were peering out. The men's jaws and foreheads and their eyes constricted against the light reminded him of his ancestors: the Adornos, or the Dorias, or the Grimaldis.

Giacinto Fieschi reached the port and managed to regain his breath after running for what seemed a very long time. He found himself face-to-face with the sea, dark and hemmed in by the docks, near a tall ship loaded with crates of tanned leather. He felt it would be easier to hide in the midst of that stench. He tore off the blue velvet stripes that were already coming unstitched, for they clearly marked him as one of the priests' boys, and he approached a man. "What do you want?" "I'm looking for work." "See the captain."

Did his calm help him, or was it God's determined hand? A short while later the ship set sail with the young Fieschi on board. Upon seeing Genoa become small, and then blurred and remote as the scent of the open sea replaced the stench of leather, he began to cry, out of longing for his mother and all the rest, and out of fear.

When Giacinto returned to Italy, eight years had gone by. He had written his mother, but had received no answer. He learned that she had died two years earlier. His father, now grown old, was living in a house in Genoa that was not the one Giacinto had left behind. Two of his sisters were there, too, but they did not receive him warmly. His father, yes, he wept out of emotion, but immediately afterward he asked to be fed. "They are starving me," he confided to that son he had almost forgotten, and his eyes, voice, and expanded girth were enough to convey the senility that had overcome him. Giacinto spent two days in that house and in the city, and he saw enough to erase his former homesickness and sense of guilt, except toward his mother; but he could now carry that remorse inside him wherever he went. Giacinto gave his sisters some money, promised to send even more, and then kissed his father good-bye and left, following the desire to travel he still felt inside. He sailed on a ship carrying slate, and then got off in Civitavecchia, where he boarded a train for Rome because he had wanted to see the pope since his days as a runaway boy. He did not even know the pope was no longer in Rome, and only learned of it from people's chatter on the train. "The pope? No one ever sees him. He has been holed up in the Vatican ever since the Italians took Rome. But you'll see, one of these days he'll emerge, just like the snails after the rain has stopped."

The train ran among fields of green wheat. To the right was the sea, and beyond the wheat fields were vineyards. Among the vineyards, Giacinto finally glimpsed stretches of a wide, green river, and brightly colored birds would fly up from the water as the smoky locomotive passed by. Then more vineyards, straw huts, and a few peasant homes. The train stopped at an excavation site where the overgrown vegetation was covered with dust. He heard a voice say, "You have to change trains to go to Termini," and a few people got off. He waited, not knowing what to do. The train continued, and took him to an esplanade nearby.

He disembarked with everyone else, and when he saw sails tied to masts towering in the sky, he knew the water was not far. He walked toward it, a calm body of water, wide and greenish yellow in color. It was the port at Ripa Grande; he did not know that Rome even had a port. He stopped to look at the boats, the barges at anchor, and the men unloading bales and barrels. But he had not come to Rome to see that, and the young Fieschi went on. To his left he passed a small white stone door in the brick wall, then he turned and continued along the wall surrounding the San Michele orphanage. He heard the sound of boys playing on the other side. He proceeded along the wall, with orchards to his left. He saw a church and walked toward it, drawn by its beautiful wide facade and the sound of its bell ringing.

Just as it had seemed from afar, the church was cool and welcoming, and since he was young and naive, the descendant of seventy-two bishops and two popes wondered, *Might it be Saint Peter's?* A source of shade after all that sunlight, the church was empty, and he walked among its columns across the tiled floor. He read and immediately forgot the inscriptions, carved by ancient stonecutters and commissioned by the pork butchers' guild, or that of the greengrocers, or the shoemakers. He reflected that he did not have much money on him, and he patted the funds he did have stored in his shirt's hem, where he had sewn them with the letter of introduction to the secretary of a minister. He sat down to rest.

In the church, deserted in the noon hour, with two candles burning at the main altar, Giacinto Fieschi prayed; he was accustomed to being alone, but had never felt as lonely as he did then. He approached the altar with a single cent, he who was a sailor, and lit a candle to the Madonna of the Roman greengrocers.

He walked along narrow streets between dark buildings without any sense of direction until instinct told him he was once again near water. There was the river, and a narrow bridge crossed it. A small, arching bridge, and Fieschi did not realize that it led to an island. He came upon a church there, which did not look as lovely as the earlier one, and a pretty bell tower made of dark brick. It looked as if the entire island belonged to that small bell tower. White-robed friars hurriedly crossed the small piazza. He left the island from another bridge and looked down at the river's rapids. In the distance, beyond the long curve of a green hill, was a large dome, truly enormous, overlooking everything. "It must be that one," he said, and this time he was not wrong, because it really was the Dome of Saint Peter.

Giacinto headed in that direction, through streets lined with humble, tightly packed houses, past old women seated at work in doorways and children playing, and he knew he was being watched. He walked without growing tired, but he felt an anxiety building within him. He had become lost, wandering aimlessly in the streets of a city that seemed without design now that he had moved away from the river. He traveled a great distance, making many turns, until he sensed water again, though faintly, and he found a small piazza on a slope, and a fountain with an obelisk above it. He did not know what that small pillar going straight up into the sky was. Nearby was a large church with columns on its facade. He inquired about it and was told, "It's the Rotonda." He thought it an irreverent name for a church and feared he had heard wrong, or had been made fun of. He did not enter but circled the great monument that had no opening on its sides; on one corner, almost in back, there was another piazza, small and serene. Giacinto turned toward it and entered. He looked very young and very much a stranger as he stopped to gaze at the sculpted elephant standing with legs firmly planted and a small obelisk on its back; it seemed to be smiling as it turned its long trunk toward him. He smiled back at the statue of that exotic animal grown tame, there on a pedestal almost too small for it, and in spite of his fatigue he felt pleased. He had become completely disoriented, but he still intended to see Saint Peter's, and he finally felt he had to ask for directions.

In a doorway, there in the piazza, stood a man not much younger than he, and Giacinto approached him, calling him "signor." He asked for directions to Saint Peter's and the man, who was about as tall as he was, courteously told him that Saint Peter's Basilica was not at all near. He indicated the direction and the streets to take, but upon seeing that Giacinto was obviously confused, he said, "But I wouldn't want you to get lost again." Fearing he might have offended, he added, "I, too, was intimidated and got lost when I first arrived in Rome. A good deal of time has passed since then. I've been living here three years now, but I understand how you feel." Giacinto said nothing, smiled vaguely, and tipped his cap slightly. Then he was on his way again. He immediately forgot the name of the man who had given him directions — if the two even introduced themselves. His name was Adolfo Venturi, from Modena.

When Giacinto resumed his walk along the street running behind the great round tambour, he heard the voices of young girls playing on the upper floors. The school bearing the sweet name La Palombella, "the little dove," directed by Erminia Fuà Fusinato, where Matilde Mucciarelli had once studied, was still located there. So it is easy for those of us in the know to say that fate was gently bringing them closer. Giacinto and Matilde would meet each other shortly thereafter in the home of the Pignalosas, mutual friends of ancient Neapolitan extraction.

For the new kingdom of Italy was even attracting southerners to the astonished city of Rome, which was now the capital and no longer under papal jurisdiction, and families of remote roots were unknowingly fated to meet there. Adele Pignalosa was a classmate of Matilde at La Palombella, and their friendship would last their lifetimes. Peppina, too, and their poor papa had found a warm, protective affection in Signora Pignalosa, Adele's mother. She also extended a warm, maternal welcome to the serious and taciturn young man from Genoa who had just arrived in Rome with a letter of introduction for the undersecretary of the merchant marine, none other than the father, Signor Pignalosa. What a coincidence!

So it happened that on Adele's birthday, when the signora had prepared 523 biscotti, four tarts, two montblancs, and three

English trifles with the help of her three daughters and a few of their friends, Giacinto Fieschi and Matilde met and liked each other. They did not divulge this right away, but on the birthday of one of the other sisters, or perhaps a friend, they made it known. They became friends, fell in love, and told each other. A few weeks later, when Giacinto obtained a position at the ministry, the two youths communicated (Giacinto by letter) their honorable intentions to their fathers. Money was scarce, but there was blue blood on both sides. True, the first to marry would be the younger of the Mucciarelli sisters, but who could say that Peppina's hopes had vanished?

During the very months that preparations for the wedding were under way, Maestro Cantalamessa's lessons became less frequent, which was certainly appropriate, if not welcome. There was so much to do in the house! A deep affection bound the painter from Ascoli to Matilde's father, but he had been given a new charge: to update the catalog of the artistic legacy entrusted to the city of Rome. That charge had been given him by the young honorary inspector for the Direzione Generale per le Antichità e Belle Arti of the new Royal Ministry of Public Instruction. This honorary inspector, though little more than a boy, was an art enthusiast who had already won several important competitions; his name was Adolfo Venturi. The royal ministry had given him the responsibility of cataloging the artworks of the new kingdom of Italy, no less! All of them! And Venturi had asked the renowned painter Cantalamessa, older and more experienced than he, to take upon himself a share of that "impossible task," as Venturi himself would write.

The Bridge

When Giacinto Fieschi, functionary at the Ministry of Merchant Marine, married Matilde Mucciarelli in 1895, the bridge named Ponte Cavour was not yet finished. People crossed the light iron bridge supported by pylons at Ripetta, the bridge "that went nowhere," which had been built in two summers and one winter by Alessandro Mucciarelli. It would be dismantled in 1901, after serving to help construct its stronger brother. The Ponte Cavour was built of stone, its parapets made of small travertine columns between walls also made of travertine; the two end pieces were in the same style, and sloped gently. The new Romans inhabiting Prati would refer to the Ponte Cavour simply as "the Ponte"; it served to "to take them into Rome."

At that time Prati was an expanse of construction sites, some open and some idle. In the middle were a few completed buildings, but the development that had swallowed Mucciarelli's money from Ascoli was at the center of what was called "the great construction crisis." The Marchese Alessandro, under the care of his English wife, the poor woman, had died shortly after Matilde's marriage without ever leaving Via delle Carrozze; it happened at daybreak, as the bells from the one Trinità dei Monti bell tower visible from his window were tolling for early mass.

After marrying in the church of Santa Maria in Transpontina, in Borgo Pio, which was the parish of the entire zone, Giacinto and Matilde were the first tenants of an apartment in Prati, in a building on the corner of Via Ulpiano and the Lungotevere.

From their sun-filled house, so much larger and more beautiful than the one in Via delle Carrozze, they could look out across the Tiber and its new white walls and see all of Rome — which included a glimpse of the Ponte Cavour under construction.

Near Castel Sant'Angelo excavation work had begun for the courthouse building that would one day be known as the Palazzaccio — the "ugly building" — destined for the administration of justice in the new kingdom. One could stay at the window all day, listening to the sounds of machinery and the voices of the workers, and watching the arrival of carts pulled by draft horses; the horses descended slowly into the pit, braced by their hooves and powerful forelimbs, held in check by the brakes on the wheels, the ropes, and the men's shouts. Other carts climbed back out carrying away mountains of earth and tufa, for the enormous travertine ashlars were being placed on a foundation that had once been a riverbed.

Giacinto Fieschi spent all his leisure hours watching the work, as if building the Palazzo di Giustizia just by looking at it. His wife and his sister-in-law Peppina were alarmed, surprising even themselves; the two girls had known only the Marchese Alessandro, who had certainly never worked, and yet they would ask each other, "Is it possible that a man who is not even thirty should spend all his time at the window?" Perhaps they were bothered by a notion of propriety, or perhaps there was a hidden and unacknowledged fear that with all his standing at the window an extraordinary novelty — the monthly salary he brought home and handed to Matilde in its entirety — might come to an end. She would tell him, "Do something, go out for a walk, you'll grow fat staying there all the time!" But her sister would say, "Let him be. The palazzo will be finished sooner or later," even though the construction, stone upon massive stone, never seemed likely to end.

How much did the great construction project really occupy the senses and soul of Matilde's husband? He was almost the husband of both women because of his mild rapport with his spouse and the profound and parallel consonance between the two sisters. Giacinto was the man of the house and they were the women. He remained the only man, for his wife and for his sister-in-law. He brought a salary home and they used it to keep house for him and his children. Giacinto Fieschi, born a patrician but without rights or wealth, and raised a sailor, was the perfect example of the new class of state functionaries; a happy example who forgot all about his work as soon as he left his office.

Then the children were born. The first one died, and since Matilde had fed him with her little breasts for the six months of his life, she feared it would be a mistake to breast-feed her second child and opted for a wet nurse instead. Titta's wet nurse came from Ciociaria and stayed two years, even after the third boy, Enrico, was born and a second wet nurse was hired. The first wet nurse was called "Nurse," and the second one "Enrico's Nurse." Then Nurse went back to her village of Trivigliano; but she remained fond of the little boy and the rest of his family, so she often took the train and then the streetcar, and then climbed the five floors on Via Ulpiano, her basket firmly balanced on the rolled-up cloth pad on her head. Inside the basket was a ricotta tart and fresh eggs for her baby and the other child. Nurse always stayed two days, and Enrico's Nurse did the same.

Peppina Candela also lived with them. She was a most refined young servant, and Matilde and Peppina had hired her on sight. She showed up in her spotless, freshly scented dress, and the sisters noticed a small rip in the shoulder seam that had been mended with such minute and perfect handiwork that they exchanged knowing glances and said in unison, "You're hired!" Peppina Candela, who was always called by both first and last name in order not to be confused with Signorina Peppina, stayed with the Fieschi family for many years. Giacinto's salary sufficed for that, too, thanks naturally to the women's careful management. And they found that the apartment, which was far from small, had become too crowded for them.

In the new century apartment buildings had risen in Prati, and they decided to move. "The Palazzo di Giustizia is almost completed anyway," said Peppina. The new apartment was just beyond Piazza Cavour, in Via Tacito — perhaps, but only perhaps, on the very site of "the land belonging to our poor papa." Matilde and Peppina liked to think so.

The building was ocher-yellow like all the ones in the new Rome. The entrance hall was vaulted; the courtyard had two porticoed walkways that concealed four sets of stairs, two on each side facing each other. Above each stairwell, dormered windows framed with wrought iron allowed light to enter, strong and bright on the fifth floor and progressively dimmer on the lower ones. The first floor received light from the courtyard, and anyone climbing the stairs would find spacious landings and handsome spiral banisters with wooden handrails of a lustrous red.

The Fieschis rented an apartment on the fourth floor. Two windows overlooked the front courtyard; others opened onto a courtyard shared by the adjoining building. The best windows looked north. In the rooms at that end of the corridor they placed the dining room furniture — with its fruit and wolf's head ornamentation — and the parlor sofa and armchairs. These were covered in red velvet, with back and armrest covers of white lace and embroidery made by Peppina. Light flooded these windows because they still overlooked an unrestricted countryside of orchards and pasturelands, even though the large yellow wounds of stalled construction sites gaped nearby. The following year a building rose across the street; then Via Gioacchino Belli was paved. On the right, before the trees in Via Cicerone had grown tall, was a wide, luminous space above the Tiber; on the left, across a few more fields, were the Vatican palaces and walls. In the morning the windows of the Belvedere reflected the sunlight. A great silence lay all around. Except when the humid west wind brought the sound of the great church bells, and then they would say, "You can hear Saint Peter's; it's going to rain."

Every morning for thirty years Giacinto Fieschi left his house to go to the Ministry of Merchant Marine to earn the family's daily bread. When he returned home in the evening he often took a short detour to see how things were going at the Palazzo di Giustizia. At home he would find the women at work near the window, taking advantage of the last light of the setting sun. Only in the heart of winter would they light the kerosene lamp — there was just one — because by then the house was illuminated by gaslight. The pipes ran along the top of the walls, and only Giacinto, with his arms outstretched, was tall enough to reach the lamps. Matilde could not have lit them, even by standing on a chair. As for cooking, they used coal.

On spring afternoons the two sisters would cross the Ponte Regina Margherita, holding the children by the hand and carrying their workbags and snacks. The bridge was older than the Ponte Cavour, having been inaugurated in 1895; from there, Peppina and Matilde glanced toward Ripetta, where they had lived during their first years in Rome. Silently the sisters harbored the same thought: that their father had then been the center of their lives, and that he had left this world not because of old age but fatigue. "He was so tired," Matilde once said, and both sisters knew to whom she referred. How their lives had changed! The children were everything for them now. They did not talk about their stepmother, and both of them felt some guilt. "Poor woman, after all," they had said when the Englishwoman was left alone; but alone they left her.

The Pincio now belonged to all Romans; Matilde and Peppina sat there with their friends, embroidering or chatting and watching the children play. There were the Pignalosa ladies with their children; Nannina Benaglia, always dressed in black due to her bleak fate; Signora Vigolo, mother of Giorgio and Mario, from Vicenza; and other mothers of children and babies quiet or loud, sturdy or frail. Among the boys, those who survived the impending war would remain friends for life. Their sisters and cousins, with flounced dresses and hair tied with ribbons, played alongside them.

Of Matilde's two boys Titta had a melancholy face that did not match his personality, while Enrico, with finer, prettier traits — *almost too pretty*, thought Peppina — was timid and pensive. They were both fairly good in school — the Marcantonio Colonna, where they wore gray uniforms — but the elder was better in mathematics, while Enrico leaned more toward literature and history.

The hours spent at the Pincio were tranquil and carefree, yet they gave the satisfaction of a duty accomplished. They were full hours. Full of tiny stitches of embroidery hard as steel like Zia Peppina's; full of exchanged recipes, tales of illnesses, pains, and betrayals borne by others. Words compassionate or cruel were uttered, but they were rarely silly; they were not gossip, a fearsome weapon that returns like a boomerang. Matilde chatted; Peppina was almost always silent, her eyes on her embroidery but her mind filled with thoughts of the future, other people's destinies. *Who knows?* she would wonder, raising her eyes toward the boys and girls and imagining stories of loves and marriages, she who had remained "without a story." She, Peppina, did not know how many of those youths would be taken away by the immense event that was as yet unforeseen.

It was still a time of prudence, there, amid the shade and perfumed air, where the water clock dripped — "It's late! Michele! Giovanni! Let's go home!" — near the oval Fountain of Moses, with its smooth, gently rounded border and Miriam in the center bending among the papyri to entrust the basket containing young Moses to the Nile . . . Each Sunday they returned to the Pincio with their husbands, in part to listen to the music, but even more for the pleasure and privilege of seeing their beloved Queen Margherita. They would then exchange greetings and smiles with their women friends in the sun, but timidly and from afar, as if reticent and aware of secret complicities.

Winter afternoons, these women gathered in one another's homes, taking turns as hostess. Matilde and Peppina received on Wednesday, and they always prepared a cake for the occasion. Many of the women continued to address one another with the formal *Lei* until the end, and there was an unspoken pleasure in that, too. That small lack of familiarity rendered their friendships precious and elegant, at times, deeper and more enduring.

The lace and embroidery in satin or shadow stitch on the children's dresses, like the handiwork on the tablecloths and tea towels, on the back and armchair rests as well as on the big matrimonial beds, would be linked to memories of this or that summer, to a pregnancy or a mourning, because women's souls retain the imprint of objects touched and seen above all.

For Matilde, 1910 was "the year my brother Carlo came back from Africa" — the brother who was almost a stranger. He was a doctor, unmarried, and he was returning to live as an invalid for a few months with his married sister, the brother-in-law he had never met, and the other sister, "poor Peppina," so called only because she had missed her fifteenth-birthday ball and remained unmarried. Carlo had returned to his homeland to die — and his sisters were absent from the Pincio for a long time. He left a few small debts and a small trunk, which would be moved to many addresses, always filled with useless and forlorn "African *mascarallicchie*." It still exists.

He lived only three months in Rome, Zio Carlo, enough time to leave an inheritance of sayings, his only wealth: "My brother Carlo, who was a doctor, used to say . . . ," or "Zio Carlo said . . ." Those phrases would be repeated in the rooms and corridors of the house in Prati for a long time.

Zia Peppina coughed day and night from cancer of the lung. Italy went to war. Soon after, Titta was on the Isonzo.

Matilde built a cooking box out of old wool fabric, cotton wool, and rags. She would bring her clay pot to a boil over the wood or coal fire in the large kitchen with wall tiles decorated with little blue stars, and then transfer it to the cooking box, where it maintained if not a boil, then a simmer for several hours. Enrico enlisted as a volunteer right after he turned seventeen, just in time to fight the most tiring and demoralizing episode of the war, the Battle of Caporetto. He walked in the mud until he was no longer aware he was still walking, exhausted by an illness referred to then as "intestinal catarrh," which most probably was amebic dysentery. He returned home with it, ghostly and ugly, and he was put to bed while undergoing a long, unpleasant treatment. It was not unpleasant for Matilde, who was happy to have her boy back; thin and sick, but home! Titta returned, too.

While his brother had attended a technical institute, Enrico had taken the state examination in classical studies. Whenever he could, he went outdoors with tablet, brushes, and paints. He did not have to go far to find the countryside; it was on the Tiber's banks and in Piazza d'Armi, the military drill ground where the Great Exposition had been held in 1911. He remembered it as immense, brightly lit, and dusty. When he was a young boy he had seen his first airplane flying there. "Flying! It lifted itself up off the ground like a chicken!" he would say. In that area, the houses and streets of the Mazzini quarter were being readied. The large bridge, built for the exposition and named Flaminio then, was later called Ponte Risorgimento.

With Enrico ill, then convalescing, Matilde liked to fall back on her memories. Seeing her favorite son paint the large trees so carelessly — at least that is how she judged it — she taught him all her secrets of painting. Cantalamessa's pupil had not painted for a long time, and even though she had been a portrait artist she would say, "You see, people look at a painting and see either the Madonna or Jesus Christ. And for Jesus that may be all right, because we perhaps know what he looked like; he had a beard . . . and then we have the Shroud of Turin . . . but the Madonna, no, we don't know what she looked like. So each painter has painted a girl or a woman from his village, or perhaps even two, whom he thought resembled Mary, his image of Mary, and it might have happened more than once that he liked her, he was a bit in love with her. Or he paid her — models are paid — or perhaps so many Madonnas were painted because the girls did not ask to be paid for being the Madonna. So there are pretty and modest Madonnas, robust and peasantlike Madonnas. They are all Mary, yet none of them is Mary, but in each there is the love of the painter and not just his hand. I, who am your mother, am telling you these things because I used to paint a little . . . Your father never painted . . . but he is the finest gentleman on this earth, remember that . . ." She spoke as if she wanted such an immodest discourse with her son to come quickly to a close.

When the war was won, the young people were overflowing with love. Inside the warm, red tambour of the Teatro Augusteo the tiny lights above the music stands in the orchestra were a locus of the soul. The hall resounding with music was filled with love, and lovers. And each one, as part of the age-old deception, contributed his uniqueness to the universal power of nature. This highest, and most romantic, form of love transcended and disdained sex; it was true for all the young women, and for many of the men.

They were both enrolled at La Sapienza, but they attended different courses. He followed her to the Teatro Augusteo and to the Santa Cecilia Conservatory. Then he went to hear her play the cello in the orchestra of the Teatro dei Piccoli. She was beautiful, her smile absolute as she turned toward her friends. She had a face of marble, a perfect profile, with a small, straight nose and her hair gathered at the nape of her neck. As he watched her play, he wondered which Madonna she was, which one of the masters might already have painted her. But no Madonna has a smile so absolute as to be inexpressive and classical yet at the same time so intimate. Enrico mulled over these thoughts, his mind churning there in the red tambour of the theater, his eyes fixed on the tiny lights.

He learned that musical name: Marta Canterno.

After receiving his diploma Enrico Fieschi enrolled in the School of Medieval and Modern Art History, which was founded and directed at La Sapienza by Adolfo Venturi. Did that name mean anything to Enrico's father, Giacinto? Perhaps he remembered the encounter on his first stroll through an unknown Rome, the morning he thought that Santa Maria dell'Orto might be Saint Peter's Basilica, and he had seen Bernini's little elephant smile at the Minerva.

For Enrico, Venturi would remain "the Professor" as long as he lived. Venturi was fond of Enrico; he preferred conversing with him above the dozen or so students who took his course, and he would tell him about his early projects and interests. He recounted the time during his youth when he fled Modena for Florence, where "art is still alive in its birthplace." At the Institute of Higher Studies he had heard about the ruins of Babylon instead of the history of Italian art. And he had understood that the book of learning was opened before his eyes, not in the school, and he told himself, *I want to see!* He led his students through the streets and piazzas, to look, see, understand, compare, and remember . . . or he took them on even longer and more adventurous journeys, to galleries of sculpture and painting. Venturi guided them with his calm and melodious Modenese accent through collections still owned by princes, and through the National Gallery of Ancient Art, the original one, born because of him in the Palazzo Corsini at the Lungara.

❖

It happened on Palm Sunday, in 1924, in Saint Peter's Square. The pope himself, Pius XI, was giving the olive branch to the faithful. Marta already had one in her hand as she walked away from the basilica. She was alone, absorbed in thought under the sun, wearing a white jacket and a cinnamon-colored skirt, with her long hair gathered in a soft chignon. But he did not see those details, he did not see any of them because he was in love with her. She was walking among the crowd without seeing it, when she felt someone touch her and heard a voice, "Signorina, violets for the signorina?" It was one of the country women dispersed here and there in the square, offering nosegays of violets to the passersby. "Signorina, violets for the signorina?" She was annoyed at first, and refused. Then she saw him, his dark brown eyes, she recognized him and smiled. He acknowledged that smile, and with clumsy fingers he started to untie one of the bouquets without saying a word. The nosegay was round and tightly packed and intensely fragrant, and the flowers were wrapped inside a layer of leaves. The two of them stood still as if in the center of the world, and the world was empty. She looked at his hands as they feverishly unwrapped the violets, his profile so serious and intent, his wide forehead and fine, wavy hair. When he finally held a small bunch in his hand — only a dozen flowers — he gave the rest to her, as if they were no longer of any use, and with great care he fastened the corsage to her jacket with a pin he had found, no telling how, on the reverse side of his own lapel. The rest of the violets remained in her hand. They walked along Borgo Pio and when they passed the church of Santa Maria in Traspontina, Enrico said, "My parents were married in this church." And considering the size of Rome, she did not believe him, because she knew — just as she had been taught — that men lie to women. He continued talking, saying he wanted to study the architecture of this building, and there was the spot in the river where he once swam as a boy. They took a streetcar together, then another. Then they walked some more, together, toward her house, but she wanted to say good-bye before they reached it. As he took his leave he kissed her hand, and it seemed to Marta that he looked through her eyes into her soul. She could feel his touch at the core of her being. So she thought. So would her memory of the moment be magnified with time.

She left him without even a gesture of her hand — he stood immobile looking at her for a long time, and she knew it. She went down the wide Via Nomentana with her eyes fixed straight ahead, confused and weighed down by a life commitment: he loved her. And since no one had ever touched her before, now she was his. But as she entered the dark, musty stairway the thought of her father came back to frighten her, and she was immediately relieved that he was so far way, still in Alexandria.

Once inside the house filled with Giacomo's children and her mother and sister's toil, Marta, who now held a secret in her heart, unpinned the violets from her lapel and hid them in a drawer. They saw each other again at the Santa Cecilia Conservatory and La Sapienza. He was in love, and she felt a commitment that was trepid and sacred, tormented and forbidden, yet she was sure it could only grow. It did, and it became the thought of her every hour. A thought that distracted her from her plans for her academic career, rendering it all the more important. Her feelings for him, although unwilling at first, had to fit in with her classes and her rhythms, with the events of her day and the hours needed for sleep at night, with the brief and always insufficient moments she found for study, with her trips to La Sapienza and Santa Cecilia, and her time spent in the cinemas in the evenings for work. What little time she spent at home was filled not with rest, but with visions of Margherita, who was content with so little, and her mother and brother, too, and his children. Marta would think, *I am different, I am worth more*, and if she added, *I am loved, I love*, she was filled not just with satisfaction but also with pride.

When Enrico learned she played in the cinema in the evening he said, "I'll come with you. I don't want you to go around alone at night; it's dangerous, don't you know?" She remained silent and blushed, because she always carried the little knife her father had given her, but she could not tell him that. So Enrico accompanied her, and the little knife became a worry and a burden as never before. What would it defend her against? Against strangers in the streets? She was not afraid of them. They went by streetcar, and ever since the Fascists had "cleaned things up" there was no riffraff around. She could not talk to Enrico about the knife, and she did not dare leave that amulet from her father at home. And it occurred to her that she might need that little weapon as a defense against Enrico himself, that stranger who left her at the doorstep every evening with a kiss on the hand that moved her every time. One night he took both her hands and said, "Marta, shall we get married? Do you want to marry me?" and she answered yes. This had not been unexpected; the question had been formulated as if by mutual understanding. In its tone, it seemed to follow other words that instead had never been said. Marta answered yes because she had long been ready to do so. Perhaps because of that, she now felt she was reciting a role. But then Enrico took her head in his large, warm hands and placed his mouth on her lips that had never been touched, and in spite of herself she felt a sensation running through her body that she had only imagined in her dreams, even though she should have expected it after seeing so many movies over the years. She understood then that nothing was finished. The moment that she had thought was the end was only the beginning. She felt pulled by him and pushed beyond, beyond anything she had known, in a precipitous carnal destiny that she would not be able to control; he had taken her away from herself in a way she had never suspected possible. Afterward, alone on the stairs and holding her cello, she could not run, but had to stop instead. She took a long time ascending the stairs, and she could not have explained it even to herself, but she knew that everything had changed. She did not sleep that night, although she was tired, her entire body exhausted, worn out by the stirrings of her soul. Her soul; indeed, that essence that Marta could not call by any other name. For everything has a name, that's what she'd been taught, that's what the book of Genesis said. But it wasn't Enrico who said, "We are getting married." It was she. One evening she said to her mother, almost with anger in her voice, "I'm engaged," and all she received for a response was, "Does *Pardi* know?" He could not know, since he was still "down in Egypt" even though in those very days he had written: "I am coming back. The books will be ready in a few weeks. I am coming back."

"You don't know . . . you don't know him . . . ," Marta kept telling Enrico. After so many years of saying *When* Pardi *comes back*, almost as a game, her childhood fears were now returning in her dreams, the vision of her disapproving father with his broad back turned against her, so small and full of tears, and unable to reach him to ask his forgiveness.

How could she write her father, her master, that another man was caressing and kissing her? "You are so virtuous, intelligent, and beautiful . . . ," he told her in her dreams. She remembered the persecution she endured because of the innocent, oblivious, mild-mannered Nicola, the son of Stelianì, and she said to Enrico, "No, you don't know him." But Enrico only responded, "How bad can it be! I am marrying you!" and she was moved by his naïveté. One Sunday, Marta spent the day writing the news to her father: "I would like to get married." And she told him about Enrico, using the wrong tone, she was sure; she mentioned his studies in art history, and his family of ancient and noble Genoese origin. After mailing the letter in fear, she did not expect the answer she received from Egypt. Her father, who was alone with his mosquitoes, Arabs, and dictionaries — as her sister-in-law Cate liked to say — her father, who out of idealism, indolence, and eccentricity had first renounced his wealth in land, then lost his teaching position (they had not heard anything else about that matter), wrote his incredulous daughter: "A conte! Your intelligence, beauty, and virtue did not deserve less. I will return soon and I will be glad to pay my regards to his esteemed father." Marta was stupefied and even more frightened of that father she had not seen in so long, while Antonia expressed new concerns about her husband's mental health. Marta was in an increasing hurry to marry and impose order on the confusion that had overcome her, a tumult from which she could not have been freed without her father's consent.

So one evening, in the orderly house on Via Tacito, Enrico Fieschi met with his father in the parlor behind closed doors. "I must get married," he said, and Giacinto was silent. He had understood the only thing a father must understand. His silence did not last long, and being an honorable man he said, "If you must get married, you will get married. Have you told your mother?" His words were almost identical to those uttered in the other house, the one on Via Nomentana. They told Matilde together, and it was easier for Enrico than telling his father had been. "A stranger!" Matilde said, "And where will you live?" and since he didn't have an answer, she said, "Naturally, in my house," then she muttered, ". . . that schemer!" but he still heard her.

"Mamma, it's not what you think . . . ," Enrico tried to explain, but she had already left the room. He turned to his father, wanting to tell him, *Her father is returning from Egypt . . . he is a strange man, she is afraid of him . . .* He didn't know what else to say, because in truth there was nothing he could say. Instead his father said, "I'll take care of your mother. But you must try to understand. She has never seen her; she doesn't know this girl." And he added, "When will you introduce her to us, this new Signora Fieschi? I am sure she is beautiful and good." That was Giacinto Fieschi's reply; once his sons had graduated from the university he knew all his duties were fulfilled, and he was certain the rest would come by itself, as if by right, by destiny. And when Enrico said, "I will work . . . I can teach," his father replied, "No, you must continue with your studies, you must complete your postdoctoral work with Venturi. Later you will work. If you want to marry, you will come to live here with us; the house is large. I am sure that you chose well. As for me, they sent me to the seminary and I have not forgiven them. I signed on a ship and knew loneliness when I was not ready for it. I was lonely everywhere, everywhere in the world before I had the good fortune to meet your mother. We have given you a home to grow up in and live in peace. That is our . . ." He paused as he searched for the word. ". . . yes, our joy. Our sense of pride. And our commitment. Your wife is welcome here."

Never had Giacinto Fieschi talked so much. He never told stories about his travels at sea, as if all he had known his entire life were the streets he took from Prati to the Ministry of the Merchant Marine, which at the time was located in Piazza di Santa Maria sopra Minerva. At the wedding in the church of San Giuseppe, her parish on Via Nomentana, everyone was present: his parents, her mother, brothers, sisters, brothers-in-law and sisters-in-law, and the children. The only one absent was Tommaso, called *Pardi*, who was still in Egypt. The fiancés of Caterina's sisters sported straw hats and very handsome two-toned shoes.

4. NUPTIALS

IN THE HOUSE on Via Tacito the couple was given Peppina's room. The entrance was in the kitchen, and an armoire was placed against the door leading into Matilde and Giacinto's bedroom. But a door is just a door and an armoire just an armoire; and just as the snoring of her father-in-law reached her, so was Marta sure the tense and quick nerves of Enrico's mother were always on the alert, listening to the two of them from the other side. Now that the sacrament demanded the carnal rituals, Marta, an educated but inexperienced bride, did not feel the sensual arousal she had experienced during her engagement.

As soon as her husband went serenely to sleep with the obstacles of his new life surmounted for the day, she continued on the long course of her studies; she lit the small veiled lamp and resumed reading and repeating Dante's *Divine Comedy* to herself. Marta wanted to have all three Cantiche memorized by the time she turned thirty. That was four years away.

In the morning after Enrico left, Marta remained in bed listening to the sounds of the house. Just five minutes, no more, because the day and her disciplined habits pushed her on. She rose, wrapped a blanket around her shoulders, and crossed the kitchen, where Matilde was already preparing the midday meal.

The first time she was greeted by a sonorous "Happy rising!" which she had answered only with an embarrassed "Good morning." The following day, when she said "Good morning," she was perhaps not heard, and the same happened the third day. Her kitchen crossings became almost furtive, and Matilde once laughed and told her, "You look like one of Verdi's conspirators!" but Marta did not even understand. She reached the bathroom in haste, where she used as little as possible of the hot water intended for everyone, feeling at once like a profiteer and a poorly served queen.

YOU KNOW A GOOD DAY FROM THE MORNING said the place mat, embroidered by Zia Peppina, on which Marta found her cup of coffee. The cup with a gold rim now faded was the lone survivor of a set bought during their days on Via delle Carrozze or, who knows, perhaps even brought from Ascoli, because Matilde "was not particular" about that meal, as she herself said. In managing the household, which was her responsibility (she had not painted since she got married), she followed rules she herself had established and with which she felt a serene affinity. Peppina's work had been complementary to hers, but it drew on higher spheres: extremely fine and difficult embroidery, refined dishes rather than ordinary meals, things with a touch of the superfluous. Peppina, who had neither husband nor children, could spend time and attention on beautiful things that weren't essential. For the young Fieschis, the period "when Zia Peppina was alive" remained a time of perfection whose fate could only have been a sad decline; the age that official culture had named "la belle époque." Matilde would refer to those happy times as "back when we had the children," and the other person included in the *we* was her sister. Matilde often said this with a sigh.

Back in her room, where she dressed quickly and in silence as she had ever since she was in Rome, Marta would look at the bed. It had no headboard, and was made from two bedsprings resting on wooden trestles. There were four mattresses, two filled with wool and two with vegetable fiber, which were supposed to go over or under each other depending on the season. One of the two bed-springs used to belong to "Signorino" Enrico but the other one, Marta knew, had been Zia Peppina's; its frame and brass bedstead were now stored in the closet under the stairs. Half of her marriage bed was the one on which Peppina had died. But which half? One slipcover was light blue and the other was white, and the mattresses' quilted borders were of classic design. How little they resembled those of Alexandria, where mounds of the whitest and softest cotton were stuffed inside cases until their seams bulged, soft and plump. Yes, every morning Marta would have liked to make the bed she shared with her husband, but she did not dare, as her mother-in-law had said repeatedly, "No, don't, not you. Let me do it with the servant; it comes out better with two of us, and Enrico likes the sheets pulled tight, like we do them. Besides . . . you must not do that." Marta did not understand that her mother-in-law's concern was for her supposed pregnancy. No, she did not understand.

Finally, they would leave the house together. It took twenty minutes to get to La Sapienza, even less on cold mornings because they almost ran, Marta clenching her arms in her too-light coat, and Enrico with cheerful strides. He had been born but a few steps away and he loved the morning air in the empty Piazza Cavour and along the walls of the Palazzaccio, the Ponte Umberto, and the new Via Zanardelli. It was during those twenty minutes that they did most of their talking; it was the best part of their marriage, at least for her. But they did not speak, by mutual and tacit accord, when they crossed Piazza Navona, and they seldom hurried. The piazza was still silent and seemed enormously long even though the first rays of sunshine were already gilding the bell towers, the facades and portals of the church of Sant'Agnese, where the obelisk rising from Bernini's sculpture of rocks, rivers, and figures was casting its shadow. Marta, who had come to La Sapienza many times from the Arco de' Ginnasi without making the detour of a few extra steps to reach the grand piazza, blurted out, "What is it?" the first time she saw it. "What do you mean, 'what is it'?" answered Enrico with surprise. Then, after a brief silence, he understood, and in an altered, deeper voice he added, "Now look. Look and don't say anything," and he guided her slowly, without speaking, as she looked up at the church and around the piazza: at the very sky inhabited by bell towers, at the palaces, at the majestic fountain and the other two in the distance. And she saw the obelisk, which did not look big to her, yet it was.

Marta walked around the fountain that day, as she would do many times in later years, watching the thin, straight shadow descend along the church's facade, become foreshortened on the pavement, and then turn with the rising sun and stretch out on the square as if it did not want to leave it. Yes, Marta would do this, in private moments when her thoughts turned to Enrico; a ritual of a pained heart.

But that first morning, "Look!" she said, pointing to the edge of the fountain. "Look!" Blue pigeons were landing on the rim and sliding down the smouth surface until they stopped on a narrow ledge. From there, with their small red feet in the water, the birds would drink. "Look!"

"What is it?"

"Look," she repeated, unable to say anything else, and she realized this leap of faith was known to every pigeon, from its first flight out of the nest — a nest inside one of the bell towers or under the moldings of one of the palaces — from that first flight through the air to the man-made rocks and the grand statues; each had discovered it, that descent of the slide, with its first thirst, and had scooped up the water in its small beak, then raised its head to let the water run down its innocent, iridescent throat . . . And Marta remembered her sparrow in Alexandria, which had slid down watermelon rinds and then stirred the water with its wings in the chipped terracotta dish that had come all the way from Alatri . . . She lingered immobile watching the pigeons, then recounted her thoughts and remote memories to Enrico. He listened with delight and recounted the history of the famous fountain and the church.

After that morning in Piazza Navona, Enrico began telling her, little by little, about Rome, offering the city to her as a gift. He led her by the hand, walking slowly, or sometimes even running in his excitement to show her "a surprise, there, beyond that corner." He combined his love for her with his new knowledge of architecture and history, repeating, unwittingly or not, the words of the Professor, his teacher, with a warm sense of pride.

He took her to the church of San Luigi de' Francesi and said, "Do you know there are two Caravaggios inside?" and she did not know, she truly knew nothing of Rome. She did not know that above the curious church they called the Rotonda there were once two bell towers by Bernini. "They were still there when my father and the Professor met here, in Piazza della Minerva. And what's more, my father remembered his name. It was buried in his memory: 'Did you say Venturi? At the Minerva! Yes, my first day in Rome, and I really was lost. I met that gentleman, who seemed so much older than I was . . . how old did you say he is? How strange!' So Papa is happy in a special way, I believe, that I am studying with the Professor, that I am in his school . . . in part because of that memory of his, his memory of being reassured and guided. Just think, my father, who sailed around the world and saw faraway cities and people . . . You see, he never told us anything. As if he had wished only to settle down for life, at home with our mother and us. Or perhaps, who knows, because somewhere he left behind memories that are too precious."

And he told her, "Here in Piazza Navona, at one time, there was a fruit and vegetable market. That was before Paul the Third Farnese moved it to Campo de' Fiori, and after it had been held, guess where? Below the church of Santa Maria in d'Aracoeli and the slopes of the Campidoglio because the papal seat was in San Marco and the pope blessed them all, the fruit vendors and the others, whether they cheated or not. But they were too noisy and they would not let him sleep, until Michelangelo completed the Piazza del Campidoglio, and our statue of Marcus Aurelius, which before that had been in the Lateran, was moved there."

And he continued, "Don't you see? Rome is made up of houses from the seventeenth, eighteenth, and nineteenth centuries. Of course, it looks full to us, and we feel it is now being emptied so new, ugly apartment buildings can be built, and it's true. But can you imagine how it looked in the Middle Ages? Those dark years? Because they really were a dark age, and it was a serious, evil time for the people then. It was an age of bleak poverty, and plagues, and wars that seem foolish to us today, when in truth no war is ever foolish. The poverty of the people worsened and became more widespread because of the use made of those wars by the priests. So even after Christopher Columbus brought the dark ages to an end, conditions that should have improved became even worse. Christopher, a distant cousin of mine, reached land over there, but here there was pestilence, flooding, and the sack of Rome. And by the end of the fifteenth century this city that for ten centuries had been building its dwellings — which weren't even houses, but hovels — from the crumbs of the great edifices left behind by the Caesars; this city was not a city. It was a heap of ruins, and it did not have one single palace! Can you imagine that, Rome without palaces? And yet that was Rome, and it was ruled by the pope.

"Where did you live? At the Arco de' Ginnasi? The Corso Vittorio Emanuele was already there when you arrived, but did you ever wonder what it looked like before then? Now the ruins in front of the Teatro Argentina are being excavated and removed. That part of the city has been destroyed and we will one day forget what it was once like. Then bit by bit it filled up, as the ancient bricks crumbled and the houses collapsed, as the rocks piled up, and everything became covered and sealed in mud. Meanwhile, the rafters were consumed by fire and, sooner or later, by woodworms. Just think, Martina, in Florence the Medici were building fountains and spiral columns. They had palaces — did they ever! But here a hapless populace, miserable and sick, superstitious and enslaved, were living in houses and alleys filled with their own rubbish. But the pope was rich; rich was his family, his nephews and children. Rich were the cardinals, who were all relatives of the pope, and his minions . . .

"And across that sea of alleyways, there was then only one church that was not made of wood. Yes, none other than Santa Maria sopra Minerva, so named because it was built, as you know, on the remains of a temple to Minerva . . . yes, as a matter of fact, so was the church of San Marco. But as I was saying, while Christopher Columbus was sailing the ocean, there was just one palace in this sea of alleyways . . . What about the churches, you say? Sure, there were churches, but other than those with the catacombs, which were all outside the city walls, there was Saint Peter's, and San Giovanni in Laterano, and Santa Croce, but they were made of wood . . . As for palaces, there was only one palace! White, large, and majestic, it overlooked that sea of hovels near the flower market . . . you know where? Do you? Right over there . . . on the street that was once called Via Florea, which in fact ended at the flower market . . . because the market was right here then, yes, right here. And that beautiful big palace — I'll show it to you now, large, white, magnificent! A cardinal by the name of Riario had it built. He was barely thirty, but he had been a cardinal since he was seventeen; he was the pope's nephew, and the pope was the great Sixtus the Fourth . . . della Rovere, of course, come on" — and he would pull her by the hand — "come on, it won't take long, it's right here, at the corner of Via de' Balestrieri. Go on, read it, your Latin is better than mine. Let's read it together!" and he recited the inscription by heart, which explained how Via Florea was constructed by the *magistri curatores viarum* of Pope Sixtus IV. "See?" he continued. "Look at the date! Read it, go on: one thousand plus four hundred, and fifty plus thirty — that equals eighty — plus three! That is the date of the opening of Via Florea. In those days it was a thoroughfare linking this great piazza — yes, the Campo de' Fiori — with Ponte Sant'Angelo, which was known then as the Ponte Elio. It was the only bridge in Rome at the time. Meanwhile, that city-building pope had his very own bridge built on an ancient foundation; that's right, you already know which one it is, because it's called Ponte Sisto. And the great young cardinal, Riario, was building himself a palace with gambling money he had won from Franceschetto Cibo, the son of Sixtus's successor, Pope Innocent the Eighth. He, too, was from Genoa, and a distant relative of ours . . ."

Enrico Fieschi would stop and say, "Do you like this? Do you enjoy having me tell you about Rome? There is still so much more . . ." And Marta would smile and blush, because the stories of gambling cardinals and popes' sons reminded her of the scandals of her uncle priests in Ciociaria — the one who had a son and the one who drank too much. As she listened, she almost felt she should confess, but confess to what?

He continued, "The funniest thing is that no one knows who designed the palace. It's now called the Palazzo della Cancelleria because the Apostolic Chancellery has resided there for the last three centuries. But look, the facade seems like something from the Florentine Renaissance, and above all, it's made of stone! It was built to withstand the erosion of time, unlike the Roman facades of that era, when even the palaces of princes were made of wood. Can you imagine the people's amazement upon seeing such a palace? On the other side, though . . . here . . . come with me. This side was built later, it's more recent, sixteenth century, can you see? But here, yes, here is the work of Bramante! . . ."

Enrico told Marta so many things, she could not possibly remember them all. But she would not forget the way he presented them to her, his eyes happy, warm, and clear, his hands guiding her along the streets.

Under the porticoes of La Sapienza, in the shadow of Saint Yves where footsteps had a different sound than in the street, Enrico and Marta parted with a secret, chaste handshake during those early days of their marriage, for Marta still blushed when bidding her husband farewell. Then they went their separate ways to attend their classes.

Marta would return home, her mother-in-law's home, at noon, for the midday meal, her marriage resembling life in a boarding school, with fixed and ritualized hours, places, and moods to be endured before a better life, her true life, could be earned. Marta was busy defending herself against those rituals, nothing more. Taller than anyone in the house, beautiful and quiet, so timid she appeared to be proud; in a house where the mistress talked all day, she was called "the Egyptian mummy."

"Not once has she helped out in the kitchen," mumbled Matilde, who was not honest enough to acknowledge that this was impossible, as she had refused all of Marta's offers to help.

"Once upon a time I, too, did something only for myself . . . I painted," Matilde told her, and in that *I, too* there was a hint of regret, but also pride in having sacrificed painting for her family and children. *You, too, will see* . . . , she perhaps wanted to threaten, but she could not. Matilde, who talked endlessly and about everything, was silent with her daughter-in-law because "something was not right" with that girl. By then, they had been married two months, Enrico and Marta. At least one month earlier . . . Matilde was torn between two suspicions, both ugly.

Matilde Fieschi, née Mucciarelli, could never imagine how far from the truth were her suspicions about the Egyptian mummy, nor how unhappy Marta was about her domestic ineptitude. She could not imagine her tears, her hidden rage. Who knows, perhaps she would have given her some affection.

Marta always arrived in time for the midday meal. By then, Matilde's chattering had ceased as she tended to the demands of serving and nourishing everyone, which is the duty of every good mother, especially toward the men in the family: her husband and sons. The father enjoyed every dish, which he praised, along with every story told by his sons. The wine flask wore a "table dress" because Matilde did not permit straw from who knows where to touch her tablecloth.

Marta ate in silence and seldom smiled. They ignored her, and her silence did not intimidate the happy gathering. But at the end of the meal when she folded her napkin and placed it in its embroidered pouch (which, given the hasty wedding, was the only one without a monogram), there was a moment of quiet. And amid that silence she left the room. The first few times this happened, Matilde had said, "Poor girl, it's clear she doesn't feel well at this hour of the day," and her words hung in the air along with the aroma of orange peel and coffee. But now? Everyone had been convinced a new little Fieschi was growing inside Marta, but a month had gone by, then two, and now the third month was beginning. The Egyptian mummy woke in the morning and went to the university. (*What will she do with a doctorate, anyway?*) She returned, was seated and served at the table, retired to her room, and then almost always went out again. They looked at her. They looked at her from the front and then in profile, and Matilde would say to her husband, "Do *you* see anything?" Marta's belly was not growing; it seemed the same as ever. Rather, it wasn't there. At last the mother spoke with Enrico, asking him, "Well, is she?" He had to admit — and it was not easy — that they hadn't gotten married "because of that." He added, "Mamma, how in the world could you think that? It's just that her father is a strange man. He was about to come back, and Marta was afraid he would have been against it . . ."

"Not at all, my dear, you led us to believe that . . . that there was some urgency . . . You made fools of us!"

Only then did Enrico see that the two women most dear to him would never understand each other. He did not mention that conversation to Marta, but his mother could not rein in her voice that carried through the closed doors, or else she did not want to, "Why has he married her, then?"

Marta heard her but no new resentment rose within her. She asked herself the same question: *Why?* And she knew the answer to be out of love for Enrico, yes, but above all because of her fear of her father and a desire to leave the house of her sister-in-law, Caterina.

She had married in September, and during those brief afternoons that turned quickly into evenings she would pay visits to her mother, to her sister, to her father. That first winter of her marriage the days seemed shorter than they had the previous year, and to her surprise that phenomenon of nature still caused her to suffer. In Egypt, the daylight hours of the brief, mild winters were only slightly shorter than those of its splendid summers. At home, Marta had a burning desire to play the piano, her piano. (She no longer played in the cinemas, so she had no earnings to bring to her mother, but Antonia wanted nothing after *Pardi*'s return.) She played Beethoven. Perhaps the aroma of Stelianìs *glookistàs* came back to her. Could she see, could she sense, any emotion in her father as he sat listening to her? Perhaps. But she was not aware of how her sister spent her days. She was not aware how sad and wrinkled Margherita had become, how old she seemed, yet she was little more than twenty. She did not know — and perhaps she never would know — about the affection that had blossomed between Margherita and Enrico's brother, Titta. She did not know that her mother-in-law Matilde had decreed, "In our family, one Egyptian mummy is enough!" And she never would.

Margherita says:

Then, when your uncle — who only invited me one time to the movies in all those years — when he met Elena and fell in love for real, it was Signora Matilde who said, "Margheritina, do Titta a favor," and she sent me to deliver a letter to her. And I did! He had seen her from his office on the Lungotevere. A young blonde who had come down from the north with some documents. From the window he saw that it had started to rain, and she pulled a red wool beret with a pom-pom from her purse. She put it on with a casual gesture, tucking some of her blond curls inside it. She did it without even looking for a mirror! It was this gesture that impressed your uncle. That, and the fact that she did not look for a mirror. Men really are silly. Elena was studying in Rome, and she was staying in a pensione. I brought her the letter, she thanked me, and she gave me a chocolate bar and said, "This is all I have." Then they got married. But it's true that theirs was the best marriage of all, and it was the one that lasted.

❖

When Tommaso Canterno returned to Rome he demanded a room to himself, the one that had been Marta's. Antonia continued to sleep with Margherita, and if that made her unhappy it was certainly not the first time she suffered in silence; to live is only to abide by Allah's will. In a corner of Tommaso's room books soon began piling up, one on top of another. He would leave the house saying, "I am going to see how Rome has changed," and he would walk up the Nomentana, past the buildings and ministries along Via XX Settembre — the date, he would remind himself, of his birth. At the Quattro Fontane he turned right and passed below the tall iron grille of Palazzo Barberini. When he reached the piazza, which had lost its age-old rustic air, Tommaso Canterno felt thirsty, as often happened to him in those days. After drinking the water of the Nile for so many years, he enjoyed the fresh, pure water of his homeland. So he crossed the piazza to the fountain and looked up from below at the ancient Triton and drank from the steady, gentle stream flowing from the conch shell. From behind the Church of the Cappuccini the wind would bring the odors of the countryside, and Tommaso remembered when the fountain had stood at the other corner of the piazza, at the intersection with Via Sistina; but he had not been thirsty then. He had been away from Rome all the years of the new century, and this homeland of his had changed. He had changed, too; he had come back sick, although now his illness was in remission.

The period following the departure of Tommaso's favorite daughter, his wife, and his other daughter had been one of discontent and rebellion, even before his ungrateful country had deprived him of his salary. He had not wanted to see anyone then, particularly not Nicola, Stelianì's gentle son. Nicola sensed this, and once he received his diploma he moved to another part of Alexandria. He took the few pieces of furniture left in the house, so that all the rooms in that house open to the four points of the compass were soon completely invaded by Tommaso's books. He had closed the windows after the first *hamsin* and he had left them that way because the books were in the way. Then the rains had come, and the book covers and pages made of parchment and cloth, of rice, lead, and silk paper, had stuck together and mildewed, becoming food for insects and mites. Finally, Settemunìra grew worried and said, "He needs a hand, for men don't know how to live alone," and she sent her youngest daughter almost every day to put things in order for him.

It was then, too, that the professor of Latin and Italian, discharged by the school and free to roam about, went back to walking the streets of Alexandria with his long, bouncing stride. This time, though, he was better dressed than during the days when he had a wife, for the young girl liked to iron his shirts and his ties, which she tied around his neck in colorful bows, laughing just like a daughter. Tommaso let her do this, and when she led him to the mirror he laughed, too — like a father. But during that first year after he stopped teaching and his visits to the port became more frequent, Tommaso Canterno had already fallen ill.

After drinking from the Barberini fountain, Tommaso dried his mouth with his shirt cuff, wet his forehead, and let it dry in the fresh air blowing off the hillside. Flanked by a row of eighteenth-century houses on his right, he descended to Piazza Colonna then cut through Piazza Capranica, the Rotonda, and along Via di Torre Argentina until he reached Via degli Staderari, where he loved to linger, for scales and steelyards had always fascinated him. Finally he arrived at the market in Campo de' Fiori, just as he had in the past. Perhaps he remembered other scents, the confusion of the long Attarìn, the singsong voices and the strong odors of the fish market in Alexandria; or perhaps he was transported even farther back, to his childhood.

Without a doubt, when Tommaso Canterno walked down to the old heart of Rome, it would have been a Wednesday. Because on Wednesday in Campo de' Fiori there had always been, and there still is, the book market. Once again Professor Canterno would buy as many books as he could carry under each arm, and he would slowly make his way home, reciting poetry to himself, as was his habit when he couldn't read from books. He went by the Botteghe Oscure and crossed Via dell'Arco de' Ginnasi, which harbored no memories for him, even though he had written to that address for so many months from Alexandria. He paid a visit to the Chiesa del Gesù, then passed between Palazzo Venezia and Palazzo Doria, barely noticing the great white monument to Vittorio Emanuele II, which had appeared while he was a student there and had grown while he was away. He walked along dark streets to the Trevi fountain, where he stopped to refresh his eyes, lungs, and ears. He sat down and placed the books beside him, stretching and bending his arms to rest them, then he picked up the books and climbed the Quirinal Hill, up the steep Via Dataria and the stairs, and then retraced his steps along the street of his birth date. In returning to Rome after a lifetime, Tommaso Canterno realized that the lights and odors of Rome had somehow always remained inside him.

But not at first — says Margherita. Because when he first came back to Rome, Papa didn't feel at all at ease. He stayed home and didn't want to go out. "Where would I go?" he said. He had grown fond of Alexandria. He was used to its shops and its streets, which were so much different and certainly much simpler . . . I was the one . . . well, yes, who perhaps saved his life. I told him, "Papa, you must go see the Porta Pia again, you must see the Quirinal . . . and you must go to Piazza Colonna." Then it was Saint Peter's: always farther and farther away. I taught him how to use the streetcars, but he almost always went on foot, and I would accompany him. I took him with me to the Polish Academy, which was at the Botteghe Oscure then, and he returned often by himself. He understood Polish, he could even speak it, because he was a genius! There was even a lady who became interested in him, very interested! Poor Papa, he was still a handsome man. As for me, I was studying at the Institute for Oriental Studies and I never learned Polish well. It's very difficult, Polish is. But I learned Bulgarian and I even knew it rather well. And Russian, too, which is such a beautiful language . . . but I never did anything with it.

❖

Caterina's life, though unburdened by thoughts of household matters, was one of preoccupation, moving from one season to the next, from an opening to a "fiasco" to a "success beyond words." Friends came to the house, she dashed off to the houses of friends, always for more conversation and laughter. She returned home, saying she was "done in" or "dead tired." She bought more furniture, including a sideboard with beveled edges and doors of frosted glass with etchings of dolphins and nude women in silhouette. She bought sixteen long-stemmed goblets and told Margherita, "Don't you dare break them!" The new sideboard was called a *buffet,* in the French fashion, and all it held were those glasses.

Margherita embroidered. She embroidered initials on bed linens, tablecloths, and bath towels, with no sense of time or or any idea what she was waiting for. A husband, certainly; but what is a husband? And how do you find him? Perhaps Cate's sisters knew, but they had nothing but eternal fiancés. Only Cate had a husband, and she was about to leave him. Other people's lives were frightful messes and it was best not to intervene. "You'd have done better to become a nun," her mother would say.

For Cate had returned from a tour with Pavlova, and one night words and shouts were heard coming from the bedroom she shared with Giacomo. He left the house at dawn without anyone seeing him. At eight o'clock, an unusually early hour for her, Cate-Marika did something new and unexpected: wrapped in a cloud of perfume, she gave her mother- and sister-in-law a hug and a kiss, told them, "I love you very much," and left.

She did not return for the midday meal. Giacomo, however, did return at the usual hour, his face ashen. At the table he stared at his plate and announced, right in front of the children, "My wife has left me. She is not coming back."

Antonia flinched, raised a hand to her mouth, and immediately looked at the children, who were stirring their minestrone with their spoons. Margherita blushed deep red and lowered her eyes, full of pain and shame for all of them, and already feeling guilty for loving an enemy. Only Professor Tommaso seemed not to have heard. Breaking the silence he pronounced, "This cabbage is very good. It was a good idea to put it in the soup; you didn't used to put it in the minestrone." Then he was silent, and no one noticed the tears falling into his plate.

Antonia seldom spoke to him. She only served him, as was her wifely duty, and he did not expect much. She did not ask him about the years he had spent alone in Egypt, but once in a while, late in the evening, when *Pardi* was reading and she was sewing with the electric light on, which they had not had down there, she would begin, "Do you remember, in Alesandria . . ." And that had been her whole life. But he answered only with a sound from his throat, not with words.

In February, and it must have been 1925, Tommaso said, "Get me two pieces of bread for tomorrow; I am going to Aquino for the feast of Saint Thomas." He went on foot, over two days, with his bread in his deep coat pockets. Surely he ate something else, too — perhaps festival pastries — but no one knew if he had slept in an inn or somewhere else. When he returned, Antonia found dried bread crumbs in his pockets and pieces of straw between his coat collar and shirt. Tommaso Canterno always wore shoes of black leather, large, with rounded tips. Inside, over his socks, his feet were wrapped in newspapers, and he would say, "Cotton, cellulose, and leather are what keep feet warm, dry, and insulated." Was that the key to his long walks? Tommaso Canterno had not bought those enormous shoes in Rome, nor had he purchased them during his last years in Alexandria. He had them shipped from Cyprus, one pair a year. They were custom-made for him by Antonio, Stelianì's eldest son. Antonia called his shoes by their Greek name, *papúzie*, and she would tell her husband, "When you write Antonio tell him to give my greetings to Stelianì." Somehow, she never found the time to write her old friend, and at heart she did not believe writing was necessary to keep their friendship alive. Besides, it would have been a trial for her to write in Greek, even though it was still an easy language for her to speak, and how happily she spoke it with her daughters! As for French, Stelianì did not read it well.

Only Enrico Fieschi had any questions for Professor Tommaso. He had to plead with Tommaso to use his first name, for his father-in-law insisted on calling him "Conte" at first. When Enrico found a ninth-century inscription he could not decipher, he copied it faithfully and submitted it to the professor. Tommaso kept the note for two days, then went down Via Nomentana to Prati. At the Fieschi house, seated on the red sofa, with his large Cypriot shoes on the carpet, he assumed an air of great secrecy and handed Enrico a sheet of paper covered with his minute handwriting. "Do not tell anyone I gave this to you," he urged him. Enrico did not know that ever since the government had deprived him of his salary, his father-in-law feared that rumors were being spread about him. It was an obsession that hounded him, taking an increasing hold on him with every passing day.

Even though Tommaso liked his eldest daughter's husband, he remained obsequious and uneasy when he met with the other Fieschi counts. And how could Antonia ever establish a warm relationship with Matilde? That perfect home, which seemed so upper class to her. The efficiency, the perpetual chatter (she thought silence offered a glimpse of paradise), the waxed floors, the family dinners, the friends and cousins from Ferrara . . . no; none of this was right for Antonia. She knew nothing about Matilde and her past, just as Matilde knew only that Antonia was the "*ciociara* from Egypt."

When Enrico was chosen to be inspector for the Superintendency of Galleries and Museums after finishing his training with Venturi, he ran up the four flights of stairs to the home on Via Tacito and hugged his mother and his wife. "I won the competition, I got the job!" he said, still breathing hard. "I'm going to Palermo, the city of kings . . . for now," he added, as if already intimidated.

"Palermo!" said his mother in disbelief.

"Palermo!" whispered Marta, so softly no one heard her. It was the first time the two women had spoken the same words together. Yet they did not mean the same thing.

That night Marta stayed awake a long time, but she did not turn the light back on, nor did she study Dante. To leave Rome! Finally! To leave with him, only with him, and to have her own home! That is what her own mother had done when she left for Egypt. True, this meant leaving her mother and her sister, and all the others, but they would not be left alone. She would be leaving the Fieschi household at last! How happy she was that night. She became a little girl again, as can happen in the dark. Once again she saw her hands tying a string to a sun-bleached doorknob to attract the voracious, chattering sparrows. She saw them fly into the little room off the terrace fragrant with the scents of home, and she saw them hop lightly across the ground. Yes, with eyes open in the dark on the fourth floor of an early-twentieth-century apartment building in the Prati quarter of Rome, Marta Canterno, Signora Fieschi, maybe even contessa, longed for her lost Alexandria. There, so long ago and far away, she had left her innocent and happy adolescence; she felt this now more than ever. As she lay in the matrimonial bed that once belonged to Zia Peppina, Marta envisioned the unknown city of Palermo — a city of kings, Enrico had called it — and saw it as a return to the house shaded by mulberry trees along the banks of the Mahmudiyah Canal that she once called the Nile.

Palermo, 1925

Enrico Fieschi arrived in Sicily by train and, even though he had studied geography, he was surprised by the number of mountains. The island seemed beautiful but tiresome, alien and weary. From the train running along the coastline the green countryside clambered upward and villages perched on dark mountaintops in the distance. When at last the train reached the shores of the gulf and Enrico saw Palermo outstretched in an arc — alone as it was, with multicolored cupolas sparkling in the sun amid low, unsheltered yellow houses — he sensed in his own pale skin the intolerance to the sun he had inherited from the Malaspinas, and he felt within him the exhaustion remaining from Caporetto and the illness that had followed. But, he thought, he had come to Palermo to begin his life's work — just as Venturi had come down from Modena to Rome. What's more, he was young, and rich in intelligence and enthusiasm.

A few hours later, from a rickety desk in a hotel room that smelled of stale smoke, Enrico wrote: "My beloved Marta, here I am, in the city of Frederick II and Constance of Aragon. The journey was long, full of smoke and delays in an ever-changing, magnificent, yet tormented landscape so different from that familiar to me." And he continued, "The short crossing was not short for one like me who had never sailed before. The two monsters, Scylla and Charybdis, fought over the ship for over an hour, amid whitecapped waves concealing strong, opposing currents. The air was sharp, the sky overcast. The man who is writing to you (and would prefer to have you in his arms) was almost clinging to a seat bolted to the floor of the ship. He was surrounded by women who, although alive, looked like characters in a nativity scene, wrapped from head to foot in ample coverings or dark shawls and crouched, but with proud dignity, on large empty baskets. They were returning from what seemed to be their usual business trip to Calabria, or as it's called here: 'the continent,' where they sold oranges and other fruits from their fields. From Messina, which is all port and low houses, white and new, at the foot of high mountains — did I tell you that the entire island is surprisingly mountainous? As I was saying, from Messina I chanced to travel in the company of several characters who had dour, impenetrable faces and smelled strongly of cheese (I did not dare engage in conversation with any of them). The train puffed first through the mountains and then through a series of tunnels along the jagged coastline. Since there was only one track, we had to wait at many stations for another train to arrive from the opposite direction, while the sea pounded the shore with majestic breakers; breakers are always majestic, or rather 'always majestic are the breakers,' as I understand they say here, where the verb comes last, as it did in Latin, and as it still does in German.

"It was impossible not to take a carriage at the station. You should have heard the drivers — but you will hear them soon, very soon, I hope — their overbearing calls are almost cries for help as they vie for customers. How they weigh on the conscience of he who must choose — *right this minute!* — some stranger to conduct him by means both rickety and rank (this time, thanks to the horse) to what for many travelers is an unknown destination, as it certainly was for me! After guiltily making my choice — even though it was he, my driver, who snatched me away from a colleague — and having studied the city as much as possible, but from a distance, as you know — and that is a very different thing from being in the middle of it — I asked to be taken to the Duomo. But the driver did not understand; he just asked me again, with his incomprehensible dialect, where I wanted to go. Only after I finally used the term *cathedral*, which he translated as "the *Matrice*" — the Mother Church — did we leave at a gallop. The city has either wide streets — the new ones, built in this century — or very narrow and tortuous ones. And it is — you know my sense of smell — pungent with odors. The air is dusty, which perhaps will remind you of something you loved . . . But there is a lot to see, and we will see much together! I await you . . ."

And the following day, ". . . Good news: I was at the superintendency and it appears — although I haven't had an opportunity to see it yet — like we will have a rather large apartment, inside the palace that once belonged to the Norman kings, no less! It will be our first true home. The people I have met in my new office have shown me exquisite courtesy, and a warm welcome that has been almost overwhelming."

In Rome, in her in-laws' house, Marta received many letters from Enrico, almost twenty in just three weeks. They were long letters, written every evening to the person he called "font of all my joy and light and strength, the most beloved and adored of all women, the most beautiful . . . ," and in closing he always signed himself, "Yours forever, Enrico Maria," which was his full name, although Marta had not known it until that first letter, just as she was surprised by the writing style in those letters, so different from his usual playful and carefree manner of speakng. She reread them often, and felt love all over again, perhaps in a new way, for this man who loved her so. In the house where Enrico had grown up, during those days when he was far away, Marta felt even more an intruder on a stage that certainly was not hers. True, she was aware of her proud bearing and beauty, but she surprised herself — she who thought she didn't know how — by playing the part, amid all the puppets in Zia Peppina's nativity scene, of one who would soon fly away, like a honeybee, to a new life. Her true life. Far from her husband, Marta was conquered by love for a second time, and she felt it more deeply. She had married as if in a dream, and her wedding now seemed a spectacle: the strange crowd of new relatives, the chaos caused by Caterina's sisters and their fiancés, the children . . . Now that Enrico was sending her love letters, or at least letters full of love, something she had never received before — desire for him flooded her heart more every day. In his letters Enrico asked her to give his regards to "Mamma, Papa, and my brother"; his letters to them, she knew, were brief and infrequent. The days were growing longer, the cold of winter was giving way to milder air, and in the mornings Marta merely draped her blanket loosely over her shoulders instead of wrapping it tightly around herself when she left the bedroom; the room where some time earlier — when? — a stranger named Zia Peppina had died. But none of that mattered to her anymore.

Enrico had written about it to Marta ever since the very first letters: ". . . You know that one of the duties of my office is arranging permission for the exportation of art objects. Thus I was able to meet a person — I almost said a personage — who offers flavor and exoticism, a contrast, I should say, to this milieu that is so new to me. Signor V. F. is a northerner who lives in this south of ours as a protagonist. A conqueror and colonizer, I would say, and he is not alone. He has been an antiques dealer in Palermo for thirty years. He arrived in that city, according to what he told me, poor in resources but not in ambition or self-confidence. He has his wife (whom he imported from his own region) and six children as dependents; his is a family business that is esteemed and respected by everyone. It's immediately obvious that he is not Sicilian; as a matter of fact he doesn't even look Italian, which he is not, or at least was not. He is from Trieste, but his family name and ancestry, of which he has spoken briefly, are Slovenian. He is about sixty, and although I would not say he is likable he is certainly impressive, and also fascinating. He knows a lot, and in his bearing and blue-eyed glance there is a great power of persuasion, accompanied by a considerable contempt for many things; among them the bureaucratic requirement for permission to export. He exports all sorts of things: ancient relics from archaeological excavations (there are not yet limitations to that, but they are bound to come! We are preparing them now and he knows it), as well as works of folk art, both Sicilian and Sardinian. He can wax enthusistic about it, and I, who do not like that genre, must admire him for it. Signor V. F. has been to Sardinia several times, and I would say he has plundered it for furnishings, especially rugs, furniture, and alas! paintings, about which he actually knows very little. He has a large clientele abroad, especially in America, where the very wealthy buy all sorts of things. I must confess I had no idea about much of this.

"Signor V. F. has been very kind to me. The second time he saw me, and heard me speak, he said, 'You come from northern Italy, don't you?' and he seemed to wish to indicate something else, that he knew the origin of my name. 'Yours was a great family,' he said to my amazement. 'You are young . . . and you are here . . . alone, if I may ask?' and I nodded. In short, Signor V. F. immediately invited me to his house, 'not out of a general sense of hospitality,' he explained, but because 'I myself have experienced the terrible loneliness Palermo bestows on its immigrants.' No, I didn't think to respond that I did not feel that way, nor was it the right moment to interrupt him. 'Out of egotism,' he continued, 'I would like you to meet the entourage associated with our work. It would be a pleasure to introduce you to "my" Palermo, and I hope you, too, will enjoy it. By now, I'm doing well here, very well indeed.' My dear Marta, I assure you it was not an invitation to be refused . . .

"It was a pleasant and interesting evening, with the F. Family — its head told me that he sees that word always spelled the German way, capitalized, 'and not just because of linguistic custom,' he insisted on clarifying. Then he added, 'The sense of Family is one of the few things that I, or rather we, share with the Sicilians, and it is of utmost importance.'

"Six children, as I said. The males were not present, but the four sisters were, and upon meeting them it was striking to see how much they resemble both their father and mother. I mentioned it, and the eldest laughed as she explained, 'That's because our parents are cousins!' The eldest daughter is named Costanza and she calls herself 'the oldest,' in the German way. None of them hides her age, and they all look like nuns, thanks to their sober dress and their absolute lack of makeup, and baubles in general — as my mother would say — but they are all married. The eldest keeps the company's books, and although she seems unassuming, she knows a lot. She has such an open and intelligent face . . . She'll captivate you. Naturally they are expecting you; they are expecting my wife. And by the way, one thing in particular will interest you: some of them are musicians. Costanza, the eldest, and Giovanna, the youngest, play the piano, and one of the two brothers plays the violin. But the most amusing thing is that the father, in his youth, played the zither, an Austrian instrument I was not familiar with. Are you? It is a flat box of sorts, with the strings inside and a decorated background, and it rests on a table while it is played. It's been said he introduced it to Sicily, as if no one here had ever heard of the lyre of Orpheus. Now Signor V. F.'s zither is displayed in a case in the parlor. Above it is a large portrait of his grandfather, a country man of the hills and a Slovenian, no doubt, and his grandmother, who is offering her husband a glass of red wine. As I was looking at it, my host said, 'It's not by a great artist, I know, certainly an itinerant painter, as was once common up in those parts . . . but we like it.' Naturally that was a 'preventive' lesson for me, in case I wanted to act the specialist, which would have been completely out of place. Those were the grandparents, and that was it. So the family, or rather 'die Familie,' is expecting you," wrote the young, lovestruck Enrico to Marta.

And still more: "Yesterday I spent another evening at the family's house. Signor V. F. — that's how he likes to sign his name — decided to show me a bound volume, a typescript in German. It did not interest me, at first glance, and I handed it back to him. But he said right away: 'Do you know what this is? This is the memoir of a friend of mine, a German from Frankfurt, who was my companion during my first years in Sicily. It is a lovely journal and I would like to have it published, as is. Naturally, I am already in contact with a German publisher, and with one here. I am translating it into Italian, and I will perhaps ask you the favor of reviewing a few parts that are not completely clear to me. I translate, and Costanza types while I dictate; we devote one hour a week to this work, on Sunday. We don't have any more time for it than that, but it will suffice, provided the commitment lasts. And we are committed.'

"As for the journal written by the German gentleman, whom Signor V. F. calls 'the noblest man ever known,' he read me some excerpts; they are truly lively and throw light on the local customs of the years at the end of the last century. He is an unknown among the many foreign travelers in Sicily (at least for now!), and he begins his journal by saying that he does not 'want to emulate Goethe . . .' Ah, those Germans! I am thinking, as I'm sure you are aware, about the historians of our art, Italian art. At first — before Cavalcaselle and our Venturi — they were all German. There was even an Italian who signed with a foreign name! So we can say — modestly or not — that we, the students of the Professor, are the first Italians to study it, Italian art, in its own home, which is also our home. But as I was saying, about my new friend and his friend, I have learned that the Germans are admired here; they are the observers, the catalogers, the conquerors, they are 'orderly,' as the Sicilians say.

"In any case, there exists in Sicily a generic xenophilia that translates into a grandiose sense of hospitality — it is Greek or Arabic in character, although I am not sure how deeply felt it may be, or if it is just a formality used for making a good impression. I do not want, heaven forbid, to sit in judgment with generic, and perhaps rash, opinions . . . but it is true that in this island of Magna Graecia I find myself witness to a strange, or at least different, human environment. This, again, through northern eyes."

And later, in another letter: "The V. F. family is still an inexhaustible source of amusement and interest. They spent the war, which does not seem so far removed to me but I believe is so for them, scattered all over Europe. V. F. was an Austrian citizen then, though not anymore, and he could not conduct business on our soil. Before he could become interned as a civilian enemy, he fled to Switzerland with his eldest daughter. Two children, Margherita and his eldest son, Arturo, were then studying in Berlin. Arturo studied Latin there, and I'll tell you, he knows it better than I do, although his pronuntiation is . . . German. He recites Tazitus by heart, and I assure you it is a delight to listen to him. We have become friends. Arturo is quite different from his father, much less authoritative and authoritarian, and how could it be otherwise, given his father? He knows the four 'major' languages very well, and is equally well versed in their literatures, which is not the only goal, at least according to his father. In fact, languages are vital to their work as merchants in the export market. It appears they made their money — and they must have made a lot of it — after the war, especially from the caravans that disembarked from the transoceanic American cruise ships, although during the war and the family diaspora Signora F. and her young children went hungry. From the transatlantic ships came buyers small and large, some of them very large. From the smaller, but more luxurious ships came members of the British royal family, and a handful of Orléans dukes even came to visit V. F.'s shop and his home. You'll see, you will like my new friends."

Thus went the letters of the imprudent Enrico to Marta during the first months of his stay in Palermo in the summer of 1925. After three months of letters, Marta was escorted to the train station by her brother, Giacomo, and her brother-in-law, Titta, and she departed, alone and happy, for the island of Sicily.

❖

She arrived tired of the immobility, of the light and landscapes, the salt air and the coal smoke breathed inside the tunnels. When she stepped from the train Enrico was waiting for her; beloved, yet a stranger, so different from the Enrico Maria of the letters. He immediately apologized, "I'm so sorry about the air here. It started this morning, and they say it will last three days; let's hope not . . ." She breathed in and looked around under the wrought-iron and glass cupola over the station while an elderly porter — an Arab, she thought — unloaded the baggage. The air was indeed different from what she had left behind, but in the few steps taken on Enrico's arm as they walked to the hackney she was filled with an ancient sense of well-being. What Enrico was calling "foul weather" was a light *hamsin*, the dry, hot wind that blows into Alexandria from the desert. Inside that sirocco, which seemed maternal to her, there were ancient, beloved odors, of cinnamon and horse manure.

"I like this air," said Marta, and he thought that she was saying so out of kindness. He did not know yet that although his wife knew how to be silent, she did not know how to lie.

They were given one of the new apartments reserved for employees of the superintendency, located on the upper floors of the ancient royal palace. The windows and a long, narrow balcony faced south, overlooking a row of trees with small green leaves. The ground below was not visible, but she could see the mountains, pink in the sun and blue in the shade, and the immense garden and trees before the open country, and below, near an eighteenth-century bell tower, the red, round cupolas of a small building. Although she had never looked out on Alexandria and its mosques from above, she was quite moved. "What is it?" she asked. It was the monastery of Saint John of the Hermits with its Arabic dome.

During the days that followed Enrico went with her to visit the great baroque churches, the ancient Arabic remains, and the Norman cathedrals. Marta listened to him as he talked about the architecture of the eighteenth and seventeenth centuries, and she watched him hold terra-cotta vases and figurines between his hands, artifacts freshly dug from soil that had harbored them for two or three thousand years. And with great emotion she touched and held them, too.

In Palermo, without ever imagining it possible, Marta enjoyed a stage of life not held in store for everyone: a period, be it brief or long, where things seen and heard nourish the spirit profoundly, rendering it alert, insatiable, joyous, calm, and well ordered. Meanwhile, other things, other things in life, retreat into the background, becoming superfluous, insipid, and harmless. In those days Marta came to love her husband even more, for he showed her the world, an immense, benevolent world, ready to be possessed by her.

They hired a woman to help tend their home with its four rooms in a row, its hallway, balcony, and small kitchen full of light. Every morning she brought the groceries ordered by "the signora" the previous evening. She was the wife of one of the gardeners who worked in the park at the royal palace. The park, shaded and perfumed by immense magnolias, surrounded the palace walls and rose-arbor-crowned bastions. A narrow walkway ran along the wall, and Marta would stroll there with Enrico by day and under the moonlight, while from the countryside, villages, and mountains the wind brought in the scents of her African childhood.

"I had a very long childhood," said Marta.

"All childhoods are long."

"Perhaps so, but mine was longer." And she would look at the children playing down in the dusty expanse behind the palace, their words and shouts incomprehensible. Incomprehensible, too, were the street cries of the vendors selling fruit and squash, artichokes and bundles of bright green vegetables brought in from the fields each morning in dancing carts drawn by potbellied gray donkeys trotting on tiny hooves. The donkeys had large, dark crosses on their backs, soft muzzles, and sharp, furry ears. Small as they were, they sometimes carried their owners on their backs, with legs hanging down and feet almost touching the ground; just like in Egypt . . .

"Do you like this place?" Enrico would ask.

"Yes, a lot. It reminds me of my own country, which was so beautiful."

From the bedroom in that long, luminous house there was no one to hear her, neither in-laws nor housekeepers, and there were no ghosts of aunts. In the morning Marta went out on the balcony and was struck by the rose-colored mountain, by the floating clouds and the call of the peddler on his dancing cart, by everything she saw and heard. Her sensuality, now awakened, was stirred and fortified by what Marta could only call her soul. A new self was rising within her, an immense self. She had reached the last Canto of the *Purgatory*.

Enrico soon took her to meet his friends. From the main door on the Corso, the vaulted entryway led to a courtyard with a tall, spreading palm tree. Above and across the room, three arches let light in on the stairway on one side, opening it to the sun.

They crossed through the shade and into the sun filtering through the palm tree. Although Marta was wary of new friendships, she noticed a familiar and pleasant odor, the scent of freshly cut wood. She saw large crates stacked one on top of another, and strips of lumber in thick and thin widths, then sawhorses, and a film of sawdust on the floor. In the midst of this, a tall man was standing with his hands in his pockets and his back to the entrance as he watched an old man and two boys pounding nails into a crate. Their sharp hammer blows echoed. Enrico called out, "Arturo, it's us! Here we are." The man turned and broke into a smile that Marta felt she had long known yet couldn't place. Arturo F. came toward them across the carpet of sawdust. "How are you?" he asked, taking her hand in his own large, warm one.

Surely she smiled; perhaps she even answered that banal question, for it had seemed so sincere. The man was taller than Marta, with dark brown, wavy hair, like a boy's. "Let's go. I am going to take you to my sisters," he said, and then turned to the men working, "I'll be back shortly," he promised. They went up the staircase on the right.

"Enrico, I have finished reading your book; I'll return it to you today, then we can talk about it . . . But tell me about yourselves. Have you found time to take the signora to see the metopes before they disappear for good? You never know!"

Marta listened but did not understand; she followed them and grew distracted. She enjoyed remaining silent while they talked. They ascended slowly, and she lagged behind, observing that "new person" (as Caterina would have called him — my God, how long ago!) who seemed to have something old, something familiar and beloved about him . . . but what? His hair; that was it! She recognized it, after all those years, and she thought immediately, *Caterina does not know it, she cannot remember it, because she never saw it, she never touched it!* She felt a shiver on seeing it again: the curly, soft hair that her brother, Giacomo, had had before he left Alexandria, before he went to war and returned . . . that way; before they all came to Italy.

Seeing that hair again, she wanted to run her fingers through it. Unexpected sensations returned to her, tender yet stinging, the same feelings she experienced with Enrico at the front door on Via Nomentana. Oh God, why?

They had climbed above the spreading, upper branches of the palm tree, where the tender new shoots emerged from its core. The scent of freshly cut wood wafted up to them. From the staircase they entered an airy room full of plants, then a large hall, the first in a row of three. Seated at a writing table at the center of the room was one of the F. sisters, who rose to greet them. A window on one side of the hall overlooked the palm tree, and another window looked out over rooftops. The walls of the first room had shelves from floor to ceiling filled with cardboard boxes. On the right was a large table spread with assorted papers and rolls of packing twine. But Marta did not notice those things.

Seated on a long, low bench, three women in ample black skirts that touched the floor were wrapping oranges in colored paper. They worked with quick repeated gestures, picking an orange from a basket with the left hand, then passing it in an uninterrupted rhythm to another worker in front of them, who placed it in a small box. "Those are mandarins and oranges for Christmas," said Arturo. "They are going to Holland." Marta inhaled, and she breathed in not only the scent of mandarins, but other unfamiliar scents as well, complex aromas she found strangely unsettling.

She was impressed by the disarray of riches. Furniture covered with art objects, paintings, and majolica vases — too many to count; handwoven rugs in exotic designs and colors — "These are all Sardinian and they are being shipped to America," explained Arturo; tall glass display cases containing ancient pieces of terracotta. The colors, the many fragrances, brought forth memories for Marta of the long Attarìn, the antiquarians' street in Alexandria where she had walked as a little girl, holding her father's hand.

They left the hall where the women were working and entered another room. It had a pleasant odor of resin, and it was filled with stark pieces of furniture that were old, but not antique. There was a table set for tea, and behind it was the brothers' mother, erect and serene with a starched white lace collar decorating her black dress, gray hair knotted tidily at the nape of her neck. She looked as if she were on a throne as she sat knitting a sweater. She worked quickly, holding her short needles with their ends free in the air, set at equal angles with her hands and arms. With the tip of her right-hand needle she picked up the yarn wound tightly around her raised left index finger and passed it through the eye of the following stitch. Marta could not take her eyes off the woman's motions, because she, as well as her mother, Stelianì, her sister, and everyone else knitted in a very different way.

Introductions were made and everyone sat down. The signora continued knitting mechanically. On the tablecloth embroidered with large daisies done in a satin stitch — just like Margherita made them — were gold-rimmed white porcelain cups. The air was redolent of spices from the homemade petits-fours, pastries, and biscotti unlike anything Marta had ever seen or tasted before.

The large-bellied teapot was covered by a cozy crocheted of wool with a pom-pom on top, like a big beret; perhaps it was made from leftover yarn, as it was multicolored. A pair of woman's hands placed a platter of buttered bread slices on the table. Years later, although she had seen them so often by then, Marta still could not describe those indefatigable hands, which seemed invisible and never at rest. Tea was poured and silence fell. The signora, who continued knitting without ever turning her eyes to her work, looked at Marta and said, "So, tell me about yourself. I know you have traveled a great deal and that you are a musician . . ." Marta was alone. Enrico had turned the other way to talk with Arturo; the sisters were silent. She was alone, but felt she had to respond. And she did respond, while the signora kept on knitting, while other people moved about in the background and then stopped to listen. She said she had not traveled much, but yes, it was true she had been born and raised very far away, in Egypt. She told the signora about her father the professor and linguist, and her brother, who was a professor and musician; she spoke of her own musical studies in Alexandria and then in Rome. She said these things almost as a challenge, she who had not screamed when the wound made by the carriage had been cauterized; she who had returned to an ungrateful homeland to work and earn money for her mother; she who had been called "the Egyptian mummy" in her mother-in-law's house because of her timid and proud silence. Marta kept them rapt in attention: her husband and Arturo F., the signora and the young servant in her apron, standing with a platter in hand, and the other sister, who had just joined them and closely resembled the first one; all the while the mother's hands and her needles continued their solitary dance and their clicking. In front of all those strangers, Marta, who could not and would not act on a stage, acted out her own life, her two countries, Santa Cecilia, the Teatro dei Piccoli of Podrecca where she had directed Rossini's *Cinderella*, the piano in the movie theaters, and the appearance of Francesca Bertini while she was playing (her voice quivered with emotion) . . . It was getting late. She ended her story with a smile that lasted a bit longer than appropriate. Afterward there was a long silence. Marta looked around. She saw her husband and frowned. Something new had happened.

"So you are a musician," said Arturo. "Naturally, Enrico already told us this," he added. "And *naturally* I insist we play something together. My sister is a pianist, and I play the violin . . ."

I know, thought Marta, but she did not say anything.

When Enrico and Marta Fieschi left the building with the palm tree in the center of the courtyard, she did not speak. They went on foot; it was less than ten minutes to the ancient dwelling of the Norman kings, but the silence between them was complete. Then Enrico said, "Did you like them? And you have not even met them all. You were great; you made a great impression." She answered quietly, "Yes, certainly, I did like them. I liked the house, the rooms, those fragrances . . ." but she spoke as if tired, or else very pensive.

5. LOVES

Sunday

THE CHURCH BELLS had already chimed, and the starlings had flown from the treetops into the fields. It was a Sunday in winter, or in spring, or in fall. Some Sunday or another. All the events that make a Mediterranean morning heartwarming and fascinating were already happening when Marta climbed with solid footsteps into the carriage that Arturo had brought for them. Enrico sat beside her, and Arturo was seated on the narrow seat facing her.

Marta was looking out at the azure mountains turning to gold, and the green citrus orchards turning azure, as she breathed in the pungent scent of the orange blossoms and tried to keep her knees from touching Arturo's.

The day promised to be long and full. "The starlings are still here," he said. "Soon they'll be gone. When the warm days of March arrive, they head north. Once I would have liked to follow them; not anymore. For a few weeks, we'll see only the sparrows; then the swallows will come. They are small and silly, but very pretty." Marta drank in those words spoken to her of creatures she loved. Yes, the swallows, and how fond were her memories of the swallows on the Nile, so different from the swifts that shrieked in the sky above Via Gioacchino Belli! Marta drank in that amorous air. She loved her husband then, amid the greatest adventure of her life. But she did not love only him.

The driver was cracking the whip. Marta noticed the horse's obedient manner, the elegance of its tail and mane, and she realized she had never truly looked at a horse before. She did not say it, though; she said neither this nor anything else, and she paid no attention to the conversation between the two men. She let the sunshine envelop her; she heard words and forgot them.

Marta did not listen and she did not speak. Strands of hair were already slipping from the chignon at the nape of her neck, and her beautiful, white face was taking on color. Youth shone in her classical, serene features while the carriage assaulted the slope and the driver urged on the horse with his dramatic, throaty cries, while the perfume of the countryside wafted in from the fields, while Arturo was falling in love with her.

He talked at length of Jules Romains and Maupassant; and having gone to school in central Europe he spoke of a "good" poem and a "good" book, and he pronounced double and single consonants improperly, and she found his barbarisms elegant. "Do you know, signora, the name of the horse that is carting us? It's Ciuriddu, which means 'little flower.' Isn't that right, Pippo?" and the driver nodded in agreement.

They caught up with Arturo's mother, his sister, and Stanka, the young servant, in the other carriage. The carriages drew together side by side and the conversation opened to include all the passengers, passing from one carriage to the other as they continued on the long uphill road, the road to Mezzomonreale.

It was that trip, or perhaps another. Those Sunday outings with Arturo's family became confused in Marta's mind, and in time they melded together, becoming the memory of a single, glorious outing, in which everything happened.

Or else it was in the streetcar. The streetcar to Monreale ran smoothly along tracks on an elevated grassy median in the middle of the road (it was, and still is, called Corso Calatafimi), which left the city between rows of modest houses. They were all wearing boots and knee socks turned down to the calf; socks that Stanka had knitted during the winter afternoons, with her shiny braids tighly wound around her head and her clean "afternoon" apron on. They all carried backpacks of heavy canvas with leather straps. Arturo remained standing, with one hand in a ring that hung by a leather strap from the roof of the streetcar. The other handholds danced freely, and Marta thought about the Roman streetcars, whose handholds she had grasped — with gloved hands because of the cold — while cradling her cello in her arms. It had remained in Via Nomentana, her cello. She smiled from time to time, and felt her cheeks blush at his big, embarrassing smile; or else she looked away.

That smile had no end; it embodied a word she had pulled from unfamiliar depths, the word *disarming*, with all that it implied. She looked out at the houses lining the dry and dusty sidewalks, at the shuttered windows and Dutch doors with their bottom halves closed.

"Yes, that's the way it is here," Arturo explained. "The door also serves as a window. During the day they keep the upper part open and the lower part closed; often there is only one room in the house, with a bed in it; in other words, the bedroom *is* the house. There's a flowered curtain; do you see it there, and another one, over there? The right side of the fabric is facing out, to keep passersby from intruding, even if only intruding with their thoughts. Naturally the flowers printed on the fabric are visible on the inside, too, but only through the light."

"You are very observant," murmured Marta, and it was the most audacious phrase she had ever uttered.

"And you aren't?" replied Arturo, smiling again. And with that smile, right in the middle of that smile, he added, "You will be, one day." By now they were alone in a sphere of love. Outside it, beyond its confines, waited Enrico and the Castellaccio, the backpacks, and the serene face of Signora F.; serene, but thin and tight-lipped. The cathedral of Monreale loomed overhead, and above it was the mountain, green with grass and white with rocks.

But Stanka shifted her hands and forced them to return to earth, among the others: her husband, her new friends, and everything in that new country where Marta had come to stage her true life, at last . . . Except that this life had brought her face-to-face with a violent truth that exceeded any feeling or challenge she had ever experienced. She knew nothing would ever be the same. She should have protected herself, stopped everything; but it was too late.

Another time, another Sunday, Marta rode on the back of a mule — she who had always been afraid of horses — and found herself higher above the ground than ever before. Arturo had walked by her side. He told her stories, explained and recited, and the rest of the time they spent together in silence. The animal swayed its warm, large flanks, and Marta felt the heat against her legs. The stony path descended through bare red earth and patches of bright green clover. Each small blade of grass that caught her eye was full of life; just like each foolish, divinely beautiful butterfly, and the clouds in the sky, and the very footfalls of those hooves on the sparkling white stones or the soft, silent earth, on the asphodels or on the wormwood that immediately released its enigmatic perfume.

As the blue and red dragonflies had flown over the Nile, so did Marta's glances fly through that clear air toward hidden waters. She drank in the colors, fragrances, and vibrations, lazily, without asking herself why.

And that time or some other time she heard:

Les amoureux fervents et les savants austères
aiment également, dans leurs mûres saisons
les chats, puissants et doux, orgueil de la maison . . .

It was Arturo's voice, near her. Perhaps as the sun warmed her face, it turned her cheeks red. His long silence flowed into hers; she heard him say with a changed voice, "*Les fleurs du mal*, remember?" She turned to him then and smiled, a fleeting smile just for him. "Never read them," she admitted. "I haven't read much, but I will."

The mule continued over the soft, red soil. "Is that a promise?" Arturo murmured, so softly Marta might have thought she imagined it. It was also as if instead he had said, "No, don't do it, I will do it for you . . . I will read you everything I know . . ." But Arturo was walking in silence; he had said none of those things. Years later he would confess to her that he had thought them.

They reached an emormous tree with a round, dense canopy that cast its shade on black earth where no grass would grow. They stopped and ate bread and cheese, and the deep flavors of the bread penetrated that excellent cheese, so fresh, lean, and dense. "It's called tuma," said Arturo.

Marta, through divine grace, had a right to everything. She had intelligence, beauty, skill, and virtue. She had a husband who loved her, and another man who loved her in a different way, who recited poems to her. These were Marta's thoughts, and they made her brim with happiness, as did the shade tree and the bright green countryside beyond its shadow.

". . . Yes, I used to raise silkworms, in Egypt, but it was easy. I would find them on the mulberry trees along the road, and we had only to take them home. They ate continuously. Then they made their cocoons, always at night so as not to be seen. And the butterflies would be born, big and heavy, with short, useless wings. They couldn't fly."

"Didn't you produce silk?"

"Silk? Oh, no. You have to kill the worms do to that; you throw the cocoons in boiling water . . . But why raise them first and then kill them? I was not interested in silk; what would I have done with it? No, I let them be born, those butterflies. They made a hole in the cocoon, but then they didn't know where to go. I would take them back to the tree; who knows, maybe then the birds ate them . . . there were so many little birds . . ." Thus Marta recounted her story in Sicily, without knowing that a silk thread connected her to Matilde, her forgotten mother-in-law. The two women had never spoken to each other about silk and silkworms, and they never would. But Marta's daughter knows it, having listened to them each tell their stories.

The Temple of Segesta appeared, solitary against the mountain.

"Right here," said Arturo, "right here, every time, I fear I will not find it again, I fear it has disappeared. Disappeared like everything else; it is so grand as to make one think the city must have been quite grand, too. Segesta isn't here anymore, hasn't been in a thousand years. All that remains is the temple, the theater, and a few tombs, but the city has never been excavated, it has never been brought back to the light of day. It is down here, all around us, under our feet." A sound of bells was heard. "Yes, those are sheep, and shepherds. The shepherds are sick with malaria."

Arturo's words remained suspended in the air with the sound of the bells. Beyond the trees, the temple now rose against the sky. "Signora, you saw the Pyramids, but I hope you will find this even more beautiful. This is alive . . . still alive, and it is human . . . the Pyramids . . ."

"I — I have not seen the Pyramids . . ." She was truly ashamed, and she blushed since ignorance, for her, was the worst of all failures. Her justification for not having seen the Pyramids was that her father had never taken her there. She said, "I am sure that this is more beautiful."

Caper bushes were growing from among the stones of the tympanum, just as they had bloomed among the white stones of Fort Napoleon; capers and passionflower, a name she had been taught by her mother.

They reached the temple, climbed the steps, and stood among the columns on the short grass. They did not speak, nor did they draw close together once inside that roofless temple, as if fearing each other's touch, or else the superimposed memories of others who remained there, invisible through the centuries, to spy on their ill-fated adventure. She knew she had to leave aside words, and even thoughts, because they were all inadequate, coarse, and out of tune; they all fell short. The winter asphodels breathed the spring air. The ground was covered in a carpet of flowers, dark blue flowers with yellow hearts, minuscule blue star flowers, and succulent, green-and-blue orchids with velvet petals, giant umbellifers, and swaying, purple lilies.

A black-and-yellow bumblebee busied itself around them. "Who is to say that the buzzing of the bee is not a conciliatory offering as well; or that the flowers that detect the bee's approach — the sound, the vibration, who knows what a flower can sense? — might not produce more nectar, more pollen, out of emotion and fear? For emotion is always fear, too . . . isn't it?"

He was speaking about her, and they were unable to resist looking at each other. Marta fell into those eyes, and she knew it was forever.

The bumblebee was still flying among the flowers. Large and fuzzy, it looked a bit ridiculous, its legs loaded with pollen to take home. "You see that part of the legs, where the pollen is stored? We call it the basket, but who knows what the bees call it. Think, Signora Marta, how many names we arbitrarily assign to beings that are born free . . . and without a name."

It was then that Marta saw the lily. Alone and striking, it stood with blooms fully open in the middle of the field, towering above everything else. Because it was by itself she did not recognize it at first. But when she realized what it was, she stopped and blushed. Then she made a confession, and in giving it to Arturo instead of Enrico she was guilty of betrayal: "A field of lilies, the entire, immense field was lilies; I used to cross it when my father took me to the seashore. It was the Mediterranean, but on the other shore, the Egyptian . . ."

Thus she had entrusted herself to Arturo without reserve, her past and her future as long as it would last. With her words and images she was also giving him — and she knew it — something else, ineffable, bursting with a mysterious vitality: her soul.

They stood alone for a long time, without smiling. Then a smile appeared on their faces, consuming them, as another bumblebee approached, black and yellow, heavy, ridiculous, even bigger than the first. It buzzed loudly and busied itself in a patch of acanthus flowers. Arturo and Marta smiled at each other, sharing the same thought: *Here he comes to feast and make fertile the flower of the most classic of all plants.*

It had happened and they both knew it, but Marta believed they would never speak of it, that it was even possible not to admit it to herself. Without speaking, she lay that night by the man she loved as he slept. She was brimming, not with thoughts or feelings of her other lover, but with a sense of completeness that lifted her heart and senses.

Music

A cello was borrowed for Marta. Costanza, "the oldest," sat at the piano, and Arturo, naturally, had his violin. Through the long twilights of summer, the short afternoons of a mild autumn without fog, and into the nights of a rainy winter they practiced Beethoven's Trio, opus 1. The sun did not set as early as in Rome, nor as quickly as in Alexandria.

By November relatives from above Trieste had already sent the top of an enormous fir tree from the northern forests. They shipped it by rail, addressed to a seventeenth-century palace in the ancient and impoverished "city of Kings," which was located on a parallel very close in climate and flora to that of the Holy Land.

The last days of the year arrived, and Enrico and Marta received an invitation that was "an exception to the rule," as Costanza confided. "Our family's Christmas is always just for us, because here in Sicily it is celebrated differently. In Rome, certainly, you must have your own traditions. But you are special friends, and like us, here you are considered foreigners. You would be alone, and we will have none of that. We are expecting you."

The staircase overlooking the courtyard was decorated with lit candles nestled into boughs of fir. The odor of resin and burned pine needles mingled with the scent of Stanka's biscotti as they ascended the staircase. Costanza was waiting for them there, at the top of the stairs. She wore a long dress and her hair was tied back in a softer arrangement than usual.

"It smells so lovely!" exclaimed Marta as Enrico exchanged Christmas greetings with the young hostess and kissed her hand.

"Yes, Stanka has been making biscotti for a week. She has almost starved us in the meantime, and tonight we're fasting . . . it's Christmas Eve . . . perhaps we should have warned you. We're eating only biscotti! Come on, come inside."

They were dressed with a solemnity befitting the occasion as they waited in the green sitting room, and the door to the adjoining grand salon remained closed. The only one missing was the head of the family. "Father is getting things ready," explained Costanza, pointing to the door just as it opened.

The lights were out in the parlor but the enormous fir rose triumphantly in the center of the room, almost touching the vaulted ceiling and flickering with the lights of innumerable tiny candles. The tree stood on a table covered in red damask that fell in folds all around, and a hidden gramophone played organ music by Bach. The birds and butterflies painted three hundred years earlier on the ceiling seemed to flutter, and the shiny majolica floor shimmered in the dancing lights. Near the base of the tree, which was held upright by a copper stand, an empty wooden cradle rested under the attentive eyes of the Madonna and Saint Joseph. Behind them two angels prayed, their wings touching the ground. The figurines were about twelve centimeters high, and carved of wood.

Enrico and Marta were overwhelmed by the unexpectness and beauty of the scene. Slowly, silently, the entire family — brothers, spouses, and parents, along with Arturo and Costanza — gathered beside the table under the lighted tree, and at a nod from the father, they started singing. Softly at first, solemnly and sweetly. It was a slow German hymn that filled the room and their souls. The song was "Stille Nacht, Heilige Nacht," but not even Marta with her musical training was familiar with the melody, although it would soon become known throughout the world. She was deeply and indelibly moved.

Enrico was fascinated in spite of himself. Baptized twenty-seven years earlier in Saint Peter's, he tried to resist its spell, he would have liked to belittle it in true, cynical Roman fashion, but he could not do it. He could not do it.

Marta was now singing along with them, and he would have joined in, too, although without words. Poor Enrico! How many years had it been since he had entered a church for anything except to look at frescoes and paintings? Christmas in his own home now seemed just a celebration of *cappelletti in brodo* and English trifle. His mother, Matilde, who had given her sons a proper upbringing — very proper — and had always gone to mass on Sunday, could not find the time for it in those days. The nativity scene, yes, she still made one, with the same old figurines, but more in homage to the sacred memory of Zia Peppina than as an act of devotion. Poor Enrico! When he looked at his wife he saw, he truly saw, that this northern holiday, celebrated on the wrong parallel, was carrying part of her away, and the realization stunned him. He saw that "die Familie" — dressed in white lace over dark blue velvet — was not singing its love for the newborn God, but for itself, for its own traditions and its proud nostalgia — real or imagined. For a lost fatherland, and for remote, perhaps only fabled, happy childhoods. It was a contagious nostalgia, even if it referred to other locales. A nostalgia for other places, far away from where they were on that twenty-fourth of December, even if in error. An error that could be remedied.

The fir needles were already starting to crackle as the dripping candles expired. The candles, they were told, were custom-made by an artisanal candlemaker, for in this city anything could be found; one need only search diligently and ask courteously. The room's exotic atmosphere was becoming more warm and intimate. Clustered around the small nativity, the members of the family began to sing a traditional Sicilian carol, "The Three Kings of Orient," a tribute, they explained, to this land, too, "which has received us, which hosts and nourishes us . . ."

After singing "The Three Kings" there was an exchange of gifts, and Stanka's tray of biscotti, which had not yet been touched, was passed. Then it was time for the other music: their own.

They played the Trio, and in the parlor there was only their music and their souls. Then, with the last chord resonating in the air and the bows lifted from the strings in the brief, sacred silence before the applause, Marta set her instrument aside and gave herself over to that world she had forgotten. And perhaps, for an instant, her eyes gazed into Arturo's. Perhaps. Or perhaps it was less than an instant. He, with violin and bow in his hands, smiled and bowed to the audience, his family. Costanza, the pianist, did the same. Marta rose to her feet and nodded with her eyes, allowing her soul a moment's rest, a moment she wished she could prolong. But then she raised her eyes, still transfixed, and met with the signora's stare, which called on her conscience. It called to her, after the music, reminding her of what she had learned, with or without words, in her days, nights, and years; something she knew all too well. *This is simply not done*, said the eyes of Arturo's mother. *Not ever*, they insisted; it surprised her that someone could still think this way. Slowly, even though her smile persisted — genuine at first, then feigned — Marta straightened her back and raised her head. She felt an old wound reopen, the memory, deep-seated and terrifying, of her father's undeserved reproaches. As if the signora had said, *Get dressed; we are going out*. Because this time she knew her crime and she was certainly guilty, but at the same time she felt — she knew — she was divinely innocent.

Marta did not say to Enrico *Let's go home*, because she was not accustomed to having weariness be an excuse. She remained silent throughout their celebration. There was no place to flee or hide, if others deemed what had happened to be a crime. Nor did she have to hide or flee from herself, because never before finding herself in love with both Enrico and Arturo had she felt so much herself, so complete, rich, and grand.

Three weeks later Enrico said, "We are moving to Naples. I was named to the superintendency there. That way we will be closer to Rome. We will have a beautiful home there, you'll see. You'll like it."

Marta threw up. Her period was ten days late; she was in the twentieth day of her pregnancy.

Naples

Enrico Fieschi, inspector of the Neapolitan Superintendency for the Fine Arts, located at the royal palace, took up residence at Villa Floridiana, on the Vomero hill. The white building looked out on the avenue across a lush green lawn shaded by hundred-year-old pines. Above the arched entrance portico was a small balcony. On each side of the palace winding avenues cut into forests of holm oaks and disappeared from sight. Blackbirds sent out their rich, complicitous calls; if they showed themselves, it was with bounding leaps, with seductive quick steps, or they bobbed up and down on the lower tree branches, their tails never still.

"It looks grand, but it isn't; it's grandiose," said Enrico. "There you are; from the palace of Frederic, the famous enemy of my uncle, Pope Innocent, I have brought you to the palace of Ferdinand. What more do you want?" And Marta felt her heart ache with remorse. Because she knew well what use she would make of Enrico's words, *grand, grandiose*. She knew, eagerly, the moment he uttered them, and she would not forget. Because every day she wrote letters — brief or long — to the man who occupied all her thoughts.

The apartment was on the top floor, under the roof. It had a wooden staircase and low ceilings. The windows in the facade, designed by Niccolini, were small, but they let in plenty of light. A long, graceful staircase descended to the garden. Below it was all of Naples and the sea, and in the center was a fountain that trilled chastely. Marta heard the sound rise up to the rooms; she heard it from her bed. Yes, she would write about that, also. Her secret heart had remained in Palermo, with Arturo, a thought that took on inalienable rights with the separation that had been imposed on her. She was far from him, but why deprive herself of that which fulfilled her — beyond words, beyond imagination — by divine will?

The sun touched the pines in the park, surrounding them in a golden halo. It made the tiny glass windows glimmer throughout the immense city and turned the sea to lacquer. It woke up the thousand birds of the Floridiana, and soon Marta was nursing a sparrow that had fallen from its nest, as she had done in Alexandria. The sun rose and set, marking the days, the nights, the weeks, while a fog grew inside her, disrupting her sense of time now that it was measured by her pregnancy. She was always sleepy. Surprised and annoyed at having lost her freedom, Marta responded to Enrico's happiness with silence.

He rode the funicular down to the city in the morning and returned only in the evening. He said, "I have invited a couple of friends for dinner tomorrow. Let's have a meal fit for company." But the following day, time flew mercilessly. "Don't be upset, signora," said the porter's wife, and she helped her prepare the meal. That evening Enrico returned to find his wife nervous but beautiful. His friend Sergio Ortolani kissed her hand. "Oh," he said, "how lucky is our friend Enrico." And when Professor Don Aldo D. R. looked at her he tilted his head "like a chicken" — for although he was not old, cataracts impaired his vision. He bowed without even touching her hand and said softly, "Enchanted." Later he took her aside. "Of all the Madonnas our Enrico has seen, you are the most splendid. And I know you are talented as well as beautiful. I hope we will be lucky enough to hear you." She smiled, almost without understanding.

At the table it was Enrico who offered the various dishes, saying, "Please, have some more," while the porter's wife, who had done the cooking, said, "Just relax, will you?" Enrico laughed, an unfamiliar, artificial laugh. Marta looked at her husband and he seemed superfluous. There was a child inside her, a child who belonged to him, too, but what did he know about it? What did he understand about her? Nothing. He knew nothing, and he was laughing with those friends she did not know. The smoke from Vesuvius was white at that hour. Marta felt dizzy and thought, *My true self is someone else*. But that someone was far away.

They had visitors: Costanza and her husband. As soon as she was alone with Marta she said, "My brother Arturo sends his greetings. He told me that if I didn't promise to visit you, he wouldn't let me come." Marta blushed and said nothing; she petted the sparrow perched on her shoulder. But Costanza had disturbed the waters that reflected Marta's soul; by her words, by daring to mention his name, she had stirred up the memory of that most distressing and delightful day. The visitors left and Marta went to bed. That night she dreamed.

When her pregnancy was almost at full term, Arturo himself came for an entire day; a long day filled with unforgettable details. She wished she could have concealed her size from him, and denied it even to herself. But Arturo gestured playfully toward the baby who would soon be born and said, "What good fortune! You must be so happy." Marta felt dismay at the sincerity of his words, for he seemed so much greater and more generous than she, so much more worthy of being loved. Then he added, "Ever since you left, music holds no more beauty for me, but I play more than ever. Because only music remains constant throughout time; only music can give time back to us. It is the only bond between life and the eternal, beyond time." She did not speak, and the silence bound them even more tightly. They strolled for a long time. Arturo was taller than Marta; his serene voice would remain suspended in the tree branches forever. They walked side by side without touching. She wore on her shoulders a shawl that outlined her figure. He said, "I'm glad we didn't try the Sonata opus 47; it's difficult and perhaps truly dangerous." She furrowed her brow slightly. Although he knew he had spoken audaciously — the words fell out of his mouth before prudence could intervene — he never imagined she would not understand. But in fact Marta was not familiar with the famous novel, nor did she know that a significance had been attributed to the Kreutzer sonata that was not strictly musical.

They returned to the villa but he did not want to enter. He said good-bye, murmuring, "Next time I will bring my violin. I wish I could return tomorrow; waiting will be miserable." Then he bent as if to kiss her hand. And he did. At once overwhelmed, exhausted, elated, and miserable, she remained immobile on the white threshhold of the small portico, knowing the man who was walking down the street, the man who was now turning to wave, would not forget her. When he disappeared around the curve beyond the lawn, she experienced a moment of unbearable suffering. She reentered the house, climbed the wooden staircase with heavy steps, and went to lie down. The child inside her started to kick, and Arturo's words returned to her. Were she not so despondant at the thought of not seeing him again, she might have asked herself if *You must be very happy* was a hypothesis or a command. But she did not. Years would go by before she wondered about it. That evening she just cried.

Her mother and Margherita came from Rome for the delivery. It was October. The labor lasted three days, during which Enrico did not go to the funicular but walked instead in the garden. Marta made an appearance there, too — "Take a walk, signora, take a walk, it will be good for you." — but after taking a few steps she turned back. She leaned against the wall, and with a fixed gaze put her hand to her open, silent mouth. The midwife came twice to say, "I'll be back tonight." In the evening Dr. Roccatagliata grinned, "Yes, we're almost there, good, very good!" A storm was unleashed during that long evening and the pine trees thrashed in the wind. A large branch fell on the roof, and the electric power failed. Inside the house the porter's wife gathered all her children. "Pray!" she ordered them. Margherita, seated on a chair in the kitchen, prayed against her fears amid the darkness and lightning.

And in the company of the angel who had come from Rome by train with her, Antonia prayed to Saint Anne, protector of women in labor.

After three hours she paced back and forth in the bedroom, and with the screams of each labor pain she raised her arms to the rafters, opening and closing her hands in reproach, "My dear Saint Anne, how I've prayed to you!" At last, toward midnight, with the doctor repeatedly threatening, "Signora, I am going to have to use the forceps!" a little girl was born by the light of thirty candles. "Brava!" said the doctor and sewed her up. The father cried with happiness, and the midwife washed and dressed the little creature, so compact, pink, and faint of voice. Margherita, forgotten once again, looked in from the doorway, gazing at the bassinette that she herself had given its finishing stitches. "Thank you, Saint Anne!" said Antonia with relief. The storm ended.

The little girl was healthy. Her name was Adriana. Before dawn, the doctor had returned to Naples to rest, and the midwife had done the same. The new mother slept. Antonia went to the kitchen and took out a white bowl. She poured a bit of olive oil and water into it, and stirred the mixture with a silver fork she had brought from Rome expressly for the purpose. The precious fork that had been bought by Tommaso, in Alexandria for Marta's birth, when they still lived in the wealthy quarter of the city with the children, Giacomo and Maria. Outside, the raindrops on the pines of the Floridiana were reflecting the first rays of the sun.

The newborn was visited by her other grandparents, the Fieschis, who were complete strangers to Marta in that house and park. Nursing had made her more beautiful. The baby was photographed in the arms of one grandmother and then the other, then with the grandfather and even with Zio Titta, who had come down from Rome, too. In those days Marta did not think to sing lullabies to her daughter, but after her in-laws had gone she took stock of her situation and decided she was the most important person in the world. Intelligent, cultured, and beautiful, she was a mother, and she was beloved by more than one estimable man; not only Enrico and Arturo, but now Don Aldo, whom Enrico addressed with *voi*, the Neapolitan formal "you."

Arturo's letters kept arriving. They opened with "Dear friends," or "Dear Enrico and Marta," and before that his postcards had come from Germany, where he had stopped on his way to Naples. Once in Palermo, he made a lengthy recount of his trip, and then he continued to write, about his home life and work, his latest readings, his observations and thoughts . . . In short, he wrote about anything. Enrico replied with two brief letters, then told Marta, "You answer. I don't have the time. I'll add my greetings at the bottom." Then even that was forgotten. A correspondence between Arturo and Marta had started, and after a few "greetings from Enrico," Marta's husband knew nothing more about the letters. It was not that Marta hid them; she simply forgot to mention them. Soon, and without being asked, the caretaker at the villa's gate began setting aside Arturo's letters, only Arturo's, and handing them directly to Marta, even though they were addressed to "the Fieschis."

When Adriana was six months old, Annita came to stay at the house, and although the baby had never seen her before, she immediately wanted to be held in her arms. Dark-haired and small, with round black eyes, Annita could neither read nor write. She did the housework with the baby in her arms, and she prepared the baby's pabulum and fed her. At the same time, as if following her, Sinesio also came to live with them; he was a small tabby, a scrawny stray from some district of poor cats in the city. Sinesio did not forget his old sufferings immediately, for violent convulsions periodically left him lying on the floor as if dead. Then either his owner or Annita would pick him up and place him in his shoe box bed. Sinesio would remain there for the entire day, and when he finally rose on trembling legs he was thin as a rail. Dr. Roccatagliata said, "In a year his convulsions will end; until then there is nothing to be done." So it happened, and Sinesio became almost a beautiful cat.

Among the Fieschis' friends in Naples was Francesco Flora, the historian of Italian literature. Tall, with a round head and curly hair, he arrived at Villa Floridiana along the broad, winding avenue, accompanied by the author Gino Doria, who in those years was writing his *History of Naples*. Doria was always impeccably dressed in light-colored suits. When Sinesio ran to meet them Flora would say flatteringly, "Bravo, Sinesio, bravo! What a beautiful cat you are!" And the cat would brush up against the legs of his trousers, which were always gray or brown. "Liar and seducer!" Doria would mutter under his breath, for he felt no fondness for cats and he always wore immaculate white pants. And then he exclaimed, "Liar and deceiver! How can Sinesio love you? Everyone knows cats don't love tyrants." Francesco Flora would smile and continue petting the cat without answering. So that small, ugly tabby was the center of attention and the topic of conversation among those great minds; at times, in a playful way, he even diverted the attention from his mistress. And when one evening Marta Fieschi silenced her guests by reciting "*Les amoureux fervents et les savants austères* . . ." with the flawless pronunciation she had learned from Professor Bocara, Enrico said proudly, "Brava!" He then added, "You know, I was not aware you were so cultured." But she looked at him without seeing him. Instead she saw the Temple of Segesta and the acanthus flowers; she saw the solitary bumblebee, still making them fruitful.

During those months she dreamed of Arturo as she strolled along the avenues in the shade of the tree canopy, as she walked over green and brown moss that remained damp even in August. Distance let her love him without constraint, free from guilt because he was so far away. His ghost was ever present in her solitude, nourishing her love for him, filling her mind and body. She walked slowly, her legs shortening their instinctive long stride to make the outings last longer, and her limbs were invaded by an intense languor. She was a beautiful sight, although no one saw her except the blackbirds hopping quietly about the meadows as she filled that earthly garden and the sky with her inexpressible torment.

At night vivid images and memories of the scents of her childhood came back to her, an innocent, ingenuous time, full of the first stirrings of life: Steliani's *kollooras*, the mulberry trees on the road, the sound of the silt running down the canal banks — as if her senses and the events of her life came together in the darkness and exploded within her. It was then that Marta possessed both men she loved. She felt complete, and she gave herself over to thought, that most precious of human gifts. She would lie there fully awake, contemplating her new ideas as if they were suspended in the air above her. She would put them in order, define and articulate them, in order to put them on paper.

In the light of day, she wished she could share that immense love with Enrico, give it to him as it filled her to overflowing. But she kept putting it off, remaining silent out of an inherent shrewdness, not out of self-interest or fear; she felt perfectly innocent, beyond reproach. Her thoughts focused inward, Marta did not *really* think of the two men she loved, nor did she consider their feelings. She knew she was loved by both of them, and their love was one of her great riches, her divine masterpiece. *I love both of them*, she would tell herself. *They are different, and I love them differently.* Thus had it been for the wives of the Arab: the fertile, slender Settemunìra and the fat, sterile Bambi; loved and loving, both of them, according to Allah's will, in order to make their common husband richer.

Their friends dedicated poems to that perfect woman, but she retained no memory of the poems or the poets. Ever since the last months of her pregnancy she had abandoned the cello and returned to the piano; she practiced her part in Beethoven's Sonata opus 47.

And she went to the porter's lodgings with guilty determination, hoping for a letter. Although she never permitted herself to run — she couldn't, and didn't want to — her heart was in tumult. The porter once handed her a letter with a knowing smile, complicitous and insolent. She managed to wrinkle her brow and fix him under a stern glare, never lowering her eyes, aware she had been on the verge of losing her regal freedom. It was a moment she would remember with pride and satisfaction for a long time to come.

Then she walked back to the villa. Her fingers, yes, now they were trembling as she opened the envelope, and at that first reading her eyes could not linger on the words to penetrate their meaning, but instead skimmed over them lightly, as she told herself, *Ah! I'm an adulteress* — then, *No, I am not!* — and each time it seemed as if it was the first time she realized she was lying. But she refused to believe it, saying, *I do not tell lies!* She had been trained to perfect herself every day. Now that she was fulfilling the greatest dream of her life, she could not, must not, taint herself with lies. If there was a contradiction in all that, Marta did not see it.

No, she would not retain memories of the friends who recited poetry for her, nor would she remember the debates, the discussions about this essay or that — "just published" by Don Benedetto, philosopher and historian, or the great Flora, the elegant Doria, the illustrious Ortolani — he, too, a former student of Venturi — or the refined critic Carlo Barbieri with his softly rolling *r*'s . . . Fearful, perhaps, of being unable to describe — on a sheet of paper to be sent in an envelope — the games played by that group of fine minds, she maintained, behind a mask of splendid timidity, an attitude of classical reserve.

With dogged determination, even during the difficult evenings of early motherhood, she continued to memorize Dante. She had reached the fifth Canto of the *Paradise*.

Then the day came when Enrico returned home at a run without so much as his customary joyful whistle to announce himself. He climbed the stairs two and three at a time, hugged Marta, and announced, "We're going back to Rome! We are returning to Rome! I obtained the transfer. We are going back to Rome! I will be inspector at the Museum of Palazzo Venezia. I'm to begin my duties in a week." Enrico was happy. Marta cried. No, not Rome. And what about Arturo? And that Marta made of light and music, made to nurse her child? And the letters in the porter's lodge, the descents into Naples by funicular, the park, their friends, even Annita . . . all of it would end. No! That evening, in bed, she asked, "Why? Let's stay in Naples. It's so beautiful here. It's perfect . . . I am happy," and she was sincere.

"Yes, certainly, it's beautiful here, but Rome is something else again. It's my city, our city . . . Don't tell me that your city is Alexandria! As far as I am concerned, between Sicily and Naples, I have spent enough time in Africa. Sure, Adriana is fine here, as long as she is small. She has the garden, and Annita . . . but she will grow up. You wouldn't want her to grow up here!"

"Why not? There are so many happy Neapolitans. And Annita . . ."

"Annita? We are going to take Annita with us, if she wants to come."

Their thoughts were moving in opposite directions. Did they know they would never again think alike? Only Marta did. She kept silent, feeling as though she were entering a silence that would last forever. Because it had been Enrico who wanted that transfer, and it was he who rejoiced over it. Marta pressed her lips together, and she let her eyes grow hard in the darkness as a cold, triumphant smile spread across her face. In just this way, at times, a break — a divorce — becomes established. No, she wasn't the one who wanted it. In that smile seen by no one there was resolve for the future. For her life and the lives of others. When Enrico fell into the slow, deep breathing of sleep, Marta sat upright in the darkened room, in the middle of her matrimonial bed, like an empress towering above everything and everyone. No, she would not let anyone take away the perfection she had attained!

But the following day (as had happened to Antonia so many years before in Alatri) she realized her milk had dried up. It wasn't a great concern; the baby was already ten months old. That same day she wrote Arturo an exuberant letter, although the only mention of the imminent departure was in a brief postscript.

The following week Enrico Fieschi took up his duties as inspector at the Museum of Archaeology and Art History in Palazzo Venezia. For six days and five nights of the week he stayed at the apartment in Via Tacito, where once again his breakfast of bread and prosciutto awaited him on the place mat embroidered in cross-stitch by Zia Peppina. On Saturday at two o'clock he boarded the train for Naples, and on Monday morning he returned to Rome. At the end of his workday there was a bowl of minestrone ready for him at the house in Via Tacito; no one in the world made minestrone like his mother. Happy to have returned to Rome "forever" (as it would turn out to be), Enrico was delighted with his little girl, and with the beautiful, affectionate wife he found waiting for him, like a reward, every Saturday. Soon he even enjoyed his commutes, which afforded him time twice weekly to rest, to think, to study. After the train ride and the funicular, the dozen paces to the gate and the obsequious greeting of the porter, Enrico walked down the avenue whistling his "theme song," the opening bars of the Eighth Symphony. Then Sinesio would run to greet him, his tail straight up in the air, and his little welcoming cry could be heard under the tall pines. Enrico talked to him, saying, "Sinesio, you beauty, you rare beauty!" and Sinesio, scrawny but happy, turned toward home with him, convinced he was leading the way. Annita would call out, "Here comes Dr. Enrico!" and Marta would descend the stairs to meet her husband with their daughter in her arms. It was true happiness. On Sunday Enrico enjoyed spending time with Adriana, amused by her unsteady first steps, by her charming first words. In the afternoon, after his only nap of the week — taken with his wife, and safeguarded by Annita, who watched over the little girl in that hour when even blackbirds take a rest — their friends would come to call.

They came to call in the large parlor with its red floor, with its low ceiling and small windows letting in light. They arrived one by one or in pairs, and their steps resounded on the stairs. Sergio Ortolani came, paramour of the beautiful, widowed American pianist who would become his wife; she was there too, already at the piano tuning up, and before he greeted anyone he stopped a moment to look at her. Luigi Schininà came, a violinist with the San Carlo orchestra and a noted Schubertian. He said. "Have you heard? I won the competition and I will be going to Lübeck, where they will call me Scininà," and he laughed behind his thick glasses. During those first ten minutes only Ortolani was listening, already settled into one of the two mismatched armchairs. And the musicians laughed and chatted, they tuned their instruments and traded quips while languidly rubbing rosin across their bowstrings or leafing through music books.

Don Aldo joined them, greeted with the respectful *voi*, although in that atmosphere its use seemed a bit ironic. More conversation, the aroma of Annita's *tazzulelle 'e ccafè*, the woodstove kept hot, or so it seemed to their outstretched hands, until the arrival of Carlo Barbieri, Gino Doria, and the great Francesco Flora, who was not wearing an overcoat in an obstinate albeit bone-chilling tribute to his northern origins. As usual, they were late, for the long Neopolitan afternoons lasted even longer for them. Sinesio was playing the Sphinx by the stove. Enrico stayed on the landing to greet the latecomers and keep them from interrupting the concert that had already started, and his eyes and heart brimmed with emotion as he listened. His daughter played with Annita in the kitchen. Marta's face was tense with concentration as she listened, her eyes on the music score and the pianist's every move. Her expression intensified with the high notes, when the hand and arm had to follow the melody down, down the strings, and it relaxed, beautiful and distant, in the Adagio. They were playing Beethoven's Third Trio.

On another occasion, after the smiling Schininà had set down his violin, Marta played the First Sonata for Cello and Piano with the future Signora Ortolani. Everyone fell silent in the haze of blue-gray cigarette smoke, and Sinesio's soft fur was caressed by hands now warm and distracted; bound by emotion, everything else was forgotten, nothing but the sonata filled their minds. Then they critiqued the music, or they discussed who would stay for dinner and who would not, as the moon illuminated the Niccolini facade, and then the portico overlooking the lawn and pines on the other side. Each Monday, Marta accompanied Enrico to the door and watched him briskly cross the lawn. She waved good-bye, and as he turned to look at her, he waved back. Then for him there was the gate, the street, the funicular with the same Monday-morning faces, the train, and Rome. So it went for an entire, perfect winter.

Her weeks were filled with work and study. Rarely, she went down to Naples to shop. She wrote, all winter, to Arturo. In the meantime she studied the piano part for the Franck Sonata for Violin. Arturo's violin. She imagined him there, behind her, as she sat at the keyboard. The two instruments conversed, the violin pursuing the piano, then the piano chasing after the violin; the violin harmonizing with the piano, the two voices fleeing entwined, talking to each other, and Arturo's presence became almost real. As she came to the last staff on each page, she closed her eyes for a moment, and as she turned the page it was as if his hand was doing it for her. The Kreutzer sonata was set aside for the moment; she wanted to study it someday, with him.

Rome

They returned to Rome. They had left the house in Prati as a couple, and they returned as a foursome, with their little girl and Annita. They shared their old room with Adriana; it was still called "Zia Peppina's room," while Annita made her bed every evening in the kitchen.

When one of Arturo's letters to Enrico arrived in Via Tacito, Marta said nothing. He said, "Those Germans! The way they regale you with what they did yesterday, you'd think they were talking about the feats of Frederick the Great. I'd almost forgotten them: him, them, and their island of the sun . . . I'll answer him, but now I don't have the time. In the meantime, you write him." That was just what she had hoped for, and Marta wrote him then, and many other times. Once again, she paid attention to the daily arrival of the postman down in the courtyard smelling of rot, and a new chapter in her magical long-distance love affair had begun.

The piano was moved to Prati; Marta's piano, which had cost forty-seven hundred piasters in Alexandria. It was carried by hand, brought up four staircases lit by skylights, and then placed in the parlor. After a long and perhaps envious silence the lady of the house said to Marta, "At last! Now you can play something for us!"

Marta did "play something," but no one listened. But at least no one was bothered. She played Beethoven first, from her old volume *Sonaten für Pianoforte Solo*, as she had done in Alexandria and at the Arco de' Ginnasi, but then she tried the Franck sonata and the ghost of the violinist returned to sit beside her. Soon the house in Prati was filled with the sound of Marta's playing.

In two years it happened several times — five to be exact — that Arturo would come to Rome and pay them a visit. "A friend from the south," said Enrico, adding, "A friend from Palermo who came to see us in Naples, too."

"Ah! Even in Naples!" murmured Matilde. She said nothing more. Marta, however, knew that her mother-in-law had gotten ideas in her head. She was overcome by an impulse to defy her mother-in-law, and the rest of the world. She, the Egyptian mummy who never said a word in that house, started to talk. She spoke about Arturo, about him alone, although she never called him by name; she was certain that no matter what she said, no one knew she was thinking about him, talking about him, or to him. Indeed the others did not understand, but Matilde did, and she could no longer look her beautiful daughter-in-law in the face. In her suffering she came to feel ashamed, Matilde did, about what was happening to her son. But she couldn't discuss it with a soul.

How long ago it now seemed since Zia Peppina lived there, when they went to the Pincio with the children! And Matilde, whose happy marriage had been granted by destiny and safeguarded by the benevolent climate of the era, felt her love for her husband rekindle and become even purer. For a couple's love, she would repeat out loud as she walked the halls, is like a child, a creature that changes and grows with time. She no longer revealed the source of all her sayings, be they her own, or quoted from her books, or from "my brother Carlo the doctor," or "my sister Peppina, poor thing," or from "the grande dame Nonna Caterina, the Marchesa Malaspina." Nobody asked her where they came from, or perhaps no one paid attention anymore. The music of her eternal talking throughout the house was like the perpetual chattering of the yellow parakeets in their cage — from whose eggs two chicks were born, unexpectedly; a blue one and a green one, as proof of some unknown law, or whim, of nature. "What a shame!" said Matilde. "Zio Carlo, the doctor, could have explained it to us."

Nonno Giacinto was called Nonno Già.

"Did you go for a walk with Nonno Già? Did you cross the Ponte? Did you go downtown?" asked Matilde with her grand airs, because for people living in Prati in those days to cross the Ponte — which was the Ponte Cavour, naturally — was to "go into Rome." Matilde could remember Prati as she saw it the first time, with its vineyards covered in snow. And how she had seen it grow — after the construction, use, and immediate demolition of the iron, brick, and mortar bridge at Ripetta, the bridge that had swallowed up all the money belonging to "poor Papa," the Marchese Alessandro, from his aristocratic origins.

By happenstance, the apartment on the floor above became available. Giacinto Fieschi told his son Enrico, "We're crowded here. There are four of you, and besides, it's only right." So the young family went to live in the apartment above, which had low ceilings but was large and airy, although there was no "Peppina's bedroom" next to the kitchen. Enrico now had a studio, and he worked at the desk he used as a student at the Mamiani *liceo*, and then with Venturi. Marta's heart was touched as she watched him study and write. And she felt an increasing desire to include him in that beautiful, revelatory thing that possessed and enriched her life. As if she wanted to make him a gift of it. Marta had never decided anything for herself or for others, she had never chosen anything except her complete devotion to her work and studies, where only perfection was a permissible outcome. But the present was too overbearing a taskmaster to allow her a glimpse into the future. She could not read inside her husband, or even herself — she had never been able to, but she did not realize it. She read music, from the first beat to the last, each note in a logical order, and often there was a da capo at the end, return to the beginning, because music has repetitions, and its execution, its realization, improves only by practicing and practicing again.

In the meantime, precisely as the two parakeets had produced their two chicks in new colors by a fluke of nature, Titta married his girl from the north. So the Fieschi family hardly noticed when Marta enrolled Adriana, age five, in a kindergarten: a small event in itself.

❖

At the Augusteo a piece by a "modern French composer," titled Bolero, was performed for the first time in Rome. Enrico and Marta were in the audience. The curtain went up, and from the deep silence a drum began to beat, so softly it could barely be heard. Then, above it, trumpets sounded, a song that was not a song but a simple, provocative statement. New and unforgettable as it was, it seemed ancient. Then, with exasperating and tenacious sluggishness, each instrument in the orchestra rose out of the silence to join the chorus, the parade, the nation of instruments until the sound swelled up, pressing against the ceiling of that round theater unique in all the world. It ended with a great, broken dissonance. The crowd in the Augusteo remained uncertain for a prolonged moment, then the applause began, sporadic and weak, but growing, growing until it became a single great shout of approval. Everyone stood up. Enrico placed his two hands on Marta's shoulders and said, "Come on, come on, clap your hands, applaud!" But she rose for only a moment and then sat down again murmuring, "Music is over." Marta, the conservative, the classicist, did not say *Music is dead*, but that is the thought that pained her soul after such dissonance; at least for that evening.

The elder Canternos, with Margherita, had temporarily rented an apartment from a friend of Giacomo's, a Jewish doctor who had been called out of town for a period of time. It was a beautiful place in Via Spallanzani. On the other side of the street there was — and still is — the Villa Torlonia wall, covered in climbing vines. Margherita liked to walk beneath the wall, for she enjoyed the sound of her steps echoing in the solitude, and the way the ivy seemed to shield her from the sky, so thick it offered shelter when rain began to fall. But at the "little house" — she didn't know what else to call it — on the corner with Via Antonio Musa, were the guards of Il Duce. One of them, a dark-haired man with a mustache, started following her, walking right on her heels and breathing hard. His breath was foul, his uniform had an acrid odor. Several times he followed her and then disappeared, but one evening he caught up to her, and as she tried to flee he forced her against the wall. "Stop, pretty girl, don't go away," he said, exhaling that fetid breath; she was used to obeying, and he was one of Il Duce's guards, a figure of authority. Her legs gave way. He grabbed one of her shoulders, turning her toward him and pressing her against the wall. "Look, pretty girl, look what I have here for you," he said, and no longer needing the wall to restrain her, he grabbed her by the back of the neck and forced her to look down. And she saw something in his other hand, down low, something she had never seen before. At the time, she did not know what it was, but it filled her with terror. She managed to free herself and flee. Once home, she did not speak for two days, and night after night she had terrible dreams, or else she could not sleep. But she still had to go to her lessons: violin, Russian, and Bulgarian — the Slavic languages her father wanted her to study; she still had to go out, to do the shopping or see her sister, to take Adriana for walks, or visit her sister-in-law and the children . . .

The man did not show up again for a few days, but then once again he appeared beside her, speaking with his low, cavernous voice and fetid breath. He uttered a word she had never heard, and although it had no meaning for her, she knew it was an insult. Still, she didn't dare look the word up in a dictionary, even though the house was full of them.

In the morning, every morning, Marta took Adriana to kindergarten. She held her by the hand as they crossed Piazza Cavour, and two of the little girl's steps equaled one of her mother's. Adriana enjoyed the walk, for even though she did not like the dark, severe Via Vittoria Colonna, she loved the Ponte Cavour. She loved its open sky and clean sidewalks, and she loved looking between its columns at the green water flowing downriver.

And how ever changing seemed the length of that bridge! Adriana could not see its other end, which, like the beginning, was on an incline. She closed her eyes and walked, feeling secure in the hand that was leading her, the large hand of her mother. As a game, she imagined she was still at the beginning of the bridge and still had its entire length to cross; thus she was always surprised when she felt the ground slope under her feet. If other people came toward them, or cars drove by, Adriana paid them no mind, erasing them so they would not intrude and spoil her surprise. That was her game of the Ponte, the game of Time, the game of Eternity: to walk on a bridge that never ends.

Adriana never knew about the night that winter when her mother yielded to the desire to speak to her husband about what, by then, had been on her mind for a long time. She never knew the words spoken by her mother to her father, the words that would undermine everything. Unable to refrain from uttering them, Marta had let them fall one by one, beating to death an innocent man, the unwitting, innocent man who was her husband, Enrico. The following morning, like every morning, Marta accompanied Adriana to kindergarten. They crossed the bridge, as always: she with her eyes closed, led by her mother's hand.

Part Two

THE DAUGHTER

1. DISTANCES

Rome, 1936

"YOU CAN HEAR Saint Peter's. It's going to rain."

They always say that when the wind comes from the west, but this time Annita is saying it to antagonize me, because I want to go out after spending so much time inside the house. I couldn't even peek out onto the landing or go down to see my grandparents. At last I have shoes on my feet instead of slippers. I keep jumping, now out of anger, from one white tile to another, right there in the corridor.

The doorbell rings, the short ring, barely audible, of Zia Margherita. I run to the door and hang on the brass handle to open it. Once inside, she barely looks at me and says to Nonna Matilde, who has appeared with tiny steps, "We're going out, and then we'll be right back; just for a little stroll as long as the sun is out, it's the warmest time of the day . . ." She speaks in the ugly voice she uses when she talks to grown-ups; Zia Margherita, who is not grown up at all. I am the only one who knows what she's really like, really and truly, my dear Zia Margherita, and that is why I love her; more than anyone else.

Annita finishes dressing me: a scarf up to my ears, the coat, a wool cap, and then the gloves with their unending torment of fingers that do not go into the right places. Kneeling on the floor,

Annita whispers, “Good-bye baby. Be careful, you hear?” as if trusting me more than Zia Margherita. Perhaps she, too, knows that my aunt is not a grown-up at all.

We go out in the bright light of the staircase. We descend the stairs and Zia Margherita holds my wrist imprisoned in her thin, timorous hand. She does not speak for the entire four floors, to make sure we don’t stumble and, more importantly, to keep from being detected by the unknown, malevolent ears that are doubtless spying from behind closed doors. I’m happy, because that silence is good for us, it is necessary. We need it to confirm that indeed we are “just the two of us” as she likes to say. But this time my aunt doesn’t even feel like talking after we’ve reached the bottom of the stairs and are crossing the courtyard. Finally she utters her usual “This time we’re really going to chop that building down, aren’t we, baby?” But today her words only prolong the silence and make it worse — all the way down the vaulted entrance hall and through the front door into the wind and cold on the sidewalk.

“And then?” Silence.

“And then?” I repeat, speaking into my scarf angrily, as if I were someone else.

“And then. And then, you already know.” There is that elusive, distracted, offensive voice of hers again. Then why did she come to get me? She could have left me with Nonna Matilde, yes, she could have. The ground seems to move under my legs, which are still weak from my fever and so many days spent indoors. She looks left, right, and back again, then we cross the street at a run and reach the wide, clear sidewalk of the flower beds in Piazza Cavour. At last she lets go of my numb wrist and says, “Run, run around a bit to warm up,” and that, too, sounds insincere, as if recited.

I remember this as if watching from the outside, Zia Margherita and Adriana. Adriana, alone and wishing for something else, waving her arms like a windmill as she runs in circles over the sidewalk warmed by the winter sun. After a few turns she draws close to Zia Margherita, who is walking slowly with her head lowered. She looks at her aunt's face and her hardened eyes. "God makes them, and the devil pairs them up," Margherita says sullenly, just as she had that other time.

Then Adriana runs faster and farther away, fleeing. She starts running in circles again, her steps pounding to the beat of those words that keep echoing in her head. She cannot free herself from them, those obscure words, and by now she does not want to, not even when Zia Margherita calls her to take her back home, for the sun has already set below the building, the one they always say they want to chop down. Instead it is still there, spreading gold dust in the sky and casting its cold shadow on the piazza.

Only then, when I was sick, did Nonna Antonia ever come to see us on Via Tacito. "And now what's wrong with this little one?" she would say, touching my forehead and neck with a rough hand redolent of the scents of her home. For me, every illness had become a celebration with plenty of guests. Nonna Antonia would remove her hat, which was held in place by a hatpin with a pearl on the end. (In those days there were so many hats, and so many ways of taking them off!) She sat by my little bed and told me stories from the Holy Bible: Noah's ark, Jacob's sheep of many colors, and Joseph sold by his brothers. She even told me about Esau and his lentils; Esau, who was "hairy as a bear," although neither one of us had ever seen a bear. She told the story of little Moses, entrusted to the waters of the Nile, imagine that, and she would add, "It's large, the Nile, I've seen it." And then she would tell me about the plagues of Egypt and the parting of the Red Sea. So many magnificent and terrible stories! Then she told me about Stelianì's cat, and she sang, "Stelianì, she had a cat — and the cat's name was Flora . . ."

I was so enthralled by those stories, nothing was better than being sick. Nonna Antonia's stories were full of flying angels, luminous and very beautiful. They brought messages. Nonna Matilde's angels, on the other hand, were of a different sort entirely, and one of them was decidedly mean. Whenever I cried they said, "Oh how ugly you look! Watch out, Adriana, if an angel passes overhead and says, 'Amen,' you'll stay like that forever."

In her apartment below us Nonna Matilde has everything: lemons, string, glue, bundles of paper bags of all sizes, and corks. Nonno Già has rubber bands, pencils, and gum arabic, which only he can use. It comes in a square, flat bottle, and inside the lid there is a small brush that never gets any air, poor thing, as it is always immersed in the liquid. Nonna Matilde has scissors of many different sizes, and one pair is expressly for making eyelets. It has a screw at the base of the blades and it looks like a crocodile. Each scissor has a ribbon of a different color. "You don't say *scissor*, you say *scissors*," Mamma corrects me. But Mamma can never seem to find her own scissors.

"Now go downstairs and see Nonna for a bit," says Mamma, and Annita accompanies me to the door. She leans over the banister, her proportions changing as I descend the stairs holding the curly wrought-iron bars. That first time I went down the stairs alone, one step at a time without using the banister or the wall, I arrived at my grandparents' apartment in no time, without even thinking about Annita. It was a Sunday, because Nonna Matilde's kitchen had a special smell on Sunday, different from the rest of the days of the week. She had tall, dark cupboards that reached to the ceiling, filled with jars of food. Beyond the kitchen, at the end of the corridor, was "Peppina's bedroom" with Nonna Matilde's sewing machine and "all your trinkets," in other words, my toys, Adriana's, that were always kept there. In the apartment upstairs Annita's kitchen is more spacious and clean, but it has only one smell, of the onion she slices on her cutting board, and on Friday evening there is the scent of the nutmeg that Annita puts in the potato soufflé. There is no "Peppina's bedroom" on the floor above, nor the Singer with its cover for riding horseback-style when Nonna puts it on the floor; in fact, Annita never uses a sewing machine. Still, she mends Papa's socks, seated in the kitchen chair — the one I can climb on even with my shoes on —

and then she falls asleep. The wooden darning ball drops and rolls clumsily on the floor, waking her up, and Annita says, "Eh? Eh? What is it?" The floor is made of hexagonal tiles, all alike, red, and a bit rough. But when Mamma sews, she sits at the edge of the bed, dressed to go out. Sometimes she already has her hat on, and the room is a mess. I watch her silently from the doorway with a knot in my stomach. My dear mamma, I adore her.

In those early years there was Old Zio, whom Papa called "Professor" and Mamma called "Don Aldo." We saw him only in winter. He had a tender, broad smile that enveloped and embarrassed me as his trembling arms lifted me up, holding me close to his face, for he was almost blind. Being the object of his affection and yet wanting to avoid him always filled me with anxiety and pain. Old Zio was a heavy smoker, and he emanated a pronounced, pleasant odor. He gave me notebooks — notebooks of graph paper — for drawing figures, which he would then examine, bringing the notebook up close to his old eyes and invariably admiring and praising my work. Half blind though he was, his profession, like my father's, was art; he lectured and wrote about painting. Winter evenings and afternoons, the three of them, Papa, Mamma, and Old Zio, gathered around a desk covered with papers and photographs, and they discussed art by the light of a lamp with a red silk shade and curls of cigarette smoke rising inside it. Lying on my stomach on the red-and-blue rug, I watched them and was happy. The gramophone played the overture of *Egmont*, which would remind me all my life of that rug and those three dear people in the red light of the fringed lamp shade. Only many years later did I learn that the Professor was in love with my mother and was on the verge of suicide because of it, or so it was said. Thus he had given Papa his fur coat, for soon it would no longer be of any use to him. But Old Zio got married instead and gave up his ideas of suicide. The fur coat stayed in a closet; it was a gray coat lined with black, heavy fur. My father would wear it a few times during the war, but not until then.

❖

There are all sorts of guests, and each person rings the doorbell in a unique way. Arturo announces himself with a long ring, and he arrives carrying the smell of his motorcycle and the red-and-blue-checkered shirt he always wears — a shirt unlike any other. He is tall and prepossesing, Arturo, his voice is strong, but clear and beautiful; everything about him is extraordinary. Even his words are extraordinary, and they fill the house. "Do you want to do a somersault?" he says. And then he makes me do a thrilling somersault as only he can do, while my mother looks on and smiles, though with a trace of fear in her eyes. "Did you already drink your milk from your bowl?" he asks me; he calls it a bowl, but it is actually a large cup that he gave me, a strange cup, tall, wide, and colored. It isn't smooth like most cups, but slightly rough-textured, like cream of wheat. I like to touch it, but I don't use it much because Annita doesn't want me to. She says she is afraid I'll break it, but I'm sure she doesn't like it, just as she doesn't like Arturo, although she says that isn't true. But once in a while Mamma serves me milk with barley coffee in Arturo's cup, saying, "Drink it, drink up."

Arturo tells stories about Sicily, and I can't distinguish the word from the Santa Cecilia, mentioned by my parents and my music-playing uncles and aunts; but I don't know anything about her, either. Mamma plays the cello, and Arturo plays, too; he plays the violin, which is a small cello that he holds under his chin; good thing it doesn't have an endpin. When Arturo brings his violin Mamma sits at the piano, but they do not always play; they talk, and sometimes they don't even do that. Arturo, though, does not want to be called Zio, just Arturo, which is all the same to me. When Arturo comes, we don't stay in the house, because he is too big and noisy to stay inside. So we go out, to Monte Mario or to the shore at Santa Marinella, which is full of rocks, and not sandy like the beach at Ostia where my mother and Zia Margherita take me.

"Grab on here," says Arturo, and this, too, is an extraordinary phrase, used only by him, but it's not beautiful because there is hardness in it; then he takes me on the high sea swimming with broad, calm strokes. My father does not swim like that, but with his head underwater, then he lifts it out to breathe, always on the same side, stretching one arm after the other. That is the right way to swim, the "manly" way — I think — but I like to be taken on the high sea by Arturo. His hair becomes curly when it gets wet and it falls on his forehead as he turns around, smiling. Papa, on the other hand, takes me out on his back, but only where I can still touch bottom, then he sets me down and tries to teach me how to swim, but I'm afraid. On the Santa Marinella beach, Arturo collects round rocks in many colors — and they are even more colorful when wet — and he runs with me on the shore's little stretch of sand, and then he skips stones on the water, a special game that is only his.

When we go to the meadow among the trees at Monte Mario, Arturo has two pots that fit inside each other, and a ring that he perches on stones to hold his little spirit-stove. We boil water for tea in the smaller pot, which has a lid, and everything smells wonderful, although you can't see the flame in the bright light of the meadow. And Arturo has a camera that he keeps inside a brown box with a button closure. It's larger and, to tell the truth, more beautiful than Papa's small, flat one. Even Arturo's motorcycle is redder, larger, and louder than Papa's, and I'm not happy about that. When the three of them leave, Arturo, Mamma, and Papa, I stay with Annita and my grandparents. Then they come back smelling of gasoline and sun. Arturo leaves immediately, and then sends photos of the three of them, small and smiling at the entrances of unknown churches.

I remember Nonno Tommaso — the "other Nonno" — behind a wall of books. You couldn't see his desk: books were piled up on the chairs, and they were stacked against the walls, scaling them like tenacious climbing vines. Nonno Tommaso with his white beard and sweet smile, infinite and distant behind his books. Zia Margherita and Nonna Antonia called him *Pardi* and talked about him under their breath.

❖

Too many, though. Just too many. It was a mania and that was how he used up all his money. After filling our house in Alexandria and Stelianì's after that, he started up again in Rome. Mamma even scolded him. Not so much because of the money, but because they took up so much room. It was dangerous, too; books are heavy. But there was nothing to be done. We could have bought the house on Via Spallanzani with that money! Instead, we had to move, with all those books! I was the one who moved everything because I wasn't working then. It wasn't then, but two years later, that your mother made me apply to the libraries. The application was for Group C, which was support staff. But I didn't start right away, not then.

"Come, Adriana, come, the band is going by," calls Annita, then she picks me up and holds me against the edge of the windowsill. The leader throws his baton in the air, spins it around in one hand, and then lets it fly again. After the band come the soldiers, lots of them, marching in silence. Their boots beat in unison on the cobblestones, making the ground shake as they proceed down Via Gioacchino Belli, and even after the band has passed by, beyond the trees of Via Cicerone, that low, menacing beat lingers at our house. The strong odor of sweat still remains, and never have there been so many soldiers as there are today. They continue to turn up in new formations from the corner of Via Tacito, and who knows how many more there still are. They wear heavy helmets, each one fastened with a strap that doesn't reach under the chin, but just rests on it; why don't they make those straps a little bit longer?

Now my mother is standing next to us, and perhaps it's the first time she has come to watch the band and the soldiers. Then I realize with terror that Annita is crying. She is speaking, but not to me, not to us. "Poor boys," she says to herself, "where will they be sending them to die? Where?"

"To Africa," says Mamma, and she is crying now, too. She cries and murmurs, "Damn them, damn them all!" and nothing so terrible has ever happened before. I want to run away, to slip from

Annita's elbow and flee, but now Mamma is clutching me, holding me close until all the soldiers have come out of Via Tacito and disappeared behind the trees of Via Cicerone. As if the three of us at the window should not forgo saying good-bye to even one of them. One of those boys who are going to Africa to die.

But this was before; it was 1935.

That is right, it was before, or after. Before or after what? I don't remember the exact sequence of events in those years. It was the time of the game of Eternity on the bridge. I walk holding my mother's hand, with my eyes closed, and I imagine being at the beginning of the bridge forever.

Once across the bridge, we walk down Via Tomacelli and our steps echo off the tall, windowless side of the church. Then we are enveloped by the aroma of the banana kiosk. Next comes Largo Goldoni — at once a name and a place for me, with no other significance — then Via Condotti, until here we are under the lights of the Spanish Steps. We cross the piazza at the base of the steps, near the Barcaccia fountain with its curves and placid water. Mamma seems taller than ever, incredibly tall, and I feel as though I fit inside her hand. I grow weary from exertion as we climb the innumerable white stairs (I'm only five or six years old), and Mamma says, "Come on, up, up. Let's plant a flag at the top!" And we really do plant one, right on the white balustrade. One day she does it, with a broad sweep of her arm, and another time I do, with a puny wave of my coat sleeve. It is an enormous imaginary flag, and it waves its colors until evening over the entire city. On mornings when it has rained, water fills the black holes in the travertine, and in late spring the big black swifts fly under us, a bit threatening with those mean eyes of theirs.

Finally we head down Via Sistina and then the precipitous Via Zucchelli with its tiny dark cobblestones. The kindergarten's door is on the right; a narrow courtyard, a small classroom, and an enormous terrace among the rooftops. The fräulein is red-haired, freckled. She wears a sky-blue apron over her dress, and men's shoes. She is kind and smiling, but I can't understand her. The children are German, too, and I don't understand them, either. And yet their little faces, each and every one of them, have stayed with me; and from then on in all my classes I would find a hint of resemblance in this or that classmate, an erroneous copy of one of my companions from those days of ring-around-the-roses and nursery rhymes.

After two years of kindergarten I knew many nursery rhymes, but I had not learned a word of German. Looking back, I understood that neither the teacher with her men's shoes nor my classmates had ever attempted to teach me anything. Why should they have? I was ignorant, of course, but I was also alone, among children who always had plenty to say to one another.

It was in 1936 that my mother won "a scholarship" (something unheard of at the time) and because of that she left for Germany.

Zia Margherita says: So I will learn German and then I will teach it to you. But you were tricked, my poor Adriana. You stayed with us, and we took care of you, Nonna Matilde and I. Do you remember? We shared the job, because you were six but you were still stubborn as a little donkey. Yes, once she left, I was the one who took you to school, but not every day. And then at home . . . you remember, baby?

Of course I remember. Nonna Matilde pulled out one of her books, a beautifully illustrated volume with PRIMER on the cover. The book had the letters of the alphabet in lower- and uppercase, in print and in cursive, underneath pictures of girls skipping rope, their hair tied back in ribbons, and Nonna taught me to read from it. And every day Zia Margherita tore a sheet of paper from her notebook and had me write a note "to Mamma who has gone off to the land of Germany, who knows why, but I think I know." She dictated not word by word, but letter by letter, and always in capitals. I still have them, those little notes, because Mamma brought them back from "the land of Germany," but they make me so sad, I don't like to reread them. The following year I was in first grade.

Where? Naturally, after the useless kindergarten, I went to a French school! However, with the exception of prayers and recitations, we were taught in Italian. I liked it, and after the first year I was promoted to the third grade. So I actually completed two grades in one year, thanks to Nonna Matilde's primer and Zia Margherita's dictations. But after that, when I was promoted to the fourth grade, I was taken out of that school that I liked so much, where the girls spoke Italian like me. Why?

. . . because your parents had separated, and they were afraid the nuns might talk . . . That's why they put you in public school for the fourth grade, right near home, at last!

Yes, at last I had a real school, large, full of light, where the girls wore white smocks with blue bows at the collar, and the boys had blue ones with white bows. And it was right near the house! I could see it from the window overlooking Via Gioacchino Belli. My school. I had heard the sound of children's voices coming from there for so long, children who were waiting for me, and finally I could join in as they sang the hymn to Rome, "You shall not see anything in the world — Greater than Rome, *maggior di Roma*." Who knows why the Major of Rome would not be allowed to see anything in the world, the poor Major!

Meanwhile at home, "You said your piece," Enrico had said. "I won't bother talking about me, about how you've hurt me with all this . . . this presentation of the facts, this sudden inspiration of yours . . . all this talk about perfectionism. But I do have something to say. I am still your husband and we have a daughter. You haven't said a word about your plans. I don't know what kind of an arrangement you've made with that . . . gentleman."

"I have no plans. We've made no arrangements. I haven't talked with him. I wanted to tell you first."

"You haven't talked to him? It's even worse than I thought. Or better . . . Even though, after what you've told me, I can hardly hope you might rethink the whole thing . . . Or will you . . . ?"

"No," she said in a low voice, looking at her hands. "No. Unfortunately not."

"You can spare me the *unfortunately*," he replied harshly. "I'm very sorry," he added, his voice pained. "Whether you have plans or not, you must understand that I can't let you throw everything away, not in the state you're in. You are still my wife. I can't begin to guess that man's intentions. And you're telling me you haven't even spoken to him. You're more of a perfectionist than I feared. You're a moralist, that's it! You'd better understand that I have the right to expect anything from you. Still, no matter how good his intentions toward you, no matter what he promises, things will take time. There are a few legalities to take care of before . . . he can take charge of you. Provided I assent. Because I could stop you, you know that?"

There was a long silence while each waited for the other to speak. (But no one else, no one else was present, and the writer wishes she didn't have to think of that moment of silence, reconstructed on the basis of the little she was told by her father, many years later.)

Then his voice could be heard again, sounding far away, and he repeated his words as if time had turned back on itself, "He can take charge of you, of my wife!

"You say that you have no plans. I understand. After all, it's the first time you've ever destroyed a family. Your family, but it's also mine. And our daughter . . . Oh, Marta, if it were possible. I . . . I would do anything, you know it . . ."

"Enrico, don't. You have been . . . you are the best of husbands, but . . . this is stronger than I am . . ." She burst into tears. He turned toward the window, pushed the curtain aside, and looked down at the black pavement. There was a section that had just been repaired, and there was still sand showing between the new cobblestones. He counted those cobblestones, looked at them and counted them without thinking. Without turning around he continued speaking. "You must find a job; you must be independent. I will not let you go like this. You are the mother of my daughter. Get a job; a state job, with a state certification. But it takes time for positions to open up. Look into it." His voice had grown tired. "I'll be waiting to hear from you." He left the room looking like an old man.

For Marta, for the daughter of the polyglot professor who had been relieved of his teaching position without explanation, for this woman who was beautiful, cultured, and beloved, "a job" meant sitting behind a post office window stamping envelopes and packages. She could not imagine anything else, could not see anything else. He had said "a job." He had also said . . . She straightened her spine, the beautiful Marta, and accepted this new challenge. She would take an examination to stamp packages and envelopes. And send telegrams; she would do that, too.

She had forgotten, Marta, or perhaps she had never clearly understood, that the teaching position her father had lost for reasons unknown to her (reasons she had never asked anyone to explain) was a job. A state job. Enrico, too, was employed by the state. Perhaps she had always thought in terms of "the university" or "the museum." Perhaps she'd never given it any thought at all. She was not accustomed to thinking about practical matters, financial matters; she had not been brought up to do it. Clerks stamped letters. And she would learn to stamp.

By the time I was in the third grade with the French nuns, my grandparents had already moved out of our building. Left behind with Annita and my parents in the apartment above theirs, I felt like I'd lost half of my shell. I stayed in bed during the days of their move, so as not to witness the dismantling of those rooms so dear to me. I heard noises and voices, then silence, and in that silence I imagined life going on as usual in the apartment below. But when I descended the stairs the first few times, holding Annita or Zia Margherita by the hand, the door below seemed to be lying silently in wait with a mysterious, lifeless wind blowing through its cracks. My grandparents' home became a fable, but not a happy one. A fable no one spoke about. So I kept a memory, although I didn't dare mention it to anyone, of the window in Nonna's parlor with its two heavy red drapes that reached the floor and hung on wooden rings from a rod that sagged under their weight. Behind the drapes, below the window, was a bench that was too high for me. It had two firm cushions covered in the same fabric as the drapes. I would throw the pillows on the floor, one next to the other, and stretch out on them, taking measure of that space between the window, drapes, and ceiling (the ceiling was decorated with a relief painting that I liked to pretend was real — indeed I once thought it was real). A space, there behind the drapes, that escaped into infinity, rich with mystery.

In winter the window, with its white shirred curtains and frame painted a dark and warm brown, like chocolate, was closed. But in summer, when the sashes were open and the shutters drawn back, that tall alcove between drapes, window, and seemingly infinite ceiling became an extension of the outdoors, resonant with life. I could hear the sweet song of the fountain at the corner of Via Gioacchino Belli and Via Cicerone, which was not the case at the corresponding bare window on the floor above. From up there, I could see sky above all, then the eaves of the building across the street, and finally the gables and windows of the top floor, with nests under the eaves where triangular heads of baby swifts peeked out and then disappeared. But the adult swifts were too black and too large, too fast in their impatient returns, too loud and close as they screeched, and I could not like them. So at sunset in summer, when the sky above Via Cassiodoro became red and yellow and white at its greatest heights, and without depth except for the faraway cries of birds so high they seemed motionless in the air, the furious, lightning-bolt dives of those swifts filled me with fear, even though I did not know what I was afraid of. But in autumn when an echo of bells could be heard from Via Cassiodoro, making Nonna and Annita say, "You can hear Saint Peter's, it's going to rain," I would feel consoled and protected by the nearness of the sound.

Of all that, only the ghosts of memories remained.

The office of Adriana's father was in Palazzo Venezia. The entrance was on Via degli Astalli, through a heavy, dark door and up a steep stairway immediately on the right. At the top of the stairs was Michelino, the typist, who always smiled and called her Dolly. He was the only one who called her this.

Papa threw back his hat, uncovering his forehead with his customary gesture, and climbed the stairs two by two asking, "Any news?" Young Adriana paddled after him, looking at her shoes. The distinct odor of Palazzo Venezia grew stronger as they climbed, the pleasant scent of wax for the tiles, and for the wooden floors — which creaked — and for the bookshelves with their orderly rows of books. The entrance hall was large and rectangular, and the view from one window was of nothing but leaves from the trees that grew next to it. Michelino worked by the window, typing up whatever Papa had handwritten in his large, broad script that morning, seated at his desk at home; an outpouring of words with no thought for saving space.

And there was Getulio, with his flattened nose and wide grin, who always kept his jacket collar turned up because he was cold. He was the superintendent's driver. Then there was Renato, restorer of paintings and ancient tablets, with his soft, smooth manner of speaking. He suffered from asthma, which made him breathe with a dull echo, and from which he would one day pass away amid unspeakable pain. Innocent and full of affection, throughout his life Renato fed an entire army of cats, the cats of Palazzo Venezia.

At the end of the corridor was the study of Professor Hermanin, a towering, white-haired man. It seemed to Adriana that the professor intimidated her father, so she felt intimidated, too. The odor of wax, among other odors, was strongest in the professor's room. Set in the thick wall at the far end of the room was a window underneath a small arch; it was almost a room unto itself, with a step leading to it. She dreamed of leaning out that window, so small and far off, across the entire length of the room (which is why the lamp on the professor's table was always turned on). It had cream-colored curtains with thick pleats that reduced the light from outside even further — too much. She didn't know if the room had a view, or even if the window was real.

Finally, after desiring it for so long, Adriana was able to cross the room and look out the window. Right in front of her, vast and gray with darkened shadows, was the dome of the Chiesa del Gesù! She was beside herself with emotion, and even felt shame at the sight of the low, flattened dome, as if she had caught it by surprise in an unseemly, embarrassing position.

Yes, all this happened earlier, before the summer of 1937, when Nonna Matilde and Nonno Giacinto had moved from the house on Via Gioacchino Belli and gone to live in Monteverde.

In Monteverde they lived on a new street that ended abruptly above a steep red earth escarpment full of cement debris and broken bricks, overgrown by weeds. Spreading majestically at the bottom was an immense, ancient orchard called Scarpone's, and the people who tended it looked like toy figures from such a distance.

"We enjoy living here; it's like always being on vacation," said Nonno Giacinto, but Nonna Matilde did not say anything, and she moved without a sound among the pieces of furniture, which were too large for that small house. The parlor and dining room were now one room, and the sewing machine was kept out in the large, bright entryway. The red drapes were not there. Had they remained on Via Tacito? Had they become ghosts of her imagination?

In the small dining room Nonna Matilde had twice given me a sharp look and squeezed my shoulders with her bony hands. "Ah, your poor papa!" she murmured, as if it weren't she who was speaking, so I avoided being alone with her in that room. Then Papa moved to Monteverde, too.

Even Annita left Via Tacito, taking what little remained of my childhood with her. During the last few days before she left, Annita only cried and could not speak, and I vomited over and over again.

"Why is Annita leaving?" I asked my father. "Why is everybody leaving? And why don't you stay with us anymore, either?" It was raining, and in the cold, foggy car Papa had done something terrible, frightening; something absolutely forbidden. He had cried. From then on I could never ask him anything again. Not ever.

Then there were the summer holidays of those years. I spent the months of June and July with my mother in mountain villages in the Alps, above Bolzano. But there, too, everyone spoke German, even the children (*go on, go play with them*), just like the children in my kindergarten, and I didn't learn to speak with them, either. In September my father would take me with him to Rimini, where he was involved with the restoration of a large church called the Tempio — the Tempio Malatestiano — whose facade had shifted and cracked. We went by car, his "509," and the trip lasted the entire day. Along with water and *panini* prepared by Nonna Matilde we always brought a yellow-and-green-checkered blanket, "just in case." We left, "just the two of us," he liked to say, with a particular tone that always caused me a subtle anguish, and as we crossed the Ponte Milvio he would say, "Do you see this? This is the oldest bridge in Rome." Then we entered the countryside along the road called Flaminia, just like the baker woman on Via Tacito. Along that road through the country, but only then would Papa sing the songs that Mamma used to play on her cello when we all lived together, although he always made mistakes. I never said anything because I liked his singing even then. He would say, "Look, look at that mountain, and that other one; they look like faces, in profile. And you will soon find that in the mountains everywhere, sooner or later, a profile will appear; it's just a matter of patience. With many other things, too, it's only a matter of patience. Time is a gentleman." That is what my papa said, but I did not fully understand the meaning of his words.

We used to stop for our midday meal at L'Osteria del Gatto, the inn of the cat — but where was the cat? — and we went up to Urbino once or twice, although the winding road made me nauseous. "Did you know that Urbino means 'little city'?" he would say. After a few more dreadful curves down the steep road we would finally reach the plain and then the sea. "Look, look at those three mountaintops, the three peaks of San Marino, 'the azure vision' of the poet Pascoli; but you haven't read him yet. Heavens, you are still so young, poor little creature! Now it's your turn to tell a story to me." But I couldn't, for fear my stories would be too small and simple, too childish for him. And I was afraid he would say, "Now who put that idea into your head? Your mother?" as he had before.

During those trips I was sometimes taken by a poignant, tender longing for Zia Margherita, and thoughts of her offered a private shelter from the loneliness and discomfort I felt with my father on that long, winding road.

When at last we reached the sea the sun would not yet have set, but it would be hidden behind the mountains, and Papa would say, "Do you see? Do you see how different the sea looks here? It's more poetic, more humane, I would say. Well, no, perhaps I'm asking too much of you . . . It's less deep, anyhow. Look, it's like a long, sandy gulf, and at the top, yes, at the end of it is Venice!"

It was a violinist from her days in the orchestra of the Teatro dei Piccoli who told Marta about the competition for "positions in the professional ranks of the state libraries, Rank A." A doctorate in letters or languages was required. Marta presented her diploma and her other credentials: her fellowship, and the certificate of participation for the course in musical aesthetics in Berlin. She declared a thorough knoweledge of French, English, and German, in addition to Latin and Greek, both written and spoken. She also spoke Arabic. She did not mention her diploma in music for the cello. At the written examination she translated from and into Latin, and from Greek. For her orals, she drew a research project in French; the paleography exam was "child's play." Marta was tall, very beautiful, and timid. But now even she marveled at the things she knew. She left the building where the exams had been held, the General Direction for Academies and Libraries — located in Palazzo Doria in Via Plebiscito — bewildered and happy. She won the competition. Immediately after, she enrolled in a course of library science directed by Ettore Apollonj at La Sapienza.

We all know that frequently used common names can sometimes take the most specific and singular meanings. For instance the name *mamma* becomes a proper noun when referring to one's own mother. The same thing can happen with the term *professor* when referring to one's own beloved teacher. That is what had happened to Enrico with Venturi, and it happened to Marta with Professor Ettore Apollonj. Because of his vast knowledge and his warm nature, he immediately became "the Professor," even though the course she had taken from him lasted only a few weeks. He would remain the Professor for the rest of her life.

Cardinal Girolamo Casanate (1620–1700), a Dominican from Naples, former governor of the Sabine and inquisitor at Malta, was a Vatican librarian. A scholar and a great theologian, he organized and cataloged the documents of the Vatican Library pertaining to the early church, and was made a cardinal by Clement X in 1673. In Rome he founded the library that bears his name, and left it to the Dominicans of the church of Santa Maria sopra Minerva, who increased and enriched its holdings. The entrance to the library was in back of the church. In 1873 ownership of the Casanatense Library passed to the state, and the building was accessed by an entrance on Via di Sant'Ignazio next to the Church of the Jesuits. An overpass behind the apse of Sant'Ignazio allows access from the Casanatense Library to the Vittorio Emanuele National Library on the other side of the church.

Designed by Carlo Fontana, the Casanatense Library is one of the largest and most beautiful in Italy. In the main hall — the most spacious library hall in Italy — wooden bookshelves extend twenty-five meters from the floor to the windows half hidden in the vaulted ceiling. Against one wall is a statue of Cardinal Casante in Carrara marble, the work of sculptor Pierre Le Gros. Perched high on a pedestal in front of the shelving, the statue's right hand is extended in a warm and welcoming gesture. The library holds more than three hundred thousand volumes, more than two thousand incunabula (the first printed books, from the end of the fifteenth century), and over six thousand manuscripts of great historical and religious interest. The aspiring librarian Marta Canterno, serving on probation after winning the competition, was assigned to the Casanatense Library, which was directed in those years by Luigi De Gregori.

When she began her work at the Casanatense, Marta's duties included organizing the collection of ancient texts. At the time only some of the oldest printed books in the Casanatense — the incunabula of the second half of the fifteenth century and the sixteenth century — were cataloged and placed on shelves. Many of the sixteenth-century incunabula, in bundles, were simply indicated as such and lay with other packages of works and documents in storage. This had been the case since the time of the materials' removal from the old building of the Benedictines behind the church of Santa Maria sopra Minerva, where the bequest of the great Dominican had remained for almost two centuries. And they were in considerable disarray: uncataloged volumes, misplaced tomes, forms left inside books or even between the parchment pages of manuscripts. There was an old catalog "by author," compiled in volumes after 1760, but by now those very volumes were useless for modern cataloging, and they had become works to be collected and cataloged themselves, with their own call numbers. In modern times, as Marta knew, as she had been taught by her Professor, catalogs had to be compiled on single file cards so that cards could be inserted in alphabetical order for new acquisitions; and there had to be two separate catalogs, one "by author" and one "by subject." Thus each volume, represented in each catalog, is retrievable "by author" and "by subject," and its location, or the place assigned to it, is one and one only, determined by the work's dimensions so as not to waste space by placing small (short) volumes next to large (tall) ones. In sum, the placement of a work is done on the basis of shape, not by subject, or author.

Marta was enthusiastic about her work from the very first day. "There is nothing in the world better than working in a library. I did not know that. And . . . I thank you for encouraging me in this direction," she told her husband, Enrico. No, she would not have to stamp packages and registered mail. For the rest of her life, Marta would feel pity for postal workers.

And while she organized and arranged the volumes in alphabetical order, memories of her first years were coming back to her, warm, colorful, and rich in fragrance, as memories of Africa always are. "Alpha, beta, gamma, delta, epsilon, zeta, eta, theta . . . rho, sigma, tau . . ." and also: "e, f, g, i, l, m, n, o, p, q . . ." just as her father had taught her, her beloved papa. She had memorized the two alphabets, Greek and Italian, while riding on his knees: the right knee for Greek, and the left knee for Italian. Then she had repeated those alphabets while jumping rope in the street with the other girls, or bouncing the ball against a wall, two skills at which she was a master. They were indelibly committed to memory, those two alphabets, from her earliest years. An indisputable truth, the alphabet. Why even discuss it, since it's not based on logic? Instead it's agreed upon, a matter of faith. In the same manner her father taught her to memorize any series of words, as if they were music. And she understands both languages, that of words and that of music. They are different, certainly, but not always. The language of music is more direct, gentler, without interventions, because music is not translated. The language of music is also a voice . . . God's voice? No, she won't say such things, but sometimes the thought does enter her mind.

Now, Marta's thoughts have brought her back to the piano room, in Alexandria. She is playing an Invention in Two Voices by Bach, and her blue pigeon is dancing. As soon as it hears her play, even when far away, it flies in through an open window. It cannot resist that call, and it lands on the piano (which is always covered by a piece of green cloth) then moves its little red feet, first one and then the other, in time with the music and bobs its iridescent head. She is ten years old and has just started school. In her first class in the *ginnasio* there are ten girls and a boy. Marta is the tallest, and in truth the most beautiful — although no one dares say so — and she is happy. That day, or perhaps another, her father called her — actually he summoned her, as he does when reprimanding her for something — and he said, "Get dressed, we're going out." She is terrified, and searches her conscience for whatever it is she might have done wrong. Her father waits for her in his study with his back turned. He says, "Sit down," and she does, now even more terrified. Then he turns around, and he is smiling! In his hands he has a large book, which he gives to her.

"This is the most precious and sacred of all books," he says. "It's yours. Take good care of it. I will teach you how to use it, but — and don't you forget — don't ask me any more questions because you can find everything in this dictionary."

It was the Georges, the great, glorious, Latin dictionary. The memory of it moves her still, and she smiles as her eyes begin to tear. Her mind's ear fills with the singsong words of the Greek nursery rhyme:

Zimbi zimbi tonantò
tonantò to stavriotò
Puzzimbuni Uraní
Pupèsone angelí,
but also
Mina Mina mìn
Anà Sultàn!

Which of course is Arabic, even if it is a little nonsense song. It is a shame that Marta did not learn to write Arabic, because there are Arabic manuscripts at the Casanatense, as well as Persian and Turkish. What a shame! Will she ever have time to study again? But she isn't worried. "I will study it, written Arabic." And the time? She will find it. "You can always find time," thinks Marta, and she even says it out loud. She loves to study, she loves putting books in order. "And they're even paying me to do it!"

In the meantime her knowledge of ancient texts (Marta had obtained the highest grade — cum laude — in the paleography examination) and her fluency in Latin and Greek had been of great help to her in working with the fifteenth- and sixteenth-century incunabula. But now that she had access to even older materials, and not all were cataloged or organized, she encountered some extremely ancient volumes, even works from the eighth century written and adorned by the monks of Montecassino, for the first illuminated manuscripts were in fact made in Montecassino, at the hand of Benedictine monks.

Once in Alexandria her father had shown her a fragment, scarcely a dozen sheets of parchment written centuries earlier. He had only let her look at it, his eyes shining among the wrinkles she loved so much and his hands trembling, and she had not dared reach out her hand to touch it. He had bought it "for a small sum" from Papadopoulos, an old man, half blind and lame, who had an antiquarian shop in El Attarìn market. "Look, Marta, this book is five or six centuries old, maybe older, I don't know. Do you see? It's not printed. You can see the ink and the imprint of the pen, it was a goose quill — or a chicken's, perhaps — and it was written . . . look at the beautiful calligraphy . . . by a monk . . . A holy monk . . . so many years ago. And these . . . look here . . . these are musical notes, for singing . . . but we don't even know how to read it, the ancient music that monks and nuns used to sing early in the morning, in church, in the cold . . . the music they now sing in paradise. I am not an expert in these things. But who knows, one day you might study, and understand, and learn ancient writing . . ." How, how could she, his daughter, have forgotten it for so many years? For years Tommaso Canterno had made sure that that book, and only that book, did not become buried under the volumes piling up on the floor of his house. That little, mutilated breviary, and only that one, he had kept separate, alone, in the top drawer of one of the few pieces of furniture in the house, the highboy chest that was now in Rome, in the house on Via Tacito.

So her two great loves — the new one, Arturo, and the living memory of her beloved father, who was now ailing — were always with her.

Marta worked two years at the Casanatense, studying, describing, and cataloging more than one hundred incunabula never before put on file. During those two years she observed and admired many ancient manuscripts, including French works of the thirteeenth century, as well as older works of the Beneventan liturgy from Casanate's original library. She developed an eye for the calligraphy of diverse hands — the tight, fine northern script, and the soft, round writing of the south — and also for the illuminated figures, the miniature drawings of the most ancient texts and the larger, more lively figures of later years. She had the opportunity, at first almost secretly and then under orders from the director of the Casanatense himself, to study manuscripts stored in another Roman library, the Biblioteca Angelica of the Agostinians. And at last, the Vatican Library.

With her mind so actively engaged, her guilt for her abandoned husband began weighing less heavily on her conscience. The lawyers were at work. Adriana was growing, between a bout of scarlet fever and an attack of acidosis; not exuberantly, but she was growing. Accompanied by Annita or Zia Margherita she went to the Pincio, and to the new grounds around Castel Sant'Angelo, where the old moat had been transformed into a public park. Yes, she had once glimpsed a look of abandonment on her daughter's face — the time her grandfather Tommaso had left their apartment with his eyes full of tears. Adriana had followed after him, had even tugged on his coat, and he stopped. He turned and hugged his granddaughter, shaking his head without saying a word. And Marta had felt more pain for him than for her daughter. Which was only right, she thought, for Adriana "would understand when she was older."

After school lets out Adriana runs to her father, who is waiting with a broad smile just for her, a smile unlike any he has ever given her before. She doesn't see anything but that smile as she runs. "Go, go and play; I'll stay here and watch you," says Papa after hugging her briefly. She returns to the crowd of children chasing one another, but it is awkward and embarrassing to have your own father look at you with loving eyes while you are playing and the others can see.

He came to pick her up in his car, but because he gave up his motorcycle for the car when he moved out of the house, Adriana does not like the car. "Do your friends' fathers have cars?" he asks, with a hint of pride that makes her feel ashamed, just as she is ashamed of terms like *fathers* and *your friends*. She has no friends because all her classmates are different from her; she arrives at school from the house across the street, but at noon she goes away with her father, and by car, no less. Her classmates do not know where she goes, but she always fears they might ask. Then he says, "Tell me what's new," and she has nothing to tell as they drive, passing through the streets, and by the trees along the Tiber, and garden gates and, an advertisement, CACHET FIAT, between the enormous gloved hands (why?) of an awful man with an ugly hat. It is a long ride for her, always the same but with plenty to look at, and every day she hopes in vain it will give her something to talk about.

But up there, in Monteverde, everything is bright. Adriana finds Nonna Matilde the same as ever in her large flowery apron, humming, laughing, and running busily from kitchen to dining room with her tiny steps. Immediately she says "grate the cheese," or "put the glasses on the table," without so much as a hello, and she accepts a kiss on the fly, saying, "Let me go now, the pot's about to burn," as if twenty-four hours have not passed and they are together again forever. Yes, there is a victorious gleam in her grandmother's eyes, and she has prepared dishes that were once reserved only for Sunday, just for them — her son who has come back to her, and her beloved granddaughter. They eat, all four of them, around the oval table with the slit in the center where they once inserted one, two, and even three leaves for holiday meals, when the cousins from Ferrara came, and Nonna Matilde's friends, "alone all year long, just like stray dogs, poor things." But not Arturo. He had never been at the holiday table among the guests with flushed faces and eyes shining from the wine, from the pork sausages and lentils and all the rest. Not as far as Adriana can remember, and ever since it arrived in Monteverde the table itself has not needed extra leaves. They eat, the four of them, and through the window they can see the nearby walls of the Janiculum covered with passionflower vines. A pine tree juts up from behind the wall, and in seeing it Adriana thinks of the unknown and thus frightening world of which it is a part. What could there be behind that wall?

Now it is the sad autumn of 1937, and as Adriana does her homework at her grandparents' oval table, her papa sits on the edge of a chair with his legs outstretched and his hat pushed back to expose his forehead. He is agitated, his mind elsewhere as he reads the paper angrily, with sudden outbursts of "dammit," and then he folds the paper up into a stick and strikes the table as if swatting a fly that isn't there.

Nonno Già would like to help her with her homework but he admits he does not know how, muttering, "All I remember is my old seminary Latin." She has never heard this term, but thinks of *seminare*, "to sow," and assumes he's talking about a vegetable garden. When she is finished with her homework, Nonno Già takes her to Prati; during the short days of winter they take the streetcar, the one that ends it run at the Porta San Pancrazio. Handholds dangling from leather straps swing back and forth from the white, arched roof. Those straps, don't they ever break? They dance in the yellow light as the windows fog up. She thinks it would be great fun to take hold of two of them and swing, but it's not allowed. It's dark when she gets off with Nonno Già to catch the Circolare Nera at the Ponte Garibaldi; it's dark at their usual stop under the bare trees in Via Federico Cesi.

But throughout the lengthy spring they go on foot, she and Nonno Già. They set out along the wall, and she likes to walk along its travertine base, which starts out low, then rises up high above the street, and when it drops down again she holds her grandfather by the hand and jumps to the ground. There is a fountain nearby that shoots a stream of water into a trough for horses to drink. The water reflects the sky, and she drinks from it even when she's not thirsty. They pass the great gate of the Janiculum and she would like to run, but her grandfather sets down his cane at each step with an exaggerated sweep of his arm and she stays by his side. Halfway down the avenue Nonno Giacinto sits on a bench and looks at the Villa Pamphili. He rests for exactly five minutes as measured by his gold watch with a chain, and during those five minutes she envies the boys and girls who play hide-and-seek among the busts of Garibaldi's soldiers, running free on the forbidden grass. Then they reach Piazzale Garibaldi, where her grandfather shows her the palaces and villas of Rome under the last light of the sun, but she does not always understand where he is pointing with his cane, nor does she care. They walk on in the steady light of evening, and the repeated clanking of iron bars issues from Regina Coeli prison. "You hear that?" explains her grandfather. "They're checking to make sure no one has sawed through the bars." She will never forget that sound echoing in the sunset. They walk under the Gianicolo Lighthouse with its three eyes. One is red and another is green, so when the lighthouse rotates, it sends out three colors, the colors of the Italian flag. "Argentina sent it as a gift," her grandfather explains, and Adriana thinks it was the Teatro Argentina and cannot understand, but it doesn't matter to her. After a bit they descend a gray stairway between dark stones. Ancient steps — too worn, she thinks, human shoes could never have worn them down that way — wind below and around a horrible tangle of wood and iron stakes. "This is Tasso's oak," says Nonno Già. "The poet. But you haven't studied him yet. He came here to write under this tree, but back then it provided shade, or at least let's hope! But then it was struck by lightning, maybe more than once — in five hundred years!" Now it is Adriana who guides her grandfather as he walks with unsteady steps down those ugly stairs. They pass by the white friar — is he real or fake? — who waters tomato plants in the minuscule vegetable garden on the slope under Sant'Onofrio, and the word *seminary* comes back to her. They walk down the steep cobblestone street called "the descent of Sant'Onofrio," she running boldly, but Nonno Già goes slowly, very slowly, using his cane with care, saying "If I fall, all you'll have left is a pile of bones." At the bottom of Sant'Onofrio's descent is a stairway between two walls where one can rest, and Adriana waits for her grandfather there. She waits a very long time, but she enjoys it, and imagines that "pile of bones" in the street. She looks at him and thinks many things during that time to herself, a stretch of time when she can do whatever she wants, or so she feels.

The Arc of Santo Spirito, then the approach leading to the grand confusion of Saint Peter's, where the houses along the Borgo Vecchio are being demolished. Nonno Già shows her the house of Raphael, which, he says, will be moved stone by stone. And in fact that is what happened, for the house is now on one side of Via della Conciliazione, while it used to be right there in the middle, bordering a piazza along with other less valuable homes.

Castel Sant'Angelo with its great moat, then Piazza Cavour; and here at last the sky disappears and the air is again redolent of the past, of home, of her early years. The building that Zia Margherita wanted to chop down because it blocked the sun during their meager outings has actually been destroyed, but it no longer matters to them now. But where was Zia Margherita then?

Here is the street, the house, the front door. Adriana gives Nonno Giacinto a kiss (taking pains not to touch his mustache!) and he gives her a light pat and says, "Go on, now, go up. And be careful." He does not say what she is supposed to be careful about.

Alone, she enters the cold entrance hall, crosses the foul-smelling courtyard, and starts up the stairs she has climbed so many times before. She walks slower and slower with each step, but not because she is growing tired. She looks at the dusty lights high on the wall. Adriana is alone for the first and only time all day, and she is not in a hurry. She likes it, being alone. She looks at those weak lights and prays, as if in its solitude the stairway is a church. She prays for her father and mother to get back together. She says "my father and mother" in her prayer, not *Mamma and Papa*, because it seems more solemn, more official and legal. So that God will understand for sure; so that He cannot pretend He hasn't understood.

But there on the stairway she never stops to think, not even for a moment, about Nonno Già, who is returning to Monteverde all alone.

Her mother comes to the door in a hurry, busy in the kitchen now that Annita is no longer there. Adriana throws her satchel on the trunk and walks idly through the hallway. She goes into the kitchen to watch her, her mamma, rosy-cheeked and a bit tired; a wrinkle has appeared on her forehead.

They eat in the kitchen, alone, laughing and joking. Marta tells Adriana stories of when she was a little girl, like the one about Flora, Stelianì's cat, who liked to walk along a certain cornice. One day it collapsed, and the cat fell right onto the turban of an Arab. She immediately jumped to the ground and darted through the front door into the house, while the man looked around without seeing a soul and then ran off invoking Allah, his hands raised to the sky. Her mamma tells stories as if reciting them, and when she is happy she seems a lot like Zia Margherita. But only then does Adriana see the resemblance, even though they are sisters.

They sleep together, the two of them, in the room at the end of the hall, the only one that the little gas heater manages to keep warm. Never did Adriana feel so close to her mother, never so happy, as when her mother came to bed early and slept with her in the very same bedroom. She looks at her greedily, jealously knowing she must hold those moments in her memory. Mamma asks, "Have you said your prayers?" as she once did — and how long ago it seems — but she no longer demands that Adriana recite them aloud. Adriana quickly makes the sign of the cross and says a hasty Hail Mary, having already given her undivided attention to her true prayer while coming up the stairs to the apartment.

"Turn over and go to sleep!" orders her mother in a playful tone, as if trying to preserve the formalities of their relationship, which their new living situation might undermine. Adriana rolls over happily and looks at the wall and her shadow as she listens to the rustle of her mother undressing, to her voice as she sings softly. She smells the stove and hears it breathing as it sends up a spark that flutters near the ceiling — a star cut from a piece of paper folded and refolded into little triangles, then cut on the folds and opened again . . .

Then her mother walks across the room. She bends to kiss her and goes to bed. Adriana turns toward her, and in the deep silence of that dark empty house, suspended between the ghosts of her grandparents' home and the night sky over Via Gioacchino Belli, she watches as her mother reads. She recites aloud, memorizing by the light of the night lamp with its parchment shade. Adriana listens to the words in bits and pieces — unfamiliar words, or words she can't quite make out — and her sleepy eyes grow transfixed on the shadows in the room. By magic, time turns back and repeats itself — just like the game of the Bridge — as her mother recites the same passage two, even four times! Thus, without knowing it, Adriana listens to Dante. So it went that entire winter of fourth grade, and throughout the spring that she walked up the Gianicolo with Nonno Già.

At the end of the year Adriana skips a grade — "So you won't waste a year," they say, but what does that mean? Through her great patience and their frequent walks, Zia Margherita helps her prepare. They sit on the steps of the ancient moat around Castel Sant'Angelo, where somebody has planted a lawn, and she learns the tale of Chichibio and the Crane from *The Decameron*, which she finds stupid; likewise the story of the emperor without clothes, but they are required reading. The examination for skipping a grade is held in another school, a school she has never seen, without her classmates and her teacher. It's the school where Zio Giacomo teaches, called the Collegio Nazareno, and it is far away, in a dark, severe building, and she has to take the MP bus — Zia Margherita's bus. Then it's vacation time, and she leaves with her mother. They go to Sicily, which is an island on the map and has nothing to do with Santa Cecilia after all. They are going "for a visit."

Only Zia Margherita accompanies them to the train; she waves a handkerchief, a wet handkerchief, but she says, "Don't pay any attention, baby, it's nothing; it's just a speck that got in my eye." This business about a "speck" (a mysterious object) is an old excuse that Adriana knows well, but she certainly can't let on to her aunt because she loves her too much. Perhaps she, too, would like to cry, but she's not sure. Her stomach is in knots but she is too thirsty and nervous to vomit. Then the train departs and immediately rounds a corner, so Zia Margherita disappears from sight, and inside and out there are things to look at, but not to understand, not to understand at all.

She sleeps all night. One always sleeps well on a train, and now it's daylight again, a new day, and Mamma is saying, "Look! Do you see how beautiful it is?" and "This is the Strait of Messina!" The train runs close by white pebbled beaches and then tunnels through the mountains and there is the odor of smoke. Then the train does what it is famous for, it boards a ship — called a ferry — which is a thing unlike any she has ever seen, and she is afraid.

Looking back, Adriana regards that first trip of hers to Sicily with little curiosity, for she is not accustomed to novelty and it does not impress her. The train runs slowly along the shore — "A real island, just imagine!" — right by the water, past pure white beaches and large black boulders — lava stones, her mother tells her — that have rolled down to the sea from Mount Etna. A terrible, fiery volcano; that, she already knew, but to see it looming so high in the sky, covered in snow even in summer . . . "It's a real volcano indeed," her mother says. "You were born at the bottom of Vesuvius, but you don't remember, and this is Etna, the largest volcano in Europe, as you learned in school." But why is her mother telling her these things? She doesn't know why, but it all seems excessive, forced. Or did she just think so later?

The warm breeze entering through the window blows through her hair and lifts the collar of her mother's dress, her beautiful mamma, who says to her, "There's a surprise waiting, you'll see." And "Guess who'll be waiting for us at the station!" Marta does not say anything, at least not that she remembers, for the game of Yes and No is too charged, and even though she does make a guess, she won't say it out loud because she is secretly ashamed of what she has wished for. Waiting for them at the small station — a toy station, says Mamma — by a low and silent sea is Arturo himself, deeply moved, with a smile on his face and his curls falling over his forehead. "Give me a kiss!" he says in his strange but beautiful voice, and she does, and immediately everything changes, becomes special, and she opens her heart to him, and yes, she is happy. There are new scents. Mamma looks splendid in her navy-blue dress with the white polka dots and wide collar. Arturo carries the suitcases and they climb into a carriage drawn by a horse with a horse's odor. They climb higher and higher — the poor horse! — up a long road winding through a briary countryside fragrant with rich, new odors. Tall vines with incredible purple flowers unlike any she has ever seen cover the wall along the road, and at every turn the sea becomes more vast and deep, more blue and incandescent in the sun. Mamma doesn't say, "Look, look!" anymore, instead she talks with Arturo. Adriana doesn't listen, and she will not remember, but when the two of them fall silent — as they do for long stretches — that vast silence of theirs fills the world.

After a tight bend in the road, her mother says, "Look, there is the house, it's that one up there with the two towers." She points into the distance, as if to another mountain, and Adriana wonders how her mother already knows this, if she has never been here before. She doesn't know, Adriana, and will not know for years, that in fact her mother has been here, several months earlier — but only for a day — to receive the blessing of a dying man (Arturo's father) there, in that house that seems to be on another mountain. She does not know that Arturo is now "at peace with his conscience, and justified in the eyes of the world and God to receive his fiancée and her daughter in his home for a month."

The carriage climbs up and up, passes an ancient door, and continues climbing and winding above the village to a gate in a redbrick wall. Taormina is silent and fragrant. Arturo's house has a large, overgrown garden, and the untended vines have almost scaled the top of the mountain.

A whole month! She should write her father. "Be sure you write your father, write to him often!" whispered Nonna Antonia as she said a sorrowful good-bye and hugged her tight.

A long month, rich and full. In the villa — as the house and garden are called — live Arturo's nephews and nieces, and she plays with them — new friends who know things unknown to her. Arturo goes with them to the "cistern," which is a large open tank for holding water, and she has never seen one before. Inside the cistern, which actually has very little water, there are many stones and fat, lazy toads that close one eye at a time with a funny look on their faces. Then he takes them to the grotto behind the house; a grotto in the rock, no less. Inside the grotto it is cool, and bottles of wine and "provisions" are kept there on shelves called *scaffe*. And then there is the attic! From the sloping wooden beams — from inside you can see that they really do hold up the roof — a sweet, warm odor descends, and beyond those beams you can see the underside of the roof tiles and blinding rays of light shining through the cracks. She had never seen an attic, or the underside of roof tiles, and those truths move her like undeserved revelations, or confirmations of faith.

A very full month, and writing to her father becomes more and more difficult every day. What can she tell him? She has already told him about her new friends, and the hut she has built with them under a carob tree; but she just called it "a tree" because she doubts her father knows what a "carob tree" is. Then she feels that she has betrayed her new friends — her only friends! — by writing to her father about them, as he will certainly never meet them. She feels as though her own world has enlarged, yet his will always remain the same: sad and poor. She also knows that her father has been preparing a new house, for her also, but she hasn't seen it, so she doesn't want to think about it. How can you think of a house that you've never seen? Too difficult, such problems, and so her desire to write her father goes away; especially when her mamma says, "Have you written your father?" What's more,

Adriana feels that her mother stumbles on those two words, and will never again refer to him simply as *Papa*.

Then one day her mother (yes, with your friends that's what you say: my father, my mother) says, "Now you can write him at the new house." She gives her the new address, and Adriana falls into an even deeper remorse. She writes a short, meager letter to that address on an unknown street, and she feels as if she is throwing it into the void.

Mother and daughter are again on the train, alone and silent in the compartment. Adriana is lying down, and looking out, filled with a sorrow that words cannot express, and time on the train is passing slowly. A few eucalyptus trees up in Calabria, cultivated fields on the slopes of the mountains, and a clear sky where one, two, three wires run by. The wires go from one pole to another; on each pole is a crossbar holding porcelain spools. She is thinking of her vacation that has just ended, and she is in tears because she misses it already. She thinks of the new house, never seen, where she will go to live. Then, imperceptibly at first, the image before her eyes enters her soul . . . those wires. Animated by joyous hope, by naive boldness, the wires go up with increasing velocity, brash, happy, as if wanting to disappear into the sky, but . . . mercilessly, the pole (Destiny) reaches out and hits them, downing them. Each wire falls down dead, or rather dying. Dying, without breath or hope. And yet a faint spark of life remains; it must not be touched, not even by a glance, not even with the hope that it is still alive, for fear it will be hurt. And slowly — don't look, you might hurt it! — in the lowest, calmest zone (is it an illusion, or is it truly serene?), hope and breath are reborn. Once again, the wire (a living creature) slowly starts to rise, eluding fate by joyous hope and naive but blessed boldness, because so it must be, because it is God's will. And so it is for Adriana.

But Marta does not look outside, and if she does she pays no attention to the sights of the countryside, the houses and wires. She looks straight ahead and does not see anything, not the advertisement posters, not the wall, not the chestnut-colored luggage rack. She is reminded of the taste of iron, as if from blood in her mouth (from when she once bit the inside of her cheek) as she rereads the words of the letter, the story, she received "under separate cover" from the lawyer. "Dear Madam" — the letter says — "here is the story: You must go to a notary with four witnesses . . ." and the letter ends, "Very respectfully . . ." Even there, in the train, Marta still blushes deeply from shame. She blushes, as anyone could see from looking, but her daughter is not looking, she is still following the drama of the wires that continues to unfold, always the same, with the arrival of each pole. The redness slowly fades as the memory returns and penetrates the "shameful story"; which at any rate cannot be shameful precisely because it is a story. Everybody knows, or they will know — she'll see to it somehow — that the whole story was fabricated, invented "for everyone's sake." A lie, certainly, but not Marta's lie, because she was not the one who created it. It's the bureaucracy that wants it, and the notions of bureaucracy are alien to Marta, as they were to her father, who let his salary be taken away without a complaint, and suggested in despair that his wife and younger daughter should "hire out as servants." Those were his words in that forgotten letter from Alexandria, the one where he had asked Marta to look for a teaching position to feed the family. Bureaucracy is vulgar, anyway, because you pay money into it, and money is "the devil's dung," as her father taught her. Vulgar but necessary, like certain rituals of nature, so emotion (always a lofty thing) justifies it. Besides, her professionalism has already intervened in that cheap story, as if instinctually, to correct and repair the errors. She remembers, she "sees" those words, written by a typewriter she has never seen, which rests on a table she has never seen in some unknown room — a smoky room, most likely — in a remote city she does not know. Brno. She hasn't even looked for it on a map. Three consonants and one vowel; nothing more exotic and improbable, nothing so unheard of, and she does not want to know where it is. Now, in that train, alone even though her daughter is by her side, Marta feels as if she has those papers in her hands, right before her eyes, while in truth they are locked under the cover of her piano. Those two sheets of paper trembled in her hands and she wrote on them, first in pencil, modifying and correcting words and expressions. She could not refrain, and she allowed those expressions, those papers, and the story itself to come under her dominion. For Marta would not, could not, refrain from putting any text into good Italian, especially not that one! It was a task for which she was particularly well suited, an obligation she owed herself. There on the train, working by memory, she returns to the task of correcting those lines, mitigating in whatever measure the lie she has to accept as the only means to attain happiness. The happiness God has promised to grant to her, His perfect creature. Because of His decision, His commitment and promise, she is allowed, even entitled, to have anything. She took the corrected documents to the lawyer's partner; the two of them are taking care of her divorce, which in truth is an annulment. The partner's office is in Via Crescenzio, just a few steps from her house. And then the papers, with their modifications, were returned to her — from Brno — for her signature. A web of necessary lies and suffering. The goal was to obtain a civil annulment after the Tribunal of the Sacra Rota refused to grant a dissolution of the marriage bond. The case and subsequent decision had been discussed with and consigned to her husband; she had never even been granted a hearing. But the Brno lawyer had assured her of obtaining results within six months — or within three to four weeks, for an additional fee — provided certain things were left unsaid . . . a sea of lies and "truths unsaid."

The phrases written by the lawyer came hammering back to her, in a jumble one after another, "Dear Signora, here is the story we will tell . . . with four witnesses . . . who will testify . . . they will make a declaration as follows, and the notary will then set it down in legal form . . ."

Weighing heaviest on her heart is the testimony required of four false witnesses — one of whom would be her young sister, whose word was needed, she was told, because they had always lived together under the same roof. They were to testify that "she had bound herself in matrimony out of fear of a violent brother" — Giacomo! — "and therefore her consent had not been freely given." "No, not my sister!" she had exclaimed, but no one listened. Not when she first asked the lawyer in Via Crescenzio (she had never spoken with the other one), and not when she returned in tears and pleaded, for surely the bureaucracy could not demand that Margherita perjure herself. But at last she had obtained that much. The actress Caterina had a sister who declared herself ready to utter "those few words on the altar of Love, since it wasn't true testimony and everyone knew it" . . . just as the oath on her Fascist identity card wasn't true, either. Caterina herself would have willingly "performed that role, too," but she was told she couldn't testify against her own husband.

All this Marta remembers, while her daughter looks out on the continuing drama of the wires. She refuses — as long as possible — to think about one other fact, which no one has mentioned to her directly: she will be facing excommunication. Her mother, Antonia, will come to know of it soon enough.

Adriana switched schools for her first year in the *ginnasio*. Just two weeks later, in mid-October, her mother left. "I'm going away to play music," she said. "I'll be back soon, my precious, you'll see. I'll be back, and I'll bring you a present. Tell me, what do you want Mamma to bring you?" But Adriana only shook her head, keeping silent in order not to cry. "All right, for now, you don't know. Let's do this, you think about it, and then you write to me. All right? How does that sound?" It's the first time she asked her to write; the first time that she left to play her music. But why wasn't she taking her cello? Why did she leave it in its case to languish in silence? Adriana noticed the cello a few days after her mother's departure and thought, *Perhaps she has gone off to play the piano*. Indeed, it had been some time since her mother had played the cello with her musician uncles; instead she played the piano. She played it by herself, occasionally singing a separate melody.

❖

Adriana now lives in Monteverde. She had never seen her grandparents' house in the evening light before, and she feels a certain trepidation; whether from restored familial warmth or from fear, she does not know. In the last hours of light, a possessive fog settles in and hides Scarpone's immense orchard down at the end of the road. Farther on is the dark strip of the Villa Pamphili pines, but Adriana is not looking in that direction, nor does she look at the cold, starry sky or the haloes of the street lamps. She sees only the warm colors inside the house, and Nonno Già next to the radio with its four long, curved legs and cloth grille speaker where the voice comes out. It's nice, the radio; it has a wide red tuning dial for a mouth and two knobs for eyes. Papa arrives and Nonno says, "Did you hear? Did you hear what they said on the radio . . . ?"

They eat soup, a frittata with mozzarella, and chicory salad. Then there are apples, small, red apples, but she is not hungry. "Eat, my little Adriana, eat!" says her father with a sad, distracted tone that makes her heart ache and her appetite disappear altogether.

"Do you have everything?" says Nonna Matilde as Marta and her father are leaving. She speaks with a note of alarm, as if they are departing on a journey rather than leaving to go to sleep, the two of them, just two blocks away, in the famous new house that is actually only a flat. Two blocks in silence in the car, then the sounds, one after the other, of the car turning and braking, and then an even deeper silence, a long, painful moment of hesitation for both Marta and her father that marks the end of the day. A day they each frittered away doing things they don't recount to each other, and now that it has ended it suddenly seems as though they have dragged themselves through it with the same weary sorrow. Her father pushes back his hat, exposing his forehead with the familiar gesture that was once cheerful, but not now, and he sighs as he says, "Amen!" Yes, the day is over. But still to come is that awkward and improbable, yet intimate and affectionate time they spend preparing to go to bed in that cold, tiny apartment, a place that smells of emptiness and the coffee her father made that morning while she was sleeping under the weight of countless blankets pulled up over her head.

Mamma said "a short month" when she left. Adriana doesn't ask anyone else about it. Her grandparents and Papa do not speak of her mother, who lists her address as the name of a hotel, because musicians stay in hotels, even for long periods of time. In her letters Adriana writes, "When are you coming back?" She puts this in small script at the bottom of the page, as if slipping it in, ashamed, in order to conceal the pain of waiting and afraid of the answer.

Why autumn? Why autumn with its short days and rain and new school year? Why?

A package addressed to Adriana arrived at Monteverde. It contained a brown cardboard box about twenty-five centimeters long with rounded ends — a thin, sturdy container molded into an almost oval shape without stitching or pasting. The top and bottom halves fit together, one inside the other, with a puff of air, and the inside was filled with white wedding almonds wrapped in white silk tissue paper.

"Whose are they? Who got married?" asked Adriana, and Nonna Matilde frowned without a word as if to say, *I don't know and I don't care*. Then she said it aloud, her voice sounding strange, "I don't know."

I turned the box in my hands. I liked it immensely, and I looked again at the address written on the card in an unfamiliar hand, large and beautiful. "Whose could they be?" I repeated, but now with reluctance, an obscure disinterest.

There was no one in the room anymore. Nonna was in the kitchen as if she had been there all the time. I picked out an almond with two fingers, put it in my mouth, and started sucking it slowly, almost forcing that liberty on myself; they were mine, were they not? But more than one? Never. And there were so many! I never thought it possible to have so many wedding almonds all at once. In fact, perhaps when they came in such quantities, wedding almonds had nothing to do with weddings. I shrugged. I was happier with the beautiful box than with the candy. It was mine, that was certain. I put it on top of the sideboard, under the wolf's head and the wooden fruit shiny with wax.

When the adults had their coffee, I stood up and murmured, "Ah, there are almonds." That phrase had echoed in my brain throughout the meal. My father and grandparents watched as I went to get the box. Embarrasssed by their silence, I placed the open box on the white tablecloth. I lifted the tissue covering the almonds and everyone looked at them; no one was watching me anymore. Then I went around to each of them, all the way around the oval table even though there were only three of them, and I offered the candy, but neither my grandmother, nor my grandfather, nor my father took any, making me feel embarrassed that I had eaten even one. "You eat them, Adriana, if you'd like," said Nonna Matilde, and it seemed as if she meant all of them, which was incredible, even stupid, but also offensive somehow, so I closed up the box, unhappily, and put it in the other sideboard, the one with glass doors that was kept half hidden from sight and seldom used, because by now I was ashamed of that box of wedding almonds.

Then my father said, "Come with me," with a voice so grave as to make me fear a reprimand. We left the house, and as we walked along the sidewalk toward his apartment he looked straight ahead, at the ground, with a terrible scowl on his face. In this same fashion Marta and her father had walked along the yellow streets of Alexandria, but I did not know that.

Then he stopped and said to his daughter, who was almost trembling, "Those wedding almonds . . . it looks like she couldn't find any other way to let her daughter know." At first Adriana did not understand, perhaps overcome by her fear of being scolded, or else because she could not, or did not want to understand.

They paced back and forth on that same stretch of cobblestone and dirt sidewalk instead of heading up the narrow street toward home, and her father continued speaking. He spoke at length, but only his initial words remained with her. She has no memory of anything else he said; but that first pronouncement, yes, that she did remember.

When Zia Margherita arrived two days later — she had telephoned first, with an annoying, feigned voice — they went along the Janiculum Wall covered in lichen and moss and entered the public park at Villa Sciarra. It was already that hour when the peacocks call lugubriously and retire to the highest tree branches, an early autumn evening. Zia Margherita held Adriana's wrist as tightly as ever, unable to say what needed to be said. Adriana did not try to wrest herself away out of added defiance, because her aunt had said, "I have something to tell you." She repeated herself two more times, "I have something to tell you, little one," without saying anything else, and Adriana felt an angry tension that gave way to an oppressive sense of boredom unlike anything she had ever known, as if that useless stroll would never end. Because she knew what Zia Margherita had to tell her, she knew it better than Zia Margherita or anyone else did. She had known it *forever*, at least that's how it seemed to her now. Zia Margherita had accepted the duty (shouldn't she have been ashamed of herself?) but in her role as messenger she was so pathetic as to elicit annoyance instead of pity. With unkind nonchalance Adriana would have been able, she herself, to communicate what her aunt had come to say but did not know how. Finally Adriana frowned without realizing it and stopped in her tracks. "What is it?" asked her aunt, immediately alarmed and on the verge of uttering them, those words. But as the streetlights high along the wall gathered the early evening mist around them, the only words to reach her ringing ears were, "It's getting cold, baby, come on, let me take you back home . . . ," as if she were still a little girl. Indeed she felt little, and her aunt's anguish upset her even further. They turned silently toward home and she thought: *Now she won't say anything*. On the contrary, Zia Margherita wanted to fulfill her duty, and as the house came into view she whispered ashamedly, "Listen, the thing I had to tell you is this: Your mamma and Zio Arturo got married."

Adriana blushed, "I know," she whispered, her voice no longer spiteful. "They sent me the wedding almonds."

Margherita stopped. "The wedding almonds?" and it was clear she truly did not understand. And Adriana jumped up and hugged her, poor Zia Margherita, as if asking forgiveness for who knows what offense, and hoping to console her at the same time.

That night — or was it another? — she found herself in bed with the door to her bedroom closed, perhaps an oversight by her father. A thin ray of light shone beneath the door. Just as in her early childhood, she was frightened. She ran to the door in tears and sought refuge in the arms of her father, who was writing at the desk covered with papers. He held her in his lap for a long while, caressing her hair without saying a word, and when she had calmed down he took her back to bed, saying, "Otherwise, you might catch cold on me, and then what would I do?"

Nobody talks about the house in Prati. As if it is forgotten. Only Nonna Matilde mutters, on occasion, "Eh, when I was in my own house . . . ," but she doesn't finish her sentence and Adriana isn't sure if she is referring to the house in Prati, or the other one, the legendary house of her nineteenth-century childhood, when she lived in Ascoli with the grande dame, Nonna Caterina, the Marchesa Malaspina. Likewise the long walks along the Gianicolo with Nonno Già the year before had been filled with silence, for they never spoke, the two of them, of their destination. Of the old house's ambience, all that remains intact are the odors in the drawers of the sideboard. And linked to these odors are memories. With great agony, it is now that Adriana develops and refines the art of remembrance, of losing herself to the dilation and artificiality of time.

Nonna's friends come to visit her in Monteverde, little old ladies grown ever smaller and more pallid — biscotti broken into by ill-fixed dentures, tea sipped by latecomers from Japanese teacups (at the bottom of each cup is a tiny figurine, visible when held to the light). Welcome! All the way out here! Enrichetta Giorgi, the cousins from Ferrara — Chiarina and Norina, as alike and fat as ever — Emilia Salaroli, Adele Carcani . . . There are always three or four of them seated on the red sofa. But now their most refined knees all but touch the dining room table, because parlor and dining room are a single room, and a small one at that.

"If you don't stop it, I'll send you away," says Lucia.

"You are not sending me anywhere. This is my house," declares Adriana, enraged.

"Your house, my foot! It's Nonna's house."

"It's mine. More mine than yours!"

"That's what you think. You are her granddaughter, but I'm her maid. Your Nonna couldn't get by without me. It's more my house than yours, you want to know why? Listen up. If your Nonna were to come and find you here, alone, eating a slice of bread, she'd ask, 'What are you doing?' But if she found me alone, even with an entire bowl of pasta, she wouldn't say a word. Understand?"

Days pass, then weeks, growing colder and colder, and the "short month" has long since ended. Adriana is not counting the days anymore, nor the flowers in the tiles; she no longer knows what to count. Mamma has written no more letters, and Adriana writes wearily to her — to that same hotel address, a hotel in Palermo — without revealing a thing about what is in her heart. And she no longer understands that pain herself, stupefied and homeless as she has been for so long, with no one speaking to her about the past or even about herself. Even Lucia knows she has no home.

Yes, Zia Margherita comes once in a while, but she doesn't say anything; she only asks silly questions about school; if she tries to talk to her as she once did, when they played a game that started with, *One day, when Zia is rich . . .*, that old pastime now sounds childish and overacted, and those visits only make her feel more displaced and unhappy.

Then Zia Margherita telephones with her "official" voice and says, "I called to talk to you, Adriana," but her voice does not change.

"What is it?" she asks with immediate reluctance.

"I must tell you something."

"What?"

"Your mamma will be here tomorrow. She won't be alone, she'll be with . . . how do you call him? Zio Arturo? I suppose you could call him that . . . I'll come to get you. If you want. Then your mother will tell you . . ."

Adriana looks at the floor. Her foot fills the length of one brick, perfectly. Mamma. Tomorrow. In a second she hates her for not writing to tell her so. She is coming back without telling her, and in that way! After more than two months, she is returning to force her into submission once again. She hates her. And as soon as she begins to hate her, she is not free to hate her anymore, because she is coming back. Because she loves her. She cries, in silence, with heavy sobs that remain inside her. But Zia Margherita is still there, on the telephone. "Adriana, baby . . ."

She remains silent a moment, then says, "What?"

"I'll come to get you, baby, all right?"

"All right!" she screams. Then she slams down the telephone and races down the stairs to the garden, where she slows to a walk, taking long, deep breaths to calm the tumult she feels inside. It is cold in the twilight, the air quiet and still, the bare trees motionless with an air of expectation. Tomorrow. It has no meaning. After two months, tomorrow! She'll see her again tomorrow, but she won't be the same. Papa explained it to her the day of the wedding almonds, as they walked along the ivy-covered wall. He explained everything to her. "For a while," he said, "occasionally . . . it's better not to make a tragedy of it . . ."

She shrugs two, four times, and that gesture remains with her, unwanted, even later at the silent evening meal. She says nothing. Minute by minute she says nothing; she does not tell them anything about what will happen tomorrow. Nor does she ask herself if they already know.

That last evening, an evening she had dreamed about for so long, she walks with her father down the quiet street with no sense of comfort or happiness. Instead she feels regret. Her father already knew. Yes, he knew about it. He didn't speak about it all evening, but later, when she curls up in her cold bed with her eyes wide open, he stays with her for a bit without turning on the light. He sits there beside her, warming her hands, then he kisses her and goes away without a word.

She opens the door and Zia Margherita says, "Let's go, get your coat," like when she was a little girl. But they do not leave right away, and her aunt sits on the sofa talking with Nonna Matilde. They speak in strange, hushed tones, in surprising agreement, as if Zia Margherita has suddenly overcome the timidity she usually experiences in front of Nonna Matilde and a new, unthinkable complicity has emerged between them.

Zia Margherita brought the children's magazine *Corrierino* for Adriana, a ridiculous repetition of an old habit, but Adriana threw it to the floor in a rage. She waits to be scolded, to see if they will *dare* to scold her, but her aunt says sweetly after a bit, "Well, let's go," as if she and Nonna Matilde had not really seen the newspaper fly to the floor. And she goes to pick it up. Nonna remains seated, looking miserable there on the sofa that doesn't give under her slight weight. With her hands on her knees and her thin forearms resting on the bulge made by her legs under her skirt, she is leaning forward as if she wants to get up but hasn't made up her mind to do it, or else she does not know how. The look on her small face is intense and distracted, and it makes her seem very old. Adriana, rigid and silent, doesn't say good-bye to her as she follows Zia Margherita; she is taller than her aunt by now. She sees her mother again in the hallway of the house in Prati. Determined as she is, she is already tired, and she immediately surrenders. The mysterious tones of that beautiful and beloved voice, her perfume; in an instant she is turned into a happy slave. They embrace with eyes closed and Adriana tells herself, *Later*. Exhausted, she allows herself a few seconds, a brief moment of secret oblivion. And immediately, the hate is not real. Or perhaps it is; a horrible sin to be erased only by forgetting.

Arturo arrives grand as ever, "How are you?" he says, giving her a warm, strong hug. But that *How are you?* is a sincere, innocent question, and it deserves an answer. Amazed and relieved, feeling as if her feet are transporting her of their own will, she follows Arturo into the kitchen; the kitchen that belonged to Annita, but it is all different now, because there stands none other than Nonna Antonia, who has moved in along with Zia Margherita and Nonno Tommaso. Zia Margherita didn't say a word about it! And Adriana doesn't ask why. She has no room for any more whys.

The entire house is different. It has different odors, although some of the old ones remain, faint and strange. On the marble table Arturo has placed a bundle of artichokes, saying, "Here, Mamma, I brought you some artichokes. Do you like artichokes? I love them, the Roman ones." He calls them *carcioffe*, mispronouncing the Italian word *carciofi* and giving it a feminine ending. Worse, he calls Nonna Antonia *Mamma*. Adriana blushes. In an instant she sees that Arturo has largely supplanted her father on grounds unfamiliar to her. And now there she is, with her chin resting on the cold marble kitchen tabletop, little defeated Adriana. What is to be done, what can she do, if that is indeed what has happened — so mysteriously, so completely — and how did it progress so far? Defeated and exhausted, she is suddenly sleepy and, after so much time, perhaps she is hungry.

In the kitchen everyone is now laughing. But why? The pot on the stove starts to sing. "It's boiling, Mamma," says Zia Margherita, no longer preoccupied with Adriana. "Put the pasta in, put it in," says Nonna Antonia. Her aunt throws the spaghetti in, pushes it down with the palm of her hand, and keeps laughing. But what is she laughing about?

Then they eat, there in the kitchen, with just a tablecloth on the bare marble as would never happen at Nonna Matilde's house, and Nonna Antonia laughs again silently, shaking her white head. Arturo laughs as he pours everybody water; Zia Margherita laughs and laughs, gay and nervous as Adriana has never seen her. She laughs and keeps repeating, "This is madness. Madness!" Her mother also laughs; her long hair is tied back loosely at her shoulders, a bit tousled. She is beautiful. And she is hers, Adriana's; that is certain in spite of whatever may have happened.

Yes, Monteverde with her taciturn grandparents, with Papa and his cold house, is far away. A shadow too sad and suffering to be loved. "How are you going to prepare the *carcioffe* tonight?" asks Arturo, and Adriana thinks she won't eat the *carcioffe* with them tonight; she will come back up before dark and have some soup, some boiled chicory, and a piece of cheese. Then an apple. She already knows which apple. She knows where it is at this very moment: in the fruit bowl on the sideboard, in that other world she carries with her in her mind's eye. She is already at fault for laughing, for having felt so happy in the old house, with them.

At Monteverde they will perhaps have questions for her.

But the evening that she returns to that shadow, accompanied by her aunt to the front gate, but only to the gate, no one asks her anything. She hates them, her father and her grandparents, because they dare, with their silence, to reproach her.

She prepares her suitcase with Nonna Matilde's help; rather Nonna packs it for her, silently, as she watches and sinks into an anguish that leaves her mouth and eyes dry. But the next morning, when it comes time to leave the place where she spent those two eternal months, she cries in Nonna's arms, and then in Lucia's, in spite of herself, miserable and with no sense of certainty.

Seated in the car next to her father, the short road to Porta San Pancrazio — which she has traveled on foot a thousand times as if it were nothing — now seems very long and rich in details, some familiar, while others she realizes she has not sufficiently explored and appreciated. Her father does not speak, but at the Piazzale del Gianicolo he slows down, pulls off to the right, then stops the car next to the wall where the cannon is fired each day at noon. He helps his daughter get out, puts his hands on her shoulders, and says, "Take a look at Rome. Do not forget her. Return soon. Right now, and for a while, you won't have any say as to how much time you'll spend away from here. I told your mother that you can stay with her for some time, as long as you are little. She'll be waiting for you. And so will I."

As he said *she* her father made a gesture with his hand, pointing in front of him. *She* is the city: Rome. Adriana blushes, overcome with impatience and resentment at her father's words and theatrical gesture. How can he take advantage of her like this? Can't he understand that the rest is already too much for her? Does he want promises and some display of emotion? He will not have them. She has already said good-bye to the Aurelian Wall, to the fountain at San Pancrazio, the plane trees on the avenue, and Nonno Giacinto's bench. What else do they expect of her? To show her Rome from the piazzale is shameful and cowardly. What does she care about the whole city? The more she closes in on herself, Adriana, the harder she becomes. Hard as stone. And she can't know how heavily that moment will weigh on her soul for the rest of her life; and with it, the guilt she feels toward her father.

She feels hardened and cold as they drive by the lighthouse (a gift from Argentina, her grandfather always says), and she presses her lips tightly together as the road curves, and as they pass under that ghastly, ridiculous burned tree she doesn't look, doesn't even raise her eyes. But at the bridge to Castel Sant'Angelo she does glance up at the line of angels. *Why didn't I ever look at these before?* she asks herself. *They can wait.* Her father hasn't spoken since they left the Gianicolo, and he races up Via Tacito as if not even planning to stop at the front gate. But suddenly he does stop, and he says, "You will stay with your mother for all the holidays. You'll spend Christmas with her . . . with them. It's not as much fun with us, anyhow. Write me. If you are not comfortable there, write and tell me. But you'll be fine, you'll see. They are very likable, those people down there. So be happy, have fun, and every once in a while think of your old grandparents, alone by themselves. And think some of me. Go on now, go."

She gets out. Her father gets out, too, and gives her suitcase to the porter, who has rushed to his side and greeted him — after so many years — almost timorously. Papa briefly responds to his greeting, and as the porter disappears into the entrance hall with the suitcase, he embraces his daughter quickly. "Go!" he repeats, mouthing the words. Adriana enters the cold passageway to the courtyard as if her feet are walking of their own accord, for she would perhaps prefer to get back in the car. But when she turns around, her father's car is already leaving, and she remains there stunned and unhappy, halfway finished with a project she will no longer be able to complete.

The hallway upstairs is filled with suitcases and Zia Margherita — not her very own Zia Margherita or one of the many she has known, but another one yet — awkward and surly, says, "Do you have everything, little one?" She talks on and on, muttering that they are going to miss their train unless Adriana stops chattering and gets herself ready to leave. "Come on, let's go!" she keeps repeating, and it seems to Adriana that the hallway in the old house is dim, very dim, and maybe the lightbulb in the milk-glass globe has been changed, the light that once lit up the hall where she raced on her scooter. Her wonderful red scooter, a gift from her godmother, she had forgotten all about it — where could it be? She stands among the suitcases, a little girl once again, as they say good-bye to Nonna Antonia, and then one by one the suitcases surrounding her are picked up and taken out the door. She is left with nothing at her feet, and she might not have even taken a step had Nonna Antonia not pulled her toward herself, hugging her tightly and saying, "Write to your papa, you hear? Now go on with them, go."

She sets out after them, and Zia Margherita returns halfway back up the stairs. "You carry this. Can you do it? Eh? Can you make it?" and she does not let her trail behind, but keeps her in the middle, between the other two and herself. Nonna Antonia leans on the banister and they say good-bye at every turn of the staircase.

Arturo goes first, carrying the two large suitcases and looking more prepossessing and uncanny than ever, there on the steps of that old house. Mamma follows him, carrying a small suitcase, a hatbox, and her purse. Zia Margherita carries a suitcase and two of Mamma's coats, and she keeps repeating to herself, without any hope for an answer, "This is madness, what are you forgetting?

This is madness. Baby, go slowly, can you make it? Say, can you make it?" Adriana nods. Her suitcase isn't that heavy, and besides, it certainly wouldn't be her aunt who lightens her load, overburdened and nervous as she is.

She imagined, while in bed in her father's apartment, that she would be able to say a private good-bye to those stairs that had once been like a church to her. Instead everything is fleeing, as her father had been at the entrance. So all that remains of the emotions she anticipated and prepared for is the pain of her urgent need to understand and remember. And Nonna Antonia remains. "The other grandmother," strange and new in the old house, with her hair as white as a spiderweb reflecting the light. She becomes smaller, more removed, and more emblematic with every flight of stairs.

During the drive in the taxi, darkness falls and it starts raining. They keep silent, there inside, and the windows fog up. She sits on the folding seat and looks at no one. She looks at the shiny, black streets, at the colored signs in the storefronts, and at the driver who clears the windshield with the back of his hand from time to time. She knows that gesture because her father does the same. Where could he be now, her papa? She asks herself already, but it is only the first time.

At the station she walks behind Zia Margherita, who proceeds with quick, strained steps. Her aunt talks, but not with her.

Now they are in the compartment, her mamma, Arturo, and Adriana. Seen from above, Zia Margherita looks small on the platform. She is free again, and maybe even cheerful, although she keeps repeating, "This is madness, this is madness!" like an unconscious refrain.

Then Zio Giacomo arrives, reaching them with long strides through the crowd and appearing very tall even when seen through the train window. She barely knows him, except for New Year's and Epiphany celebrations. He boards the train and kisses his sister Marta and his new brother-in-law. He kisses his niece Adriana on both cheeks. "This is for you," he says, handing her a small package. "When the train starts moving, you can open it, baby, all right?" He, too, says *baby* just like Zia Margherita but with a different tone in his voice, and he even caresses her timidly, that uncle of hers, with his sad eyes hidden by the shock of black hair covering his forehead. Then Zio Giacomo turns to her mother and says something Adriana does not understand, although she knows it's Greek. Her mamma and her aunt speak that way at times; it's a familiar music and she likes it. Now they seem to be amused and they laugh, brother and sister. They are still speaking Greek, but what are they laughing about? Then Zio Giacomo says good-bye — embracing everyone, including Arturo — and he leaves. Adriana leans out and sees him walk away with long strides through the crowd of people holding handkerchiefs. He goes away alone, just as he came, leaving Zia Margherita there by herself, even though she is his sister.

When the train moves and her aunt blows them kisses with her handkerchief clenched tight in her nervous fist, the departure she had long feared finally happens, with dreamlike, unbelievable speed.

"Close the window, it's raining," says Mamma. Arturo stands up and closes the window, and immediately all that remains of Rome are ghosts of streetlights drowning in the dark.

Zio Giacomo's package contains a box, or rather a small basket made of strips of a tender, light wood; shiny, yellow straw peeks from the spaces between the strips. The basket is tiny, and it looks like the ones the vendor in Via Tacito uses for holding eggs or even chicks. This one holds candy, yellow like the thin paper straw on which it rests: honey candy. The box is the prettiest Adriana has ever received, even prettier than the one with the wedding almonds (which she mustn't think about), and she plans to keep it forever. She holds it in her lap and gazes placidly at her mother and Arturo, who are talking quietly to each other as the rocking of the train grows steady and the rain streams in slanted lines across the dark windowpane.

Palermo, 1937

It's my mother who wakes me. "Get up, we're in Naples!" and once again I must try to understand many things at once. The train has stopped in a silence broken by strange voices, men's voices. Mamma is on her feet, standing tall, tying her sky-blue silk scarf around her neck. I think, *Now, only now I could* . . . The urgency of feelings never put into words, incomplete and heaped together, is pressuring me to speak, so I go to pull on her coat but I'm rendered mute, paralyzed by that "now or never." Curled up in the corner where I slept, I can only brush her coat with a finger. And I do not wonder about Arturo.

"Let's go, we must get off here," says Mamma, carrying only her purse and hatbox. "Let's go," she repeats without looking at me, and I follow her. Arturo is there, in the train's corridor, handing the suitcases to a porter. Everything is gray.

It's raining lightly. The wet ground is black and covered in dimpled squares of flagstone. I carry a small suitcase and walk with my eyes on the ground. Yes, I had imagined and feared many things, but this I could not have foreseen, such a different pavement; not flintstones or asphalt, and not like my own sidewalks, with their smooth flagstones and white travertine borders . . .

I walk looking at that ugly pavement; I have not yet seen the boat. Still, all the light comes from there; the light reflected by the wet, black flagstone comes from the immense ship. A ship! I have seen them only in books.

"Do you like it, Adriana? Before today, you had never seen one, never seen a boat so close. And just think, we are going to go on board, and tonight we are going to sleep inside it." I say nothing, but I do think about it as I take the last step away from land and climb the ladder behind Arturo; but it's not a ladder, it's a gangway, uncomfortable, with rungs nailed at distances that don't match my steps, while with his long strides Arturo remains oblivious to them, those rungs. Looking over the side of the ship I can already see a band of black water between the ship and the pier, and suddenly I feel frightened and dizzy.

On board the ship, Adriana is now afraid of the silence, of the hot, nauseating odors. Everyone keeps quiet, there inside, where only the attendants are moving about. The men are in white jackets and appear tired and unkempt, old and worn out in one way or another, while the women wear ridiculous domestic's costumes, with aprons and starched white hats on their heads, like at the theater. They, too, look tired. They seem resigned, as if in a trance; accomplices in some mysterious, treacherous game. They all have roles, and they play their parts well. Just like Zia Cate, who changes her voice and her costume for the theater, because an actor doesn't go about on stage as she would at home or on the street. But one time — so long ago — when the house was full of guests and she had asked her mother, "It's all pretend, right? Just like at the theater?" her mother hadn't understood at first (or else she pretended not to; was she playacting, too?). Then she threw back her head and laughed, but with the exaggerated, phony laugh she reserved for strangers, and Adriana was immediately ashamed of her question and regretted asking it. That was just it: Mamma — a concert player — never really knew how to do that laugh. That evening, seeing her at the piano, Adriana realized she had offended her with that question, for an artist cannot betray her secrets. But not even when her daughter asks her to?

Thus Adriana has reached the second act of the great play staged just for her by all of them. All of them, even Papa with his flat in Monteverde (although he put on a poor performance at the Gianicolo), and Nonna Matilde, who said good-bye without a smile or a word, she who always talks so much, and even the innocent but deceitful Zia Margherita, and Nonna Antonia at the top of the stairs with her spiderweb of white hair. Yes, Nonna Antonia herself unlocked the secret to the game, because she made the absurd move to Via Tacito with Zia Margherita and Nonno Tommaso (and her aunt didn't say a word about it out of shame!) only to keep the house from being empty. And as soon as this idiotic game of new marriages, relocations, and other absurdities is finally over, they will give the house back — to her, and Mamma and Papa. Annita will come back, too. She hasn't gone away forever; that would be impossible, she has just taken a little trip. And on that day everything will fall back into place and be right again. Perhaps even her grandparents will return to the floor below. Who knows? And finally, Nonno Tommaso will return to his sun-filled house in Via Spallanzani, surrounded by all his books just as they left him, one by one, when they said good-bye, since he never accompanied anyone to the door. Thus Adriana finds consolation in the past. She is suddenly happy, almost exultant, and she follows one of the puppet-waitresses down the long, narrow carpet of that vibrating, caricature of a house with its curving corridors and low ceilings — like in Alice's fable — to make her believe she is really inside a ship. Ridiculous!After the steamer leaves the pier — is it possible they are actually floating? — and the three of them are on the bridge breathing the black wind and watching the lights of Naples like a crèche in the distance ("Look, Adriana, that's where you were born," but it is too much for her to understand), she is overwhelmed with anguish by the growing distance from Rome, from her grandparents' house, from her father's sad, cold apartment; water and railroad tracks across dark and unknown distances. Then Arturo takes her by the hand and has her touch the wooden edge of the parapet. It is wet, and he says, "Feel the sea salt? The salt in the sea breeze? It's always wet here, because the salt sticks to the wood and attracts humidity. It only dries out in the sun, or perhaps the parapet pretends to be dry to make the sun happy, and as soon as the sun sets it gets wet again, like this . . . What do you want to bet that tomorrow morning if we come to touch it, it will be dry?" And Arturo shows her the water below, with its terrible, unfathomable depth, and the white beard of foam left by the ship, a wave that tries to flee and is swallowed up by the night. Then she and Arturo run to the bow, where the ship ends in a point, among gigantic coils of rope, and Arturo says, "Doesn't that seem excessive? Do you think they'll ever need that much? I say the captain has read too many novels, what do you think?" and she is pleased. Then he adds, "How many sea adventures have you read? What, no Corsair? None of any color, neither Red nor Black? Is it possible at your age? Well, I'll give you some to read, you'll see. We have so many books you'll like, at home."

He said *at home*, and for an instant she becomes serious again. But then they race off, the two of them, to where they left her mother, and it is as if they are returning, together, from a long voyage that has further strengthened and matured a secret, deep, and old friendship. She is standing with her back turned, holding her hat against the wind with both gloved hands. They shout, "Boo!" and she turns around, smiling, and she is absolutely beautiful.

And so I sleep for the first time in a ship's berth, holding Zio Giacomo's basket of candy by my side. The sun is shining when I wake up. Mamma helps me dress, which she hasn't done in a long while, and before closing her suitcase she pulls out the old tattered yellow teddy bear that I haven't seen in years. She holds it up to me and says, "Do you want it?" but without waiting for an answer. I take it, vaguely offended and embarrassed, but feeling sympathy for her. Soon, among so many new sensations, I forget all about the bear lodged in the crook of my arm, held there more by my heavy coat than by me. Then, on the bridge, as the ship slowly enters the port and the wave rising from its nose breaks lightly over the deep cobalt sea, I put my hand on the sun-warmed parapet and I feel that it is dry. I look at Arturo and we exchange a secret, complicitous smile, and I experience a flutter of happiness.

The quay is full of people. They shout cries of welcome to those arriving, wave their hands, blow kisses, and raise young girls dressed like dolls above their heads. As we disembark I pay attention only to where I am placing my feet, and at the end of the gangway I land with a jump on large paving stones like those in Naples, but these are light-colored and dry. In Arturo's shadow as usual, and followed by my mother, I am now in the middle of that strange and noisy crowd. Island inhabitants; indeed, I am standing on an island. I test the ground with my foot, almost expecting to feel it move like an immense barge.

Yes, for the first time Adriana was walking on an island. She didn't count Taormina, perhaps because she got there by train. The island was covered with houses and streets, and the mountains were very close, not like Monte Cavo, which was barely visible. Of course on an island the mountains must be clustered more tightly together.

"This is Adriana," said her mother, pushing her forward. Adriana turned around and looked at her mother; she was beaming. Before them was a grand signora, prim and proper. She had a smooth face, smooth hair, and a gray, smooth dress. With her long arms and large, strong hands, the signora took Adriana by her shoulders and pulled her close. She bent down and kissed her silently, a clean kiss pressed on her forehead. The signora wore no perfume or lipstick. Her hair was pinned on the nape of her neck, and her cheeks were red from tiny veins under her cheekbones. Then the signora let her go and held her mother in a long embrace. Adriana knew nothing about that woman. The entire scene had been silent and no doubt ridiculous, too. She looked at Arturo and saw that his eyes were teary. The smooth signora also had tears in her eyes, and Adriana realized with horror that it wasn't from the wind. The two of them started speaking in German, but only briefly. Then the signora said, "Adriana comes with me." She took her free hand and placed it under her arm, holding it under her gray sleeve made of men's fabric. "Come!" she repeated. "Do you know who I am? I am the sister of . . . how do you call him? . . . I am Zio Arturo's sister. My name is Costanza, and if you want I will be the Zia Costanza for you. I would like it, and it will be simpler for you." (Simpler? Simpler than what?) Once again the signora placed her warm hand over Adriana's cold one tucked in the fold of the gray coat, and Adriana felt even more like a prisoner, and all the while the stupid teddy bear was still clutched in her other hand.

Arturo and a tired porter with a strap over his shoulder were carrying in the luggage. The light was penetrating. By now docile, Adriana allowed her hand to remain in that of the signora who wished to be called the Zia, but she touched her as imperceptibly as possible and walked quickly to keep up with her stride. "How did you like the trip on the postal?" asked Arturo's sister, but Adriana didn't understand, so she did not answer. So the signora repeated, "How did you like the crossing on the boat? You see, we call that boat the postal because it brings us the mail." (*That's it, the island* — Adriana thought.) "And that one, see? That is our Monte Pellegrino, not Monte San Pellegrino as the people from the mainland say. It's a most beautiful mountain, and we have a great appreciation for it. The poet Goethe appreciated it, too." Adriana did not respond. She looked at the mountain, then at "the Zia Costanza" (an aunt with an article), and she felt smaller and more lost than ever, there on an island whose natives appreciated mountains. Did her mamma appreciate them by now as well? *Those from the mainland!* Was she one of them, too?

She looked for her mother and didn't see her. She was overtaken by panic and her feet stuck to the ground. "What are you looking for? Are you looking for your mother? There she is," said the signora with her lilting, foreign accent. Mamma was ahead, with Arturo, and she was not thinking of her . . . she had abandoned her on that island. Adriana took a few hurried steps, and the signora let her go. But she slowed down, contrite, and she slipped her hand back under the signora's arm so as not to offend her. The signora said, "Bravo," using the masculine, and pronouncing it with hardened consonants. She blushed. Then she looked at the sea, the land, and the ship, and silently saluted the "postal" that had brought her there. She could not ask any more questions.

The carriage, pulled by a small shabby horse, was already filled with their luggage, and it creaked as they climbed on board. *Poor little horse*, thought Adriana. But she liked climbing up and sitting on the narrow seat in front. The carriage took off with a jerk at a grunt from the driver and it rocked along noisily. She had been in a carriage only once before coming to Taormina, with Nonno Già, but here it was different. From time to time the noisy wheels got caught in the ruts between the gray paving stones, tracks made by thousands of other carriage wheels. Around them were not streets but dissonant and dusty spaces, somber buildings with closed windows and no eaves; they seemed surprised at reaching so high into the sky. The carriage was traveling along what Adriana later learned was "the Via Roma," because the natives used the article with street names, just as they did with aunts. It was a noisy, meandering, tired street. Or was it the dusty sheen that was covering everything? She was reminded of the game of Topsy-turvy she used to play as a small child, where she imagined buildings and other objects to be mirror images of themselves. It was a game she played with Zia Margherita. Images: things that weren't real, not truly. And places. Those new places weren't real, therefore they weren't definitive. Just like the bridge, you had only to close your eyes . . . So this journey of hers was just a temporary adventure, not final. Then, exactly as her mother Marta had done a dozen years earlier, Adriana heard the horse's steps slow down as the carriage turned into the entrance. The sound of hooves and turning carriage wheels echoed off the walls and vaulted ceiling, solemnly announcing their arrival, and they passed into a bright courtyard with a large palm tree that filled earth and sky with spiked leaves and jagged shadows. Once again the ground was paved with pockmarked slabs of stone. The horse stopped, and the carriage groaned as Arturo got off. Part of the courtyard was filled with wooden crates. Men hammering the crates raised their eyes from their work, and Arturo went up to them, standing taller than them all. Her mother rested a hand on Adriana's hair in a caress, but the girl withdrew; her mother was not looking about, because she had already been there. This was a return for her, a return home.

Adriana climbed the stairs, seeking comfort in the small things she saw around her: the rounded corner of the gray steps, the peeling walls . . . She walked among these things toward her future, and the more she saw of it, the more mysterious and obscure it became. As the staircase opened on to the sunlit courtyard with its columns and archways, the Zia Costanza took her again by the hand. She looked at her mother a few steps ahead, carrying the hatbox she had brought with her from Via Tacito, and it occurred to her that it still contained the air of Rome. How many times throughout the years would she make that same pointless observation!

The landing between the arches, with its dusy banister of ornate wrought iron, overlooked the palm tree. The sound of hammers and the smell of sawn wood rose through the air, and the palm looked like an artificial tree, but a tuft of tender green foliage sprouted from its inhospitable core, stretching toward the light and free of dust. "Who knows, when that new leaf unfurls I might . . . ," but of course Adriana had no idea how long the leaf would take to unfold. And with the heart of that palm in the courtyard Adriana invented a new pastime, the game of making plans for herself in a future she was trying to give a familiar, protective face.

Arturo has joined them. They enter, and it is not a house but three rooms conjoined as if to make one immense room. Against the walls, on tall shelves made of dark wood, are hundreds, perhaps thousands of boxes; new cardboard and wooden boxes, large and small, piled up according to size. Did she search for them? She later asked herself if she had searched expressly for them, because on one shelf she saw dozens upon dozens just like "that one." Light brown, oblong, just like the box filled with wedding almonds! Adriana blushed and could not take her eyes off those boxes.

Seated on invisible stools were five women in black full skirts, their arms bare to the elbow. With a quick turn of the wrist, they were wrapping small jars and placing them in cardboard boxes. On each jar was written ORANGE BLOSSOM HONEY, but she did not understand. The women cast indifferent, cold and obstinate glances at her mother. Adriana realized with discomfort that her mother had opened herself up to stares like that, and she moved closer to her. She saw a telephone on the wall. She had never seen one like it, a rectangular box with a hook on one side holding a long receiver, in three parts instead of one curved piece. In that city there was no one for her to call, not her grandparents or any of her classmates from school.

They passed through other rooms with vaulted ceilings painted with flowers or other scenery. There was one (her mother pointed it out to her, as she did not usually look up at ceilings) with a painting of a banister that lined the walls. In the center was a sky with clouds, birds, and butterflies, and overlooking the banister were seven little angels. It was the most beautiful ceiling she had ever seen. Low to the ground and in a private home, it seemed more beautiful even than those she had seen in churches. But at the time, Adriana didn't even think of churches.

She even liked the floors. They were made of tiles painted with a floral motif, shinier and more colorful than any she had seen, except the ones in Palazzo Venezia, which were smaller. Indeed, those large, square tiles were painted, but in the center of the floor, and in places of heavy traffic, they were worn down to a soft, opaque red, the pale red of terra-cotta, and she liked that, too. Air warmed by the sun streamed through the tall windows, and the windowsills were so deep that a woman was ironing on one of them. But the long windows with their deep sills did not resemble the bay window in Palazzo Venezia, the alcove where one day she had finally seen the Cupola del Gesù. Such open spaces in a home — she realized it now — held a surprising element of the familiar for her, as if from a dream world or a fairy tale; could they be unconscious memories of Naples? This, then, was the bright and sonorous world from which Arturo had come. He was a disruptive stranger in their house in Prati, a place that immediately seemed too small and humble to contain him and all his charm. In her first house, well-known and beloved voices had only harmonious, valid things to say, but here the characters were silent, like the women rustling papers as they wrapped jars of orange blossom honey, or else they made surreal pronouncements with high, strangely lilting voices, *a most beautiful mountain . . . we have a great appreciation for it.*

She met Stanka, who smelled of butter and sugar and biscotti. She had shiny braids held with bone hairpins just like Nonna Matilde's, and yet the two were so different. Stanka (what a name! it would be years before she realized it was not *stanca*, "tired," but a diminutive of Stanislanka) and the Zia Costanza, along with her husband, called "the Zio," lived on the building's upper floor.

The apartment had a makeshift air, with small, low-ceilinged rooms, thin, sometimes curving walls, and frameless doors with pretty handles. It was a house full of light, with two balconies whose undulating floors were also made of painted tiles, each one different — mismatched and very old. "It's an old building," Mamma had said, "from the seventeenth century. You will like it, you'll see." She remembered that her mother had spoken of the house, not the people. The balconies' walls were cracked, stained, and crumbling. In the middle of the one they called the great balcony was a mysterious square covered by a black grate, and underneath it was the skylight in the stairway. Adriana had never seen a skylight from above.

On that first morning so rich in events for Adriana, a festive breakfast of tea and Stanka's pastries was waiting for them on the upper floor. They were still in the apartment of the Zio and Zia when a young girl burst through the door. She was homely, with a flattened face and large mouth. Stray wisps of hair were escaping from two thin braids. She hurriedly took off her coat and threw it on a chair, but it fell to the floor. "Laura, pick up that coat this instant!" scolded Stanka. The girl tore off her black school smock as if it were on fire. She stared at Adriana and asked, "Aren't you peeved?" and Adriana did not know what to reply. The girl continued, "You *should* be peeved, what with your mother getting remarried. Did you sleep on the postal? In the lower or the upper berth? I always want the upper berth, otherwise I won't go. Because we take a trip every year, with the Mamma, the Papa, and Stanka." (Even with *Mamma* and *Papa* they used an article on that island!) "Come on, I'll show you the kittens, the mother cat won't like it when she sees us, but she has to learn. Don't touch her, though, or she'll scratch. Look what she done to me!" she said, holding out a plump hand covered with scratches. (She said, *Look what she done*!)

"Come on," she said again. She took Adriana by the hand and pulled her into the kitchen. "The kittens are in the woodbox," she explained. One of the walls in the kitchen had a small door midway up, running about a meter from the floor up to the ceiling. The girl dragged a stool across the floor, climbed up on it, and opened the door. Inside, light filtered between the beams supporting the roof, and there was a draft rich with the scent of old wood and mold. Laura put one knee on the edge, then the other, and Adriana followed. The cat hissed as they looked in on the kittens, or what little they could see. Whispering so as not to disturb the cat, Laura said, "Aren't they cute?" This, too, was a new word for Adriana; not that she hadn't ever heard it, she had just never used it. "In my opinion, they're even cuter than the ones Stanka boiled last year. She says they ran away, as if kittens this small could run off!"

"They could," murmured Adriana, but the girl did not hear. Or perhaps Adriana had not yet uttered a word. And the other girl explained, still whispering as they crouched there with their hands on their knees, that the only way to keep Stanka from boiling these kittens was to outsmart her and find owners for them as soon as possible. "Indeed, in my opinion" — a girl so young who actually said *in my opinion*! — "let's do this: you take one, and we'll give it to the Zia Marta, since she's a signora who lives in another house, and that way Stanka won't be able to say a thing."

The Zia Marta! That was her mamma, and no one had ever called her Zia before. Not only had she become an aunt, she was the Zia! Although the places seemed inexplicably familiar in this new land, or at least they were just as she had imagined them, the people and their way of speaking made her feel very much like a stranger.

They were two full months for Marta, those final months of 1937, and rich in memories. There was her marriage, of course — she had worn a splendid skirt and jacket (the word *tailleur* was not yet in use) of warm gray with a hint of red in the weave, and she looked beautiful — but there was also her new position. At first "temporarily assigned," then "permanently transferred due to marriage," Marta Canterno, newly Signora F., had taken her post at the National Library of Palermo. The National Library was, and is, a large, long eighteenth-century building on the Corso Vittorio Emanuele, on the right coming up from the sea, immediately before the piazza and the cathedral and almost directly across from the building where Arturo's family had its antiquarian shop.

The building has three stories and a rectangular courtyard, with porticoes on two floors. Of these, the long side on the Corso is the Reading Room. Under the portico on the right-hand side a baroque staircase rises in four shaded flights.

Marta was the assistant librarian, Class A (those with a doctorate), working under the director. The latter, a young Florentine, entrusted her with the care and oversight of the Consultation Room where, as was customary, rare volumes were available for reference, but only in that room, and only to scholars approved by the directorial staff.

There a half-light reigned, and one could breathe air scented of wood and wax, parchments and old ink, which for Marta were the scents of thought, prayer, and the union of mind and spirit. It was the same air and silence as in the Casanatense. But the silence of the Palermo library was all the more precious, secluded from the hot lights and dusty air, from the excessive noise of a turbulent, confused city, as compared with the tranquil Roman atmosphere of Sant'Ignazio. This air of Palermo, enclosed in tight quarters and illuminated only by the golden sunlight from outdoors, resembled the air once breathed in *Pardi*'s room, in his forest of books written in all the languages in the world. Thanks to heavy drapes of raw cotton, that air, too, had been safe from the mild but perpetual tumult of footsteps, singing, peddlers' cries, and children playing in the streets.

Thus, by way of the senses — the most primordial being those of smell and touch, which help lost cubs return to their lair, leading them back to their mothers — Marta was finding her own nest in the library. Yes, thanks to tactile sensations, too. With fingers accustomed to ivory and ebony piano keys, to gut strings pressed against the ebony of a cello, she felt the texture of ancient papers and touched sheaves of parchment with sensuous pleasure. Odors from her past returned to her, of pigeon coops and Stelianì's *kollooras*, of camels with their bouncing gait on the dusty roads, and of the mill water on the nearby banks of the Mahmudiyah.

A beautiful room, entirely lined with wooden shelves, and with only four reading tables. In the most private section were groups of manuscripts on parchment, tied in bundles, all formerly belonging to the Benedictines of San Martino delle Scale Monastary, and then transferred to Palermo pursuant to the law of 1866, which assigned possession and ownership of estates once owned by religious communities and organizations to the new kingdom of Italy. This "historical" event had never bothered Marta, who was familiar with manuscripts at the Casanatense that had also "passed to the Italian state," but without changing location; they had always remained in the same place, part of the collection of Cardinal Casanate and the Dominicans of the Minerva. Ancient codices, Bibles, Gospels, and breviaries — objects from the kingdom of the spirit where money is a laughable value — belonged, in her view, to everyone and to no one. But it now seemed to her that these manuscripts of the Benedictines of San Martino delle Scale had been stolen from the church and held prisoner by the state. She didn't even dare to touch them.

Then she did touch them. First she undid the ribbons that bound the smallest packet of those holy volumes. SAN MARTINO DELLE SCALE FUND was written in ink on a sheet of paper poorly pasted to the shelf. Some startled silverfish ran away, frightened; insects, she well knew, that avidly devoured old paper, glue, and parchment. She moved more packages, and more insects fled. Someone needed to protect the manuscripts, she thought. *I must do it*, she told herself, and her reticence to touch the manuscripts had disappeared. *They are entrusted to me.* She called an attendant, had him bring rags and petroleum, and the two of them set to work. After closing hours, she worked alone.

❖

At home, during the long hours of night, her thoughts returned to those manuscripts imprisoned in "her" Consultation Room. Her baptism in the great Italian illuminations — those noble decorations in holy texts, handwritten one at a time by monks before the advent of the printing press — had come at the Casanatense Library. But then her marriage had been going under, swept away by hurricane Arturo, and her life seemed to have exploded, bereft of all serenity. Now everything had been achieved, everything had been conquered, albeit at a price that caused great pain and created an invisible but lurid stain that made her mother weep: excommunication. A fact that could not be erased. But Marta's life was now this, and this would forever be her library. These were her manuscripts to protect, to make sure their lives exceeded hers, like children, but older than she. It was a privilege to touch and know them.

The following day Marta carefully untied the ribbon holding a stack of parchment papers together — an unbound manuscript. It was small, barely fifteen centimeters high and ten wide, but it contained many pages, the last of which was numbered 148. The text, in Latin, included a calendar (written in black and red), the Office of the Holy Spirit, the Office of the Passion, the Mass of the Virgin, the four Gospels, and the Office of the Virgin.

There was a single illumination — a square, about five centimeters per side — containing a decorated letter D at the beginning of a chapter. But the first page of almost every other chapter was missing. Those pages, evidently adorned by miniatures, had been taken away by an "unscrupulous collector," as Marta would write: that is, a thief. The missing pages had all left their imprint on the preceding (or following) page with which they had been in contact. And that proved that the theft had taken place early on, when the illuminations were still fresh, although there had been enough time for the humid air to permeate the pages and create an imprint by transferring a bit of pigment and gold foil from one page to the next.

But that was not the only thing she noticed. Marta could tell immediately, from the calligraphy and style of the written work as well as the colors both vibrant and delicate of the remaining illumination, that she had a Franco-Flemish manuscript in hand. The small but perfect picture inside the initial D was of a devotional scene. Three monks — two tall, one short and fat — with tonsures encircled by black crowns of hair were singing by the light of four candelabra as they read from a large book resting on a catafalque. Meanwhile, four nuns — two standing and two kneeling — were reading from another book.

After admiring the illumination, it was the lettering on the pages of the Latin text that captured the scholar's attention. The style was clearly northern, fine and closely spaced (she recognized it immediately as French gothic from the first half of the fifteenth century). But several pages in a different hand were interspersed throughout the manuscript. The writing on these parchment pages was larger and more round, less angular and tightly spaced. Indeed it was gothic script, but written by a southern Benedictine monk. A Sicilian monk. A Benedictine from San Martino! He had made the additions, and they were not in Latin but in the Sicilian vernacular. And they were *different* prayers.

In reading those additional letters Marta experienced a profound and genuine set of emotions, far more than just the excitement of a scholar. Not only weren't the prayers in the customary Latin — like those by the French monk — they were in Sicilian vernacular and they were meant to be read by a woman! They were written for a nun or, more likely, for a lady of such high station as to allow her the ownership of an illuminated manuscript. But she had not been able to read Latin. In order for that woman, that signora, to recite them, a Benedictine from the time of Antonello had written the prayers out in the language of King Enzo and Emperor Frederick, the mother tongue from which standard Italian descended. A language still spoken by monks and other cultured people in the fifteenth century, as the moving prayers that Marta held in her hands testified. A language deemed not unworthy of being written and useful for addressing God in prayer.

They were communion prayers, versions of those attributed to Saint Thomas Aquinas, which as Marta knew, appear in the Roman missal. The prayers Marta held in her hands were writtern *per una peccatrichi*, for a woman sinner. The last one, which referred to the Panem Angelorum, the Bread of Angels of the Eucharist, ended with:

> . . . *as it must be and is necessary for my soul.*

Now Marta, the scholar, wept inside. She, the sinner, could not partake of communion anymore. It was no longer allowed because of the event — that divine gift — that had unsettled her and brought her there, to a new life, a new city, and a new library, at once pulling and pushing her. She knew it well, it was the hand of God that had pulled her and pushed her there, inexorably, inevitably. No, it was not fair. *But what is?* she asked herself.

". . . as it must be and is necessary for my soul." She had been excommunicated. She was not even worthy of reading or saying that prayer. Once again she could see the procession of white heads moving toward the piazza of Saint Catherine, led by Père Quilici. Or perhaps not, she didn't see it; this is only rhetoric, gossip, and imaginings. Is the soul a figment of the imagination? What about God? Can the church — the Church! — excommunicate, deny the sacraments and expel from the community someone who has loved so deeply? Someone who has been pushed and dragged by God's own hand? Justice will come, but meanwhile . . . The soul of that other sinner had been saved. Yes, hers. Meanwhile, time runs on and disappears, and her mother, Antonia, innocent of everything, continues to weep and pray as she has always done, although for other sorrows and never for something like this: the excommunication of her own daughter!

May Marta forgive me, if she can, these fantasies, these inferences. The bibliographical note in the journal *Aevum* (1940) of the Catholic University of Milan reads, "Two prayers in Sicilian vernacular in a Franco-Flemish manuscript."

Palermo, 1938
My school was in the building across the street, on the other side of the Corso; the entrance was behind the cathedral's apse.

"Arceri, Arena, Ballo, Battaglia, Bologna . . . ," and the roll call continued down to my last name, which was only uttered there. In Palermo that name was mine, not my father's, and I didn't know enough to be happy about it. It made me feel defenseless and alone. And I never talked to my classmates about *my father*, or *my mother*. I rarely spoke with my classmates; I felt they were fortunate and they perhaps felt I was haughty with my subjunctive and conditional and past perfect tenses. My desk mate invited me to study at her house. I went, and we did our Latin together, in a study with dark, barrister's bookcases and yellow curtains. When my mother asked me what my friend's house was like (permission to go to this classmate's house had been discussed at length with Arturo), I replied, "It's normal." But a few days later when my classmate said, "Today I'll come to your house," I blushed and answered, "No, not today." After two days of suffering I asked her to come, that very day or another, but I had to warn her that I didn't have a house with stairs or an elevator, but a door that closed and that was all. "And the door won't have my last name on it, but a different one," I told her, and when I explained why, I felt nauseous, and only later did I realize that I should have kept quiet. The girl remained silent for a moment, and then she said, "Well, then I won't go there to study with you." So friendships with my classmates always remained inside the schoolyard walls.

"In my opinion, you should hate everybody here. You can tell me, because as soon as I have the money, I'm leaving this place." Laura was playing ball and her words matched the rhythm of the ball bouncing on the wall. She continued, "You know . . . the story . . . of the wedding almonds . . . when . . . your mother . . . was acting crazy . . . because they sent you . . . the wedding almonds?" "The wedding almonds . . . ," I said, voiceless. Laura threw the ball on the chair and sat by me on the step that led to the balcony. "Listen to me. When the Zio Arturo and your mother got married, and she didn't wear a white veil, just a skirt suit, they gave out wedding almonds anyhow, even to the women who do the packaging. Then Stanka made packages of almonds to ship to Austria and Switzerland, because, you see, we have friends there. I don't know them well, but when they visit I have to greet them in the parlor, which is a big pain, and they say that I have grown so much, and there's nothing I can do to get out of it. They all see to it, even Stanka, as a matter of fact she's first in line, and she bakes cookies just like at Christmas. But my father, no, truly, he really doesn't care if I greet them; it bores him, too, in my opinion. So Stanka made packages for the relatives in Taormina and all the others, and my mamma addressed them and she even sent one to you, one of the packages, which your mamma said they weren't supposed to do, but she didn't know that they had mailed it, and it seems it was your papa who wrote to tell her, and that's how she found out, and she was crying and saying 'I'll never forgive myself' and things of that sort. In my opinion you cannot not forgive yourself, besides she hadn't done anything, and then, after she and the Zio Arturo were married, what did it matter that they sent you wedding almonds? Better almonds than nothing, in my opinion. But your mamma, wasn't she a musician in the theater, but then she stopped playing?"

That was Laura. She talked without stopping, skipping from one topic to another, and liked to say *in my opinion*. With her, I didn't have time to stop and be miserable. I also thought Laura was the only one who wasn't acting out a role. Or was it because she was just six years old? I loved her, Laura.

Once I'm ready for school I come to the table for breakfast, and Arturo is already there. "Tell me, how far have your read?" he wants to know. I tell him about the book I'm reading; he was the one who gave it to me, and he knows the story, surely, because he has read everything, and the memory of it moves him. So he picks up the story and I am enchanted by his wonderful storytelling. He is even better than the book, and when he tells a story it is all the more fascinating and rich in hidden details. A story told by Arturo cannot be forgotten! Even though I remember hearing in Rome that Arturo is "nothing but a shopkeeper," I admire and love him. Why? I wonder. Perhaps because of his ability to tell stories that move me so. Is it because of that? Or because of my mother? Or because he, too, is a musician? Or because he can recite poems by heart, even in English and German and French?

A *shopkeeper!* In Arturo's work and throughout the entire building Adriana now sees fascinating, far-reaching links with marvelous, romantic places she has never seen. America, Australia, England! Where unknown, strange people, dressed who knows how (she would never go there, never!) wait for orange blossom honey wrapped by the women packers. And they wait for Sardinian donkeys (surely no one else ships live donkeys) for their children, furry toys "that eat and poop," says Laura. So, too, her bowl had been something of a toy and not the genuine article. And so was the invisible flame of the gas burner in the meadow at Monte Mario. The red scooter stayed in Rome. It was a strange scooter, different from all the others, with just one pedal to press while standing on the foot plate. Laura has a wooden scooter, small and very old, and she rides it in circles on the terrace with her little braids flying. Adriana would like to tell her about her own scooter, so large and strange and difficult to ride — difficult because it won't go if you're touching the ground. But then she thinks Laura wouldn't understand because she wouldn't know how to describe it . . . and besides, what does it matter? Laura will never see it, her scooter, and now she is almost ashamed of it. Adriana herself won't ever see it again, and she feels, more profoundly than ever, that she won't see any of the rest, either. Nothing, ever again, of her old life. But along with her newfound suffering a sense of relief, of liberation has sprung up, and a new sense of guilt. Yes, she is thinking of her father on the Gianicolo as he shows her the city. Her poor papa! On the contrary, in July, along with a load of her mother's things, the scooter arrives, red and metallic. And she and Laura take to the wide, dusty sidewalks of the marina under Stanka's watchful eye.

❖

Mamma does not talk to me about him and that does not displease me, by now. Instead it is Arturo who asks me, "Have you written your papa?" and that makes me blush. "Let me see." At first that indiscretion offends me. What's it to him, Arturo — I have never called him Zio, what kind of foolishness would that be? — what's it to him whether or not I write my father? But after glancing at it he says, "What a stingy little letter! Take another sheet of paper and start over. Tell him about you, about what you do, your school, the walk you took yesterday . . . I think your father will want to receive more than just 'dear Papa I am well' from you. Go on, you'll make him happy." I return to my room, offended, but I do take another sheet of paper and start again. This time I write something, but against my will because I am ashamed, although Arturo doesn't know it, or perhaps he does. I am ashamed to say who I've been with, and to say "I did" instead of "we did"; I am ashamed to tell him about my scooter rides with Laura by the seashore, and the funicular to Monreale, so full of mystery. I am ashamed of enjoying simple, childish pleasures, and of revealing these things to my father, who wants me to grow up as soon as possible. Simply, I don't want to tell my father that I like being in Palermo very much.

"Did you rewrite it? Let me see," says Arturo, and I reluctantly give him the letter. But he doesn't read it. "Three pages," he says. "Good. See, you had plenty of things to tell him. He'll be much happier, your papa." And I am not ashamed of my letter anymore.

Returns

"I will come later," said Mamma. But when, when? Arturo accompanies me. Zia Margherita is waiting at the Stazione Termini. I see her from the train window, but at first I pretend I haven't seen her. Once I'm off the train I let myself be embraced. "My, how you've grown! Look how tall you are, why, you're taller than I am!" Immediately Zia Margherita's voice, her perfume — which I never really noticed before, and which I certainly haven't thought about in all those months — plunges me back into the past. The train did not stop by the Roman ruins as it once did, but quite a distance before them. There is quite a commotion at the station, and we have to walk a long way to reach the bus — the old MP. "Look here, what a disaster, just look what a mess they've made of the piazza. Who knows what they're aiming to do, hmmph!" mutters Zia Margherita as we walk amid the calls of the porters and the chatter of the crowd. The chatter of "before," the same as always, the way it should be. "Soon you'll tell me all about it, baby, soon," says Zia Margherita, and never before have I realized how beautifully she speaks. Or is she perhaps overdoing it a bit just to please me, with her lovely *r*'s, her effortless, perfect vowels, and the consonants falling so softly after them? Suddenly I am very content.

Then, as I look out through the window of the MP (which means Macao–Prati, Papa taught me), I rediscover the dimension of "my" streets: here in Piazza Cavour are "my" sidewalks, here the white borders of travertine (*lapis tiburtinus*) with the crescent-shaped joints. We turn onto Via Cicerone and I am met with scents I haven't thought about in months, yet they have waited patiently for me. Now I am walking in front, with Zia Margherita behind me, full of questions, and then Arturo. Tired from so much thinking, I do not listen to them, only breathe and look.

Adriana turns the corner at the fountain, and partway up Via Gioacchino Belli a car is stopped, pulled over to the left side of the road. Upon recognizing it, she is momentarily stunned, wishing it were not true. But indeed it is her father's Topolino. She can't tell through the car's tiny window if there is someone inside, but she slows her pace and when the door opens from inside and no one steps out, she begins to run. Inside is his smile, his hand holding the door open. She kisses him, but he says softly, "Go on, go say good-bye," and she hears the emotion in her father's voice. She pulls away then, and steps back a few paces, slowly. Zia Margherita walks up with Adriana's suitcase, but Arturo, no. Arturo has disappeared. Adriana is not capable of understanding, of saying, *Where is Arturo? I want to tell him good-bye.* Zia Margherita is still dragging the bag when her father reaches her, and he takes it, saying, "Thank you, and good-bye," and Zia Margherita vanishes, too. Her father talks on and on, and he is happy, yet he is so much uglier and older than she remembers! She is silent and her papa's stream of words finally dries up. They reach the Viale del Re and he lifts a hand from the steering wheel and caresses her head. "My poor Adriana, what can we do . . . You will learn . . . We will learn . . ." Once again his tenderness is embarrassing, but perhaps it is his way of offering forgiveness for offenses unwittingly commited. "Wait until you see how happy your grandparents are to see you, poor old ones. Nonno Già has aged, he had a bad fall not long ago. I wrote a bit about it in my letters to you, but I don't know if you understood. You don't really answer my letters. You didn't even answer — not that I wished you to, I know you can't really understand what it means — when I wrote you that they made me director of the National Gallery of Ancient Art at the Palazzo Corsini . . . I don't know if you remember, but I did tell you that it was the first national gallery of Italy, and it was founded by my mentor, Adolfo Venturi . . . do you remember? Well, anyway, there are many paintings inside . . . surely you remember the gallery, you went there with me several times. One of these days I'll take you there, would you like that?"

But she is lost in her thoughts of Nonno Già, and it frightens her to know she will find him changed. She has not thought much about him, or about Nonna Matilde and Lucia. Now she wishes she would never get to Monteverde, but they are already going up Via Dandolo, then Viale Glorioso with its streetcar rails, and then Porta San Pancrazio and the fountain the same as ever. At the gate her father says, "What are you doing, aren't you getting out?" and he is already whistling as usual, and here comes Lucia, walking down the stairs with her bosom bouncing under her checkered flannel dress (a housemaid's uniform, made for her by Nonna Matilde), and she gives her a kiss on each cheek without any further fuss. Her grandmother is waiting at the top of the stairs with a broad smile and her thin arms outstretched. Behind her, Nonno Giacinto seems to her the same as before, only a bit smaller, just like all of them, even her father. She smells the scents emanating from the house and at last she feels a sense of cheer. Nonna and Lucia have prepared a big meal for her, she who survived all the adventures of her trip, as well as her return home.

But that evening in bed, she is unsettled by thoughts of her mother and by something else: she did not say good-bye to Arturo. The fact that he had chosen to slip away does not appease her remorse, and it soon becomes a sourse of resentment. Days go by, and the resentment becomes — once again there is that need for order — approval for what she had done: she taught "them" a lesson. But when Zia Margherita — days later, indeed many days later — dares to telephone and tell her that Arturo has departed and bids her farewell, she almost hates her — her poor, innocent aunt — in a new burst of regret and love for the man she wishes she did not cherish so deeply.

A long, lazy, drowsy summer. A summer filled with boredom. She likes to go down the escarpment leading to Scarpone's orchard and take refuge from the sun. Her grandfather's expression has changed. He comes to the kitchen doorway but does not enter; instead he stands and stares blankly at Nonna Matilde, as if from a great distance. He stops in the streets and stares in the same manner. Yet with an almost morbid diligence, Nonno Giacinto never misses the evening news on the radio.

Just as a dog experiences joy or fear depending on the tone and gestures of its master, Adriana looks to her father, who is standing at the window. The sound of his words still hangs in the air, frightening. She feels the same knot growing in her stomach as in the early years, the same dull pressure telling her she is about to vomit. She feels small and vulnerable, as she had when in Annita's presence, as well as responsible for creating such unease. Because now, as he has never done before, her father has said, "Pray." His profile, the contours of his white shirt against the window, is illuminated by the sun. And Adriana pours all of her anguish into her prayer, whispering, "Please, God, make them get back together." The ancient incantation has come by itself, for those are the words she whispered so many times on the solitary landing of the stairway on Via Tacito. But if she once fell to sleep crying with those words on her lips, now they roll around in her head like an annoying refrain. She understands this, and the wave of nausea rises again with her rejection of that request that no longer applies, and out of fear. Pray! But if God had not listened to her prayers for such a small thing involving so few people — so insignificant, as far as He was concerned — why would he listen when the prayer was for something so much bigger, and for so many people? War! Papa said, "Pray that there won't be a war." Let others pray, if they wish. Petulant, Adriana refused to talk to God. Let someone else pray!

My father's flat, which during the winter months I had known only by night, had always seemed cold and sad. But now that I was there by day I found it was actually quite cheerful. As soon as you entered it smelled of chocolate. "Life has dealt me its share of blows. But I like chocolate, so I buy it. Eat, my Adriana, take as much as you wish, for this is your house, too. In all your life, never let yourself be without chocolate!" The chocolates were kept in a flowered porcelain candy bowl with a domed lid, a gift from who knows who, but a recent one, because it hadn't come from the house in Prati. Sometimes there were so many chocolates the lid rested on them and could not close.

Early mornings my father made coffee and set to work at a desk covered with papers and photographs of paintings and works of architecture. At seven thirty he made himself another pot of coffee, and came to my bed with his old *cabarè*, a tray containing the Neapolitan coffeemaker just upturned, two coffee demitasses, and the sugar bowl without its lid. He placed the tray on a nearby chair, then sat on the bed and talked, tapping the coffeepot from time to time. I followed his words, but my mind wandered to other thoughts as well: that the object Annita had called the *cabarè* was a "glove tray" in Palermo; that my father had his coffee at the foot of my bed — because it pleased him, of course, but also so that I would one day retain a memory of it — and then I would look at his smile and listen to his words with sharp attention. "A drop for you, too, because you're practically grown up by now, no harm will come of it, although I'll bet your mother, down there, doesn't let you have any." I would blush and remain silent. I always drank that bit of coffee, although I would have preferred not to. Then we would make the beds. "I'll have you know that out of all the women I've known, and I've known a few, only my mother — your Nonna, that is — truly knows how to make a bed. You can trust in her — not only for that — and me. Pull, come on, pull, and don't worry about the sheet. We have plenty of them anyhow, plenty, and when they're worn out, we'll buy more, don't worry. They've made me start over with more than just linens, in my life!" What a pity those hours were ruined by a continuous stream of offensive comments about that other life of mine. Why did my father have to spoil what could have been precious moments of intimacy between us with his flimsy, overgeneralized, misguided "philosophy"? No, I could feel no compassion for his unhappiness then. And as I had once done on the Gianicolo, I thought, *Isn't he ashamed of himself?*

I was even tired of the fear of war, because every day my father would buy a copy of *Il Piccolo* from the newsstand at Porta San Pancrazio, and then he would read it in the sun and swear, and every day Nonno Già would remain glued to the radio all day long, always listening to "the same old thing," as Lucia used to say. So in the hottest hours of the day I would stretch out on my belly on the red sofa and read back issues of *Domenica del Corriere*, one after another. There were at least ten piles of them, tied with string. I first searched each issue for an "Unbelievable but True" feature, but these were rare. The few that I found I read over and over again, as if in secret, ready to turn the page should anyone enter the room. And yet I'm sure no one would have prohibited me from reading them! What lovely stories they were! The most striking story told of two men who lived in the same house, but they could never meet each other for they were actually the same person. Naturally, they weren't ever supposed to see each other. At the end of the story the narrator — who claimed the story was true and included his name and address so as to be "available to the public for any additional clarification" — forced them to meet, and with a scream of pain one of the men faded away and disappeared . . .

Adriana shivered happily. Years later when she read Dostoyevsky and Conrad she would recall that scene, just as she had imagined it on Nonna Matilde's red sofa.

And in that house shaded with the green shutters painted by Nonno Già, she read serialized fiction, transferring each edition from one pile to another while Nonna and Lucia did their housework and Nonno read peacefully on the balcony where it was cool. But Papa would say, "Why do you stay inside with your grandparents all day? Go out with your friends. And come see me at the gallery sometime. I would enjoy it, and you might even learn something."

I went, and the cool air smelling of paint reminded me of years past. But in his office I felt I was a nuisance to him; he sat at his big desk and didn't have time for me. "Walk around," he would say."Go look at the paintings." I didn't care about the paintings. I didn't know where to put my hands, didn't know what length and rhythm to give my steps in the rooms where even the custodians intimidated me as they said hello. Then my father, without raising his eyes from his papers and books, would ask, "So, tell me, what did you see? What did you understand? Tell me what you liked most, and why." *Why!* I didn't know how to answer, and couldn't wait to be gone. "So?" he would ask after a while, but as if he had already forgotten. "Come here, look!" he would say, holding a photograph, "Look, this was painted by the same painter who . . ."

No, it didn't work. Her father, who wanted her to grow up quickly and espoused his philosophies of coffeepots and chocolates and how to shine shoes, was able to say only a few clumsy words about his one true passion, painting. And Adriana found herself making painful, heart-sickening comparisons between the "other man's" fascinating way of speaking about the things that moved him most, and her father's reserve: a sense of propriety ancient and genuine and holy, she well knew, but that fortold further suffering, and silenced and embarrassed them both. However, when that sad father of hers appeared cheerful and playful among his friends and made them laugh, she was torn by jealousy. Like the time the "grown-ups" put on a skit in Santa Severa at the home of the Ceccarellis. He had worn a shirt with starched cuffs jutting out from an odd black coat, and he sang — in a surprisingly mellifluous voice — a long song that she had never heard, which started with, "We were once so in love . . ." How could he dare? How could he show such indifference? She was sure she would never forgive him.

A lovely summer indeed. I would go to Via Tacito to see Nonna Antonia. Silent and unhappy visits. Visits that tore me apart and left me feeling miserably homeless. No one in Monteverde ever talked with me about those visits, and I carefully avoided any reference to them. And neither Zia Margherita nor Nonna Antonia ever talked about the house on Via Spallanzani. I asked about it, but my aunt responded in a strange, frightened voice, "Don't ever mention that house again, never again, understand?" Meanwhile, thanks to the application her sister had given her months earlier, and the exam she had passed, Zia Margherita was now employed in Class C at the Casanatense Library where her sister had worked.

I went out one afternoon to do the shopping with Nonna Matilde, and when we returned we found Nonno Giacinto standing at the top of the stairs waiting for us. "My Lord, Giacinto, what is it?" said Nonna, frightened, for the old man seemed drained, and it looked as though he was about to tumble down the stairs. Instead he was laughing merrily, with his loose, decayed teeth and his receding hairline — how his son resembled him — and with his voice cracking involuntarily as he called out, "It's not going to happen! It seems it's really not going to happen! The war, dear

Tilde, the war! It looks like they've reached an accord. It's a miracle!" He descended two stairs toward us and she walked up to him, and he embraced her awkwardly, such was his excitement. The radio was broadcasting the commotion but he looked as though he'd never pay attention to it again, after all those months of tuning in. I ran to the kitchen to be alone with the thought weighing heavily on me: *And I didn't even ask for it!* My soul blushed before God for not having joined the others in prayer, the prayer he had granted, the miracle. I, who was still asking for the same "small thing for a few people," and by then I was asking without faith. In the shadow of that remorse, the Monaco Peace Accord offered no relief.

That relief would not last long for the rest of the world, either. At the ministry they did not put much trust in the Monaco Peace Accord, at least not right away, and they made contingency plans to protect and safeguard the artistic patrimony of the nation: the churches, the museums, the art collections of so many royal palaces. And the Italian patrimony was much richer than it had once been, ever since the state and not the convents and religious institutions had come into possession of so many artistic treasures. It was a commitment required by all once the winds of war — as the saying went — had begun to blow. Danzig was in 1939. The Second World War was beginning.

In October the director of the National Library in Palermo received a circular from the ministry asking him to make immediate plans for the transfer of the most precious and important volumes to a secure location. These plans were to be reported to and discussed with the director general. A professional visit to Rome was authorized toward that end, as it was advisable that comunication with the *camerata* director general take place in person and with the greatest secrecy. Every letter from the ministry ended, above the signature, with the set phrase: "Long live the King! Long live Il Duce!" The functionary's closing was an enthusiastic and clear "*Eia, eia, alalà.*"

The fact that those sounds had no meaning was certainly a good thing.

In the same mailing the director of the National Library of Palermo, Dr. A. G., a Florentine reserve officer, was also called up for a period of military training in the field. Dr. G. was to appear within four days at his district command. After a sleepless night, the director called Marta Canterno to his office. She entered his office, giving the obligatory Roman salute. The director invited her to sit down and gave her the letter from the ministry to read. She read it, wrinkled her brow, and made no comment. Then he handed her the other missive, the call to defend his country. She read it, made no comment, but stared at him with distress in her eyes. "Oh, my God!" escaped from her lips.

"As you can see, Dr. Canterno" — he used the requisite Fascist *voi* — "we have a job to do. As you can also see, I must leave. I charge you with this job, as the first in rank after me. You are a woman, but you do not lack competence and ability."

She bowed her head and murmured thanks. Blushing, she hid her fear behind her modesty. But she had no choice. She would be going to Rome in his place, with an official letter of introduction for the director general. She did not know who the present director general was. Dr. Canterno remained with the director for more than an hour, discussing plans for protecting the most precious works — everything conceived, prepared, and organized in that brief span of time. Immediately, the next day in fact, they would go together to Monreale, site of the ancient Benedictine cloister, to speak with the archbishop in person, if possible.

The following Monday, under the director's authorization, Marta left for Rome on a Tyrrenian ship, the old *Città di Tunisi*. In Rome she immediately went to Via Tacito, and the house seemed larger, sad, and very cold. Her father greeted her with a smile, but she wasn't sure he recognized her. She kissed her mother, but did not see her sister, who was at work in the library at that hour, at the Casanatense of course, and then she left at once. She took the CP (Colosseo–Prati) in Piazza Cavour and got off at Palazzo Venezia.

The offices of the director general were in Via del Plebiscito, in the Palazzo Doria. The director general was Ettore Apollonj, her beloved Professor! She had not known this, something unthinkable for anyone else, as she was not interested in bureaucracy and never remembered the positions held by others. The pupil was deeply moved to find herself in front of her Professor in that role; moved and reassured. And the assignment that had caused such fear and loss of sleep immediately seemed much easier.

When she left the Palazzo Doria after meeting with her former teacher, Marta was excited and flushed in the face. She was happy. Perhaps much work lay ahead, and not just in the library. Perhaps. Because if things between Germany and England and France could be settled — but how? and alas, now there was talk of Russia, too — or if Italy could remain outside that mess, as might still be hoped, nothing would be necessary. It was only in the worst case that she would need to be ready. She felt, and not for the first time, called on to accept a challenge. As the Professor had said, it was necessary — and yes, it was her responsibility — to make arrangements, not only with the Benedictine authorities in Monreale to shelter a good number of precious volumes underground, but also with at least one other episcopal seat, one that was even farther from the city. And secret.

It had begun to rain. When she boarded the CP to return to Piazza Cavour and home, Marta was possessed by a familiar and powerful sensation: pride. She would be taking part in a great plan. She, yes, she who had been excommunicated, would be working with the Benedictines and maybe even the Jesuits. Perhaps. Should it become necessary . . . In her heart of hearts Marta found herself hoping that the dreaded intervention of Italy in the war would indeed take place. And that secret and insufficiently ashamed hope kept growing, for when certain winds rise up and begin to blow even the finest souls, even the innocent and the unaware, can be sucked into the vortex.

Adriana returned to Rome for Christmas, a snowy but sad Christmas. Along with the odor of mold, her father's icy and inhospitable little house still contained a faint scent of chocolate from the porcelain candy dish now long since empty. They felt cold and told each other without complaining. There was an intimacy between them, and her father was now more serene and cheerful in his own house than in the house of her grandparents. But Adriana was again counting the days until her return to Palermo, and those days, although few, felt like many.

"Such freezing hands, my poor little cricket!" In the doorway to Palazzo Corsini her father stopped to talk with the porter. There were two staircases, and he went up the one on the right. In the center, beyond the entrance gate, was the open air of the garden, but little light passed through the opaque glass to the stairway. "Run, warm yourself up!" said Papa, but she did not feel like running, just as she hadn't felt like it in Piazza Cavour the time she was there with Zia Margherita. Her father said, "Stay with me, if you like that, but I think you'd be happier moving about, looking at the paintings. Go on, take a look around, choose a painting, then come back and tell me about it."

And she went, walking from one room to the next with quiet steps so as not to attract the attention of the caretakers. To choose a painting! She went from one to the next with resentment, trying to imagine what he would say about her choice and why. She did not choose battle scenes, because she certainly would not have known how to talk about such things; nor that woman with a pillow on her head and a jewel on her forehead, who carried a platter containing — what a horror! — a man's head with his hair and beard. And she could not choose a crucifixion as she didn't want to face questions about religion, and she couldn't report back on that dark-eyed Madonna looking tenderly at her baby — at the bottom it was signed Murillo — because she couldn't make any references to mothers and children with her father. In the end she was able to choose one by eliminating all the others; and in that painting, what struck her was the sky. She also chose one as a reserve, although she ended up by preferring the latter, as far as she was concerned: a hare among the greenery, with nails and hair that looked real; it truly looked beautiful to her.

"Well, did you choose your painting?" he asked, but not immediately upon seeing her, and the girl thought he might have forgotten the task he had assigned her. But when she led her father to the landscape painting with its few small figures and grand clouds, her father broke into the broad smile she knew so well, with his mouth closed and a little bulge under his left cheekbone. He looked at her, then nodded and said, "I see. You are a little rascal. But it doesn't matter. You are right, not I. You are right. Children are always older and wiser than their fathers think. Brava, it is a magnificent sky, and the use of such small figures makes it appear even greater; you will allow me at least this observation. Now, however, your father will quit his boring job in this freezing building, and we will go, just the two of us, out for a stroll. And we'll buy some pastries, too. My poor little daughter, this, too, shall pass. At least for you, it will pass for sure . . ." In part because of those words that were more than enough, and partly as a gesture of gratitude to her father, she also showed him the other painting, the hare. And he said, "Oh, the rabbit!" Instantly cheerful, he added, "You're right, it is truly a most beautiful painting, done not only with an attention to detail that you notice right away, but with love. And it's old, much older than you realize . . . and German, by a German painter named Dürer." Suddenly Adriana was quite pleased with her morning, and she decided to spare her father the correction on the tip of her tongue: *This isn't a rabbit, it's a hare!*

In Palermo, Dr. Canterno found the letter from the director — he had already left for an unknown destination — conferring upon her the duties of acting director. Marta would make decisions and sign for him.

She decided to seek shelter for the manuscripts as far as possible from the city. She had sworn fidelity to her country, her administration, and to art, and she thought of those manuscripts — all of them still to be read and studied — as creatures whose salvation depended on her. And so it did.

The first time, Arturo accompanied her when she went to Polizzi, the city Frederick II called *la Generosa*, the generous. A long, unforgettable journey, first by train in the dark of a winter morning, then by the blue bus of the Madonie Mountains up hairpin turns among orchards and pastures, then in the fog, all the way to the "regal city" of Basileapolis, founded by the Byzantines, then used as a Norman stronghold against the Arabs. A small, ancient city, with churches from every epoch on the prow of the Madonie Mountains rising up from the island's inland plain.

The city was hidden by fog, but when they reached its height they saw it from the final bend in the road, its sharp profile mirrored in the azure haze — a unique sight indeed: two cities, one high in the sun, and the other reflected in the blanket of fog below it!

"Did you expect this?" asked Arturo, his voice wavering. She shook her head without a word.

At the sight of it, a city reflected in the fog, Marta was seized by a sudden, joyous religiosity. She found herself thanking the Creator, Lord of heaven and earth, for such privilege. To find a place of such beauty — this was the only adjective that came to mind to describe it, but it would suffice — to safekeep her precious volumes: the Offices of the Blessed Virgin, the Bibles, the illuminated manuscripts of the Gospels. She, the excommunicate.

"Marta, what are you thinking about?" he asked her, and she answered, "So many things . . . nothing . . . I don't know what to say . . ."

Far away, above and beyond the azure fog reflecting the city so spectacularly, beyond the mountains and the hills, a large, majestic white triangle sent a white plume into the cobalt sky. It was Mount Etna.

Among the many churches of Polizzi is the Matrice, overtopped by an octagonal tambour. It is the center of a large complex that includes the city hall, formerly a Jesuit school, and a library endowed with more than thirty thousand volumes. It was there, among their brothers, that Marta would hide "her" manuscripts. She looked forward to studying all the other volumes that had made their way there, from the Lancia di Brolo collection, and from convents across the region.

The manuscripts of the National Library, most of them small and priceless, were wrapped and packaged under her watchful eye. Slowly and discreetly, in truth, with utmost secrecy, they were transferred to the underground caves below the city hall, the ancient Jesuit convent. They were placed in bags and carried by hand, transported by bus and on the backs of mules, up from Scillato by two clerks from the National Library. Accompanying them was also the acting director, Dr. Marta Canterno.

I knew nothing of those secret trips made by my mother to Polizzi in those months of winter and spring.

Adriana was quite fond of Professor Ratti, her French teacher, because she spoke Italian beautifully. The notebook she handed in to Professor Ratti was always well written and neat.

During the school year 1939–1940 the Fascist assemblies became more frequent. In the morning they all went to school in Fascist dress to be called to order. Then they crossed the city, stopping frequently and waiting at length in the cold wind or under the sun, until at last they came to Villa Gallidoro, where they stopped in the full sun, men and women, with parched throats and aching heads, waiting to be reviewed by the Federale, although one Thursday the inspection was done by the prince of Piedmont. Adriana saw the Federale only once, but she never saw the prince of Piedmont. On one of those occasions at Villa Gallidoro, among the waving fezzes and shiny black boots and the leaders running about giving orders to anyone who would listen, Adriana saw her, her beloved Professor Ratti, with golden eagles all over her uniform.

At school there was talk of war. She kept quiet. And she was all the more happy to return home, where there was no radio and no one spoke about that thing for which Papa had urged them to pray. Yes, Arturo spent more time reading the paper, then he uttered a long sigh and said, "Mah!" And with that he seemed to bring the topic to a close. Winter went by with walks among the deep green clover, a brief spring went by, and summer exploded in May. Professor Ratti missed a few classes, then came to school in her black uniform and spoke about the war that Italy would fight, and about "the ignoble defeat" of the French. Adriana looked at her; she had loved the French language, and even France a bit — or so she thought — all because of Professor Ratti!

Then, on June 10 — it was 1940 — Adriana was lying on the floor reading when Laura passed by at a run, shaking the floor supported by ancient beams. "The war broke out!" she shouted. "I'm so happy because my papa will come home soon." Adriana turned her gaze back to her book, to a nonsense rhyme.

> *Staccia abburatta*
> *Martino della Gatta . . .*
> *La Gatta andò al mulino*
> *Le fece un covaccino*

And she thought that if she could continue reading without believing Laura's words, she could erase the war.

2. WAR

IN PALERMO THE FIRST alert of the war sounded on a Sunday morning. It was seven o'clock. Adriana went to close the shutters. The June sun filtered unremittingly through the cracks. Explosions from the anti-aircraft weapons could be heard. *This is it*, she thought. There were a few shouts in the courtyard, and then silence. The city, hushed, was listening to the war. That was it; it wasn't terrible, after all. She wasn't afraid; she felt only an excitement that was almost cheerful, the joy of something new.

Afterward, Adriana realized that during the entire duration of the alert she had not thought about her father. Nor did she think of him the afternoon of June 24, the day of the French bombardment on a city dismayed, incredulous, and unprepared; the day they carried away the dead in vegetable carts. But when it came time to write her usual letter, she would have preferred not to say anything about the bombing to her father, for the thought of it filled her with shame.

It was still possible to travel during the first few months of the war. And Marta traveled, by train and bus through the Madonie Mountains, and by train to Rome. In the train, during that incomparable free time away from all her other commitments,

Marta thought about the manuscripts, taking notes on the images that were so vivid in her mind; the manuscripts of the San Martino Foundation in the National Library, those of the City Library of Catania, and those of the School of the Jesuits in Polizzi. And, as always, the manuscripts of the Casanatense, the Angelica, and the Vatican Libraries. Ever present in her thoughts was the memory of the Vatican Library manuscripts decorated by illuminators of the Ferrara School. "For some things, the memory cannot be trusted," Professor Apollonj had taught her, but since she could not be everywhere she had no choice but to use it now, her memory, just like aboriginals and painters and illiterates. She looked outside and did not see the landscape, whether the train was moving or stalled because of a bombing in progress or damage to the tracks — stations destroyed, rails littered with rubble or in need of repair. Instead she drew her memory on paper. She did a second drawing and compared it with the first. With eyes closed — whether the train traveled or stood still — she again saw the small painting with its enameled colors, and additional details emerged. She had not forgotten them, they had just escaped her mind's attention. She repeated this with not only the figures but the writing and the script: Greek characters: ancient, medieval, and Byzantine . . . and Latin . . . and the vernaculars — she envisioned them just as she, being a musician, could write out a melody on an imaginary staff. She was even able to make attributions from drawings done by memory and, almost feverish from the urgent need to see and compare the original ancient figures, she developed the ability to recognize, using imaginary comparisons, the evolution of the decorative elements of the ancient texts that she herself had been obliged to move to safety (unthinkable that it would be otherwise) in Polizzi and Monreale for the near term — until the unfathomable war should end.

When in Rome — a Rome ever more disconsolate, bare, and tiring — in the house at Prati that was colder and gloomier each visit, its inhabitants more impoverished and hungry, she would find her father, mother, and sister waiting. Her father's jacket hung from his shoulders like a rag from a stick. He dragged his feet as he walked.

"Sit down, Papa, sit down, I have something to tell you . . . Good, and I'll sit here. Remember, do you remember when you bought a small manuscript from Papadopoulos in Alexandria in the market El Attarìn? Do you remember? And you told me I should study the ancient writings, the ancient texts? Those written by hand by the monks . . . before the printing press . . . do you remember?"

He smiled and nodded.

"Well, you know, Papa, I did a bit of that, I'm still doing it. I studied . . . and I learned new things beside what you taught me, things I didn't know. I studied the ancient texts and also a bit about how the monks decorated those first books; and the first monks to decorate manuscripts were precisely the Benedictines of Montecassino . . . But you already know those things . . . ," she whispered as he slowly nodded. She continued, in a louder voice, caressing his hand, "Do you know that the first designs were geometric patterns, or floral and animal motifs, and they drew them along the margins, then around and inside the initial letters, which were drawn very large . . ."

She spoke to him as if he were a child. He smiled and nodded. At times he even wept softly — she saw his tears.

Then she closed her eyes for a moment, his daughter, and she was encouraged to think that although he followed her only with great effort, it gave him pleasure, and it was good for him. Good for his mind, that dear, irreplaceable mind that was slowly retreating and fading away. "Yes, so many of the things you taught me, and more. The most beautiful and decorated manuscripts were the breviaries, the Gospels, and the Bibles, copied by hand and then painted. At first only with *minio*, ferrous oxide, that's why they were called *miniatures*, and then with other colors, too. The monks wrote and illuminated beautiful ones, to be given as presents, yes: gifts to the pope, a king, a bishop . . . to an abbess. So, the most beautiful manuscripts were destined to travel from place to place, from one country to another."

He nodded. Did he follow?

Out of love she steered the discussion toward what could have been topics of his old lessons, even if it wasn't so. Did he understand?

"But you see, Papa, the monks never signed their works, out of sacred humility. So just think, Papa, there are manuscripts made in Montecassino that are now in Spain, or France . . . and no one knows where they came from. Other works were illuminated in Ferrara; in the fifteenth century a monastery there was famous for its illuminators. Those manuscripts were sent off to France, Russia, and who knows where else. There were manuscripts given as gifts and manuscripts stolen, perhaps taken as war spoils; they are easily transported, and they are beautiful!"

He looked straight into his daughter's eyes, his beloved daughter who was warming his hands in hers, and he smiled and said yes, yes. But did he understand?

She did not stop. She told him, no one else but him, other than Arturo, about the study she was undertaking, the study of the attributions of manuscripts that had migrated from one place to another, those northern manuscripts she had found in Sicilian libraries. "I found one in Palermo, just think, Papa, that was without any doubt illuminated by a great painter of the Ferrara School. His name was Martino da Modena . . ."

On her last trip to Rome while her father was still alive, Marta was able to take him her first important publication on illuminated manuscripts from the ninth to the fifteenth centuries; a study that she would pursue for the rest her life, becoming one of the greatest experts in the field. It was titled "A Breviary from the National Library of Palermo Illuminated by Martino da Modena." The dedication, written in my mother's beautiful script, reads: "For my beloved papa," but I don't know if he was able to read it.

He did not want to believe in the first war — says Margherita — refusing to believe that human beings could be that stupid, but the second one killed him. From the moment he heard that Italy had entered the war, and his obsessed son left even after he told him not to go, he was no longer right in the head. And for two years I lay myself down to sleep outside his door. Because he tried to go out at night. He couldn't sleep, so he would get up, put his shoes on — he never took a step without putting on his shoes — he would grab his coat, go to the door, and try to go out. So I slept right there. I would get up, take him by his wrists, then by his shoulders, and lead him back to bed. Who knows, perhaps he thought he was still in Alexandria.

My returns to Rome are increasingly filled with misery. I am accompanied by my mother, or Arturo, or even Zia Margherita when she comes down for a few days — an estranged, pathetic companion. I no longer find happiness in the streets, the lights, the ancient smells of Rome. And, especially if I am traveling with Arturo, I am overcome by the urgent desire to have him leave so I will not have to think about him, about him and the charms of his voice, his words and memories. This impatience to return to Monteverde, to my other life, as soon as possible gnaws away at me. My mother's letters are miserable things, and mine to her are worse. The first one is always the most difficult: putting the old deceptions on paper once again to please her, or to not displease her. To be at peace with my conscience. For a genuine letter would have been a cry of regret, of nostalgia and yearning. But I won't do it, because it isn't part of the game. Thus I, too, have a role to play. If the first letters are a house of lies that leaves me even more dispirited, the others, the later ones, become more and more true. True, yes, but nothing more than a dialogue between a new Adriana and a Mamma made of paper, great and glorious like the writing on the envelope and the two blue, perfumed sheets of paper with the word *Mamma* at the bottom. I begin to cling to this habit. It is convenient, and with the passage of time it becomes easier and easier to lie with my pen. Perhaps it isn't lying, but another thing entirely, though I'm certain it isn't a means of forgetting in disguise. By now I'm older, much older than my mother realizes. My heart instinctively skips a beat out of happiness at seeing her letters in the mailbox, but what follows is resentment — just a whisper, but resentment nonetheless — for the violation of the peace I have atttained, and for forcing me to regain contact with that world. A beloved world indeed, but guilty of being too far away, not to mention illusory, naively innocent, and childish. And if at times — brief but painful occasions — I find myself speaking sincerely to my mother on paper, I have only to reread about some suffering that I've put into words and I turn red in the face and tear up the paper. I take out a fresh sheet and start again.

But: "What does your mother have to say? Tell me something about that land," says Nonna Matilde. For years, she has not even mentioned her, my mamma. In those questions asked by Nonna Little (that's what I used to call her), who has grown even smaller, I sense a wish to be kind, and perhaps even heartache for me. There is no catch, only goodness. And yet, I barely answer, sullen and offended by this new violation.

"Tell us something, come on . . . at least tell us about what you eat there . . . what's the matter? Have you lost your memory?" says Lucia. I really have forgotten. And I wish it would continue. I wish I didn't have to give an account of anything to anyone, ever again.

War in Rome is dull, and while everybody says, "When will it end?" it seems to Adriana that the war has always been there and it will do nothing but grow. Yes, she does remember when the city was full of lights and there were storefront windows full of pastries, but she had never cared much about things like that. Just as it hadn't meant much the time her father took her to the cinema after dinner and said, "Grow up soon, my little one, and you will enjoy yourself even more!" But that was a fairy tale, and this is reality. Enjoy oneself even more! On walls across the city are posters of a spy of dark and sinister complexion and expression. He wears an English helmet — that's how we learned to recognize it — and cups an equally dark and sinister hand to his ear. The caption says: BE QUIET! THE ENEMY IS LISTENING. Anyone who saw it could not possibly forget.

❖

Meanwhile Zia Margherita has a dream, a dream "that has nothing to do with anything," but who knows? She says, I am entering a place that is large and dark, but I am not afraid, only curious, and I walk on. I go on and on, and I realize it is a big church, a cathedral. There is a bit of light, now, and it comes from the other end, and I keep walking and the light increases, and at last I see that at the other end, instead of an altar, there is a throne, and on it there is someone. I come closer, and it is Carlo the Fifth on the throne. Yes, it's him all right. He says, "I've been here for centuries now, and I still haven't seen God's light! Help me!" What kind of a dream was that? And when have I ever given a thought to Carlo the Fifth? So it must be true. And now I even have to pray for Carlo the Fifth, as well!

Nonno Già gets up from his armchair, hunched at first, then slowly straightening himself while leaning on the table — he insists on doing it himself, and won't let anyone help him. He unrolls a sheet of tar paper and hangs it over the stairway window. "There! Our own dark ages," he says every time and returns to his seat, more limber and agile for that bit of exercise. And with the sky shut out, night begins. Had times ever been any different? Perhaps, but not for her. Even before the war, when she returned to her father's house to sleep, the roads had been dark because they weren't yet part of the city. Only now the two of them go on foot. And when Nonna Matilde complains that she can't shop for any of this or that, Adriana never remembers enjoying these things. With bony hands gray from the cold, her grandmother makes shapeless slippers out of rags, "for that poor father of yours, alone at work in that miserable cold house," and Adriana blushes and runs away, ashamed of her mother and herself at having her secret revealed: she is not a true companion to her father, she who betrays and abandons him daily with her desires. This, too, is war for her, the cruel, slow reassertion of ancient sufferings.

But then Nonna says, "When will you go pay a little visit to your other grandmother, the poor old woman?" and she goes on foot, alone, down through the Gianicolo, down the steps past Tasso's oak and the stairway to Sant'Onofrio, and in Prati she finds Nonna Antonia and Zia Margherita, grown thin and gray-haired. And yes, they ask her about her mamma, has she written, and so on, but as if they really didn't want to know. When she tells them, they say "Oh, really?" but they seem hesitant or distracted, perhaps annoyed, as if they have forgotten. She heads for the windows overlooking Via Gioacchino Belli and finds the shutters closed; dim light and muffled noise. She would like to open them and lean out to see the swifts under the eaves across the street, or the flagstones in the road; she would like to see the fountain with its water filling the black basin and overflowing softly down its crumbling base. But in truth she doesn't feel like opening the shutters; she stays there awhile and listens, then walks away.

Adriana doesn't know, cannot possibly know, what really happened to her aunt after they left Via Spallanzani. She does not know what frightened her aunt, who was so young then, and left such lasting sadness inside her. She does not know why, in that cheerless house in Via Tacito, her aunt never complains of missing the beautiful home in Via Spallanzani, while Nonna Antonia always remembers it with a sigh. Adriana does not know, she cannot possibly know. It will be many, many years before she puts together the pieces of the shameful, inane, and cruel event at the heart of the suffering that will last throughout Zia Margherita's life.

No one speaks any more of France and the French. At home, in Palermo, they were almost never mentioned. But Arturo reads and recites in French, with tears in his voice, from small volumes with cream-colored covers inlaid with blue and gold. Almost every day, British planes can be seen in the sky above the city.

Yes, bombs are falling, but they are far away, on the outside, and this is home. And once, as the Aunt Costanza plays the piano while her mother sings, Adriana looks at them, she looks at the picture they make so as not to forget, and she thinks that if a bomb should fall at that moment they would all be transported to paradise together. Still, deep down she remains convinced that the bombs are meant for others, people she does not know and will never meet, people who exist expressly to die under the bomb in order — who can say? — to spare them. Like the passengers traveling on the train in the other track. But that is a sin. For Arturo (who, like everyone, never wants to discuss these things) once said, "You see, Adriana, those who dare say — surely you've heard them — that 'war is to men like motherhood is to women' have truly sinned against the Holy Spirit."

Artichokes boiled whole, with their thorns left on (Roman artichokes don't have them), are eaten leaf by leaf with oil and salt. Arturo says, "Taste them, taste how good they are, then follow up with a sip of water and you'll find it has a unique flavor, sweet and pure." It's true. Those flavors, those warm, affectionate voices in the full light of the gas lamp, Adriana knows they will return to her with a guilty nostalgia when she is next in Rome.

In December 1941 we declared war against the United States. Yes, we declared it against them. In Palermo the bombings took place at dawn, during school hours, at midday, in the evening, and at night. "They have no schedule," people said. The Americans did not abide by the customs of Arturo's family, they obeyed nothing associated in any way with "home." They were nothing but destructive, frightening, and numerous. The deep rumble of their inevitable approach could be heard, shaking heaven and earth before the bombs fell. Dust and white sky over the city, "continuous waves," as the radio broadcast referred to that inhumane, dreadful din. Adriana saw them, the "flying fortresses," from the Castellaccio mountain pass. Big silver insects in the clear sky, so far above the futile cackle of the anti-aircraft fire, and the city below, unable to escape. She saw the explosions at the port and everywhere, silent at first, and the columns of white and gray dust that slowly rose and melted into a single immense cloud, tragic and beyond comprehension. She was with Laura and the others. They watched, immobile and speechless. Except Arturo, who murmured something in German. It was a curse, and he was weeping.

❖

Arturo. I never called him Zio, always just Arturo. I don't really know how to speak of him, although my memories of him are most vivid. Without a doubt, the love I felt for him rivaled that which I felt for my father. And my affection, guilty on account of its very existence, has confounded my every attempt to describe him. "A handsome, stalwart figure," he would have said in jest, with a high forehead and dark, wavy hair. His eyes were of two different colors — one green and the other blue — and they were always smiling. His whole face smiled, even with the thin lips he had inherited from his Slavic forebears. His mother had a mouth just like his, only cold, and so did his father. At least according to the photos; I never met the old gentleman who extended his welcome to my mother before taking leave from Taormina and his earthly existence.

He had a strong, beautiful voice, Arturo. He loved music, along with classical literature and theater. But he could be moved by any good story, or by watching a child or other delicate creature. Or the sky. Likewise with poems, either read or recited, since he knew so many by heart.

A pacifist, he said that in school we'd been taught our history — the last hundred years — as if it were nothing but an immense madness. He was among a number of Sicilians (even though he didn't feel Sicilian, and he wasn't by blood, not having been born in Palermo) who claimed life under the Bourbons hadn't been so bad.

He would recite D'Annunzio: "*Eravamo sette sorelle. Ci specchiammo alle fontane. Eravamo tutte belle.*" He told me, "Listen, little mouse, listen and see if you can understand. It's beautiful, this one, it really is:

> *. . . L'ultima per cantare*
> *Per cantare solamente*
> *E non voleva niente.*

Yes, I loved him, and felt guilty of betrayal for doing so. He was the first one to leave me.

For him, unlike for my real parents, war was not a time for action. Because of his shipping and antiquarian business, and also because of his nature, it was a time of stagnation, of incredulous, outraged waiting. He played Bach and Mendelssohn. His antiquarian dealings, at first temporarily halted by necessity, came to an end with the bombing that destroyed his building; he was able to start up again afterward only with great difficulty. All his holdings were buried under the ruins with the collapse of Palazzo Santa Ninfa during the last bombardment of Palermo in June 1943. But this didn't seem to have much importance to him. His love for my mother and her accomplishments was great, and it never diminished. I do not know how to speak of him, but a star has been named for him: Arcturus.

Rome

> *The Cicada with her little belly full*
> *and her unceasing raucous melody,*
> *Sang all summer long*
> *And didn't think about the other seasons.*
> *But when winter comes cold and harsh,*
> *and not a mouthful to eat has she*
> *To the Ant she turns and begs for help*
> *a little grain, that's all.*
> *"And what did you do during times of plenty*
> *When the sun's rays were warming the earth?"*
> *And she responded, "Night and day*
> *I sang to passersby with dulcet voice . . ."*

Here Nonna Matilde always pauses because she doesn't remember the words. Then she concludes in a rush:

> *"Now listen well to what I have to say:*
> *If you sang then, my dear, now it's time to dance!"*

The tragic, vulgar fate of the cicada is not unlike their own. Nonna Matilde spreads oil on the bottom of the pan with a brush, and the oil is no longer in the green two-liter bottle kept in the kitchen cupboard on paper stained with circles of grease. Instead it is in a small flask under lock and key in the dining room sideboard. "Will you ever understand that there is a war on?" she screams in her thin voice, angry at no one in particular. Her hair is pulled back in a minuscule bun, and the bones of her head are almost visible.

Now it is Adriana who puts up the tar paper over the window in the stairway because Nonno Giacinto only sits in his chair all day listening to the news on the radio. The paper, now four years old, is torn in several places and the frame is bent. *We should repair it,* Adriana thinks, but she doesn't want to do it. She doesn't want to grant the war that satisfaction, does not want to tell it, *Go ahead, you can continue.* But one evening she finds it has been glued back together. It was Nonna Matilde who did it, with the old gum arabic.

Night falls early, and there is a curfew.

Each night after the evening meal, Adriana goes to sleep in the same little house, her father's, two blocks away. He leads the way with the pale circle of light from a dynamo flashlight that works by repeatedly squeezing a lever with your hand as if signaling so many *ciaos*. The distance between the two houses is no longer magical; still those moments are precious, traveled primarily in silence. The rare conversations that ensue are never about small or mundane things, thus their nightly walks have become a solemn ritual. One evening, walked in silence until they reached the narrow cobblestone road, her father stops and says, "Adriana, you are not a Fascist."

It is a statement containing just a hint of doubt. He turns the flashlight toward her face. She closes her eyes, unable to bear his glance, even though she cannot see him in the dark. She answers in a firm, smooth voice, "Certainly not, Papa." In fact she is not certain of anything about herself, she who has written compositions at school full of "supreme goals" and "glorious futures" because she knew it was expected of her. She feels herself blush in the darkness and only hopes the redness will disappear before they reach the house. On the landing her father takes out his key, turns on the light, and opens the door. He seems serene, as if he has forgotten. But just when she believes his thoughts have shifted to other things, he says quietly, "Don't betray me in this, too."

Nonno Giacinto had gone away forever, "quietly, and without disturbing anyone, just like a little bird," said Nonna Matilde, and she decided to leave the house in Monteverde, which she had never been fond of — for it had too many stairs, among other things. She went back to Prati, or almost, to a ground-floor apartment in Viale delle Milizie with her son Enrico, who was again a bachelor, and Lucia. Adriana went to visit her there during the summer vacation of 1942; a vacation that started early because of the bombings.

A long summer, and Nonna Matilde, even smaller and thinner than before, loved to walk with Adriana along her old streets, the Lungotevere, and the bridges. They would walk up to Piazza Cavour, which had once been the center of her life. Or at that special hour of the day when the sun was beginning to set, they would walk slowly across the Ponte del Littorio along Via Flaminia to Villa Borghese. In Via Flaminia they would buy — for one lira and eighty centesimi — a quarter kilo of black olives. They looked like Sicilian olives, but Adriana didn't say as much, for she never spoke of Sicily and the nostalgia that filled her days. That quarter kilo of olives evoked a combination of pleasure, guilt, and hunger, and before they reached the Villa Borghese she had finished them. Then grandmother and granddaughter would walk under the dark canopy of ilexes to the Fountain of Aesculapius and sit on the bluff bordering it. It was the year Nonna Matilde turned eighty. She talked and talked, Nonna Matilde, as she always had, but she seldom asked questions, as if she was not curious about Adriana's other life, or else she did not want to know. She was happy, in her old age, just to observe every step of Adriana's present life.

A long and languid summer. In front of the house, beyond the double line of plane trees, was a wall enclosing the air force barracks. The ground at its base was not asphalt but yellow earth and stone, and pairs of soldiers and servant girls would linger there in the shade of the trees. The girls' legs were visible, thick calves and heels overhanging the backs of cork sandals discarded by the signora of the house. The couples always spaced themselves evenly apart. A summer filled with radio broadcasts, bombings at La Valletta; Il Duce at Derna, then El Alamein, and then again at La Valletta, La Valletta . . . Malta was a huge island, immense; the geography she had learned in school didn't mean anything anymore, dimensions and distances had changed. Sicily was a distant island, unreachable. Places, houses, even the very stones she had known and touched. A flood of memories came back to her: the rough texture of those stones, sweet odors, warm bread, the knob at the end of the stairway banister — they were nothing now but fruits of a sick and evil imagination.

CENSORED was printed on the blue strip that resealed the envelope containing her mother's letter. The letter came from a place that now existed only in her imagination, a place swallowed up by the reality of the dead of La Valletta, the dead in Russia, the dead of El Alamein and Tobruk. She had actually grown fond of those names, but she could no longer abide the voice of Titta Arista, who read the news on the radio. She turned off the radio when she could, but never until after the war bulletins, never until she had heard about the bombings. And Palermo was always hit, though only once a day now. It was now Nonna Matilde who sat by the radio all day as Nonno Già had once done. She would say, "It was a light bombing, did you hear? Only fourteen dead and fifty wounded. Just don't think about it." She meant well, poor woman. Adriana could only shrug and pretend she was not interested in the news. And she never responded, *There is no one left there anymore. No one and nothing.* Then Giovanni Ansaldo's rich, weighty voice would come out of the radio, almost singing: "Is it true, or is it not?" If her father happened to come into the room just then he would scream, "What kind of filth are you listening to?" and turn off the radio. He was thin and pale, her father, with lines on his face. His shoes were made of cheap canvas with cardboard soles, and his tender feet ached inside them. They were the summer shoes Nonna Matilde had made for him, in addition to his winter slippers made from rags.

Adriana and Lucia made shoes out of rope. They went to buy supplies in a shop on Via Luigi Settembrini where a rare impression of opulence still reigned: raffia and hemp, enormous spools of twine of every thickness on the shelves, long coils of rope hanging from the ceiling. "The hangman's paradise," Lucia called it, and in fact the store was full of goods, everything but food. They bought the rope by weight, which also made Adriana think of abundance, who knows why. Once home, they hung the rope from the handle of the kitchen window. Then Adriana braided it tightly, a difficult job that brought blisters to her hands. Harder still was the task of sewing it onto the sole, using heavy thread and a big needle that grew hot from friction as it passed through the braid. She pulled and pulled; the thread could show through on one side of the sole but not the other, the side that would face the ground, and she sewed and wound the braid in one direction for the right sole, and in the other direction for the left one — a mysterious act, symbolic of who knows what — but it also seemed natural, like the funicular at Monreale, whose two cars always met where the track was split in two . . . Adriana braided and sewed, and all the while she counted the hours, waiting to return to Palermo — to her mother, Arturo, and all the others. The steps in the entranceway were five, like the months of the long vacation that stretched until October; the tiles in the corridor were in rows of twelve, which was the number of the remaining weeks; and the days of those weeks corresponded to the number of tiles above the sink in the bathroom. With her time thus divided, she made it disappear bit by bit, in silence. The deadline was October, when the schools would reopen. But one day in August her father said, "Come on, let's go for a walk, you and I," and she followed him reluctantly, fearful of a scolding or any unexpected news, like that time with the wedding candy. They walked along the Lungotevere, crossing not the first bridge but continuing on to the Ponte Risorgimento, where her father finally spoke. "You've heard the newscasts, and you know that things are going badly in Africa. Poor Italy, those scoundrels have ruined it. And the worst is still to come. For all of us, but for them, too. That's right, for them, too, but that is meager consolation." He stopped speaking. Linden trees in full foliage and bloom filled the air with an overpowering perfume and blocked the river from view. She saw the fence with its crossed pickets like the ones at Villa Borghese and felt an instinctive urge to make one of her foolish calculations of time, of weeks and days remaining. But just as she started counting the wooden stakes, her father spoke again. "I promised certain things to your mother, just as she made promises to me. I agreed to let you stay with her during the school year, and I intended to keep that promise. But you've seen how they are bombing Palermo. Perhaps your school isn't even there anymore. Perhaps nothing is left. I don't know, and I don't want to know. At any rate, those gentlefolk we're calling your relatives have left for the countryside, and rightly so. The pope is here in Rome, so although we suffer from hunger, we are without a doubt safer. So I have decided you will remain here this winter. I have already written your mother about it, and she sent me a reply. In sum, and with the exception of an outlandish statement about a possible Italian counteroffensive in Africa, she agrees with me. Perhaps she wrote that sentence for the benefit of the censors. Anyhow, you will stay with me. If it is the Lord's wish for this catastrophe to end soon — unfortunately I doubt it — you can go to Sicily next summer, or whenever possible. I'm sorry I had to tell you this. Unfortunately, it's not open to debate. It is, as we say in such cases, for your own good, assuming a father is still allowed to do anything for his daughter's good. Right now I believe it is my duty. And I hope you'll still love me in spite of it."

Adriana was crying. Her pain was searing, her sense of loss complete. Oh, that idiotic fence! But she could not let herself fully accept her father's words, not at that moment. She thought the military situation in Africa might indeed turn itself around. The war might end soon, or another miracle might occur: all those relatives could come to Rome, where it was safe under the pope. The tenacity of that hope, that dream, sustained her for yet a few more days, even in her letters to her mother — or were those letters only lies by then?

In September her father said, "If you want to go for a few days, before winter sets in and school starts . . . Yes, I have already enrolled you at the Mamiani, which is nearby. It's the school I went to. I was saying, if you want, you may go, to get your books and winter shoes, to say good-bye . . ."

She went by train. The relatives had escaped to San Martino delle Scale, the place where they had once spent so many Sunday outings. She was able to spend the last Sunday of September there, in the little house they rented. A small stone stairway led up to a square terrace off a kitchen and two rooms. The two families stayed in the two attic rooms, and Stanka slept in the kitchen. She cooked outside on the terrace, over a fire fueled by kindling she gathered in the woods. Oh, that scent! The pots became blackened, the soup was scented with smoke — "Take the cover off, take it off!" — and Stanka would go to the stream to scrub the aluminum pots with lemon and sand until they shone again.

At sunset they visit the Roccuzzas. Their small house is white and gray; the black and brown tiles on the single-sloped roof are covered with gray lichen. Next to the door, running along one wall, is a bench. To one side, beyond an open area paved in stone — an ancient threshing ground, to be sure — there is an oven. The Roccuzzas are three old women, sisters and sisters-in-law; they have already kneaded the bread that afternoon. It has risen under a black woolen military blanket and is now waiting near the door on a worn plank. Five loaves. One Roccuzza prepares a fire, from lemon and orange tree cuttings, in the domed oven made of brick and stone. Gray, fragrant smoke comes out of the single opening, and when the fire is reduced to coals and the oven's vault is white, the woman calls out, "It's ready!" The second Roccuzza sprinkles seeds on the five loaves, and the third one traces a cross on each loaf with her thumb. Meanwhile the first Roccuzza has run into the house. She returns with one arm raised to the sky, holding the plank with the five loaves on her open hand. She props the plank on the mouth of the oven, and with an ancient rhythm she slides the loaves inside, one by one. When she carries the plank back to the house she holds it low at her side, and there is no longer anything of the sacred in her pose. The oven's door has been closed and sealed with a wet rag shoved into the crack; there is nothing left to do but wait. The three Roccuzzas sit down with their customers — villagers, evacuees, and a carabiniere — who are talking or resting quietly. Occupied with their thoughts in that silence, they gaze at the azure and black mountains or at the still branches of the trees nearby.

Eight days only; she knew it already. Adriana enjoyed those first few days from one hour to the next, but now she is already counting down the sunrises and sunsets and the loaves at the Roccuzzas'. And although she is trying to watch the others with the detachment of someone who is about to leave and would like to feel mature and wise, it is no use. She soon despises those few remaining days and the increasingly absurd calculations they will cost her. Then she asks them for forgiveness, one by one, as if each day were a living creature offended at being insufficiently loved. Those days belong to her, because for the evacuees time does not exist; there is only the bell at the Benedictine convent to mark each passing Sunday. Stanka, who rises up again perennially like an aster, is eternity. Eternal, too, is Arturo as he reads while sitting on the low wall or in his old rattan chair, or while walking or standing still. Likewise her mother is eternal, as she sews and sings: "*Che farò senza Euridice? — dove andrò senza il mio bene? — Euridice! Euridice! — Ah, non m'avanza — più soccorso — più speranza — né dagli uomini — né dal Ciel!*"

Is it possible? Could it be that the arc traced by the needle and thread, or the sound of her mother's singing, so pure against the endless evening summer sky, is sincere, and not done just to burn and leave a cruel and indelible yet untrue mark upon her soul? On her last night, Adriana doesn't cry. She lies in bed motionless, with her eyes on the ceiling. The next day at the station, when she first dares say to her mother, "Come with me!" and her mother doesn't respond, Adriana knows she is right. Her mamma can't return with her to Rome, not now. "All of you, come," she then whispers, but softly, and she immediately hopes her mother hasn't heard. She is ashamed of those hopeless words, as if they were a sin.

Autumn came to Rome, bringing night fog among the trees, a new school, and more hunger. Her father had returned to his reticent ways, and had grown even more thin and ugly. There was no municipal gas and Lucia used the coal she got with her ration card to heat the quart of milk they gave to Nonna Matilde because she was old, and to Adriana because she was not yet fifteen. But this did not last long. Soon it became a pint. Her summer of black olives and strolls to the Fountain of Aesculapius had ended, and she was occasionally seized by a furious craving for canned tuna that made her salivate and constricted her tongue. Her professor was teaching Homer, and she saw Odysseus eating canned tuna at the table of the Phaeacians. She went often to the house on Via Gioacchino Belli, more often than she let on to her grandmother; pilgrimages back to her childhood, to a time she was already pretending was filled with precious happiness, all the more so with the distance separating her from her mother.

The Red Circular tram was infused with the odors of the broad sidewalks and the plane trees lining Viale Giulio Cesare. The war was there, too, in those smells, and in Adriana's steps, made with nostalgia for the strolls she used to take amid the red earth and mountain rocks. War was in the water dripping from the flasks filled at the fountain, and in the lines of famished people waiting to buy half a kilo of partly rotten potatoes. Alone and silent, Adriana brimmed with lengthy, imagined conversations as she walked past city gardens and barracks walls — pretend conversations with those who would return one day, discussions held in an invented future disguised as the present out of necessity. Those trees along Via Alessandro Farnese! She did not know how many there were, and she turned away to keep herself from counting them each time she passed by. For she had said she would return to Palermo in as many days as there were trees. But instead of days, the trees had come to mean weeks, and then months.

Instead her mother came to Rome, for three days in March 1943. She had not written Adriana to tell her. Zia Margherita telephoned, as she had done once before, saying only, "Come, Mamma's here." Adriana had not understood at first, and thought she was speaking about her own mother, Nonna Antonia. But she saw that Nonna Matilde and Lucia already knew — perhaps her aunt had called earlier, while she was at school — and they let her go without asking any questions. "Come back as soon as you can" was all her grandmother said, as if Adriana had a duty to fulfill. She ran along Via Marcantonio Colonna and crossed Piazza Cola di Rienzo as if in some other season of a joyful year, and then she walked up Via Tacito and was home. Home! Once again the shutters on Via Gioacchino Belli were open, and she was wildly happy, but for only one day. The second day it was already necessary to think about tomorrow. She went to school, but once there she did not say anything to her friend Camilla; she did not tell her, *Today I'm not returning home to my usual house because my mother is here in Rome.* And when she left school she was almost unhappy, certainly she was less happy then she had been the day before, and after a few paces she turned back to the other house, to Nonna Matilde and Lucia, with the excuse of having to leave her books. "Will you be eating here?" they each asked, and twice she had to say no. Her mother left the next day. She was thin and beautiful and unreal, yet so desperately her only reality . . . She accompanied her mother to the station on the Black Circular — in those days there were only the two Circular trams — and they hardly spoke a word. The train was late, but neither mother nor daughter knew what to do with that half hour, which had seemed like such a generous gift. Adriana cried for days after that visit, for although it had made her happy, it had broken an equilibrium. The trees along Via Alessandro Farnese had become frightening ghosts.

That winter of 1943 the conductors on the few trams were women. Everyone went on foot, dispirited, in a constant search for food, wearing makeshift shoes that hurt their feet. Under the guidance of their mathematics professor, her classmates exchanged samples of edible plants gathered from Monte Mario or the Gianicolo or Villa Borghese. In June, Adriana's father bought a bicycle. Adriana would ride out past Porta Latina with Camilla and her brother, and sometimes even Lucia, on a bicycle borrowed from Renata, the gatekeeper. They went in search of eggs. As they rode past the railroad bridge into the countryside fond memories would stir inside Lucia, raising her hopes that within a few hundred yards from the city provisions could still be found in abundance. They returned with a sack of fresh shell beans and a string net bag full of eggplants and sweet peppers. Those were the first string net bags, an important invention, and Adriana and Camilla would learn how to make them. The peppers made her angry with their empty, wasted space inside. Nonna and Lucia cut the eggplants into thin slices, strung them on a thread, and hung them like garlands throughout the kitchen to let them dry. They would be used that winter to make dark, leathery patties, bitter but good. And they steeped old newspapers in water, rolled them into balls, and let them dry on the windowsill to make fuel for the fire and the stove.

Tommaso Canterno died in 1941. The house in Via Tacito remained overrun by books. Margherita's hair is turning white. She is hungry, hungry every moment of the day. She no longer sets her hair in curlers before leaving the house, if only to buy milk in the evenings — that pint of milk allotted to her mother because of her age. Only her memories remain. She doesn't mention — to whom could she speak? — the camels with their big teeth that frighten her so, but she thinks of them; she thinks of the sparrows — they must weigh a pound each, she says — hopping amid the feet of the children playing in the street, and she remembers the nun with the headpiece with white wings who held her by the hand as she waited in the doorway for her brother to pick her up from school; but Giacomo has forgotten, and she says to the nun, "I know the way home, I can find it myself," but the nun replies, "No! All alone in the street? No . . ." She remembers the grand flights of the pigeons as they left the dovecote, mornings and evenings, when their keeper came to gather eggs for the market . . . In Alexandria there are shops that sell only eggs: from those small pigeon eggs to big goose eggs . . . Or perhaps Margherita does not have these sweet memories I'm now giving her, to comfort her in those times. She has no memories to console her as she walks the streets of Rome. Margherita has only hunger. Her mother says nothing because she never complains, but she, too, is at the end of her rope. She makes do, as ever, but there is not even enough to buy anything on the black market in Via di Tor di Nona. There is nothing left to eat in the house. Only books. They line the walls of the bare corridor, stacked up two meters high from the floor. No one will ever read them. Margherita leaves the cardinal's library and returns home to even more books. In *Pardi*'s room books are everywhere, and she doesn't enter so as not to see them. Perhaps they are even valuable.

Margherita knows French and English well, along with Greek and Arabic (not written, however). She can read Cyrillic characters because she studied Russian and Bulgarian at the Institute for Oriental Studies in Via Lucrezio Caro. She could organize those books by field, subject, and language. She certainly knows how to do it, and she starts in. But she is overcome by nausea and her nose begins to run heavily in an allergic reaction to the dust. She is hungry and cold; that room is colder than any other. No one helps her, but who could?

After a year the books are in an even greater state of confusion because the old heaps have been joined by new piles of her own making, big and small ones with labels on top that are prone to floating off. Finally her mother responds to the question that has gone unasked: "Go ahead, sell them," she says.

Because she is so frugal, or else incapable, Margherita has never purchased a good pair of shoes, so she has painful objects on her feet, and chilblains. Her lips are cracked and she is cold. In summer she is thirsty. She walks a lot, entering antiquarian bookshops — so many strings of bells hanging in doorways. The vendors aren't always interested in buying, but they always want to have a look. The books are heavy, and she carries them in two canvas bags sewn by Antonia. For months she refused to take the books, or rather take them back, to Campo de' Fiori, but when she finally changes her mind — at the end of 1943 — it's too late, people are too hungry to buy books. And she is ashamed indeed, there in a corner of the piazza, the corner with Via del Biscione, when one vendor or another turns a tome between his hands and says, "I know this book, I sold it to an old man . . . wasn't he your papa? Eh, poor old man. Signorina, I'll buy it back from you, but not for much. I'll never sell it again; you can't eat books, you know . . ."

For three years Margherita tried to sell the books. She succeeded with a few of them, after much pain and difficulty, and very little profit. But the piles of books in the house never seemed to diminish. So she started putting them in the trash, and this, too, was a delicate operation, as she was convinced her mother would be displeased if she ever found out, and perhaps it was even forbidden. For in her heart she knew, by means of some unwritten yet deeply felt law: culture is not to be thrown away.

In the spring of 1943 my father sat at the table without even a newspaper; he heard the news outside, in the evening he listened to the broadcast from Radio-London. He ate what little there was in silence, with a voracity sad, pensive, contrite. We ate everything down to the last crumb, even licking our plates clean.

He gave me money: "Go on, go find something. Eat, you at least should have something to eat." But he no longer said *you, who must grow up*. I bought lupini beans and ate them with a little salt, or with none at all, searching in their bland flavor and texture for hints of delicacies from the past. Ravioli filled with ricotta! How good they were, and now how remote! In the early days of July, mail service from Sicily was broken off.

On July 10 my father said, "I saw some Maccarese grapes at the fruit stands. Go buy some to eat, my dear! All for yourself." The Americans had landed in Sicily, and we had grapes from Maccarese.

On the nineteenth I set out along the Lungotevere, my eyes barely able to see over the parapet, I was so small. I walked to Ponte Regina Margherita, and then on to Ponte Cavour, for it had always been my bridge. I crossed it amid a gaunt crowd, hurried and distracted women carrying the usual patchwork shopping bags made from scraps of leather. They held their bags greedily with two hands, resting them a bit on their hips so they wouldn't seem so heavy. Only sometimes they were heavy. I continued past Palazzo Borghese and crossed the entrance to Via della Scrofa. Then the alarms sounded, and the bombing immediately followed. Anti-aircraft guns started firing from nearby; rapid, clean bursts in the bright, still air.

"Hey, girl, come here!" I heard someone call. An old man was gesturing from inside a doorway on the other side of the piazza. There was no one in the entire piazza, no one in the streets. "Come here," he called again, and I obeyed reluctantly. A few women were inside the entryway with him. "What's the matter with you, are you deaf? Those are bombs!" they said. I went to stand by the wall, sullen and proud. As if I needed to be taught that those were bombs! Of course they were bombs, and even closer than the night before. "Last night they hit the San Paolo station," a woman said. ". . . and Ciampino," said another. Then everyone started talking, and by now there were about twenty of us in the entryway. The door was ajar and I looked out through the crack on that bit of empty piazza; I saw a corner of the midday sky, and I knew I was sinning against the Holy Ghost. Because I was happy that Rome was being bombed. It had ended: the city that was holding me prisoner had lost its immunity! And that truly meant it would all end soon. Even though the end of the war, which everyone was hoping for and talking about, was nothing but a meaningless phrase to me, for I could scarcely remember a time when the war did not exist. But the end of the war would mean I could have my mother back, and forever! Was it possible? I couldn't believe it; I didn't think it could be true. I felt *the end of the war* was just another deception, idle talk used by adults to fuel that relentless, superfluous chatter of theirs.

But when the bombing ended and the city lay motionless in a strange, vast silence in the middle of the day, the last flash of explosions shattered the air like bursts of laughter, giving me a sense of euphoria, of urgent longing. A longing to run and shout, happy and free.

Before the sirens sounded the end of the alert, Adriana fled from the doorway and no one tried to stop her. She reached the sidewalk and ran back to Palazzo Borghese and across the bridge. The July sun beat down on the smooth water of the river, on the empty Via Vittoria Colonna. Cavour, leaning on his pile of books, seemed closer across that emptiness, and ironic. Adriana's feet burned inside her homemade shoes as she ran silently, madly, across the dusty gravel of her old piazza and turned into the deserted Via Tacito. She wanted to find Nonna Antonia and Zia Margherita. The door was ajar, as if in mourning. She slipped inside and drank in the ancient air, cool and musty. She stopped. She wanted to see them, but she knew they would be upset to learn she had been out and about during the alert. They would try to detain her, surely they would. She heard voices next door, in the porter's apartment. They were there, she saw them sitting there, Nonna Antonia with her rosary in her swollen fingers, Zia Margherita staring blankly, with a suitcase full of valuables at her side. She saw them, and that was all she needed. She backed up and disappeared through the narrow gap in the door just as the sirens started sounding. No longer running, she headed for Viale delle Milizie. The empty, lost stare on her aunt's face had stayed with her. She did not know — she couldn't know — that the dream that would become recurrent had appeared to her aunt that night for the first time: the dream of "that scene."

Nonna Matilde was waiting at the window, and she made the sign of the cross when she saw Adriana. Her father had also come back after the second bombardment, and she realized she had hoped things would be different between them after the bombing of Rome. They ate potatoes cooked without oil, seasoned with a bit of onion that had burned in the pan. Her father said, "Come on, Adriana. Get your bicycle and we'll go see what's happened. They say it was at San Lorenzo. Let's go!" They rode through the streets in silence, side by side, each playfully trying to pull in front. At the mouth of the Traforo — the tunnel — which had been turned into a shelter, there was a great commotion. They rode up Via del Tritone then pushed their bikes up the hill to the Tre Fontane, which were dry. There were clouds of dust, people moving on foot, a few military vehicles moving slowly. In front of the Stazione Termini they saw the first groups of men and women, mattresses on their backs and children clinging to their sides. Her father was sweating and flushed, in spite of being so lean, and he did not look around as he pedaled. She pedaled behind her father, looking at the women's dusty, sobbing, stunned faces, at all the misery, and she was glad her father could not see her face, could not sense her shame for her thoughts of two hours earlier. Although she felt more energetic than her father, she had no desire to pass him. When the church of San Lorenzo came into view her father stopped and muttered something that Adriana did not understand. The piazza was crowded with people and carts — where had they found all those carts? — loaded with mattresses, children, bewildered old women and men. Women were screaming, men were weeping. But Enrico Fieschi headed straight through the crowd toward the basilica. They reached it, and the portico was gone. The front was still standing, but the roof had collapsed, and there was no telling what was left inside. "The bell tower didn't come down. I didn't think it would still be standing," mumbled her father. Adriana thought he had come only to see the church, and she felt a newfound sense of shame.

The invasion of Sicily was under way. Adriana walked through the streets or rode her bicycle with Camilla. They rode without saying a word. The canopy of the plane trees formed a roof overhead, fragrant and penetrated only here and there by the sun's rays. She didn't understand, had almost learned not to think. She no longer ached from counting the days and months now that her days were no longer planned out; instead she had only hunger. Hunger, and an awareness that she should not think. She went to church, kneeled, uttered words or made silent prayers that devolved into strings of profane images as her thoughts wandered. Of course she said, "Protect her, protect them," but she could not think beyond that, she could not say anything more, or at least so she thought. How can one envision the worst without fear of evoking it? Still, and to her surprise, she was seized by an unrestrained joy when she heard of the landing at Salerno.

And that July, on the night of the twenty-fifth, I, too, ran laughing with my father in the streets, and we stayed for a long time there in Via Fornovo, watching the crackling bonfire of papers and furniture thrown from the windows of the Casa del Fascio. Papa spoke on and on as he had never done with me. He revealed that he had been in communication with an underground party for months. "We did it! We did it," he kept saying. "Do you see? All it took was four bombs on this old city of priests to put an end to this comedy. These delinquents have destroyed Italy, but they didn't destroy all of it. And we'll make sure you know, you poor children. We've let you grow up in this climate of buffoonery and crime, but we'll make sure you know, God willing, the true Italy." I blushed. I blushed from all those patriotic Mazzinian words, which, then and always, seemed so excessive and ridiculous. But I trembled. My father did not notice it, but I was trembling with disappointment. With every step I took on his arm, my father's arm as he spoke more freely and happily than I had ever known, I felt more estranged and alone. He was all I had, but he was different in his joy.

When we turned toward home the cheering crowd had disappeared and Viale delle Milizie was dark and deserted. Just the two of us and nothing else. The true Italy, he had said. For me there was only a frightening loneliness. That other world of mine — which Papa never mentioned and I had learned to ignore, even in my soul — no longer had any semblance of reality. Maybe — I knew it, I just knew it — it had even been destroyed. The Allies in Salerno, the Allies in Sicily . . . Names, names of places that weren't real, perhaps imaginary, certainly unknowable. Just like the clear, silent water at Mondello. It had not been real, either.

And in the days that followed, from then until September, Adriana did not speak. She threw herself on the bed and stared absently at the ceiling. The bombing on the city continued, the "open city"; that was another joke, and it made her laugh. Horrible bombings on all the other cities. Naples. Naples! Who knew if Annita was still alive. The radio didn't say a word about Palermo. Palermo no longer existed. Now the news bulletins were signed "General Ambrosio." Now the radio no longer broadcast "*l'orticello ogni mattina*" or "*và, giù per la via — che conduce alla staziòn!*" She had grown fond of those songs, which were among the few pleasantries she remembered from those winter months. She had sung them while walking under the trees of Via Alessandro Farnese, and had included words and phrases from those lyrics in the letters she had written to Laura and her mother. Now she couldn't write anymore. Neither could they, if they were still alive. But surely, surely they were still alive. If not, how could she possibly be lying there, playing with the fringe on her cotton blanket? Or maybe not. They were all dead. Dead — indeed, that was the word. But it was just a word, nothing more than a few sounds. And images. How could one defend against them? What difference would it make to that blanket if they were all dead? What difference to her fingers that were touching it? They weren't bombing Palermo anymore, the news bulletins weren't mentioning the number of dead — just a few, do you see — hardly any! — or the wounded. Nothing but dead silence — that's how they said it — from over there. The island had vanished, sunk. In fact she had never thought it very stable, from the first day she set foot on it.

Or maybe not. Maybe her mamma is down there now, cooking ravioli, and Laura is grown up, and she's putting her balls of cheese round as pumpkins in a big pan full of olive oil — olive oil! Oh, those cheeses, if only she could eat them! She is so hungry!

Time stands still, goes nowhere. She visits Via Tacito and her grandmother's fine hair has thinned and gone completely white, revealing the pink skin underneath. Her aunt is emaciated and has started chewing continuously, nothing in her mouth, the result of some new tic. "Did you bring me anything nice?" she asks teasingly, but immediately regrets it and offers Adriana something to eat, something they purchased with their ration coupons; they who have so little. All the same, Adriana accepts, sullenly mulling over the words they always tell her: *You must grow big and strong*. Indeed it seems that only while eating, only while remembering flavors now experienced just in her dreams, that her real self breaks forth, wild and strong and free of doubts. Adriana does not know — she cannot know — that a dream has been visiting Zia Margherita during those months of hunger and cold and profound despair. With her beloved brother on the Russian front (and how he would return from it!), and no news from her sister in Sicily, and her mother grown old and so unkind, this dream had settled and taken root in Zia Margherita's mind. Many years later, in a delirium, she will describe it. "I'm returning home and I'm carrying my bag with the bottle of milk, the pint allotted to Mamma because she's old, and the lid doesn't have the date on it because the dairywoman poured milk into it from another bottle, but who cares about that. But I think about that date and now I know why. Because it's a different date, years later; a day that has yet to arrive. And there are two men in front of the entryway. I know one of them, but not the other, and they come up to me so quickly I don't have time to run away, and my legs are too heavy, they can't move. The one I know is him, the guard at Villa Torlonia, and he grabs me by the arm and repeats that word, shouts it, and he twists my arm until I bend and fall to my knees, and I think about the bottle of milk because it might spill, and then what would I tell Mamma? Now I'm kneeling on the hard, cold sidewalk, the gray flagstones right in front of my eyes. I was destroyed, on my knees, and I begged for mercy" — she can't recount this in the present tense, so great is her fear — "but he kept swearing at me, saying that word, over and over. The other man, the one I didn't know, a short man, stood by him and did nothing. He did nothing! He didn't help me. He didn't say a word, and he did nothing! And after dreaming this scene so many times, it actually happened! Years later, after the war, right there in front of the entryway on Via Tacito. The war had finished, and my poor brother was finished, too. It had long since ended for him, but not the fear from having hidden him after he had come back, ill, from down there . . ."

Camilla telephoned; it was the morning of September 7, 1943. "Come on, let's go for a ride. We can go to the Gianicolo, do I ever have something to tell you!" Adriana took her bicycle. Camilla lived in Via Fabio Massimo, ten minutes away, if that. "I am coming down!" she shouted from the balcony window on the sixth floor. Camilla's bicycle was under the first ramp of stairs, secured with a thick chain to an iron pillar. As her friend came down the stairs, Adriana stared silently at that chained, motionless bicycle; silent and still in spite of all the trips it had been on with them. Camilla descended the stairs two at a time, and when she was on the second floor she leaned out and said, "Did you know, there's an armistice!" She continued down, skipping stairs and leaving Adriana alone for another few minutes with those words in her ears, and the bicycle and chain were still there, silent against the crumbling wall, and nothing had changed. Then Camilla jumped the last four steps to the ground — she always did — and put her hands on Adriana's shoulders. "Do you understand? They've signed an armistice, the war is over!"

Her mind was blank. Camilla continued, "I know it's true, my father said so. They signed it in Sicily. In your Sicily."

She blushed, without a word. That was nonsense. Signed in Sicily. But Sicily did not exist anymore. Signed? What was signed? And by whom? As if to humor her she asked, "Who signed it?" "Boh!" said Camilla. "The king is here," said Adriana, "and the pope, too." "The pope? What does the pope have to do with it? Are you coming with me to the Gianicolo?" "To do what?" "I'll tell you later. We're going to see the nuns." Meanwhile Camilla had opened the lock and unchained her bicycle. With a quick, practiced gesture she spun it through the air on one wheel and for an instant it looked like a saucy pony rearing up on its heels. Adriana let her friend go first, then walked behind, pushing her bicycle, the sound of its chain echoing in the entryway. They pedaled in silence from Via Fabio Massimo through Cola di Rienzo, all the way to Piazza Risorgimento. There were few people in the streets and they pedaled with delight along the Vatican walls, pulling side by side under the shadow of the colonnade at Saint Peter's. The water spewing from the fountains shimmered in the sun. The spray from the fountain on the left was almost completely missing the basin. "I'm going to take a shower!" shouted Adriana as she left Camilla's side and pedaled straight for the fountain. She pedaled around and around and the wayward stream of papal water drenched her completely. She was perspiring, and that rush of water awakened her. She shouted out defiantly, "Armistice, armistice! Where in the world is this armistice?"

"Don't believe in it then, suit yourself. How much will you give me if I'm right?"

Adriana kept pedaling, and the wild spray from the fountain seemed now to follow her, now to dodge her. Finally she got off her bicycle and threw it to the ground. She stepped over the railing and started scooping handfuls of water from the fountain's embrasure, throwing it on herself, on Camilla, all the while shouting, "The armistice! The armistice!" Camilla threw down her bicycle and stepped into the fountain, too, and after both girls were soaked head to foot, their dresses clinging to their skin, they picked up their bicycles and rode off in the sun. In Borgo Santo Spirito they encountered a German platoon. Dripping wet as they were they kept their eyes fixed on the ground and rode past the Germans without speaking. The soldiers wore their helmets lowered over their eyes, and they surely had heard nothing of an armistice. The sense of folly of a few moments earlier had dissolved. As for the Germans, the girls were used to seeing them march by in a bubble of silence. They passed under the Arc of Santo Spirito and carried their bicycles up the brick steps to the Salita di Sant'Onofrio. Now they were chattering freely, in their normal fashion, about silly, frivolous things they would not have discussed in the presence of adults. Adriana would remember nothing of those conversations, only that they had allowed her the freedom to act her age, for she and Camilla were the same age, and although she did not love her dearly — or so she thought — they enjoyed each other's company. Perhaps that's what friendship was. So they had not been headed to the Gianicolo after all, but right there, to the Salita di Sant'Onofrio. Adriana did not say that she had memories of that steep little road, as there were certain things she did not speak to Camilla about, things connected with her family, especially her parents. Camilla knew Adriana's mother didn't live with her, although she was not dead, but she didn't ask questions. Camilla went up to a small door on the left but was told to come back later. "Let's have a look around, then," she said, and they continued up the road with no destination in mind. They went up the stairs, carrying their bicycles again, to the Piazza Sant'Onofrio. To think Adriana had never been up there before! How many times had she passed below those walls — there where a white-robed friar once tended his tomatoes, watering them when she walked by with Nonno Già — and she had never been up there! Perspiring, and with their clothes and hair still wet, the air in the piazza seemed cool. They put their bicycles down beside them and sat on the gray wall dangling their legs. The breath of the city rose familiar and warm in the still of midday.

They did not notice them right away. Adriana had seen a few white clouds in the blue haze above the Colli Albani, but she paid them no attention. The rumbling of the explosions reached them much later. It was Camilla who pointed into the distance and said, "Look, they're bombing." The sounds grew louder and no doubt remained. White clouds rose and spread one after another. The glint of the planes could be seen, flying low, and the columns of smoke rose higher. "It's Frascati," said Camilla. "And Grottaferrata . . . and Albano . . . they're not leaving anything. Look at the mess they've made!"She had pulled her legs up from the wall as if about to run away. Adriana did not move. She looked at that bombardment and felt guilty. Guilty of believing — yes, she had believed, albeit in that cynical way of hers — in the armistice, in the end of the war. And this was the consequence, the first of many dreadful consequences. "What about the armistice?" she asked, almost reluctant to let the words issue from her lips. Her question was not asked out of cruelty or spite, but out of a profound sense of defeat.

"That's right, the armistice," said Camilla. "So then those are the Germans. Adriana, those are German planes! Let's go!" She picked up her bicycle and headed for the top of the stairway. Adriana followed her, without understanding, without even thinking. "Let's go home, because if those are Germans, they mean business." And they rushed down the stairs as white friars ran up, robes flapping, to look out from the spot where the girls had just been.

"They're bombing the Castelli! It's the Germans!" Camilla shouted, and they heard an incredulous friar mutter, "The Germans?"

The two girls jumped on their bicycles and set off down the road, the gentler descent that curved below the Ospedale del Bambin' Gesù, for the other one was too steep for bicycles. They raced along the Lungotevere, past Castel Sant'Angelo, down Via Crescenzio and then Via Fabio Massimo, shouting to people standing wide-eyed and open-mouthed in the streets, "They're bombing the Castelli! It's the Germans!"

But it was the Americans. Even the armistice had been a swindle. The German occupation of Rome was beginning.

The following month, in October, I returned to school and found my classmates silent. We were thin, and none of us had grown much over the summer.

"Here we are, back again," Professor Pagani said softly, and he did not know what else to say. Soon the class was reduced to only girls, because that winter the Germans started taking boys — from the streets, from school, from wherever — for labor service, so parents were keeping them at home.

Rome had been in German hands since September, and in October, Badoglio declared war on Germany. All state functionaries had been invited to relocate to the north, or else retire. My father remained in Rome. He spent a great deal of time with me, helping me with my studies in Latin and Greek, and in Italian.

One Saturday evening in mid-December he said, "Tomorrow I won't be in Monteverde. Here are the keys. Wash up, and get yourself something to eat. There's food in the kitchen cupboard."

"You won't be there?" I asked, surprised. "Where are you going?" The words came before I realized my indiscretion. He looked at me at length in silence. Finally, as if still undecided, he said, "I'm going to the Marches, at Old Zio's request. It's about some paintings, but don't you say a word to anyone, not even your grandmother. I'm not telling her, poor old woman, because it would only make her worry. I'll tell her that I've got some work here in Rome and for a few nights I won't be home. We're going — I'll be with Vannutelli, and Getulio, and Abbruzzetti . . . you remember them, don't you? We're going to retrieve a few paintings that we hid here and there for safekeeping during the war. Now we can't be sure anyplace in Italy is safe, you see. So we're going to get them and take them to the Vatican. They'll be out of harm's way there."

I knew it was impossible to travel. He added, "We'll have an escort, and a German officer will be coming with us. Now, don't you start worrying; we have every seal of approval. There's been an accord between the Germans and the Holy See . . . We'll travel at night when the roads are safe — the firing always happens during the day. Rest assured, they won't nab me. I'll bring you some sheep's-milk cheese, if I can. I'll only be gone three or four days, don't worry . . ."

It seemed like a charade, nothing but lies, and suddenly I was frightened. Without speaking I tore off a strip of wallpaper that was already peeling from the wall. The plaster underneath was rough and ugly. I watched as a flock of birds landed in the field outside and started to peck away with precision at whatever they could find in the road. *They won't nab me*, my father had said, but I could see him, bloodied, dead, lying in the grass on the shoulder of the road in the absolute silence of a foggy winter countryside. I couldn't go back to sleep, and his story of paintings to be brought to the Vatican sounded like a ruse. Which paintings, and why him? Wasn't he retired? And why *on Old Zio's behalf*? If he was still calling Superintendent De Rinaldis by that childish name, Old Zio, after all this time, then surely he was trying to deceive me. And what request could that poor, half-blind old man possibly have? And Getulio, Vannutelli, Abbruzzetti! Memories, forgotten characters from the days in Palazzo Venezia, the stuff of long ago, when there was a museum in Palazzo Venezia and not the mess that was there now. Palazzo Venezia indeed! And a German officer, no less. There in the dark Adriana envisioned her father as he departed for who knew what act of heroism, only to be killed. And she felt betrayed. Betrayed by him, too, after her mother preferred to remain down there, in the midst of the bombing, unable to send any news. So her mother was transporting and hiding manuscripts, her father paintings. What kind of foolishness was this? Was it only her divorced parents who were fighting this war? Yes, it was all pretend, another script acted out on her behalf.

He was bundled up, ready to go out into the night, when I awoke. He was shaking me gently by the shoulders and saying, "Listen carefully, Adriana. We are going by way of Narni, Todi, Perugia, Urbino. Don't forget." And he repeated the names of the cities. "It's a route that should be safe. Now repeat those names to me." And I repeated them, my eyes transfixed, staring at my blanket. He kissed me on the forehead and left, closing the door behind him quietly. I remained seated in the middle of the bed in the dark, repeating those names. I couldn't sleep anymore. It was Sunday; I took the tram to Monteverde and then went up along Via Garibaldi and the stairs below the fountain. I was upset and frightened — frightened for him, thinking only of him. I entered the cold, empty house and left all the windows closed save the small one in the kitchen. The bathroom window had frosted glass but no shutters and it allowed a bit of light into the room. I turned on the faucet and watched the water run, but I couldn't undress in that empty house with my father who knows where in the treacherous countryside. I turned the water off. I was ravenous, however, and the sound of my chewing could be heard throughout the house as I devoured the chestnut cake he had left for me in the kitchen cupboard. That cabinet had come from Nonna Matilde's kitchen in Prati. She had kept her cinnamon and cloves in it, and here it didn't contain much more. I locked the house and went away. I didn't talk about him with my silent grandmother, and that night I went to bed early, seized by fits of anger and resentment toward him for the torment his absence was causing me. I didn't go see the "two poor women" in Via Tacito during that time, nor did I seek out Camilla, because of the secret I had vowed to keep. I kept repeating the list of names of cities I had never seen. And in the evenings I stared out through the window at the dark sidewalk, damp from the condensation that dripped from the bare branches of the plane trees.

Finally, three nights later, Lucia called out, "Your father's on the phone," and Nonna Matilde came running, too, without a word. His voice was cheerful, clear, and young. He was fine. He was in Rome. "But I'm coming home tomorrow because we have a lot to do here." He did not say where *here* was.

So grandmother, granddaughter, and Lucia ate alone again that night, but they were lighthearted, even talkative, now that their unspoken fears had subsided. But Adriana could not stop thinking about the fear her father had caused her, or the prayers she had said for him on that little trip of his for just four days in the company of so many people he knew. She thought of the pain she had felt for him, and yet it had been six months now without a word from anyone in Palermo. Not one word. They could all be dead; or some of them at least. This could be true, she knew it. And she knew that if she didn't think about it, she would not have to believe it. She knew, yes, deep down she knew, that the certainty she felt about her mother's survival, which she called faith — was born of a practical law of nature to protect her: so that she could complete the deeds required of her from day to day, at school, as she studied, as she talked and laughed with her friends. She knew — yes, she well knew — that during that second winter she had missed Palermo and all of them much less than she had the year before. This was not because she was no longer able to count the weeks and months, so time was no longer tearing her apart, but only because she had grown accustomed to the distance.

For three days I hardly saw my father because he came home late in spite of the curfew and left the house early in the morning while it was still dark. Then, tired as he was, he said, "Today we verified twenty-four crates and sent them to the Vatican, paintings from Latium and Naples. I worked alone because no one was there to help me. Tomorrow, could you miss school and come with me?" I went. Rome was dark and deserted at six in the morning. Truly deserted, with only one German patrolman on the Ponte Cavour. I worked with my father in the cold under the portico in the courtyard of Palazzo Venezia. We worked in absolute silence, for even the trickle from the Doge's fountain been shut off during those months. The old custodians, Abbruzzeti and Capitani, were there with us — "my how you've grown, little one" — and around eight o'clock, when the curfew was over, the art restorer Matteucci arrived with his broad smile. He caressed the paintings with his eyes, even though they could often be seen only through the slats of a crate. His job was only to verify the presence of each work of art. The paintings then crossed Rome in two small trucks under German escort and were taken to the Vatican.

As we returned home my father said, "You don't know these things because I have never talked to you about them, and you, poor children, are growing up in a world gone mad. But before this disaster of ours, this war, we had thought of declaring Urbino an 'open city,' where we could store every possible item from our only source of wealth — our works of art. It wasn't possible, the open city, but we thought the Marches would still be the safest place since it is far from all the borders. This was when we were worried our largest cities would be bombed. So we brought paintings from Venice, Milan, and Rome to the Marches. Back then we were thinking only of the cities. And now? Now the Gothic Line runs through there, and the Allies are ready to make their way from one end of Italy to the other in their tanks, rolling it up like a rug. Naples . . . the museums of Naples moved their works to Montecassino for safekeeping, far from any military objectives. But can we be sure anyplace is safe anymore?"

We worked together for days; it was my Christmas vacation. We worked without uttering a word more than necessary, and by now the bond between us seemed loving, deep, and unbreakable. My thoughts and memories of my other loved ones no longer seemed to me like a betrayal for they belonged to another world, to a former semblance of myself.

Here was the true Adriana now, working with her father. He was not unhappy and alone and rejected anymore, and he had not deceived her. That was it: her father wouldn't tug at her conscience anymore, and he would not say, *Who put that idea in your head? Your mother?* Never again. Finally, there was a genuine friendship between us.

During that vacation from school I seldom went to the house on Via Gioacchino Belli, whose skylight had been hastily painted black so the lamps could not cast their meager light up into the night. I seldom went out on my bicycle with Camilla, and I didn't spend any time reading in my usual fashion, stretched out on Nonna's red velvet sofa. On January 4 my father said, "Do you want to come with me? I'd like to have you see and remember a few things. Today they are delivering the treasures of Naples — works from the Museum of Capodimonte and manuscripts from the monasteries. Montecassino was evacuated, and its paintings are going to the Vatican. The Göring Division itself is transporting the crates to Rome and delivering them to us."

I stood a short distance from him in the cold, empty piazza. Thirty-one German trucks drove in from the Corso, one by one, and lined up in front of Palazzo Venezia. The head of the division, General Maeltzer himself, was there to receive them, along with several officers, some retired functionaries of the ministry, and a few others. A German official gave a speech, of which I understood only a few words: "The Göring Division is gathered here today not for an action of force but . . ." Then an Italian responded. The ceremony had begun at two o'clock. I was hungry and I had a headache.

A few evenings later my father, speaking openly at the table rather than in secret, said, "I'm leaving. We are leaving day after tomorrow, if it doesn't snow." I stood up, pushing my chair back noisily, breathless with emotion and unable to speak right away. He was staring at me, my grandmother was staring at me. "I want to go with you," I said, my eyes fixed on his. My father stood up, too. He slowly placed his napkin by his plate and covered his face with one hand as if overcome by weariness or else his eyes had been strained from too much reading. Then he returned to his seat and said, "Sit down, now. Let's finish eating, then we'll talk." We talked, the two of us, alone on the sofa after Nonna had gone to bed.

We left at four in the morning with two trailer trucks. In addition to the four drivers we were accompanied by Getulio and two custodians from Palazzo Venezia, Capitani and Abbruzzetti, along with Vannutelli, and Professor B. of the Vatican Archives. The SS lieutenant T. carried permits for the two trucks and Vannutelli's car. My father and I rode in the cabin of one of the trucks, driven by a man named Nino. The rumbling of the engines broke the eerie quiet of a deserted, cold, and unlit Rome. We crossed Ponte Milvio and took Via Cassia out of the city. After passing through a sleeping village — my father said it was Otricoli — the sun began to appear on the horizon. We rounded a curve and our truck slowed down, almost to a stop. Ahead in the road was a line of dark silhouettes, still and silent. A burst of wind came through the trees and there was a rippling of tarpaulin. They were German trucks, at least twenty of them, and none was moving. A few of them were off the road, upturned; there were even two in the middle of the field, stopped in their vain attempt to escape the strafing. We watched, and none of us had yet seen our films of the war. Our war.

"They still have all their tires; it must have happened only a short time ago," said Nino. I found what my eyes had been looking for: the dead. Dark blots in the grass, small and flat in the fog. I imagined what could not be seen but could be presumed, hunched over in the cabins of the trucks, covered with blood. And I felt all the more guilty at having insisted Papa bring me with him, guilty for the fear I caused him. It was almost daylight, a gray day.

"We are at Narni," he said as earth-colored houses appeared on the left, "but we won't go through Terni and Somma because the bombing is too heavy. We'll take the Via Tiberina instead."

We were in Perugia shortly after noon. It was cold; icicles were hanging from the fountain. I had never been to Perugia, but I recognized the fountain and the staircase from the photographs taken when my parents were traveling by motorcycle with Arturo. So many things had changed . . . My father said, "Come with me, Adriana," and I followed him up the steps of Palazzo Ducale. We walked through the grand halls where the walls were covered with paintings, although many works were missing. And as paintings will do, they had left a discoloration to mark their absence on the walls. I followed my father slowly, and when I caught up with him he was in a room speaking to a gentleman who was listening while standing behind a desk. The man, who was the Umbrian superintendent, walked around the desk and stepped forward as my father said, ". . . we are here with boxes and crates to pack up the paintings. Everything is ready. The day after tomorrow the works will be at the Vatican, but I can't find anyone here, nothing . . . The art pieces from Campania are already at the Vatican, the Göring Division itself handed them over . . ."

"I'm sorry, I cannot give you the paintings. There was a meeting of superintendents in Padua, on the ninth of January to be exact, and the minister gave orders that the works already sheltered in storage are not to be removed. Those orders are confirmed by a letter sent to all the superintendents. I am surprised . . ."

"Confirmed! Confirmed! And now you're going to tell me that the minister came up with this bright idea without having been told about the arrangements made . . . not by our authorities, let's leave that aside . . . but the arrangements made by the German authorities with the Holy See. We have a small hope, perhaps the possibility of placing at least part of our artistic heritage in a safe location, at least the sculptures and paintings that can be transported; they've already been moved once to keep them sheltered, but unfortunately they are no longer safe . . . if they are stored in the Vatican they will at least be protected from the devastation . . . and His Excellency the minister decides that no, he will take full responsibility. Doesn't His Excellency the minister know that, if the Allies resume their advance, or land farther north, the smaller cities will be much more exposed . . ."

He stopped. The gentleman shrugged. "These, I repeat, are the orders, and I will obey them."

Adriana watched her father close his eyes, calm himself, and say, "Forgive me, sir. But do you, you personally, do you agree that the paintings would be safer in the Vatican than in Todi or Foligno or Spello? You personally, sir?"

"Yes, I'll allow that. But you should address me with *voi*."* A silence followed. Adriana watched her father turn pale and then redden. She moved closer to him and saw, more than heard, him murmur, "This is pure stupidity." Then he said aloud, "Let's go." But he stopped again in the doorway and said, "Please, tell me if the superintendent from the Marches was also present at the meeting in Padua."

* *Lei* is a formal second-person singular pronoun, roughly equivalent to *thou.* It was branded as un-Italian by Mussolini, and was officially replaced by the pronoun *voi* during the Fascist years. —*Trans.*

"No, he was not there. Perhaps he was unable to join us given the difficulties with travel . . . but you, now that you know the orders given by the ministry, surely you will not take advantage . . ."

But they had already taken to the stairs, the grand staircase of Perugia's Palazzo Ducale.

The fields were covered with snow. They entered the city at nine in the evening, and while the drivers went in search of a place to eat, Enrico Fieschi ran to Urbino's Palazzo Ducale to talk with Superintendent Rotondi. Adriana was with him, and she watched as her father warmly embraced that small man with the broad grin. "At last! Yes, I'll give you anything you want. Rome, the best of the Marches, Venice . . . I even have a surprise for you."

A short time later they each had a plate of mushrooms and a loaf of bread in front of them. The conversation between the two men continued, while her father was eating with gusto and delight. "Yes, I received the letter authorizing me to give you the works to be taken to the Vatican. I also received the invitation to participate in the Padua meeting, but the letter said February ninth, not January ninth. So I haven't gone anywhere yet, and I know nothing." He had delicate features and he was laughing softly. Adriana could sense his serenity, and her father's joy.

Was the German lieutenant able to follow their conversation? He was quietly eating his bread and mushrooms and drinking the wine of the Marches, new to him. A peaceful scene among smiling men gathered around a table — never before had Adriana witnessed such absurdity and human joy, so real and tangible, yet so incredible, a scene on the brink of vanishing — like so many of her recent and past experiences, which now returned to her not as images, but more precisely, as flavors, or even scents: secret, urgent, holy, and precious. Her father and the superintendent of the Marches made plans for the following day, for work in Urbino and also Sassocorvaro where several paintings were hidden. The truck they had been unable to load with crates in Perugia would carry not only "all of Venice and Rome" and "the best of the Marches," but also the treasury of the Patriarchal Basilica of San Marco, which the bishop of Urbino had received for safekeeping from the patriarch of Venice. The bishop now wished to have the collection transferred to the Vatican, too: this was the surprise promised by Rotondi.

The following day, a Friday, they set to work verifiying the contents of the crates and loading them onto trucks and trailers. In all, there were twenty-three crates of artwork from the treasury of the Patriarchal Basilica of San Marco, five crates containing works from Venice, and twenty-two crates from the Brera Gallery from Milan the Galleria Corsini, and the Galleria Borghese from Rome, as well as the Caravaggios from Santa Maria del Popolo and San Luigi de' Francesi. They continued their work in Sassocorvaro, although due to space limitations they left behind — in enclosed shelters in the rock — some of the less valuable works from the Brera Gallery and a few canvases that were too large to be transported by truck.

I helped to transport crates, verified numbers and names, and forgot about the cold and hunger. And I found myself once again seated next to my father and Nino the driver, on the road white with snow to Rome. My father spoke for long stretches at a time, with equally long stretches of silence in between. He said, "We have half of Venice here with us. Just think of it, my dear Adriana, do you know what that means?" Perhaps I did not fully understand, and I knew it.

On that same road, or another one, also covered in snow, was the destroyed German column and all the dead we had seen on the way up. We did not talk about such things. Snow was falling even on them as we carried the paintings. Thoughts so difficult they left you stunned and weary. Other thoughts, cruel and rudimentary, now seemed childlike and remote.

But from them other simple thoughts arose: that they were carrying half the artistic heritage of Italy to the Vatican with the consent of the Germans; that if the Germans had wanted to cart everything away, it had already been assembled, cataloged, and packed — Venice, Milan, Rome, and "the best of the Marches," in addition to what had once been in Montecassino — objects from Naples and elsewhere that they themselves had brought to Rome. These thoughts, too, were simplistic and ingenuous, thoughts that Adriana would never have voiced. But as if her father had read her mind, he said, "Yes, we're bringing it all to the Vatican to keep it safe during the war. It's all we can do, and we must do it at once. Everything will be together there, organized and cataloged. It might be tempting to the SS . . . but they would never do it. In spite of everything, Germany is behind them, and Germany is not just SS . . ."

Thus spoke Adriana's father, the man called Enrico Fieschi here; descendant of the Genoese family that produced seventy-two bishops and two popes; great-grandson of that grande dame Nonna Caterina, Marchesa Malaspina; and pupil of Adolfo Venturi.

My father! How well I thought I knew him, and how I had underestimated him. My father, with his old, annoying unhappiness; a man who could spend hours bent over a painting, studying the invisible restoration work of Ventura or Matteucci — Annita used to call Matteucci *capannecchia*. Who knows what she meant by that; I never asked her and now it's too late. My father, who had been so sad in the days of the Galleria Corsini; my father, so playful and cheerful on an improvised stage at the Ceccarellis' house in Santa Severa, singing, "We were so in love . . ."

Yes, Adriana remembers many things, and many things — perhaps — she thinks she remembers. For perhaps her father did not actually bring her along to Perugia and Urbino in January 1944, and she constructed her memories out of the stories he told.

As the truck proceeded through the night with a surreal whirring of tires on the snowy Salaria road, the girl turned and saw that her father was asleep. She tucked the blanket around his legs and moved closer so they could keep each other warm. Now they were on the plain. Beyond the snow, from under the black, thin outline of bare tree branches, a dim reflection in the night sky rose up from Rome. Farther south was a flicker of distant lights: it was the battle at Monte Cassino. In those hours, the landing at Anzio had begun.

❖

In Rome the graffiti on the walls made no one laugh but no one erased them. I remember: LOOKING FOR FASCIST, EVEN SECOND-HAND. And also: GO AWAY, ALL OF YOU. LEAVE US TO WEEP ALONE. Rome was famished, darkened, sad. The evenings were quieter than before, except for the rhythmic marching of a handful of foreigners in hobnailed boots. There were no gasping dynamo flashlights operated by hands aching from the cold, gesturing, *ciao, ciao*; there was no tapping from the iron tips and heels of cardboard shoes. Everything was silenced, for the curfew was now at five o'clock in the afternoon.

In addition to the Jews, the Fascists had also disappeared from Rome. They were hiding in the homes of friends, in clinics, in the Vatican, in sacristies, in libraries.

Rich as it is in theological texts, the primary users of the Casanatense Library have always been priests, young and old. But that winter of 1943–1944 it hosted many other men, in hiding there day and night. "Men whom no one saw" for weeks. Occasionally three or four would turn up, other times two or three; no one really knows how many there were. With hands in their pockets, hats on their heads, and collars upturned they roamed the immense, high-ceilinged room lined with bookshelves and display cases. At times, surely out of boredom, they walked out on the balcony midway up the shelving, or even on the upper balcony running under the windows.

Above the banister on the upper balcony large golden scrolls bearing Roman numerals indicate the sections where the books are shelved. Given their height, a man could stand unobserved behind one of those scrolls, especially since no one on the now deserted main floor ever looked up there.

But Margherita, noticing that the threadbare window drapes weren't hanging properly, had climbed up there, to that narrow balcony at such a vertiginous height, and she saw him there, face-to-face. She recognized him instantly: her persecutor from Via Spallanzani, the guard at Villa Torlonia. Later, yes, years later, she realized he could have hurled her to the ground below . . . Instead they looked each other in the eye, which she had not yet done, and like a sparrow mesmerized by a cat, she gave up. She gave up in spirit, while her lips spoke. "What are you doing here?" she said clearly, and in her confusion she even offered him her hand. He shook his head and withdrew. Without a word he backed up to the corner of the balcony, then turned and fled, not at a run, but with long strides. She watched him from above, from across the expanse of the hall, as he hugged his coat to him and raced off without looking back. She — who felt so at home in the library — did not realize at first that he was afraid of being reported. Frightened and confused, she asked herself, *Why?* Why had she spoken to him? Why had he fled? No, it didn't occur to her that that man might now fear her. The very idea was unthinkable, so accustomed was she to being afraid. She felt guilty for discovering him, for having disturbed him. And in that moment whatever modicum of peace that grown girl had ever known was now undone. Reality and dream — the nightmare that returned again and again — became entangled in her mind, and from that moment on she felt she was being hounded by the police.

Margherita changed. She became hunched and her hair turned white. But not from hunger, not hunger alone. She could find no peace, because she wanted to be forgiven. Forgiven for having disturbed that man, for having upset him. She wanted to be forgiven, but did not know how, by the police.

Then she did a second foolish thing: she talked about it. She mentioned it to a colleague she regarded as a friend, without knowing that he in fact had been the one to conceal "that man" in the library. Shortly afterward, the man offered to help rid her of the problem. He said he had a friend on the police force who could move the file opened against her to the bottom of the pile and ultimately make it disappear. And every month the file was shifted to the bottom of the stack, which, according to the colleague, was on the desk of the investigating judge. Certainly, she needed help. But at a price. And Margherita was blackmailed. It lasted several years. Half her salary ended up there and her mind was never the same. She said nothing to her mother, just as she had said nothing when one of Il Duce's guards had come upon her from the shadows in the doorway on Via Spallanzani when she was a girl.

I didn't know — no one knew, except Nonna Antonia and Zia Margherita — that by the end of 1943 Giacomo Canterno had already returned. A tall, thin man. I remember him as a stern uncle, but with a tender smile, always in uniform.

Only a few came back, the few survivors of the ARMIR, the Italian Army in Russia, crushed by the Soviet offensive of December 1942. It was a perilous journey, and it left him with a grave illness.

His son, my cousin, just back from the African front himself, came to Via Tacito to see Nonna Antonia and Zia Margherita. "I have something to tell you, but it's a secret. Papa is back. He's been in Rome for a week, but he's in hiding. It's better if no one comes to see him, if no one knows about it. I'm telling you this to reassure you: he's alive."

"How is he?" Antonia gasped.

"Not well, but now he will recover, you'll see. He is . . . a guest. Of an old friend, a woman."

The mother understood, and did not ask any more questions. She closed her eyes, offering thanks in prayer.

If they had caught him, they would have shot him, says Margherita, and it would have been worse. It would have been a dishonor, too. He remained in that signora's house, in hiding. But he needed nourishment, and that was difficult, especially since he didn't have any ration cards. His wife, our sister-in-law, was doing well in those days; she was in the movies and had resources we certainly didn't have. She helped him a lot. She helped us, too. She was always very good to us. She really was. She always loved me, and her sisters did, too. She didn't always get along with your mother, though. Why? What do you expect? They both had strong personalities.

Then, months later, during a very difficult time for me, your cousin kept a lookout for me, then came up to me in the street and said, "Don't turn around. Tonight I'm bringing Papa over. He can't stay where he is anymore. That lady can't keep him, it's not safe; not safe for him. You be ready around one o'clock. Look out of the window. I'll be driving a friend's car. I'll signal you, and then you come down to the main door."

He brought him. I went to open the main door because I had the key. I didn't recognize him; he could stand only with great effort. Thank goodness it had stopped raining. He was wearing a coat, with a blanket over it. He was unrecognizable, that poor brother of mine, and your cousin carried him in his arms up all five flights of stairs. He was light as a feather. A feather! We put him in the back room. Mamma had prepared a bed for him in the small room at the far end of the house so the neighbors wouldn't hear him when he coughed. Oh, how he coughed. Then he died, but not right away. He died, my poor brother, says Margherita, shaking her head slowly, it's a blessing Papa wasn't there to see it.

For us, the war ended with the arrival of the Americans in June 1944. Mail delivery resumed, and letters were no longer censored. But we wrote each other short, incredulous letters, full of broken, impatient sentences, unable to say what was really weighing on our minds. My mother had come to Rome by September, and I returned to Palermo with her. Laura had grown up and become quite beautiful. Arturo and the others were thin, but they seemed bright and luminous, as if detoxified.

A second adolescence unfolded for me, a happy one this time; with the soft, elusive fragrance of the flowers of the pomelia — by now it was a tree — that stood as always at the corner of the terrace with its broken tiles, although half the building had collapsed during the last bombing of the city, on June 30, 1943.

Yes, the war was over, but not for Margherita.

It was in the fall of 1946 that the policeman, Il Duce's guard who was no longer a Fascist but still a policeman, found her again. And the scene in the doorway on Via Tacito took place, the scene she had dreamed so many times before. The policeman, that filthy man, was a contemptible, grotesque inverse of Javert, taking vengeance on an innocent dove, the young girl of Via

Spallanzani, who was guilty of not indulging him then, and guilty again for having recognized him in his hiding place.

Margherita doesn't seem to remember those things anymore. Now that she has lived so many years, I take her back to her earliest memories, her only happy ones, those of Alexandria. But her family affections are always with her, and they are strong. She says:

He was a born warrior, my brother was. He fought in all the wars. Even the Spanish War. A born warrior indeed. His entire life he did nothing but fight wars. And what was the purpose of it all? Strange, I never dream of him. And yet I loved him so much.

She is the only one left, Zia Margherita, because the others have been gone for years, now. Marta, my mother, worked for the libraries of Sicily to the end. She was involved in the reconstruction of those that had been bombed and in the restructuring of all of them. She devoted herself to the training of new, young librarians, and introduced them to the study of manuscripts. She cataloged and detailed every ancient manuscript in Sicily, whether it originated there or was imported. As for my father, after the war he directed many important restoration projects and saw them through to completion. He also wrote many books on the subject.

All of that is documented and published. Other memories remain, and they are mine alone.

Zia Margherita still has her dreams.

I saw your mother, last night. She was sitting on a bench, you know, one of the green ones in Piazza Cavour. She was with Papa and they were discussing philosophy, bless them! Then she turned to me, smiling, and said, "Guess what, Margherita? They made me a Knight." "Is that so?" I said, "A Knight of what?"

"A Knight of Alphabetical Order!"

Alphabetical Order! "This is the most precious and holy of books," said my grandfather. And in those days it was. Today that convention, that brilliant device, that glorious organism, an irreplaceable instrument of knowledge that has been part of civilization for centuries, seems to be on its way to extinction.

It is almost useless, if you think about it. Because it is no longer necessary to leaf through the telephone directory or consult card catalogs in the libraries. Today you type in your question and the answer appears on your computer screen. Of course the program in the computer still uses it, if the rules of alphabetical order have been downloaded into it, but who knows if this won't soon become obsolete, too.

Perhaps one day in the not-too-distant future only a few madmen like my grandfather will remember what the alphabet was, and what it was used for. Only a few will remember what books were, and why it was necessary — and good — to organize and keep them in that given order; a unique, binding, irreplaceable order. And we will also have forgotten, with the exception of a few of us, how lovely was the scent of a library.

OTHER STEERFORTH ITALIA TITLES

VENICE REVEALED
An Intimate Portrait
by Paolo Barbaro

VOICES FROM A TIME
by Silvia Bonucci

ROME AND A VILLA
Memoir
by Eleanor Clark

The Adventures of
PINOCCHIO
by Carlo Collodi

TORREGRECA
Life, Death, Miracles
by Ann Cornelisen

WOMEN OF THE SHADOWS
Wives and Mothers of Southern Italy
by Ann Cornelisen

THE TWENTY-THREE DAYS OF THE CITY OF ALBA
by Beppe Fenoglio

ARTURO'S ISLAND
by Elsa Morante

HISTORY
by Elsa Morante

THE WATCH
by Carlo Levi

THE CONFORMIST
by Alberto Moravia

THE TIME OF INDIFFERENCE
by Alberto Moravia

THE WOMAN OF ROME
by Alberto Moravia

TWO WOMEN
by Alberto Moravia

LIFE OF MORAVIA
by Alberto Moravia
and Alain Elkann

Claudia Roden's
THE FOOD OF ITALY
Region by Region

CUCINA DI MAGRO
Cooking Lean the Traditional Italian Way
by G. Franco Romagnoli

CONCLAVE
by Roberto Pazzi

THE ABRUZZO TRILOGY
by Ignazio Silone

MY NAME, A LIVING MEMORY
by Giorgio van Straten

LITTLE NOVELS OF SICILY
by Giovanni Verga

OPEN CITY
Seven Writers in Postwar Rome
edited by William Weaver